Praise for *The Last Time I Was Me*

"Charming."
—*Publishers Weekly*

Praise for *Julia's Chocolates*

"*Julia's Chocolates* is wise, tender, and very funny. In
Julia Bennett, Cathy Lamb has created a deeply wonderful
character, brave and true. I loved this beguiling novel about
love, friendship, and the enchantment of really good chocolate."
—Luanne Rice, *New York Times* bestselling author

"In *Julia's Chocolates*, Cathy Lamb has created a passel of characters
so weirdly wonderful that you want to hang out with them all
day just to see what they'll do next. It's a ride that's both hilarious
and poignant, and all the while you cling to the edge of the
pickup truck because you'll want to make sure you stay
in for the whole trip."
—Amy Wallen, author of *Moonpies and Movie Stars*

Books by Cathy Lamb

JULIA'S CHOCOLATES

THE LAST TIME I WAS ME

HENRY'S SISTERS

Published by Kensington Publishing Corporation

To Leslie

Henry's
Sisters

CATHY LAMB

Cathy Lamb

KENSINGTON BOOKS
http://www.kensingtonbooks.com

KENSINGTON BOOKS are published by

Kensington Publishing Corp.
119 West 40th Street
New York, NY 10018

All Kensington titles, imprints, and distributed lines are available at
special quantity discounts for bulk purchases for sales promotion, pre-
miums, fund-raising, educational, or institutional use.

Special book excerpts or customized printings can also be created to fit
specific needs. For details, write or phone the office of the Kensington
Special Sales Manager: Kensington Publishing Corp., 119 West 40th
Street, New York, NY 10018. Attn. Special Sales Department. Phone: 1-
800-221-2647.

Kensington and the K logo Reg. U.S. Pat. & TM Off.

ISBN-13: 978-0-7582-2954-0
ISBN-10: 0-7582-2954-2

First Kensington Trade Paperback Printing: August 2009
10 9 8 7 6 5 4 3 2

Printed in the United States of America

To JayRae, RaeMac, and The "T" Man

with love

❧ 1 ❧

I would have to light my bra on fire.
And my thong.

It is unfortunate that I feel compelled to do this, because I am particular about my bras and underwear. I spent most of my childhood in near poverty, wearing scraggly underwear and fraying bras held together with safety pins or paper clips, so now I insist on wearing only the truly elegant stuff.

"Burn, bra, burn," I whispered, as the golden lights of morning illuminated me to myself. "Burn, thong, burn."

I studied the man sprawled next to me under my white sheets and white comforter, amidst my white pillows. He was muscled, tanned, had a thick head of longish black hair, and needed a shave.

He had been quite kind.

I would use the lighter with the red handle!

I envisioned the flame crawling its way over each cup like a fire-serpent, crinkling my thong and turning the crotch black and crusty.

Lovely.

I stretched, pushed my skinny brown braids out of my face, fumbled under the bed, and found my bottle of Kahlúa.

I swigged a few swallows as rain splattered on the windows, then walked naked across the wood floor of my loft to peer out. The other boxy buildings and sleek skyscrapers here in downtown Portland were blurry, wet messes of steel and glass.

I have been told that the people in the corporate building across the way can see me when I open my window and lean out, and that this causes a tremendous ruckus when I'm nude, but I can't bring myself to give a rip. It's my window, my air, my insanity. My nudeness.

Besides, after that pink letter arrived yesterday, I needed to breathe. It made me think of my past, which I wanted to avoid, and it made me think of my future, which I also wanted to avoid.

I opened the window, leaned way out, and closed my eyes as the rain twisted through my braids, trickling down in tiny rivulets over the beads at the ends, then my shoulders and boobs.

"Naked I am," I informed myself. "Naked and partly semi-sane."

I did not want to do what that letter told me to do.

No, it was not possible.

I stretched my arms way out as if I were hugging the rain, the Kahlúa bottle dangling, and studied myself. I had an upright rack, a skinny waist, and a belly button ring. Drops teetered off my nipples one by one, pure and clear and cold. I said aloud, "I have cold nipples. Cold nips."

When I was drenched, I smiled and waved with both hands, hoping the busy buzzing boring worker bees in the office buildings were getting their kicks and jollies. They needed kicks and jollies.

"Your minds are dying! Your souls are decaying! Get out of there!" I brought the Kahlúa bottle to my mouth, then shouted, "Free yourself! *Free yourself!*"

Satisfied with this morning's creative rant, I padded to my kitchen and ran a hand across the black granite slab of my counter, then crawled on it and laid down flat like a naked human pancake, my body slick with rainwater, my feet drooping over the edge.

I stared at the pink letter propped up on the backsplash. I could smell her flowery, lemony perfume on it. It smelled like suffocation.

No screaming, I told myself. *No screaming.*

Suddenly I could feel Cecilia in my head. I closed my eyes. I felt abject despair. I felt fear. I felt bone-cracking exhaustion.

The phone rang, knocking the breath clean out of my lungs.

It was Cecilia. *I knew it.*

This type of thing happened between us so much we could be featured on some freak show about twins. A week ago I called her when I heard her crying in my brain. I couldn't even *think* she was so noisy. When I reached her, sure enough, she was hiding in a closet and bawling her eyes out. "Quiet down," I'd told her.

"Shut up, Isabelle," she'd sputtered. "Shut up."

We are fraternal twins and our mind-twisting psychic link started young. When we were three, Cecilia was attacked by a dog. He went straight for her throat. She was in our front yard, I was at the grocery store with Momma. At the exact same time she was bitten, I started shrieking and clutched my neck, which felt as if it had been stabbed. I fell to the ground and frantically kicked the air before I passed out. Momma later told me she thought the devil had attacked my very soul.

Another example: Two years ago, when I was working in some squalid village in India, teeming with the poorest of the poor, my stomach started to burn and swell. I had to ride back to the city in a cart with chickens. Cecilia needed an emergency appendectomy.

One more bizarre example: When I was photographing the American bombing of Baghdad, I dove behind a concrete barrier as bullets whizzed by. One grazed my leg. Cecilia's message on my cell phone was hysterical. She thought I'd died, because she couldn't move her leg.

It's odd. It's scary. It's the truth.

I covered my face with my hands. I did not answer the phone, waiting until the answering machine clicked on. I heard her voice—think drill sergeant meets Cruella De Vil.

"Pick up the phone, Isabelle."

I did not move.

"I know you're there," Cecilia/Cruella accused, angry already. Cecilia/Cruella is almost always angry. It started after that one terrible night with the cocked gun and the jungle visions when we were kids.

I tapped my forehead on the counter. "I'm not here," I muttered.

"And you're listening, aren't you?" I heard the usual impatience.

I breathed a hot, circular mist of steam onto the counter and shook my head. "No," I said. "No, I'm not listening."

"Hell, Isabelle, I know you're wigged out and upset and plotting a trip to an African village or some tribal island to get out of this, but it's not gonna work. Forget it. You hear me, damn it. Forget it."

I blew another steam circle. A raindrop plopped off my nose like a liquid diamond. "You swear too much, and I'm not *upset*," I said, so quiet. "Why should I be *upset?* I will not do what she says. If I do I will be crushed in her presence and what is sane will suddenly seem insane. Mrs. Depression will come and rest in my head. I'll have none of that." I shivered at the thought.

"And you're scared. I can feel your fear," she accused. "Ya can't hide that."

"I don't do scared anymore," I said, still shivering. "I don't."

"We're going to talk about what happened to you, too, Isabelle. Don't think you can keep that a secret," she insisted, as if we were having a normal conversation. "Pick up the damn phone before I really get pissed."

I loved Cecilia. She did not deserve, no one deserved, what had come down the pike for her last year with that psycho-freak pig/husband of hers. My year had not been beautiful, either, but hers was worse.

"Isabelle!" Cecilia/Cruella shouted, waiting for me to pick up. "Fine, Isabelle. *Fine.* Buck up and call me when you get out of bed and the man's gone."

I flipped my head up. *She knew!* So often she knew about the men. She told me once, "Think of it this way: I don't get the fun of the sex you have, but I sometimes know it's happened by the vague smell of a cigarette."

See? Freaky.

"I'm already out of bed, so quit nagging," I muttered.

"Is," she whispered, the machine hardly picking up her voice. "Don't leave me alone here."

"Cecilia hardly ever whispers," I whispered to myself. "She is beyond desperate." I ignored the tidal wave of guilt.

"You have to help me. You have to help *us*," she said.

No, I don't have to help. I do not have to help you, or her.

"I can't do it without you. I will go right over the edge, like a fat rhino leaping over a cliff." She hung up.

I am going to live my own life as sanely as possible. My answer, then, has to be no. No, no, no, Cecilia.

I conked my head against the counter, then tilted the Kahlúa bottle sideways into my mouth. I rarely drink, but Kahlúa for breakfast is delicious. I licked a few droplets right off the counter when they splattered, my beads clicking on the granite.

The man in my bed stirred. I raised my head from the counter, mildly interested as to what he'd do next.

I couldn't remember his name. Did he have a name? I flipped over and stared at the open silver piping on my ceiling. Certainly he had a name. Because I couldn't remember it didn't mean he had no name.

The man turned over. Nice chest!

Surely this man's mother gave him a name.

For a wee flash of time, I let myself feel terrible. Cheap and dirty for yet another one-night stand.

"Ha," I declared. "Ha. This night must end right now."

I rolled off my counter, grabbed a pan from my cupboard, and filled it with cold water.

When it was filled to the brim, I balanced it on my head, still clutching the Kahlúa bottle with two fingers, and teetered like a graceless acrobat on a wire to the man with no known name. "Good-bye to the night, hello to the incineration of my blue-and-white lacy bra."

I ignored the three- by-four-foot framed black-and-white photographs I'd taken hanging on my wall. Everyone in them was traumatized and I didn't need to stare at their eyes today. They were people. They were kids. That bothered me. That's why I hung them in my loft. So they would never, ever stop bothering me.

That nagging question popped up: Would I ever shoot photos again after what happened?

The man in my bed had been impressed when he'd found out who I was. I am not impressed with myself. I was not impressed with him.

I put the pan down, tore my white fluffy comforter away from the man, then dumped the cold water over his head. It hit him square between the eyes and he shot out of bed like a bullet and landed on his feet within a millisecond, his fists up. Military training, I presumed.

"That was fast," I told him, dropping the pan to the floor and swilling another swig of Kahlúa.

"*What the hell?*" He was coughing and sputtering and completely confused. "*What the hell?*"

"I said, that was fast. Most men don't jump up as fast as you did. You're quick. Quick and agile."

He ran his hand over his face and swore. "What did you do that for? *Are you insane?*"

"One, yes, I am. Insane. I'm still sensitive about that particular issue so let's not discuss it, and two, I did it because I need you up and at 'em." I sat down in my curving, chrome chair and crossed my legs. The chrome chilled my butt. "You can go now."

I did not miss the hurt expression in his eyes, but I dismissed it as fast as I could.

"What do you mean, I can go?" he spat out, flicking water away from his hair.

"I mean, you can go. Out the door. We had one night. We don't need another one. We don't need to chitchat. Chitchat makes me nauseated. I can't stand superficiality. I'm done. Thanks for your time and efforts."

I watched his mouth drop open in shock. Nice lips!

"Out you go." See, this is the part of me that I despise. I truly do.

He shook his head, water flicking off like a sprinkler. "You've got to be kidding."

"Nope. No joke. None." I got up and went to the front door and opened it. "Good-bye. Tra la la, good-bye."

He stood, flabbergasted, naked and musclely and wet, then snatched up his shirt and yanked it over his head. "I thought . . ." He ran a hand through his hair. "I like you . . . we had fun . . ."

"I don't do fun." No, I was past fun with men. That died when he couldn't control his nightmares followed by the rake and fertilizer incident.

"You don't *do* fun?"

He was befuddled, I knew that—completely befuddled. I love that word.

I felt a stab of guilt but squished it down as hard as I could so it could live with all my other guilt.

"Tootie scootie," I drawled at him. "Scoot scoot."

He wiped trickles of water off his face.

For long seconds, I didn't think he was going to do what I told him to do. He did not appear to be the type of man who took orders from others well. He appeared to be the type that gave the orders.

But not here.

I took another swig of Kahlúa. Yum. "Don't mess with me."

"I'm not going to mess with you. I thought I'd take you to breakfast—"

"No. Out." Out. Out of my life. Out of my head.

He shook his head in total exasperation, water dripping from his ears. "Fine. I'm outta here. Where are my pants?"

I nodded toward a crammed bookshelf where they'd been thrown. He yanked them on, his eyes searching my loft.

"My jacket?"

I nodded toward the wood table my friend Cassandra had carved. We had met in strange circumstances that I try not to dwell on. There were smiling mermaids all over it, swimming through an underwater garden. She'd painted it with bright, happy colors. Two weeks after that, she jumped off one of the tallest buildings in Portland after a luncheon in her honor. She'd left her entire estate to an after-school program for minority youth, which I administered.

Days later I received a letter in the mail from her. There were two words on the yellow sticky note inside the envelope. It said, "Rock on."

I watched him toss my pretty, blue and white lacy bra off his shoe and onto my red leather couch. It would soon be ashes, taken away by the wind off my balcony. Hey. Maybe my bra would land on a mermaid's head!

I opened the door wider.

He stared down at me, his eyes angry and . . . something . . . something else was lurking there. Probably hurt. Maybe humiliation.

I nodded. "Please don't take offense. It's not personal."

"Not personal?" He bellowed this. "*Not personal?* We made love last night, in your bed. That's not *personal?*"

"No, it's not. This is all I can do. One night."

"That's it? Ever?" He put his palms up. "You never have relationships with people more than one night?"

"No." I tilted my head. He was gorgeous. Cut the hair and

you'd have a dad. But I would not be the mom, that was for sure. I closed my eyes against that old pain. "Never."

He gave up. "You take the cake." He turned to go, his shirt clinging to him.

Poor guy. He'd woken up with a swimming pool on his face. "I like cake. Chocolate truffle rum is the best, but I can whip up a mille-feuille with zabaglione and powdered sugar that will make your tongue melt. My momma made me work in the family bakery and darned if I didn't learn something, now get out."

I put a hand on his chest and pushed, leaning against the door when he left.

I would burn the bra and the thong and try to forget.

The rain would help me.

Rain always does.

It washes out the memories.

Until the sun comes out. Then you're back to square one and the memories come and get ya.

They come and get ya.

I grabbed my lighter with the red handle from the kitchen, lighter fluid, a water bottle, my lacy bra and thong, and opened the French doors to my balcony. The wind and rain hit like a mini-hurricane, my braids whipping around my cheeks.

One part of my balcony is covered, so it was still dry. I put the bra and thong in the usual corner on top of a few straggly, burned pieces of material from another forgettable night on a wooden plank and flicked the lighter on. The bra and thong smoked and blackened and wiggled and fizzled and flamed.

When they were cremated, I doused them with water from the water bottle. No sense burning down the apartment building. That would be bad.

I settled into a metal chair in the uncovered section of my balcony, the rain sluicing off my naked body, and gazed at the skyscrapers, wondering how many of those busy, brain-fried, robotic people were staring at me.

Working in a skyscraper was another way of dying early, my younger sister, Janie, would say. "It's like the elevators are taking you up to hell."

Right out of college she got a job as a copywriter for a big company on the twenty-ninth floor of a skyscraper in Los Angeles and lasted two months before her weasely, squirmy boss found the first chapter of her first thriller on her desk.

The murderer is a copywriter for a big company on the twenty-ninth floor of a skyscraper in Los Angeles. In the opening paragraphs she graphically describes murdering her supercilious, condescending, snobby boss who makes her feel about the size of a slug and how his body ends up in a trash compactor, his legs spread like a pickled chicken, one shoe off, one red high heel squished on the other foot. That was the murderer's calling card.

No one reports his extended absence, including his wife, because people hate him as they would hate a gang of worms in their coffee.

Janie was fired that day, even though she protested her innocence. That afternoon she sat down and wrote the rest of the story, nonstop, for three months. When she emerged from her apartment, she'd lost twenty pounds, was pale white, and muttering. At four months she had her first book contract. When the book was published, she sent it to her ex-boss. And wrote, "Thanks, dickhead! With love, Janie Bommarito," on the inside cover.

It became a best-seller.

She became a recluse because she is obsessive and compulsive and needs to indulge all her odd habits privately.

The recluse had received a flowery lemon-smelling pink letter, too. So had Cecilia, whose brain connects with mine.

The rain splattered down on me, the wind twirly whirled, and I raised the Kahlúa bottle to my lips again. "I love Kahlúa," I said out loud as I watched the water river down my body, creating a little pool in the area of my crotch where my legs crossed. I flicked the rain away with my hand, watched it pool again, flicked it.

This entertained me for a while. Off in the distance I saw a streak of lightning, bright and dangerous.

It reminded me of the time when my sisters and I ran through a lightning storm to find Henry in a tree.

I laughed, even though that night had not been funny. It had been hideous. It had started with a pole dance and ended with squishy white walls.

I laughed again, head thrown back, until I cried, my hot tears running down my face off my chin, onto my boobs, and down my stomach. They landed in the pool between my legs and I flicked the rain and tear mixture away again. The tears kept coming and I could feel the darkness, darkness so familiar to me, edging its way back in like a liquid nightmare.

I did not want to deal with the pink letter that smelled of her flowery, lemony perfume.

2

She was wielding a knife.

It had a black handle and a huge, jagged, twisty edge.

If evil was in a knife, this was evil incarnate.

She rotated it in front of my face, wearing a fixed, contemplative, detached expression. I whipped my head back, my breath catching.

"I think she'll use this," Janie said, poking it into the air. "This would do the job."

I rolled my eyes and pushed past her into her houseboat, being careful to avoid the evil one.

"You need to smile when you come through my door, Isabelle."

"I smiled." I had not smiled. I wiped rain off my face.

"You did not." My sister stood by the door, her arms crossed, that shining blade pointed toward her ceiling.

"I smiled in my heart, Janie. Behind the left ventricle."

She tapped her foot four times.

"I can't believe I'm doing this." I stalked past her, opened the door, slammed it behind me, knocked four times. More rain dive-bombed down on my head. She opened it. She smiled.

I smiled with my teeth only, like a tiger in menopause, and sidled by her. She was playing a Vivaldi CD.

"Thank you," Janie said. She patted her reddish hair, which was back in a bun.

Cecilia and I are protective of our younger sister, Janie, and her . . . *quirks*. As she said one time, "The whole planet does not need to know that I have to touch each one of my closet doors in the same place with the same amount of pressure before I go to bed each night and if I do the wrong amount of pressure on one door I have to do it again. And again. Sometimes a third time." She'd let a little scream out and buried her face in her hands when she'd told me that one.

"What do you think of this knife, Isabelle?" she asked me.

Janie's eyes are bright green. I mean *bright green*. Luminescent. As usual, she was wearing a prim dress with a lace collar and comfortable (read: frumpy) shoes. She wore sensible beige bras that a nun might wear if she was eighty and blind. She was also wearing a white apron.

"I think that knife is sharp and twisty."

She sighed. I had disappointed her.

I headed toward her great room. Janie's houseboat is located on a quieter part of the Willamette River, although you can see the skyscrapers in Portland from the front decks. The windows are floor to ceiling, and the river rolls right on by, as do storms, ducks, Jet Skis, canoes, and drunk boaters.

The rain made the view blurry and gray.

"But do you think it offers up a sufficient amount of blinding fear?"

I turned around. "Yes. I'm blindingly scared to death of it."

Janie uses white doilies and has plastic slipcovers over all her pink chairs. She has pink flowered curtains and has *tea*—tea with scones and cream and honey and sugar—every afternoon, like the British; listens to classical music; and reads the classics, like *Jane Eyre*. If she's feeling wild, she listens to Yo-Yo Ma. She takes one bite of food, then four sips of tea. One bite of food, four sips of tea.

When she's done with her tea she goes back to wringing people's guts out of their stomachs with cattle prods.

"You know, the next killer in my book is a grandma. She goes after mothers," Janie said. "She hated her own mother. Her own mother made her work all the time, locked her in closets, and schlepped her around the country in a dirty white trailer. She worked in a bar. The kid got lice."

I stopped at that. "Now that's special, Janie. *Special.* Think she won't recognize who that is?"

"I've changed her name." She said this with not a little defiance. "And we were never locked in closets. We chose to go there all on our own. To hide."

I put my hands on my hips and stared at the ceiling, imagining how bad things would get once *she* got her hands on it. Oh, it would be ugly.

"And!" Janie said, stabbing the knife in the air. "The grandma in my book has white hair, she volunteers at the hospital in the gift shop, and at night—whack and stab, whack and stab."

I groaned. "Must you be so graphic?"

Janie put the knife back in a case on her kitchen counter, slammed the lid, and tapped it four times. "Well, then. Fine. *Fine.*"

I ignored the tone.

Janie patted that bun of hers. "This grandma scares me. Last night, after I finished writing at 2:02 A.M. I went in my own closet and hid."

"The woman that *you* created scared *you?*" Gall. "So, even though she's only in your head, you hid in your own closet from her."

She stared off into space. I knew she was waiting four seconds to answer my question. Why the obsession with the number four? I had no idea. Neither did she. She told me one time it was the "magic number in her head."

"She's so uncontrollable. I can't even control her when I'm

writing about her. She does things and says things and I follow her around and write what I'm seeing and hearing and smelling. She's a sick person. I don't like her."

"Me, neither. Maybe you should embroider her out of your life." Janie has to embroider flowers each night or she can't sleep. When she's done, she sews a pillow up—always white—and gives them to a group that counsels pregnant teenagers.

She fiddled with her apron. "Stop telling me you think my embroidery is stupid."

"I didn't say that," I protested.

"You didn't need to. I can hear it in your tone."

"My tone? My tone?"

"Yes, that condescending one!" She turned around and faced the front of her house, then gasped.

"What's wrong?" I got out of my chair.

"Oh, nothing. *It's nothing.*" She turned around, fiddled with her apron.

I moved toward the front window, so I could see the walkway in front of her houseboat. I saw a man. Brown hair. Tall, a loping stride, bigger nose than normal, but not too big. Not big enough to snarf down a fish. I figured he lived in the houseboat down the way.

I turned around. Grinned at Janie.

"Don't even think about it—" she breathed.

"Is that?" I raised my eyebrows, laughed, and made a dart for the door.

"Oh, no, you do not, Isabelle Bommarito!"

I opened the door and the rain came on in.

"Come back here, right this minute!"

But I had already stepped over the threshold to the wood walkway. She was right behind me and grabbed me around the waist, both arms. "Don't you dare."

I whispered, struggling, "I can help you to meet him—"

"*I don't need your help!*" she hissed.

"Let go of me, Janie," I whispered. "I'm helping you!"

I tried to pursue Big Nose, but she held on to me like a human octopus, one leg twisted around mine, both of us grunting with effort. "Get off of me."

"Never." She tightened her arms and lifted.

I wiggled around and tackled her and we ended up in a heap by her front door. Both of us went, "Ugh," when the air knocked out of our lungs. I held both her arms down, then whisked myself off her zippity quick and got a few steps. She scrambled up after me, her footsteps thudding, and shoved me to the ground. We rolled twice to the left, twice to the right, huffing and puffing.

She yanked at my ankle, tried to drag me back in. "You're always trying to butt in—"

"I am not trying to butt in." I tried to kick her hand with my other foot as she yanked me halfway into the air. I had no idea how she got so strong. "You need to get out of the house and live," I panted. "I've been hearing about that man for months—"

"There you go again! That's your definition of living!" She wiped rain off her face. "I don't want to sleep with each stud I meet! I want to find common interests, like a love of literature and the orchestra . . . and scones and tea! Besides, some of us like preserving ourselves for marriage!"

"What marriage?" I shrieked. "You can't get married unless you date, and dating takes being able to say hello to a person of the male species from this planet."

She flew at me like a little torpedo and landed on top of me, my face smashed down.

"Do you think it's healthy to stay home all day thinking up ways to kill people?" I huffed out, rain running down my neck.

"Do you think it's healthy," she huffed back, "to put a wall between yourself and everybody else?"

I whipped her over to her back. "Do you think it's healthy to count how many steps you take to the bathroom and tap toilet paper?"

She gasped in outrage. "Do you think it's healthy to keep a huge secret from your sisters, Isabelle? We know what happened to you, but you shut us out and you hide behind your camera like it's . . . like it's an eighteenth-century shield!" (I've mentioned her love of the classics?)

"You hide behind your front door, Embroidery Queen!"

She got me with an elbow to my neck for that one.

You might think we would be embarrassed by our behavior: Two grown women rolling around fighting on a deck.

Here's the truth: We are long past being embarrassed.

We kicked away from each other—kick, kick, kick—then Janie dove on top of me and we were face-to-face. She yelled, "Sometimes I think I hate you, Isabelle!"

"Sometimes I think I hate you, too, Janie!"

We both grunted.

"Well, I know I hate you both," another voice cut through, sharp and low. "What's that got to do with anything? Now get the hell up, your neighbors are all spying out their windows wondering why two grown women are wrestling on a damn deck."

With that, our sister, Cecilia, who has swinging long blond hair, the voice of a logger, and weighs 280 pounds, *at least*, stepped over us.

Before she entered the houseboat, she smiled at Janie. As soon as she crossed the threshold she turned and scowled at both of us as if we were slimy algae. "Get the hell in here. We got big problems. We gotta get this figured out friggin' quick. And don't you two think you can say no. Your answer is yes, let's start with that, damn it. *Yes.*"

She slammed the door.

"We're together on this, right?" I panted. Janie was still laying on top of me, rain streaking down our faces. "We're not going."

"Absolutely, positively not. No way."

"Our answer is no."

"No, no, no." Janie shook her head. "No."

We hugged on it.

Within an hour I was contemplating a quick escape by cannon-balling into the river. Janie was curled up, rocking back and forth, chanting, "I am worthy of praise, not abuse. I am worthy of praise, not abuse."

Cecilia shoved a chocolate doughnut into her mouth. "Momma wants you home to help."

Janie wrung her hands, four wrings on one side, four on the other. "My therapist said going home was an antispiritual, regressive idea for me. It could set me back years on my personal development and social-psycho-ecstasy scale."

"Years from what?" Cecilia demanded. "You sit alone in this pink and white houseboat, indulging all your weird habits and number counting and rituals and you write books about torture and murder. Honey." She did not say the word *honey* nice and polite. "There's nowhere for you to go but up."

"I can't go. I'm working."

"You can kill people in Trillium River, Janie."

Cecilia shook her head at Janie, then fixed me with those blue eyes. "You're coming, Isabelle."

I snorted. Leave my loft with the view of the river? Live somewhere else when I'm still fighting all the blackness lurking around the edges of my life? Live with *her* again? "I don't think so. Nope. Can't come. Won't come."

"You can keep the lingerie companies in business in Trillium River." Tiny doughnut pieces flew from her mouth in her fury. "I need you there."

"I'm working," I lied.

"Give me a break, Isabelle. You're not working. You're too screwed up. You two mice are leaving the city and coming to the country. Hey, maybe you'll learn there's more to life than yourselves."

"That is unfair," Janie sputtered.

"That's so like you, isn't it?" I stood up and faced her. "You attack when you don't get your way. You use fury to control anyone who pisses you off. You get mean and nasty and believe that *your victim* deserved your attack and you sit back and hate them, never considering for one second that you might be wrong, never considering that, gee, you might do things that tick people off—"

"*I* attack?" Cecilia pointed at her chest. "*I* attack?" She turned red, and I could tell her Mrs. Vesuvius–like temper had triggered.

"Yes, you attack. You hold grudges, you remember each tiny thing people did to offend you, you exaggerate to the point of lying—"

"Listen up, you braided mental case and you wacko, tea-slurping crime writer, I have spent years, *years*, handling her and Henry and Grandma while you two indulged your weirdness and forced me to handle everything."

"That is not true." I wanted to smash that mouth of hers shut. "When the house needed a new roof, I paid for it. Janie paid for a remodeled kitchen. I paid for Momma and Grandma and Henry to stay at a beach house last summer. Janie sent them to the mountains because she knows that Henry loves the snow—"

"You've sent *money*. Big deal. You're both swimming in it. Janie, you've got so much money you could buy France. Neither one of you has hardly been home since you left for college and you live only an hour away. You know Momma reopened the bakery and you've done nothing to help!"

"Cecilia," I snapped. "Janie and I paid for a live-in caregiver for Grandma and Henry. In fact, we interviewed a bunch of them, hired one, and sent her over."

"It didn't work, did it?" she shrieked, stomping her feet. "I told you it wouldn't. I told you! Grandma thought she was an ancient tribesman she met on an island during her final trip around the world as Amelia Earhart."

"Why did Grandma think the caregiver was a tribesman?"

Janie asked. She tapped the tips of her fingers together. "There were no feather hats, no tribal war paint . . ."

"How the hell should I know?" Cecilia said, doughnut sugar spewing out of her mouth. "She's got dementia. Henry didn't like the caregiver because he said she resembled a gecko. He ran away and hid in the shed under a trash can and the police had to come. Momma said the woman smelled like mothballs and death."

"She didn't smell," I protested. "She was a nice lady. She was from Maine."

"Maine Schmaine. They hated her. Momma told her she reminded her of Jack the Ripper, only with boobs. The caregiver asked me if Momma was insane, too." Cecilia flung her head back, stared at the ceiling, and threw her arms up as if asking for deliverance.

Momma wasn't crazy. She was, however, a nutcase.

"Jack the Ripper?" Janie moaned. "There is no correlation, none. Jack the Ripper was a killer in England who tore out—"

"We know who Jack the Ripper was," Cecilia fumed. She picked up another doughnut. "Let me lay it on the line, you two. I'm exhausted. I've had it. I'm not sleeping at night." Tears filled her blueberry eyes, then started soaking her red face. "I go from teaching kindergarteners, to the girls—they both have problems I haven't told you about—I help *her* out, handle Henry and Grandma . . ."

She put her hands over her face and started making these choking, gasping, snorting sounds as great gobs of tears rolled down. It about ripped my heart in two. "I can't take it anymore. The lawyers are fighting, and Parker and that . . . that . . . *slut* . . ."

Janie started crying, too. She **always cries** when one of us cries. Gentle, innocent heart. Killer **on the keybo**ard, but she hates to see anyone in pain. I got up and **put an arm** around Cecilia.

"I can't take her anymore." **She sniffled** and coughed and snorted again and I pulled her in close for a hug. "And I can't . . . I can't . . ."

"You can't what?" we asked.

"I can't . . ."

She waved the doughnut. "I can't stop eating." She mumbled. "I hate myself for it. I'm getting so fat, I can hardly walk. I can't tie my shoes. My blood pressure is as high as Venus and my cholesterol reading shows I have butter in my veins. The other day I was in my car and a boy oinked at me."

I wanted to tie the boy up by his heels, attach him to a boom on a crane, and swing him around until his intestines slid out.

"Oh, oh! Bommarito hug!" Janie weeped out.

We did a three-way hug, our foreheads together. Cecilia smelled like doughnut. Janie smelled like fear. I smelled like a person who had too many regrets.

"Okay," I whispered, feeling myself spiraling into a deep chasm of doom. "Okay. I'll come."

Janie leaned against me and whimpered, "Me, too, Cecilia."

Cecilia abruptly snapped her head up, away from our forehead powwow; wiped the tears from her face; and left our warm, snuggly, sisterly hug. Her face entirely composed, she grabbed her purse on her way out, waddling quite quickly.

"Good. Glad to hear it. See you two at the house," she ordered, no sign of the tears or unhappiness in her voice at all. She grabbed another doughnut. "I'll let her know you're coming. She'll be frickin' delighted."

The door slammed behind her.

I sank to the ground. So did Janie. She put her head on my stomach.

"She duped us again, didn't she?" I asked. *"Duped us."*

"She manipulated our vulnerability. Our compassion and our womanhood. And we rehearsed this, Isabelle," Janie whimpered. "Our answer was no."

"No, no, no—that was our answer."

"I need my embroidery," Janie whined, "I need my embroidery."

Shit. *Double shit.*

* * *

On the way home I got stuck in a traffic jam. Since I was on my motorcycle, I was happy it had stopped raining. When we were near the accident, we came to a complete halt to let the oncoming traffic go by. There were a couple of police cars, a fire truck, and an ambulance. An old blue truck had smashed into a light post and the beat-up camper trailer the driver was hauling was on its side. The light post now resembled the Leaning Tower of Pisa.

"What happened?" I asked a police officer who wandered over to chat about what a great motorcycle I had.

"The driver was high. Probably meth. He's going to court next week for distributing the stuff. His truck flew through the air with the greatest of ease. Like a bird. Like a torpedo. Like an idiot." He shook his head. "What an idiot."

The driver was not strapped in, so he went through his windshield. Because he was high as a kite and relaxed, he would live, which was somewhat unfortunate considering the long criminal record he had. He was the oldest son of an old, snobby family in the city.

"Spoiled brat," the police officer muttered. "Grow kids up rich and they never turn out. Make 'em work, and you'll teach 'em how to live and respect other people."

As the tow trucks came, I stared at that trailer and shuddered.

It was a carbon copy of the one we'd lived in years ago.

The darkness pulled at me again, inch by inch, the hole waiting nearby. I had to stare at the trees on the side of the road and breathe.

She had been beyond desperate. But it was the trailer that had caused all the screaming. And the blood. All that blood.

Blood everywhere.

Once I got past the accident, I rode so fast on my bike I got a ticket.

"Nice bike," the red-haired officer told me who pulled me over. "Who you running from so fast?"

Myself, I wanted to say.

I'm running from myself.

But I'm not quick enough to get rid of me.

ᙦ 3 ᙢ

Momma lives in the Queen Anne Victorian home she grew up in before she rebelled and left right after high school but not before smashing my grandma Stella's mother's crystal punch bowl. She lives there with Grandma Stella, and our younger brother, Henry. Cecilia lives up the road on several acres about five minutes away.

The Queen Anne is situated a little outside the town of Trillium River, which nestles along the Columbia River on the Oregon side.

Trillium River changes each time I'm there. When we arrived in high school, traumatized and exhausted, it was small and dumpy. Now there are art galleries, cafés, coffee shops, bookstores, a gourmet ice-cream shop, and a classy tattoo parlor named The Painted Vein. There's also world-class windsurfing, skiing on Mt. Hood, and nature fanatics can get high on nature.

Surrounding the town are orchards and farmland. My grandma's Queen Anne home, sitting on five acres, amidst a vast expanse of perfectly green lawn, can best be described as cakelike. Why? Because it reminds me of a blue cake.

Built in 1899, it's four thousand square feet and light blue with white trim and white shutters, lacy lattice, a gabled roof, a huge wraparound covered porch on the main floor with an attached gazebo, a tower that Grandma visits often to "hide her secrets," and a sunroom filled with wicker furniture and walls of windows.

Inside there are nooks and crannies, two bay windows with window seats, built-in bookshelves and built-in china cabinets. The rooms are large and airy, with stained-glass windows in the living room and perfectly preserved antiques.

Two clematis, one with pink flowers and one with white, wind their way up and around the porch like no one's business.

I drove up on my motorcycle, with Janie behind me driving her silver Porsche. We would return to Portland soon and get my black Porsche. I had to have my motorcycle for mental escape.

Grandma's Queen Anne is the most charming home I've ever seen. Inside it smells like fresh-baked bread, vanilla, cinnamon, and history.

Our family's history.

I wanted to turn my bike and peel on out of there, one wheel up in the air.

Janie and I stood in front of the house together like soldiers before a battle, though we did not have any grenades or assault rifles with us.

The wind swirled around, like it was welcoming us home, fun and frolicking . . . mysterious.

I have never forgotten the wind here.

To me, the wind has always seemed like a person, with all the mood swings and rampaging, out-of-control emotions that we have. Sometimes it's angry and whips around corners, sometimes it ruffles the river as it hurries toward the ocean, sometimes it puffs on by, gentle, caressing.

"The wind never stops," Janie said, in wonder. "Never."

She grabbed my hand, pulsing it with her fingers. She does this when she gets nervous. She'll squeeze my hand four times, then pause, squeeze it four times, pause again. She gasped a little. Coughed. Breathed in. Breathed out.

"I feel faint," I said. "I may need a one-night stand." Sometimes I try to humor myself when things are particularly bleak.

"I need to tap and count," she replied. "In fact, I think I'll pause for a sec and count the roof tiles."

At that second, the door flew open and a man came sprinting out, legs pumping, arms waving. He was wearing a straw hat over brown curls, blue shorts, and a T-shirt that said ABC. His white shoes had Velcro straps. He had a tummy, he wasn't as tall as me, his eyes tilted, and his smile beamed, as usual.

He put his arms out wide as he hurdled toward us, screaming and laughing.

"They here! They here!" he shouted. His hat flipped off into that wind.

We knew what would happen.

"Now, Henry, no tackling us!" Janie said, so kind, because she loves Henry, but she backed away, hands up.

"Be gentle, Henry," I said. "Give us a nice, gentle hug. Gentle!" I love Henry, but I backed up, too, sticking close to Janie.

Henry was not to be stopped.

Within two seconds, Janie and I were splat on the grass, tackled by our happy, mentally disabled brother who was on top of us, laughing.

"You home!" he announced, giving us both a kiss. "You home for Henry! Yeah, yeah. H-E-N-R-Y-H-E-N-R-Y!"

I gave Henry a kiss on the forehead and said, "I love you, my brother, Henry."

Henry giggled. "I love you, my sister, Is."

Janie kissed both of his cheeks. We hugged him as my love for Henry walloped me hard.

I heard Janie counting out loud. Soon we would be with our momma, a tricky sorceress; our grandma, who thought she was Amelia Earhart; and our sister, Cecilia, who has a hurricane for a personality.

Honest to God, Henry is the only normal person in our family. The only one.

* * *

A long wood farm table slouched in the middle of the stunning, country-style kitchen Janie had paid to have remodeled so she could assuage the guilt she felt for not living here in the nuthouse with the viper.

A vase of flowers, purples and pinks, in a clear, curving glass vase sat on the table. On the windowsill was a collection of old, colorful glass bottles, the sunlight shimmering right through them. A set of French doors let in that ever-present, meandering wind.

Cecilia hugged both of us, bear-hug tight, then stood to my right, a sister-soldier in the battle against Momma/The Viper.

Momma did not bother to stand from where she was sitting at the table cracking walnuts when Janie and I entered. She said, almost melodically, "Henry, darling, would you please go and pick me a bouquet of flowers? You're the only one who can do it right."

"Yeah! Okay dokay, Momma!" Henry grabbed some scissors, blew us a kiss, then jump jump jumped out the door. "I bring the sisters in, now I get the flowers. I be right back!"

To get a full picture of Momma, blend together an older, blond Scarlett O'Hara and the steely coldness of the Queen of England. Except Scarlett and the Queen were not conceived on the banks of the Columbia River, which is how Momma got her name.

River Bommarito has ash-blond hair that curves into a stylish bell to her shoulders. When we were younger, it was either elegantly brushed or wedged onto her head. The wedging happened if she was spending days or weeks in bed, her depression getting the best of her, as she screamed at us to *get the hell out.*

One day, for some mysterious reason, after she'd molted, decayed, and sunk deeper into her own emotional pit, she'd get up, shower, apply her makeup, slip on a dress and heels, and it was like her depression never happened.

She'd get another job, usually a soul-shredding one, or her old boss would take her back because she made him so much money, and that was that. No explanation, no apology, no thanks to the three young daughters in the house for keeping things together while she dissolved into an almost-catatonic state.

No family meeting to discuss the trauma we'd recently lived through. The traumas became family secrets, never discussed or let out of the locked box.

Fortunately, after we sisters moved away, and Momma got older and the very same Grandma Momma had once called, to her face, "a wrinkled, mean hag-monster," slipped and slid into dementia, she rarely took to her bed.

Maybe Momma was hoping to enjoy as many sane days as she could before Grandma's dementia caught up with her through the gene pool. Or maybe, because she was no longer in dire emotional and financial straits, she didn't get depressed.

Or maybe she took drugs. She'd told us she didn't take medication, but I wasn't sure about that. Not sure at all.

Next to me Janie started counting, her fingertips meeting as she muttered each number. "One . . . two . . . three . . . four . . ."

I stuck my chin up a fraction of an inch.

Cecilia whispered, "Speak, witch."

Momma glared at us, like we were larvae, then stood, carefully placing the walnut cracker on the table and swishing her hands together to get rid of any nut residue, her intense gaze never leaving ours.

"So, the impossible girls have finally returned to help. Guilt has finally gotten the best of you after years of neglecting this family, hasn't it?" River is tiny like a ballerina and has the same eyes as Janie, bright green, but River's eyes are a murky sea with a light on all the time behind the irises. "I've changed my mind. Throw out those pink letters I sent you. I've decided that we don't need your help."

Ah. So it would be this way. We grew up with her demands, her retractions, the guilt trips, righteous self-anger. I know what she is, and isn't, but when I'm with her I can get things all screwed up, as if my head is in a blender and the blender is turned on to "grind." "Momma, you're going in for open-heart surgery. We got your letters, we came, we want to help you."

"I can handle it myself. Your presence here is no longer needed." Her green eyes shot tiny emerald-tipped daggers at us. We were bad larvae, she told us without saying a word. Bad larvae.

"1 . . . 2 . . . 3 . . . 4 . . ." Janie whimpered.

"You can't do it all, Momma. You can't take care of Grandma and Henry and the bakery and yourself."

"Cecilia can do it. Cecilia can help with Henry. She can move into this house and watch him and she can keep an eye on Grandma." She adjusted the starched white collar of her shirt. She wore a light pink sweater over it, pearl earrings, and beige slacks. Understated elegance. Prim and proper. "Cecilia has always been here for me."

I glanced at Cecilia and felt my chest get all tight and emotional, if a chest can get emotional. The emotional toll for being "there" for Momma had about puréed poor Cecilia.

"Cecilia works as a kindergarten teacher, Momma. She has two kids. She has other problems, you know that." For example, she has to figure out a way to fillet Parker.

"Cecilia is always the daughter who has come through for me and she will again. She can do anything. Anything."

I felt my throat tighten, like it was shrinking. *Cecilia is always the daughter who has come through for me.* I told myself to buck up. Tears never helped a situation. Never. What were they worth? Nothing.

"I've taught her everything she knows about the bakery and she'll carry on. It won't be the River Way, but Cecilia will do her best."

I closed my eyes to smother my temper. Momma always did this, played one daughter against the other. You probably think that I hate Cecilia for this favoritism. That would be entirely wrong. I feel sorry for Cecilia. Momma might declare that Cecilia is her favorite, but it's kind of like being the favorite of the devil's assistant.

"You are a separate person. You can control how you react to her," muttered Janie. "Breathe deeply."

I heard her breathe deeply, then make a humming sound as she exhaled. "Set a boundary. *Believe* in the boundary."

"You and Janie came to help?" Momma arched a perfectly plucked brow. "Perhaps Janie will teach all of us to count?"

"Momma, stop it, that is not nice," Cecilia interrupted. "Janie is here, isn't she?"

I could tell she was petrified at the thought of me and Janie bolting out the door. She knew she couldn't handle teaching and her kids and Grandma and Henry and the bakery. Who could?

No one.

"Janie's here, yes," Momma mused, cupping the bottom of her perfect hair. "But I don't understand how someone who can write best-selling novels from a houseboat in Portland can't make time for her momma."

Janie took a gaspy breath. "I do make time for you, Momma."

"No, you don't, young lady. *You. Do. Not.* Too busy being famous for your momma."

I heard Janie mutter to herself, "Janie, you can't change her, you can only change your reaction to her."

"Must you mutter to yourself?" Momma snapped. "I told you not to do that eons ago. Stand up straight, and what on earth are you wearing? Do you want to be frumpy and old? Why are you wearing flat brown shoes? And where did you get that dress? From a farmer's wife? Why do you have gray in your hair? I'm your *mother* and I don't let any gray show in my hair."

She crossed her hands in front of her. "Gray is for old women. It's for women who don't care about their appearance anymore. You girls are only in your thirties, but . . . you're getting old, Janie, I can tell. You should be working to retain your youth, not diving into middle age."

"Momma!" Cecilia and I protested.

Janie muttered beside me, her voice teary. "She's a hurt, deranged woman. You need to be strong. Rise above her pettiness."

"Stop that muttering this instant!" Momma lashed out.

"Okay, Momma, okay," I said, putting my hand out toward her and stepping in front of Janie.

Janie whimpered and said to herself, "You are separate from her. She cannot hurt you if you don't let her. Breathhhheee . . ."

How many times had I done this? How many times had Cecilia? Physically stepped in front of Janie to shield her from Momma? We were all her personal dartboards, but Momma's remarks always aimed especially sharp at Janie. Probably because Janie wouldn't fight back. I would. Sometimes Cecilia did. But not Janie. She crumpled.

"Humph." Momma's attention, diverted from Janie, turned on me. "I see you're still wearing your hair in hundreds of little braids, Isabelle. Why is that? You're not a black person, are you?"

Cecilia murmured, "And the witch speaks . . ."

"I don't believe I'm an African-American, Momma, unless there's something you want to tell me?"

"Black people braid their hair. Are you black? No, you're not. It is unbecoming on you. It is tacky. It is classless."

"Actually, my braids are cool." I met her gaze, shoulders back. In my work, I had faced down murderous warlords, scary men with mirrored glasses and guns; escaped from rioting, delirious mobs; and hidden behind tanks to avoid grenades. I could handle my momma.

Probably.

"Cool?" She rapped her perfectly polished red nails on the table. "Cool? You remind me of a hippie who might have camped out at Woodstock in the 1960s. Do you never wear a bra?"

"Not today. I needed to feel loose today, like I wasn't suffocating."

"Loose? A lady never should feel *loose*. Breasts should be in bras, close to the body, with no jiggle. So what is your excuse for flopping about in such a completely unladylike fashion?"

I resisted the urge to laugh at the hypocrisy behind that statement. "Well, I burned a couple of bras this past week on my balcony and didn't feel like putting another one on. Plus, I knew, Momma, that I would have the pleasure of your company."

She simmered. "Pray tell, what does that have to do with bras?"

"I needed to feel a bit freer, not constricted, because I know you'll make me feel like I should commit myself and beg for a straitjacket."

She drew in a deep breath, stuck her bosom out. "You will not speak to me like that. I'll not have it! It's disrespectful."

"And you will not bully Janie, Momma." I put my hands on my hips, but my whole body hurt. Why couldn't she love us like a normal mother? Why couldn't she hug us and hold us and thank us for coming?

"I sacrificed for the three of you for years—"

"Don't start in, Momma. Don't start."

"I gave you everything I had when you were children—"

"Yes, you did. You also were often as mean as a cornered rattlesnake and went to bed for weeks on end," I said.

"How dare you. How dare you!" She hit the table with her palms.

"I dare because I'm not going to allow you to whitewash what happened to us when we were kids to guilt us into staying here."

"Whitewash? I worked, I did things I never thought I'd do, I provided, I protected you. By myself. All by myself."

"I know that, Momma. I do. But we worked, too. We baked gingersnaps and lemon twist cookies and banana bread until I hated the sight of sugar with a passion, and I don't want you twisting our history into your own victimhood."

She said nothing, but her face reddened. "You may leave now." She tilted her head at me in dismissal and picked up her nutcracker. The symbolism was not lost on me. "I have decided that your presence is unnecessary."

Cecilia leaned against the wall, the color of coffee foam, shaking her head back and forth, her blue eyes beseeching me. "Don't leave me with the witch," she hissed.

"You may leave, I said," Momma sang out. Her eyes were bright. Perhaps there was a tear?

Nah. Nada. Not our momma.

Silly me.

Behind me, Janie started to chant. "I will make my own boundaries and hold myself to them, I will make my own boundaries and hold myself to them . . ."

Cecilia put her hands together in prayer, pointing the tips of her fingers at us, mouthing, "She's wicked. You must stay."

"We're all fine without you. More than fine." Momma's perfectly manicured hands did not still.

Cecilia had taken the brunt of Momma for years. She could have left, like me and Janie. But she hadn't. I tried to smash my guilt down.

"You two have lived your own selfish lives without us. Cecilia has been the only daughter who has valued family."

Cecilia closed her eyes tight, her breathing labored. "Please, please, please," she mouthed at me. "Help me!"

It was like living inside a horror flick and the resident she-devil was directing what happened.

"I can make my own decisions. I do not have to choose to stay," Janie muttered. "I am strong. I am mighty. I am not a doormat for others' abuse. I can say no. No. No."

"Janie," I told her. "Grab your suitcases. We're moving in."

Janie sounded like she was choking on a rock. Cecilia squeaked with relief.

Momma cracked a nut, a slight smile tipping the corners of her mouth.

I wanted to heave that bowlful of nuts through one of the stained-glass windows, followed by my momma.

Like I said, if you happened upon Momma, she would remind you of a southern belle. A model for petite, older women's clothes. A serene lady.

You would never guess, I thought, as I stomped out to my motorcycle, my stomach churning, my anger switch flipped on high, that our elegant, proper momma had been a stripper when we were growing up.

That's right.

A stripper. Pole, G-string, and glitter.

Va va voom.

4

Cecilia, Janie, and I trooped toward Janie's Porsche parked outside Grandma's house.

Henry bopped along beside us. "Sisters home! Sisters home! Who want to play the hide-and-seek! That game! Hide-and-seek!"

"We'll play with you, Henry," Cecilia said. "We have to get Isabelle and Janie settled first." Then she muttered, "They're moving into the witch's house."

"Okay dokay!"

I hugged Henry. He's the nicest person I know. My poor brother had survived one wrecking-ball blow after another in his life and he miraculously still found eight hundred things to smile about. "Let me unpack. How's your stamp collection?"

He laughed. "I have fifty-six stamps, Isabelle! Fifty-six! I have a stamp from North Dakota! Do you know where that is? I don't!" He clapped twice. "Do you know where Michigan is? I don't!" Clapped twice. "Do you know where Florida is?" He loved this game. "I do! They have swamps and alligators and an ocean and Disney World!" Henry loves Florida. Never been there, but he loves it. He started singing, "Mickey Mouse! Donald Duck! For ever ever ever . . ."

I noticed that Janie was not with us anymore. I stopped and turned around. Janie was crouched on all fours in the middle of the grass, her skinny body jerking as she went through a series of dry heaves.

"You think this is hard, you counting hermit?" Cecilia snapped, her usual compassionate self. "Try living with it day in, day out, for years. Know how many times I've been told I'm the size of a pregnant hippo? How she never thought she'd have a fat daughter? Get up, Tapping Queen, and suck it up." She flounced past me, grabbed two suitcases, and marched back to the house. "Get in the house, hermit."

"I'll get your stuff, Janie," I told her. She nodded weakly, went back to dry heaving.

Janie had brought five suitcases, a laptop, a sack of self-help books and her classics, a giant picture of her houseboat ("so I can visualize a peaceful place"), East Indian music, her embroidery basket, teas, a Yo-Yo Ma CD, a yoga mat, a picture of her therapist, and nine new journals to "write in when I feel like Momma will overwhelm or diminish me. My journals will recenter me, help me to find the goodness and strength within myself, and the courage to stand up tall as a person who deserves respect."

I left Henry patting pale Janie, slung my favorite camera around my neck, and dragged my suitcases into the house, up the wood stairs, down the yellow-painted hallway, and into my old bedroom.

My bedroom was painted a light sage color and had a window seat overlooking the front porch. I used to climb out this window at night to meet one boy or the other for attention and copulation purposes. My bed was a twin, with a flowered bedspread on it. Two white nightstands and a white dresser and desk completed the room.

Janie's room was pink with white curtains. Her room was smaller than mine but had a funky, pitched ceiling and two dormer windows. I knew she would soon be cowering in her closet, chanting to herself, rocking, embroidering flowers, trying not to let Momma undo years of therapy.

I already felt like the walls were sucking me in, stripping away my fragile, tenuous hold on sanity. The blackness in my head foamed a bit, bubbled, swirled. I had been an adult for so long, but a few minutes in this house and I was regressing.

I flicked my braids back and took a shuddery breath.

I was home.

Welcome back to your nightmare, I told myself. *Welcome back.*

I heard the van pull up in front of the house about an hour later. I leaned out the window of my bedroom, that busy wind blowing my braids and beads.

There she was. I couldn't help chuckling. Within minutes I heard her marching up the steps, then a brisk knock on my door.

I smiled at my grandma, a tiny woman with white, curly hair, standing in the doorway wearing old-fashioned, air force flight gear, including an antique flight helmet and goggles. It was hard to believe that until a few years ago, when dementia caught up to her, Grandma was a firebrand who'd nitpicked Momma until she could barely see straight through her fury.

"Amelia!" I exclaimed. "Amelia Earhart!"

"Good to see you, young lady." She narrowed her eyes at me, saluted, clicking her black army boots together two times. "You're familiar to me. I believe we met during my speaking tour in 1929. That tour exhausted me!" She flipped a hand to her forehead. "It was my sinuses. Clogged. Burning. Running."

"How are your sinuses today, Mrs. Earhart?"

"Better." She tipped her head up, touched her nose. "Probably because of my latest operation. The doctors had no idea what they were doing, none. Men are stupid. I'm surprised my nose is still on my face."

"I'm glad it's still there, Amelia."

I hugged her. She seemed surprised at first but then hugged back.

"My fans love me!" she declared, then stepped up close to me, flicking one of my braids back. She smelled like roses and mountain air. "I love to fly at night."

"Well, Amelia, your night flying skills are excellent—"

"Some people question my flying abilities." She adjusted her goggles over her face. "Again, they're men. Stupid, know-nothing men. Eight brain cells. Maybe. I've written a poem about them, shall I pronounce it to you?" She straightened her flight jacket and clicked her boots together. " 'Men. Slimy and rude, loud and uncouth. Never inclined to give up their booth.' That about sums them up."

"Sure does, Amelia."

"I'm a nurse, you know. I aided the soldiers in World War I and I know what I'm doing. If your arm is amputated while you're here, I can sew it back on. If your head has a bullet in it, I can get it out with a spoon. Care to fly with me soon?"

"It is my dearest wish," I told her. "It will be my pleasure."

"Women power!" she shouted, fist up and swinging. "Women power!"

I raised my fist. "Women power!"

By the time we moved in with Grandma, my first year of high school, all of us were covered in so much fear we were quaking. It practically dripped off of us. Momma was holding on by her fingernails and most of the fingernails were split in half.

Henry had regressed at least two years and was babbling, his speech lost, bladder control iffy because of what he'd been through. Janie was anxious to the point of cracking. Cecilia was furious and inhaling food. I had retired into my head and my blackness.

But Grandma's gracious home was an oasis in the midst of an ocean of night terrors come alive. We had clothes that fit. We had food on a regular basis that she cooked from scratch. We had heat.

When Momma hit blackness and crawled to bed, we were not alone. Grandma was not a saint—she had a flaming temper and did not bother to mince words—but she hugged us warm and tight, unlike Momma, who avoided all displays of affection with her daughters as one might avoid malaria, and she *cared*. Grandma cared about us.

By any account, you could say that Grandma saved our family. She was smart, strong, and ran a tight ship. As captain of that ship she hounded Momma to get counseling, to get a date, to gain weight, to button her shirt up, to go back to school so she could be "someone," to stop hiding in her bed, and her hair! A mop! Grandma reminded Momma that she'd warned her this would happen! She knew it! She'd told her! It was endless.

As I grew older I realized that Momma's relationship with Grandma was a carbon copy of our relationship with Momma: difficult, competitive, critical, demanding. Never good *enough*.

It's genetics, and we were screwed in that department.

When they fought, we hid in our closets.

Amelia and Momma, however, never fought.

Grandma/Amelia rose onto her toes. Clicked her boots. "I must be off to the tower. I have to hide my secrets again so the natives won't steal them."

I nodded sagely.

"Will you be residing here for a while with my copilot and what did you say your name was and do you fly?" She stuck her arms straight out, made the sound of a plane engine deep in her throat, and left the room.

I wandered into Janie's bedroom.

"Get out of the closet, Janie," I said.

"No. I'm in self-analysis contemplation."

"Come on. Out you go."

I opened the door to the closet. It was filled with stuffed animals. Janie's face was buried in an alligator. She was sitting on her yoga mat.

"I'm regressing back to childhood, Isabelle," she whimpered. "I can feel it. Feel the backward passage of time flowing."

I got down on my knees. "Take it on the chin."

"I can't."

"You better. She's gonna eat you alive, regurgitate you back up, and start picking at your bones if you don't."

"You sound gruesome. It makes me uncomfortable."

I rolled my eyes. She writes graphic crime novels and *I'm* gruesome? "Sorry, but it's true. Find a backbone and stick it in your spine."

Cecilia came into the room. "Okay, ladies . . . Oh, man. What the hell? Get out of there, Janie. Right now. Stop being such a wimp." She shifted her weight to a rocking chair. The chair made cracking sounds. She wiped the sweat from her brow. She was wearing a dress that resembled a green tarp, her long blond hair in a messy ball on her head.

"I have the list from Momma." Cecilia whipped out the list. It was written on pink paper. I collapsed on the bed. Janie shut the closet door.

"Damn!" Cecilia threw the list down, yanked open the closet door, grabbed Janie by her ankles, and dragged her to the middle of the rug. Janie struggled like a dolphin would if caught in the jaws of a killer whale and tried to crawl back into the closet, but Cecilia hauled her back out.

"We're too old for this . . ." I drawled.

"Oh, shut up, Isabelle!" Janie said. "You tackled me outside of my own houseboat!"

Cecilia grunted and flipped Janie over. Cecilia is fat but she's about as strong as Popeye. "Listen to me, Janie!" she screeched. "You're not going back in the goddamn closet!"

"Yes, I am, and then I'm going home," Janie wailed. "Home to my houseboat—let go of me, I was in my restorative mood, claiming my own gentleness in my journal—"

Cecilia got down on all fours and put her face two inches from Janie's. "You listen to me, you skinny, obsessive crime writer, you are gonna get yourself together and help me. I can't, I won't, do this all by myself when you hide in your houseboat, tapping this, tapping that, counting this, counting that, indulging yourself in your problems while you write about ripping people's throats apart with barbed wire and a machete. That's sick, Janie. No wonder you can't sleep at night. . . ."

"I turn off my light at precisely 10:14 at night, fluff the pillows four times"—she dissolved into tears—"tap the tables on both sides of my bed four times, drink water, touch the closets, check the front door to make sure it's locked, check the stove, check the door and stove again, touch the lock of the door, touch each knob on the stove, retouch the closet doors, get in bed, fluff the pillows, tap the tables." She put her hands on her face in complete despair. "After that I sleep."

Cecilia was speechless.

I crossed my legs, examined my nails. "Think that's exhausting? Ask her about her morning routine."

Cecilia turned her head toward me, her blond hair flipping over her shoulders. She has amazing hair. "You've got to be kidding."

"Nope. No joke. Now let's see that list you have."

Janie clapped her hands four times.

The list Momma had compiled of things we needed to do while she was in the hospital was extensive and detailed. I will not share each glorious detail here because if I did, you would probably want to check your own self into a nice, quiet, mental ward and a nice, quiet straitjacket.

Beyond obsessive detail on how to keep the house cleaned in her absence (corners, girls!) and admonishes to not eat too much or we'd get fatter (Cecilia), or too little and appear corpselike (Janie), and not to sleep with the gardener (me), Momma detailed Henry's schedule.

Henry helped at the bakery at least twice a week. He also had to be at the church on Sunday from 8:00 to 1:45. Henry was in charge of bringing the boxes of doughnuts in from Mrs. McQueeney's car. A description of Mrs. McQueeney followed: "Her facial features are a cross between a nutria and a carrot. She has large nostrils."

Henry got the coffeepots out and ready, then sat in the front row for both masses to help Father Mike, if necessary. ("For God's sakes, Isabelle, don't confess to Father Mike. It will humiliate me as a mother. *Humiliate me.*")

On Wednesdays Henry helped at the church for the high school youth group. On Thursdays he went to the senior center, served lunch, cleaned the tables, and set things up for Bunco. On Mondays and Friday mornings he went to the animal shelter and petted cats and dogs. ("If Janie is going to obsessively count the cats, keep her away!")

When Henry helps in Cecilia's classroom, "remind Henry to make Cecilia go out for recess with the kids. She needs the exercise!" On Saturdays he joined other special people for a day trip.

As for Grandma, aka Amelia Earhart, she had her activities, too. Grandma was picked up by one of those short senior buses and taken on day trips with other seniors. Not all of them had lost their marbles yet. They let Grandma come because when Grandma had her marbles still in her head, she'd made a large donation. ("Do not let Grandma bring the whiskey with her on these trips. Fred Kawa always drinks too much and ends up doing strip-teases.")

"Velvet will come in and help you with Grandma. She is a much better caregiver than the mothball you sent me last time and dear Henry likes her, bless him. She has already been informed to never, ever serve Henry orange juice. *You know why.*"

Yes, we knew why. All too well, we knew why.

Grandma had been known to give Velvet the slip, though, so I should be prepared, wrote Momma, to leave the bakery "on the spin of a nickel" and help Velvet find Grandma. "Come immediately. You have a lazy bone, Isabelle, you are riddled with lazy bones, and I know, Janie, that you will have to do odd things before leaving the bakery. I don't know where you got such strange habits, certainly not from me."

Grandma could get dressed in her flight outfits herself, although she sometimes forgot underwear. "You must check Grandma's bottom each day to make sure it's appropriately covered." I was to comb her hair, description given. She forgot to brush her teeth and would often give speeches in front of her mirror. If the speech grew too long and she was going to miss her day trip, I was to go into her bedroom, the same one she'd been sleeping in for sixty-four years, and say, "Mrs. Earhart, are you ready for takeoff? Your plane is on the runway."

Grandma would then stop giving her speech, salute, and go downstairs to the bus.

Grandma had to have bran in the morning. "She has bowel problems. Without the bran, she'll be stuffed to her ears. Make sure she eats it. She has hemorrhoids, which she calls her 'bottom bullet wounds,' and you will have to address that. Cream is on the dresser.

"Don't push Grandma to do anything she doesn't want to. I know you girls are control freaks, but control yourself. Control is important for any lady to have and you three need it." I rolled my eyes at that one.

I already knew I was to address her as Amelia, or Mrs. Earhart. I was not to discuss her husband, Momma's daddy, with her, because Mrs. Earhart would start swearing and expounding upon "killing the cheating bastard" or "He is not a man. He is a eunuch. No balls. Fucker."

My grandpa Colin was a man, as legend has it, with an ego the size of Arkansas. He was a doctor, hence the house, and died when he was having a nighttime picnic with his receptionist up on a cliff. He drank too much and toppled off.

Momma was fourteen. She told me that Grandma's response at the time was, "Wonderful. I was going to have to divorce him. Now I'll take the life insurance and dance on his grave." Apparently she did that, too. Danced on his grave every Friday night for five years while drinking his whiskey. She would scream at him, "Hey, pond scum. See who's still dancing? See who's decaying?"

So no Colin reminders.

The list reminded me that I was not to call her Grandma or "chatter on" about anything we did as kids. Ever. That confused her.

We also received directions on Bommarito's Bakery, which we had all worked and cooked in, for hours each day, all through high school, despite Grandma's protests that Momma was working us "hard enough to rip the skin off their bones."

Momma took orders, and we baked cookies, cakes, breads, you name it, using our dad's cookbooks. Ad nauseum.

"The bakery is a thriving business. Thriving. Don't ruin things for me," she wrote. "I have loyal, dear customers. I hope to the high heavens I still have them when I return."

I rolled my eyes. She then detailed her recipes (many), what time I was to get to the bakery with Janie (5:00 A.M.), what goods should be made first, and other inane details like frosting color. Again, I won't list it. Think: straitjacket.

"Isabelle, don't get into men's beds. That was humiliating last time. Do you have to wear your hair in braids? Black people wear braids. Not you. Are you black? I raised you better than that, and you know it. Janie, *please*. No muttering or chanting. Ladies never mutter or chant.

"Get this right, girls.

"Momma.

"PS Keep Cecilia from eating any more than she already does. She is too fat already. I have done what I could for her."

There was a silence when we all finished reading The List.

Cecilia's chin was quivering.

I slung an arm around her shoulders.

"I can love myself even if I don't feel loved by Momma I can love myself even if I don't feel loved by Momma," Janie chanted.

I went to hug Janie.

Cecilia made a move for the closet; Janie crawled in behind her. They shut the door.

I crumpled up the pink letter that smelled like nauseating flowers and opened the door to the closet. "Scoot over."

Later that night Henry, Janie, and I lined up his shells on the floor and studied them. Same with his collection of rocks.

When he went to bed, we sang songs, and I brushed his curls back. "I love yous," he murmured, when his almond eyes began to shut. "Yeah, yeah. I love yous. I so happy you home."

No one in my life has ever been as excited to see me as Henry always is. No one has ever loved me as much as he does, either. Darn near made me tear up, thinking of that.

We snuck out when he was asleep. Janie went straight to her room and started murdering people. "I have a deadline and I still haven't set out my doilies or peace candles, nor have I arranged a serenity corner or a positive breathing space."

I hugged her good night, then I headed out to the porch swing. Momma was already in bed. She had not liked the dinner we cooked. The sauce was too spicy, the bread hard "like a suitcase," the salad filled with salmonella.

You might think that Momma had lost it, like her Momma has, based on what she says. That would be incorrect. Momma has been like this since before our dad slung a bag over his shoulder and walked down our driveway, away from our home and swing set and into the soft lights of dawn. This is how River Bommarito *is*.

I pushed River out of my twirling mind and thought about Henry as I swung.

You would have thought that we sisters would have hated Henry for being Momma's clear favorite.

Never happened.

From an early age, he was sick, helpless, loveable, pitiful, lost, cheerful, loving, and sweet.

It was an unbeatable combination.

He was completely unprepared for the shittiness of our child-hood, for what had happened specifically to him, but unlike his sisters, he had learned to trust again. To hope. To reach out to others with innocence.

He was a blipping miracle.

I swung more, the country quiet, the wind a gentle rustle, calm, the land undulating like the soft swells of a green ocean, trees rustling overhead. It was incomparably beautiful in Trillium River.

I felt like I'd entered hell.

Cecilia took a day off work from her kindergarteners to help us get Momma to the hospital the next morning. She swung by in her van and Janie and I got Momma settled in the front seat.

The sun was peeping up, the sky golden and pink, the wind sauntering by, relaxed, as if it had all the time in the world today to see Momma off. All was still, sleepy, and content.

Except for the three of us sisters, who were twisting in the middle of an emotional battlefield filled with booby traps and land mines.

Momma was not in a good mood. The breakfast I made her was "flat." Janie was making her nervous. I hadn't snuck a man up to my room last night, had I? The kitchen was messy, she *never* had a messy kitchen. Cecilia was late. She's always late. "Not an organized woman. She's a mess. A mess."

"Stop spinning around me," Momma snapped, attaching a pearl earring. "Do not tell me to relax, Isabelle! Cease mumbling to yourself, Janie. Or are you speaking to an imaginary friend? Cecilia, for God's sakes, you have enlarged. You're bigger than you were yesterday! You have got to stop eating. One of the biggest days of my life, if not the biggest day of all because I am getting open-heart surgery, if you girls care to remember, and here you are, making me late!"

"We're not late, Momma," Janie said, tentative. "Don't you worry—"

"I am worried, Janie. I'm worried that I have a daughter who has written nine books and all she does is murder people in bizarre, twisted ways."

"I don't murder people, Momma—"

"You do! What is going on in that head of yours? This is not the lady I raised you to be!" She wriggled in her perfectly pressed blue suit and recrossed her blue heels. "When are you getting married and having children? You're going to get too old—"

"Momma," I interjected, as soon as Cecilia pulled out of the drive. "Don't miss the sunrise. It's beautiful." *Momma, don't you want to stay in the hospital five months instead of five days? Don't you want the doctors to sew your mouth shut for the rest of your life?*

With both hands, I pressed my braids tight to my head. I could feel that blackness again, right on the periphery. I fought so hard against that blackness. It had plagued me since childhood. Sometimes it won, sometimes I won. I was definitely sliding into second place today.

"Please, Isabelle! I know what you're trying to do," Momma argued. "You're trying to change the subject and it won't work. Drive by my bakery, Cecilia, immediately. I want to see the building one more time before you girls get in it and burn the whole thing down." She shook her head, tsk-tsked her tongue. "I'll be out of business before a week is up."

"You won't be out of business, Momma," Cecilia said, turning toward town. She always tried to appease Momma, as she'd tried to appease Parker for years. Cecilia had simpered and catered and smothered her own personality around him to meet his endless and unreasonable needs and wants. With Parker, she had re-created the same relationship she had with Momma. In turn, he had decimated her soul.

There was no one else on the planet she did that for, as she is a tornado with feet.

"Janie and Isabelle are going to take good care of the bakery, and when summer starts I'll be there, too, while you recover."

Momma humphed in the front seat. "Humph! And what will Henry do without me?"

"Henry will be fine," we all three said.

"And what about Grandma?" She patted her perfectly brushed hair. Twisted her pearl necklace.

"Grandma will be fine," we all three said.

"The house will be declared a waste site when I return," she muttered.

"The house will be fine," we said.

"What are you, parrot triplets? Stop. You're hurting my ears." She massaged her ears.

I groaned.

Janie gurgled.

Cecilia sighed.

It would be a long drive.

You might find me callous for not wringing my hands and diving into semihysteria about Momma's open-heart surgery. After all, this is what they do in open-heart surgery, if I've got it correct: They cut your chest open with a knife as if you are a fish to be filleted. A human does this. Then, they yank open your rib cage, like it's a closed clam, using something refered to as a "spreader."

Even thinking about this bothers me. If God had wanted our rib cage opened up, I'm sure he would have inserted a zipper in the middle of it. I see no zipper.

Then they stop your heart.

Boom. Beatless.

You're hooked up to a heart-lung machine, which does what you could imagine it should do. It beats and breathes for you, like it's a person only it has an off-on button.

Then they (often) cut open your leg and borrow a blood vessel or two without asking the permission of your leg. They use the blood vessel to bypass a clog in your artery. The vessel that is clogged may well be clogged because in your lifetime you have eaten the equivalent of nine cows, four pigs, and a multitude of yummy stuff like wagons full of fried chicken. This cholesterol clings like plaque to your arteries.

If you don't get your arteries hosed out or fixed, well, you're a goner.

So, you might think I would be worried that Momma would soon be a goner.

That is not going to happen. Why?

Because I know it.

Momma will live to be one hundred. Maybe older. I can see her living to be one hundred and twenty-one to taunt me and Cecilia and Janie. By then we'll be in our late nineties and I hope I will have lost my hearing so I can't hear her anymore and I will have lost my sight so I can't see her anymore and I will have lost my mind and will believe that I am someone else.

Like Amelia Earhart. Or Cleopatra. Or Joan of Arc.

I vote for Cleopatra.

On our way into Portland I saw a windsurfer. He had a red and purple sail. He was whipping right along on the waves of the river. Away from struggles. Away from people. Away from life. Free.

He was free.

I wondered if he'd take a shift for me with Momma.

❧ 5 ❧

We got Momma checked in to her room at the hospital. She didn't like her room. ("It's small. Dirty. I feel like I'm being housed on the inside of a vacuum cleaner bag.") She didn't like the hospital outfit. ("I will not wear this green sacklike monstrosity. Never. Bring me my pink robe.")

She complained of being hungry but she was not supposed to eat. ("I'm being starved to death. Starved. You girls can't even get your momma fed properly.") She didn't like the nurse. ("The nurse is too thin. If I need help, she'll snap like a toothpick.")

She didn't like her doctors. "Too young. One is Mexican. One is Chinese. One is short. I need a tall, white doctor."

She told them that.

"I'm sorry," I said, raising my voice to a thundering decibel to block her out. "She's always like this. Ignore it or go into therapy. The three of us have done both. Still, we're all slightly insane because of her. Want to knock her out right now with a hammer to the head? Do you have a hammer?" I made a pounding motion with my hand. "I'll do it for you."

The doctors' eyes widened in surprise.

Janie started to hum and rock. Then she whispered, "I am envisioning a peaceful place. My houseboat. On the river. Ducks. Birds. Charm. Quiet. I am in control."

"Shhh!" I ordered Janie. "Put her out," I ordered the doctors. "Not my sister. My momma. Swing the hammer, cut her open, yank the ribs apart, and fix her ticker. If you keep her here for a few extra days, I'll pay extra. Double even. Triple. Can she stay a month?"

I crossed my arms over my chest as Momma squawked and announced I was ungrateful, poorly trained as a daughter, rebellious, and so on. "You're already humiliating me, Isabelle." She threw up her arms in the pink robe. "Humiliating!"

I knew the doctors would never accept any extra money from me, but they whipped her out pretty quick, the stretcher rolled around the corner, and Cecilia, Janie, and I sagged against the wall, hip to hip.

It was nine o'clock in the morning.

"Is it too early to get drunk?" Janie asked.

Cecilia grabbed her purse. "Nope. Not to me. Get your rears in gear."

We got our rears in gear.

We left Momma's room, then waited in the hallway for Janie to go back in, check we hadn't left anything, and tap all the tables in the room four times.

We heard her tapping.

She smiled as she passed through the doorway.

We were ready to go.

"Did you smile?"

We nodded.

She made us go back through the doorway smiling.

Janie always knows when we're lying.

The three of us found a breakfast diner about two blocks from the hospital, then decompressed in our own ways.

Janie took the sugar packets out of the container and divided them into groups of four. She shook salt out of a container onto her saucer and divided the salt into groups of four. She muttered.

When the waitress, a skinny girl with dyed black hair, sauntered over, I ordered coffee and toast and a round of beers.

Cecilia ordered two breakfasts of eggs and bacon. The waitress raised her eyebrows at Cecilia's order.

"I overeat so you can feel better about yourself," Cecilia snapped, hands crossed on the shelf of her stomach.

The waitress cracked her gum. "Whatever. We got fruit y'know, you can order that, less calories . . . and all that stuff."

"I don't want all that stuff. I didn't order it, did I? Did you see me open my mouth and order a plate full of damn fruit?"

"No, you didn't. It's a suggestion, don't get your panties in a twist. A diet suggestion. Helpful, you know." She dropped her gaze to Cecilia's stomach.

"Sexy, isn't it? One day, you too could have this. You could have a stomach big enough for a small calf to rest inside."

The waitress rolled her eyes.

"Aren't you Beck's daughter?"

"Uh . . . yeah . . . you know my mom?" Now the waitress was nervous.

"Yes, I know your mother. Tell her I said you need better manners around fat people."

"I didn't say you were fat." She cracked her gum twice.

"You didn't have to. Now bring me my double order of bacon and eggs without the attitude. Perhaps sometime today you could decide in that pointy, black head of yours not to judge people's worth solely on the size of their gut. Think you could do that? Too much for you?"

"No." She scribbled on her **pad. "Shit,"** she said quietly.

"Shit yourself. Hey, Beck's **daughter, I**'ll make you a deal. I won't tell you that at first I **thought** your nose piercing was a black bugger if you lay off with your weird sneers."

"Uh. Whatever." The waitress scampered away. "Yeah."

"I hired a private investigator," Cecilia said.

"You what?" Janie asked, her head tilting up. "What for?"

"Because I want to get laid, Janie, that's why. He's going to find me a man who wants to have sex with a female King Kong."

I laughed. "Excellent. You can make monkey noises together."

"I feel so nervous when I'm with both of you," Janie complained, fingering the sugar packets.

"We feel nervous with you, too, shrink tank," Cecilia said.

"Don't ever say I'm a shrink tank," Janie huffed. "You mean sister."

This was going to get warlike. Here came the peacemaker. "Why did you hire a private investigator?"

"Because I need *her* investigated."

"Who?" Janie asked.

I didn't need to ask.

"*Her.* The husband-stealing witch." Cecilia slammed her coffee cup down. "The loose slut. The whorey home wrecker. The woman who met Parker on the Married But Unhappy Web site."

"A Married But Unhappy Web site? I didn't even know that Web sites like that existed," Janie said. "It would make a great beginning for a murder. Maybe a woman murderer—she went after cheating husbands and sliced off a ball."

"Please. I'm going to eat." I sat back in my chair. "So you're going to find out who she is, what she is, her past, her secrets . . ."

"Yep. I know she's twenty-six. Parker's forty-two. She's thin, blond hair, boobs the size of Kentucky. She knew she was cheating with a married father. He's rich. He's successful. He's a fuck face. I hate her, I already know that."

"I hate her, too," Janie said.

"Me, too," I added. Everyone had to hate the woman who took away your sister's husband. It was an unbreakable rule. "I would like to smoke her body over a fire and feed her to a cannibal. I never liked Parker."

"Me, either," Janie said, shuddering. "Scumfuzz."

"Gee! What a surprise!" Cecilia put a hand over her mouth, eyes open wide. "I'm simply shocked! Floored!" She waved both hands. "When you both staged an 'intervention' two months after we met and again two weeks before my wedding to—how did you say it?—knock some sense into my stupidity? That was a small clue. And, let's see, Isabelle, for years you came to visit me at my house only when Parker wasn't there."

"That's because Parker's insufferable."

Plus he'd made a pass at me. He was a little drunk about a year after the wedding, but drunks do what they want to do while drunk and use the drinking as an excuse.

We were out on the deck and Cecilia went inside to bake him his favorite cookie, snickernoodle, because he'd told her to. Parker took a lurch toward me, a hand brushing my boob. Instead of apologizing, he left his hand hanging in the air above my breast as if he was massaging it. "You're beautiful, Isabelle. God almighty, you're beautiful. I didn't marry the beautiful sister, though. I married Cecilia. We lost out, big-time. Big-time. But it doesn't have to stay that way. We can change this."

He moved forward to kiss me, his lips puckered, his tongue darting out an instant before his lips landed on mine.

He slung an arm around my waist and hauled me in. I do not shock for long, but for a millisecond I did. When that millisecond was over, I shoved Parker, karate-kicked him in the chest, and flipped his legs, and he went right over the railing and landed on his head after torpedoing a rosebush.

He passed out as soon as his head hit the ground and did not appear for an hour. He had scratches all over his face and a massive bump on his head.

He caught me by my Porsche before I left. (That was my first Porsche. It was red. Fast. Slick.)

"You bitch."

I laughed. "You make a pass at your wife's sister, and yet I'm the bitch. Now this is what a bitch would do, so we're clear what a bitch is." I slung my fist at his face so hard I cracked a bone in my hand, then got in my car and aimed it right at him. I swerved twice, trying to hit him (not really) and he had to scurry away, like a python with two legs.

I drove to the hospital. Sent him the bill. I was never rebilled, so I think that was Parker's way of keeping me quiet. I should have told Cecilia, but that is the problem with sisters and your relationship with them.

You know them. You know how they'll react.

And I knew that Cecilia, at that point in her marriage, would have blamed me. As twins we have a lot of history. I was the pretty-slutty-valedictorian. She was the fat–athletic one. I had been accused by her on several occasions growing up of boyfriend stealing (never, never true), so I couldn't risk it.

And Parker the Penis would have denied what happened. Cecilia would have believed me, in her gut, but she would have had to have believed Parker's version because she loved him. She would have hated me for it. I couldn't have her hating me, because I knew she needed me so she wouldn't drown.

Later I found out that Parker told her he tripped in their shed and landed on a propane tank to explain his injuries.

"And you, Janie," Cecilia spat out, still angry, always angry, "you visited—infrequently—when you knew Parker wasn't going to be there."

"I couldn't be around Parker," Janie said, "because he made my skin feel like maggots were eating it. One time he shook my hand and I couldn't use that hand for days. It felt unclean."

Parker had made a pass at Janie, too. It was about two years after the wedding. He came by her houseboat, shoved his body up against hers. She had responded by leading him out to her deck, smiling. He advanced. She shoved him into the river and stomped on his fingers when he tried to get back up on her deck.

He swam to a neighbor's dock, but Janie called the neighbor and told him that a burglar was slithering onto his property via the river, and the neighbor had come out swinging with a shovel. The next neighbor, who could see out of only one eye due to a war injury, had a gun and pointed it at Parker's head, then shot three times into the river.

The police were summoned, handcuffs were snapped.

The usual.

Their divorce was ongoing, messy, and horrible. Compare it to World War III on a microlevel.

Cecilia blew air through her two front teeth. "I should hear the first report in a few days from the detective."

The waitress brought our food and beer.

"Anything else?" The waitress was sulking.

"Ketchup. Hot sauce. Extra cream for the coffee, please," Cecilia said.

The waitress rolled her eyes.

"Hey, Beck's daughter, rude one, try not to roll your goth-decorated eyes when your customers can see you. Get the stuff, wipe the bugger off your nose, and go harangue another fat person."

The waitress flounced off, then came back and dumped the stuff on the table.

"Parker smiles at me now, with nauseating condescension, trying to convey that he feels sorry for the poor, fat ex-wife." Cecilia guzzled her beer. "He comes by, gets the kids, gives them a big hug, and in front of me raves about all the great things 'the four of them, the family' "—she again mimicked Parker's voice—"are going to do every other weekend."

I wanted to break my brain on the table I hurt so bad for Cecilia.

"I hate her even more now," Janie whispered. She separated the food on her plate from the other food. She tapped her fork four times. She shook the salt shaker four times over her omelet. "I'll put her name in my next book. It's Constance, right? I'll give her a venereal disease, a pockmarked face, long earlobes, inverted nipples . . ."

Cecilia leaned toward Janie. "You know, Janie, I'd appreciate that."

"You would?" Janie's voice pitched in hope.

"Yes, I would. You're a vengeful sister and I don't think I've ever thanked you for that."

"Oh!" Janie dabbed at her eyes. "And you're a strong Viking woman, a Valkyrie! No need to thank me!"

"I love how you want violent things to happen to Parker."

"Of course I want violent things to happen to Parker, he hurt you! You're my sister!" Janie could not go on, choked with emotion.

What a sap.

Cecilia briefly held Janie's hand and they shared a loving-violent moment together. "That reminds me." She bit down on two slices of bacon at once. "I had my review at school last week." She blushed. She coughed.

"Why are you blushing?" Janie asked.

"I'm not blushing."

"Yes, you are," I said. "I can see it. I can feel it."

"I'm not."

"Who gave you the review?" Janie asked. Her antennae were up and wiggling.

"My principal, Dr. Laurence Silverton."

She smiled when she said his name. Blushed more. It was as if she was caressing the words.

"He's the best principal ever at our school. Came from Los Angeles. He loves Oregon, the rain, the outdoors. Loves to ski and hike and bike." She paused, her eyes unfocused, a blush blooming on her cheeks. "He's very tall. Kind of big. Not big like me. But big. Taller than me. Big guy."

"So he's big?" I asked.

"Yes, he's big." She sighed. "He's nice. He's the nicest man I've ever met." Her voice was awfully soft. So unlike Cecilia.

That amused me. I winked at Janie.

"How nice is he?"

Cecilia didn't even blink, off in her own world. "He's sweet. We all love him. The teachers. The kids. I . . ." She coughed. She sighed. "He's so funny."

"How funny?" I asked, I could barely contain my laughter.

"He has a dry sense of humor. And he *sees* how things are. You know how most men are so dense? They can't see beyond words? They never want to find out how you *really* are? Never want to touch anything resembling an emotion? You know how men see *through* you? He's not like that. He's deep."

"How deep?" Janie said.

Cecilia's face got positively dreamy.

Janie stifled a giggle.

The giggle made Cecilia blink herself right out of her trance.

She watched us watching her, our lips twitching as we tried to stifle those laughs.

She sat up straighter and her expression tightened. "Dr. Silverton is a professional. I respect him as a professional and, I believe, he respects me."

"Of course he does," Janie soothed.

"Absolutely. A professional," I said, drinking my beer.

"He's a fine man."

"Yes, so fine," Janie drawled. "And big."

"Big. Very big," I inserted. "Not too big."

"Shut up, you two," Cecilia said. "Let's change the damn subject."

"Oh, let's not," I said.

"I like this one!" Janie piped up.

Cecilia's face got all snarly and vindictive again. "I've hired a private investigator on asshole's girlfriend. We'll see what comes up on that loose, amoral, plastic Barbie doll with a mind the size and substance of a testicle."

We would indeed.

* * *

We went to a bookstore next, then explored 23rd Ave in northwest Portland, which is filled with specialty shops, a few bums who converse with themselves, moms with strollers, and little plastic horses tied to steel rings on the sidewalk that were used to tie up horses a hundred years ago.

It is part of Portland's funkiness.

After fifteen minutes of aimlessness, Janie returned to the hospital. "Too much stimulus, too many cracks in the sidewalk, too many colors. I don't like the geometrics, it's upsetting my 'me' balance."

Cecilia and I entered a coffee shop and brought our coffees to a window seat.

"How are you, Isabelle?"

How was I. Not bad. Not good. "Holding. In a holding pattern. Like a jet that's not headed in a nosedive to the ground, but one that's thinking about it."

She didn't like that answer. She cleared her throat. "How did it go there?"

"Fine. It was splendid."

"No, tell me the truth."

I drank my coffee. "I don't want to talk about it."

"I tell you everything."

"And I tell you everything I think you need to know. I'm better. That's it."

"That's not fair."

"What's not fair? That you choose to share your life tidbits with me, but I don't want to analyze to death each detail of my life?"

"Shit. You shut me out."

"Live with it, Cecilia. I am."

Sometimes things are so insanely private, you don't even want to talk about them with yourself. Don't talk about them, don't wrestle with them, don't let them run you over. Let it be.

I thought Cecilia was going to fight it out, strangle it out of me, but, surprisingly, she didn't. We had enough stress in this family.

How much stress and tension can one family hold before it explodes or implodes? Must all problems be dissected? What does that help?

Cecilia nodded and placed her hand over mine.

Cecilia is not given to a lot of affection, so I was surprised.

And touched.

I thought I was going to choke and bawl and coffee would spurt out of my nose.

She squeezed my hand and I squeezed back.

And there we sat, in the window seat of a coffee shop, off a funky street in Portland, holding hands with a little plastic horse attached to a steel ring on the sidewalk.

Sometimes that's all you can do, I think. Hold hands. Because life gets so scary sometimes, so bleak, so cold, that you are beyond being able to be comforted by mere words.

People probably thought we were gay, but I'd stopped worrying a long time ago what people thought of me, and so had Cecilia. Childhood had beat that right out of us.

We held hands. We did not let go.

"She'll eventually be fine, back to her dancin' and high kickin' ways," the doctor told us after the operation.

It was the Hispanic doctor, Dr. Janns. When Momma had first met him she had asked him if he had had to spend his childhood picking berries in farmers' fields.

"No, I didn't." He had shaken his head, gracious enough to let Momma's inflammatory comment go. "My ol' man was a career military man, tougher than nails, so we grew up all over the world. Like vagabonds. We didn't ever pick berries. Too busy learning German or Spanish or Korean. New country, new language. My mom was a battle-ax." He swung his hand like an ax. "When we weren't learning how to squawk and swear in the native tongue, hell if our mom wasn't haulin' us around by the ears to the opera and ballet. I prefer the ballet, myself. You?"

Momma seemed surprised by this. "Oh. Well. Hmm."

I waited for her to change the subject. This man didn't fit her profile, so she was stuck.

"You look too young to be a doctor," she accused him. "Almost a child. Are you a child?"

He grinned at her. He had a lot of perfect white teeth. "You look too young to have heart surgery, ma'am, you gorgeous queen, you movie star, you, so we're gonna fix the ticker on up and kick ya right on outta here."

I saw the corners of Momma's smile tip up.

Dr. Janns now grinned at us with those white teeth. "Your mom came through fine. She already told one of the male nurses that nursing wasn't for men and asked if he was a sissy."

"Obviously the operation did not soften her disposition," I drawled.

The doctor grinned. "Difficult operation, hard on the body. But then, we're rippin' people open, pumping the ol' hearts for 'em and clampin' 'em back up again. What can ya expect?"

Sheesh.

"I understand that her mother has dementia and you have a special-needs brother at home. She'll stay here for a while, chill, relax, she'll dig it, then we'll send her to that movin' and groovin' retirement center in Portland to recover and get back swingin' again."

Janie snuffled. Cecilia got all teary but didn't let a tear drop, not a one. She is not into weakness. Finds it appalling. I was relieved Momma was okay and relieved that I felt relieved. It made me feel more human to myself, as if I could still love a mother like Momma.

"We've tried to get the dragon to go to the retirement center, but she's refused," I said.

"The dragon will go," the doctor almost sang out.

"Huh. You don't know our dragon."

He hummed a happy song. "I told her that there were many

healthy people there. Many healthy men. And there's dancing and trips. I had no idea your mother was a dancer in her youth."

I cleared my throat, Cecilia made a sound between a whistle and a gasp, and Janie hummed.

Yes, Momma had been a dancer. Of sorts.

"So she agreed to go?"

"Yes. Definitely. She's a character. A free spirit. A warrior." He clenched his fist and raised it. "Awesome!"

"That's one way of putting it," Cecilia said.

"Any chance, doctor, that you sewed her mouth shut?" I raised my eyebrows.

Momma was still out cold when we went in to visit. For once in her life, she seemed tiny, barely a bump under the white sheets, the machines humming, the nurses and doctors in and out, the IV line a clear snake above her.

We stared at our petite, silent momma, lost in our own thoughts.

"She's gonna be raving when she realizes she's not in her pink robe," I observed.

"She's going to have a fit because her makeup is smudged," Janie said, with worry.

"She's not going to like the food here," Cecilia said tiredly.

I didn't hesitate. "I'm thinking it's time we returned to Trillium River."

"Shit, yes," Cecilia said. "I'm with you."

"Oh yes. Let's go, let's go, let's go," Janie breathed. "The nurses can handle her and I know she'll upset my spiritual balance if I'm here when she wakes up."

"Out we go," I said, turning.

Janie was out the door first and into the hallway before I could say, "Escape, ladies, before the volcano wakes up and explodes."

She didn't even bother smiling.

Soon we were sailing by the gorge, our hair flying with the wind, like pinwheels, for once not trying to talk, our thoughts our own as they tilted and spun and finally settled into a pattern of peace as we headed back to Trillium River. Janie pulled out a Yo-Yo Ma CD from her bag and we floated along on the notes, pitching and diving and soaring.

Three sisters.

And Yo-Yo.

✺ 6 ✺

"**I**'m a practicing Mormon now."

The silence at the table would have been complete if Cecilia had not stabbed her fork into the spinach ravioli with unnecessary force at her daughter, Kayla's, announcement.

It was a typical dinner at Grandma's house with me, Cecilia, her girls Kayla and Riley, Henry, and Janie. Henry was wearing a shirt with Big Bird on it; Grandma was in her black pilot's outfit, her goggles atop her head; and Velvet, the caregiver, was wearing a blue velvet dress.

Kayla is fourteen, Riley is thirteen. They have the blond hair of their mother and the brown eyes of their father. They are sharp as tacks. Kayla studies religions and has papered her room with pictures from *National Geographic*. Riley is obsessed with physics and reads science books for fun.

"You're a practicing Mormon?" Janie asked Kayla, taking a sip of lemon tea, then putting her teacup on a doily.

Cecilia glared at her daughter.

"Yes, I am."

"I thought you were Catholic," I said mildly. Kayla is hilarious. She antagonizes Cecilia until Cecilia's about to pop.

"I go to a Catholic church, because I'm *forced to against my will,* but I'm a practicing Mormon."

"Ah. How do you practice being a Mormon?" I asked.

Grandma made the sound of a plane's engine. Then she dropped her fork and clasped her hands together. "Dear God, this is Amelia. I pray for my plane. Don't let it pretzel. I pray for my gas. I hope there's enough of it. I pray for the natives here. They seem friendly. I pray for my bottom bullet wounds. Amen."

Henry puffed out his chest. "I wear my Big Bird shirt today!"

"Well, I'm reading the book of Mormon," Kayla said. "And I'm studying Joseph Smith and Brigham Young. Did you know that a prophet named Moroni came to Joseph Smith and told him where to find a book written on metal plates? I want Moroni to come and sermonize me. I am waiting for him and listening intently."

Cecilia stabbed her ravioli again. Spinach squished out.

"Now, last month you were studying Buddhism and said you were a Buddhist," Janie said. "You told us you were going to be reincarnated."

"That's right. I studied Buddhism. I know that when I die I'll come back to earth. Maybe as a person. A man or a woman. Maybe as a leaf. I also spent time in meditation, I accepted the Four Noble Truths, and I pursued my own path of enlightenment."

"Why don't you tell them about your Jewish month, too, Kayla?" Cecilia snapped. "Let's make a complete circle here."

"Well, the month before that I was Jewish. I asked six rabbis for wisdom, three of them online, studied Moses and the Ten Commandments, said prayers three times a day, and baked challah bread."

Cecilia grunted.

"I like bread," Henry said. "I squish bread. Ducks like bread. You want go to duck pond?"

"Air traffic control, this is HRTO2233." Grandma spoke into

her empty glass. "All is well. Give me a weather update. Storms ahead?"

I nodded. "Well, you've certainly been busy with your faiths."

"It's important to explore and not naively swallow the religion that gets stuffed down your throat by someone who has never explored any other religion *in her life*." Kayla glared at her mother.

"I don't need to study another religion because I know what I am, Kayla: Catholic." More spinach squished out of that ravioli, then Cecilia attacked her roll.

I nodded. Cecilia had never wavered on her religion. Momma took us to the Catholic church on Sundays no matter where we were unless she was semicomatose with depression/fighting her mental monsters, and then she insisted we go without her.

After church, if Momma had roused herself, we had to stay so she could say a rosary. She always made us wait outside. A couple of times we snuck in because she was taking so long, then skittered right back out when we saw our momma sobbing at the altar.

"You don't even go to church, do you, Aunt Isabelle?" Kayla asked, her eyes narrowed. "Are you an atheist?"

I put down my garlic bread. Here's another genetic marker of being a Bommarito: We cannot have normal meals like normal people. Our conversations are often inflammatory.

Food has been known to fly. One time a chair. Another time an entire stuffed turkey. Screaming occurs. Cecilia reached for me one time *over* the table and landed on Momma's casserole. Janie's flipped the table. Glasses have broken. Whipped cream has been sprayed, hot dogs have been hurled like bombs, loaves of bread have been used as weapons.

It's hereditary. When we first arrived at this house as teenagers, Momma and Grandma had a fight over Momma's makeup (too much, looked trashy), and Grandma's attitude (critical, judgmental), and Momma's lack of visits over the years (she had deprived Grandma of her grandchildren). Momma threw a chicken leg at her mother, Grandma pelted an apple at Momma's forehead. A handful of corn and a roll followed. Then a peach.

I glanced at the food on the table. Gall. Ravioli. Miniature square land mines. Salad that would be so slimy.

"Jesus loves Isabelle!" Henry said. "Yep."

"I'm not an atheist," I told her.

"Are you agnostic? That means you doubt that God exists."

"I'm not an agnostic."

"You believe in God?"'

"Yes. I believe in God." I didn't think about Him much, though. One does not like to think about God, or particularly hell, when one is living the life I live. "Basically, I've tried to stay in the shadows so God can't see me."

That didn't stump smart ol' Kayla. "You can't hide from God in the shadows."

"God see you." Henry laughed. "God see you, Isabelle. He gots good eyes. You silly."

"Only if he squints his eyes and slinks around all the shadowy corners. I think I lost him a few years back when I was in the Middle East and he's forgotten about me. They're busy there, you know. Wars and famine and zero rights for women, who are treated like goats. He's got a lot of work on his to-do list there."

"He can see you, too, Kayla, and he sees a kid who's changing religions monthly," Cecilia interjected.

"God doesn't care about that. He knows I'm searching for peace," Kayla protested. "Besides, religion is what people use as an excuse to kill each other."

"The natives may kill us!" Grandma declared, wielding her knife back and forth like a sword fighter. "Watch out!"

"Not always," I said. "I used religion as a way to guzzle red wine at church."

Janie blew milk through her nose as she laughed. Cecilia choked and I had to hit her on the back.

It was the holy truth, though. We used to sneak into the

church and drink the wine out of paper Dixie cups on Wednesday nights. No one could understand why we laughed so hard while reciting our Hail Marys.

"I don't get it. It's a sister thing, isn't it?" Riley asked. She was twisting hair around her finger. I don't think she'd stopped twisting the whole meal.

"Take your finger out of your hair. What is it? A finger corkscrew?" Cecilia snapped.

She took her finger out. Riley's hair was so thin, too . . . it used to be thick. Was I seeing bald spots, or was she styling her hair in a weird way?

"So, Kayla," Janie said, picking up her teacup again. "You're studying to be a Mormon?"

"Yeah, and I'm going to church with my friend Shelley next week. She's a Mormon. There's eight kids in her family. Eight, Mom. You only have two. And they all will live together in heaven and on Sundays they have family days and they don't fight."

Cecilia stood up, arms spread, "Why didn't anybody tell me I don't have eight kids? I thought I had at least six. There's only two of you? Nobody tells me jack anymore." She patted her huge stomach. "Maybe there's one in there?" She eyeballed her stomach. "Yooo-hooo! Anyone in there? Hello? Another baby? Maybe two?"

Kayla picked up a ravioli with her fork and aimed it at her mother.

"Don't you dare," Cecilia told her. "Don't you dare."

She put the ravioli down, scowling.

I threw one of my ravioli at Kayla.

Cecilia tossed a ravioli at Kayla, too. It landed on her face. She said, "Bless you, bad mother."

I threw one at Janie. She jumped in surprise, and tossed one at Riley. Appropriately, it landed on her hair. Riley took it off her head and started squishing it through her fingers.

Henry laughed. He picked up a handful of ravioli and put

them on his head. "Look me! Look me! I have ravioli nest on my head! Ravioli nest. I need a bird!"

Grandma stood up straight, pulled her goggles over her head, and straightened her flight jacket. "I am ready to take off now." She grabbed a handful of ravioli and threw them into the air, then climbed on top of the table and sat in the middle of it. "There's weather ahead! Weather ahead!" she screamed. "Prepare for a crash landing! SOS! SOS!"

We knew what to do or Grandma would get all upset. We pretended to pull on our own flight goggles, dropped napkins on our heads, and held on to our seats while we rocked back and forth.

"Hang on! We're going down! We're going down!" She shouted into her glass, "SOS! SOS!"

We all threw some more ravioli squares, then we crashed.

Grandma stopped abruptly, sighed heavily. "We're lost."

Grandma was so, so right.

We were lost. I tossed a slice of garlic bread at Cecilia.

She caught it in midair and rolled her eyes.

Velvet helped get Grandma to bed after dinner while we girls did the dishes.

Velvet Eddow was the skinniest person I'd ever seen and reminded me of Mrs. Ichabod Crane without the horse. She was six feet tall with white curling hair she piled on top of her head and strong bones in her face. She was not younger than seventy-five and had a thick, gentle, rolling southern drawl she'd acquired after living for fifty years in Alabama. Those words left her mouth like honey, with the honey winding its way around each syllable, smooth and gold and yummy.

Sometimes she used ol' southern sayings and sometimes I knew she was making them up on the fly.

I'd watched her with Henry and Amelia Earhart. She was brilliant and, most important, kind. It did not take us more than a day to beg her to move into the spare bedroom in the house until further notice.

She gave us a hug and said, "Well ain't that the berries! Sure, sugar, I'll come help y'all. This takes the cake!"

In college the woman with the honey drawl studied engineering when it was an all-male domain. "The men didn't even know what to do with me. I wasn't their mother or their sister or their girlfriend. But I was smarter than them. They didn't get that part. It baffled the heck out of all of 'em.

"Men are easily baffled, though, darlin', don't ever forget that. Their brains think like porn. That's the only way I can describe it, darlin', like *porn*." She dragged that word out real long. "One part of their brain thinks, the other part is holding a breast in his hand, at all times. I'm givin' that to you as free advice, darlin'."

"I'll remember that, thank you."

"Men are for amusement only. They are treats. Like candy. Like ice cream on an Alabama afternoon. A dessert. They are not the main course. As soon as you have a man in your life who becomes the main course, that is the time, my sweet, when you should go on a diet. Right that second. Men are for dessert only." Envision: Honey.

"Yum, yum," I told her.

"They are yummy." She winked at me. "But never take them seriously. A bite here and there is puh-lenty. All three of my husbands died, bless their pea-brained souls, but I never thought of them as the chicken and potatoes. They were always the flamin' cherries jubilee at the end of dinner." She stared off into space. "And there was many a time, darlin', that I wanted to set them on fire."

Okay dokay.

As long as she didn't set any men on fire in the house with her cherries jubilee, we'd be good.

Later that night, about one o'clock, I headed for the middle of the grass near a huge weeping willow tree in the yard. The moon was almost smack over my head and the stars were bright white holes in the deep soft black.

I closed my eyes against my life. I thought about my loft in Portland, the view of the river, my cameras I could hide behind, and my darkroom I could work in for hours. Dark on dark.

I wanted the aloneness of my life, even though it came with the familiar thick blackness, the blackness I struggled to contain and felt lost in. I didn't want this mess here.

All the emotion.

The fighting and the stress. The total lack of control. The incessant responsibility, the small town, the Momma element.

I wanted my loft.

The wind meandered over my face.

What the hell was I doing here in Trillium River, I asked myself. *What the hell?*

One sole star twinkled at me. I rubbed my hands over my face, then breathed in a touch of wind.

I knew why I was here.

I knew.

About a year after Dad and his jungle nightmares took off, Momma told us she was a dancer. We thought that was pretty cool. She had been working as a waitress during the day but she kept getting fired because of Henry.

Henry cried when he had a sitter and if he wasn't crying he was ill with one of his many health problems—asthma, chronic colds, sleeping problems that produced colds, continual stomachaches, pneumonia, and ear infections—and she had to be home to take care of him.

So Momma would soon be fired for taking too much time off, we'd rapidly be broke, she'd get that empty no-one's-home blankness in her eyes, then go to bed for a few days or a few weeks, and the hard-core struggling would begin.

When Momma told us she had a job as a dancer the first time, we were living in Massachusetts. We envisioned her with one of those Las Vegas showgirl type costumes doing the cancan. Why we thought that, I don't know.

All I knew was that Momma started working nights and left us notes on pink paper on what to do and not do when she was gone. Janie, Cecilia, and I watched Henry when she left about two hours after we got home from school. What we liked about that job is that Momma always brought food home after her shift so we'd have it the next night for dinner.

Plus, we finally had cash in the cookie jar so we could buy milk and eggs. There is nothing like the taste of cow milk when you're a kid and you've been drinking powdered milk or water for weeks. Our water and electricity were no longer turned off and our phone worked on a consistent basis.

We threw out our old shoes, held together with duct tape, and Momma bought us new tennis shoes. Mine were pink, I remember that.

We still got free lunch at school, but Momma told us we could go down the street to get ice cream on Friday. We were stunned, beyond delighted.

It wasn't too long before we got the truth.

A girl at school told us her older brother and his friends had seen our momma, "buck naked."

"My brother said your mom is sexy. Sexy sexy. He says she's got small boobs but they stand upright. They go on Monday, Tuesday, and Thursdays now to see her with all their friends. What do you think of your mom being a stripper?"

I hit that girl so hard she had to go home because her nose wouldn't stop bleeding. She shut up about our momma, but I got suspended for five days. We knew she was lying.

When girls in pigtails and Mary Janes came up to me and Cecilia and told us our momma was a whore, we whupped all of them. Five against two. They shut up about our momma.

When an older boy, his teeth buck and sticking out, told us his daddy thought our momma had an "ass tight enough to hold nuts," Cecilia and I took care of his tooth problem and he shut up about our momma.

That took care of the overt teasing at our school, but nothing could take care of the laughter and snickers and pointed fingers behind our backs.

But Momma wasn't a stripper. We knew that. She was a dancer—feathers, sequins, and all. We knew it so well we waited around the corner from the strip club in town that we knew she didn't work at because she wasn't a stripper.

We waited and waited and we cringed with disbelief when we heard the wheeze and thunking of our ancient car and Momma drove up and parked around in the back and went in a side entrance wearing an old sweatshirt of my dad's that said UNITED STATES ARMY, her hair in a ponytail.

Cecilia and Janie and I leaned back against the wall in shock. Too shocked to cry. Too devastated to move. Too humiliated to breathe. Within fifteen minutes, that parking lot was packed, with loud, boisterous men getting out of cars.

We trudged home, heads down, avoiding the streets of town, avoiding each other's eyes, trying to avoid the truth but knowing the truth was beaming and bold and undeniable: Our momma was a stripper.

We waited up for Momma that night, one light on in our shabby, brownish family room, us three lined up on the sofa, our feet on our stained carpet.

"Momma, are you a stripper?" Janie asked, soft as a mouse, a frightened mouse.

Momma froze in the doorway. She had bruisy circles under her eyes and was pale with exhaustion. One of the take-home boxes of food she held in her hands dropped to the floor. Chicken wings fell out. I still remember that. Still remember those chicken wings. To this day, none of us eats chicken wings.

"How dare you," she said, her voice so quiet we could barely hear it.

Janie cringed, Cecilia wrapped her arms around herself, and I put my chin up.

"How dare *we?*" I asked as I stood. I was furious. So embarrassed

I could have died. Momma took her clothes off for the men in this town. On stage.

"Yes, how dare you," Momma said, starting to shake.

"You're the one taking off her clothes!" I shouted.

She sent the other box of food flying across the room. Noodles with tomato sauce spilled out. I was steaming about that, too. That pasta was dinner! I was hungry!

"Who told you?"

"Everyone, Momma! We've been beating kids up for weeks! We thought they were lying!"

She swayed.

"How could you do that?" I was so frustrated, so destroyed, I felt like the devil had set my stomach on fire.

I heard Henry start to whimper in his bedroom. Momma's eyes darted in that direction.

"You didn't tell Henry, did you?"

"No, Momma, we didn't think he needed to know about your pole twirling!"

Her face flushed. "Do you think I like what I do, you spoiled brats?"

There was silence. We were young. We didn't get it, didn't understand.

"Do you?" she shrieked, her blond ponytail swinging behind her. "Do you?" She threw her purse across the room. It broke a glass vase we'd found at a garage sale.

"You must like it!" I shouted back. "You must because you do it!"

God, I had a momma who took off her clothes!

Janie said, "Momma, we love you, but—"

"But what?" she seethed.

"But don't do it!" Cecilia yelled. "Don't strip! We gotta move, Momma. Everybody knows!"

Momma didn't move.

"Even being a waitress is better than that!" I told her, superior, snotty. "You're holding a tray in the air kissing people's asses but at least you're not naked!"

"Momma, they're calling you the River of Love at school!" Cecilia accused. "They say, 'My dad wants a sexy river.' That means they're going to see you!"

"It's a little slutty, don't you think, Momma?" I sneered.

That did it. Looking back, I'm surprised she didn't pound me into the wall. She was not known for her restraint.

"You think I'm a slut?"

"I think you're acting like one!"

Janie whimpered.

"You're judging me, Isabelle Bommarito? You, who has never had to work a day in her life? You who has never had to worry about supporting four kids, on your own?" she shot back, her bright green eyes with the light in back of them filling with tears.

Henry made a moaning sound in his bedroom.

"Yeah, Momma, I am. That's disgusting! You're disgusting."

"Isabelle, stop—" Cecilia pleaded.

Her whole body shook. "Then you do it, Isabelle. You support this family."

"I can't, Momma, I'm fourteen!"

Momma charged right up to my face. "Do you know why I have this job, you little snot? Do you have any clue? *It's because I had to take it.* I don't have any skills. I don't have an education. I don't have a husband. Waitressing, you obnoxious brat, did not pay our bills. Do you think you all were eating crackers for lunch because I wanted you to eat crackers? Do you think we had noodles all weekend because you liked them? We ate them because that's all I could afford."

She pulled away from me as if she couldn't bear to be near, then picked up the nearest item on a table—a clay imprint of my hand I'd made her as a kid—and hurled it across the room. It smashed a mirror and both the hand and the mirror shattered into a thousand pieces. I felt the blood draining from my face like liquid through a sieve.

"Do you know how much Henry's stomach medicine is each month?" she rasped out. "His asthma medicine?"

I shook my head.

I could hear Henry sobbing.

She picked up another item. It was a ceramic sculpture Janie had made last year. It was supposed to be a dog. It looked like a snake with a porcupine back. It went flying over the couch and crashed into a lamp. The lamp toppled and broke.

Janie moaned. Cecilia sucked in her breath.

"Do you know how much I owe the hospital and doctors for Henry? Do you?" She named an enormous sum. "I will never, ever be able to pay that back, but they're suing me anyhow. At least I *can* keep the lights on."

The third item that went flying was a framed photo of the four of us plus Momma.

Janie covered her face with her hands and talked to herself.

Cecilia trembled, red, flushed, scared.

Momma shoved her face, twisted with anger, one inch from mine. "I hate stripping, you get that? I *hate it*. I do it for us. Even you, you judgmental, stupid child. I do it because you're the only ones who can take care of Henry. I do it because he's sick so much and needs one of us with him all the time. I don't have a choice. Do you think I like taking off my clothes in front of leering, sick, gross men?"

She screamed then, in frustration, in defeat.

In humiliation.

"Oh, Momma," Janie wailed.

"Momma, we love you—" Cecilia started.

Henry shouted, "Help me! Help!"

I crossed my arms. "There's got to be a different way, Momma, than being naked."

I could still hear those words in my head. The biting tone, the condescension, the harshness.

To this day I hate myself for that.

"Get out of my sight," she raged. "And don't you ever open your snotty mouth and bring this up again!"

"We should move," I drawled. "Our momma is little more than a hooker."

That did it. Her arm arched, like the curve of a bow, whipping me across the face. It knocked me to the ground.

"God, I think I hate you," she seethed.

"Momma—" I stayed on the ground, crushed, stunned by her words. Cecelia had stapled the back strap of my bra together and I felt it snap.

Henry shouted again, "Help me! Help!"

She cracked me again and my head whipped back. My neck would hurt for days, the bruises purple, then greenish-beige.

"Get out! Get out!" she yelled. She moved toward me again and at first I crawled, then Cecilia and Janie hauled me up and yanked me to our room.

Henry's wails grew to a pitch. They softened only when Momma went to his room. In the darkness I could hear her soothing him, calming him.

I knew she was hugging him until he went to sleep, like a mother bear protecting a cub.

For a second I hated Henry.

I wished Momma would hug me to sleep.

I crawled to my closet and cried until my tears were dried up, shriveled, gone. Left in their place was a hollow void.

I still have that void.

The Bommarito girls were never invited over to anyone's house or to a birthday party.

Not once.

People can be unforgiving and unaccepting, and that easily extends to the offender's children. Especially when the mother is gorgeous and often naked, and when their husbands whisper out, "River," when atop their wives, they're not moaning about water.

We never talked about Momma's work again but we continued to fight our way through childhood, literally.

Momma collapsed on a fairly regular basis into a downward, whirling spiral. When she did, essentials like food and electricity were often not there. Cecilia got rashes that wouldn't go away and Janie had migraines, but we couldn't afford the medication for either. Henry's health was shaky.

An incident with a lot of blood still replays in my head like a red, vibrating vision. Another time, with evil waiting on the deck of a dilapidated house, I thought we'd sunk to the bottom of fear and poverty. But there was more devastation working its way toward us, insidious, unstoppable, shattering.

That time, though, it came for Henry.

7

At five o'clock in the morning, my alarm went off. It sounded like a torpedoing bomb and I leaped out of bed. Too many nights in war-torn cities will set your feet on fire when awoken from a deep sleep by high-pitched buzzing.

I sank back onto my bed and held my head until my heart pittered back down and I could breathe.

I showered and pulled on jeans and a V-necked black sweater, the morning so still and cold outside, I felt ice cubes in my gut.

I met Janie downstairs. She was wearing a pink skirt, white blouse, and white tennis shoes, with her hair in two braids wrapped around the back of her head to complete her frumpiness.

"You look like a cupcake."

She put her hands on her hips. "Nothing wrong with a clean, crisp outfit."

"You look like a clean, crisp cupcake."

She put her nose up a fraction. "I like my clothes."

"Me, too. Tasty."

"Funny. You're hilarious, Isabelle. Hilarious." She stomped toward the door. "We don't all want to dress with suggestive-ness!"

I took a gander down my shirt. There wasn't *that* much cleavage showing.

Before we left the house, Janie checked the stove and the iron and the hair dryers. She locked the front door, got in the car, then ran back and rechecked all her checking, locked the door, tapped it four times, and ran to the car.

"Tap tap tap," I sang out, starting her Porsche.

"Shut up, Isabelle. At least I don't lay naked on my counters when I'm upset."

"I lay naked on my counters when I'm happy, too, so there, tap tap tap."

"You're never happy, and at least I don't show people in skyscrapers my boobs."

"They like my boobs."

"At least I don't drink Kahlúa for breakfast."

"Kahlúa is yummy."

She put on Vivaldi.

We drove toward town, no one else up and around at this time because they are sane. The sun even seemed tired, the golden globe slowly rising, as if she was getting out of bed and only now starting to slough off her hangover and begin thinking about the colors she would spread across the morning sky.

Trees arched over the road and I saw familiar homes, remembering who lived where when I was in high school. Nice kids and mean kids and kids who got in trouble and kids who were trouble.

It had been a long time since I was here for any length of time. I had run far and long in my work as a photographer. I'd lived for years in France, Israel, Lebanon, and London, with stints in various war-torn, war-crushed, war-raped, war-demoralized countries in the serenity of Africa and the sweet tranquility of the Middle East.

Seeing people's bodies blown apart in different directions—a foot here, a head there—because a few men have decided they can't sit down at a table and figure things out isn't pleasant.

Arriving in a village that's been obliterated by a tsunami isn't, either, with mothers screaming that they can't find their children and children screaming they can't find their mothers. Running from the Janjaweed as they swish the jungles with their machetes is a heart-stopper. Famine offers up an especially lovely glimpse of how other people wait on the porch of death, barely able to stand, their stomachs swollen as if they've ingested a watermelon whole.

Strange diseases that we never see here thrive in other countries, their symptoms cruel, debilitating.

I'd photographed all of it.

And it was actually here that I'd come to love photography.

There was a photography class at school and only nerds took it. I took it because I thought it would be easy.

The teacher was a nerd, too. His name was Mr. Sands. He had a friend named Mr. Reynolds.

We all knew they were gay.

I thought they were the nicest men, besides Father Mike, that I'd ever met. Mr. Sands gave me a camera and told me how to take photos. I used to go with Mr. Sands and Mr. Reynolds to take photos in the mountains and by the river. Cecilia and Janie tagged along, too.

From an old, battle-weary perspective, I now realized they "got" our home life. They had met Momma one morning after she'd been in bed for two weeks. She had not showered, her hair was straight up and gnarled, her robe stained by food and grape juice and mental collapse.

She took one shocked glance at the men and slammed the door. "How dare you bring men to the house when my hair's not done!" She slapped me across the face, her eyes still fuzzy and unfocused. "What do they want with a young girl? They're perverts, aren't they? Perverts." She slapped me again.

No, Momma, I wanted to say, but they care if I live or die, which is more than I can say for you. "It's my teacher and his brother. I'm catching up on my work."

She ran two shaky hands through her greasy hair before bursting into tears. "Fine. Go. Go!"

Mr. Sands and Mr. Reynolds patted my arm all day and bought me a root beer float.

I was soon hooked on photography. I think it was because when I was with them, I started to feel clean. Not completely clean, that couldn't happen—I had a momma who appeared to hate me, a reputation growing uglier second by second, and cataclysmic memories I couldn't shut down—but around their gentleness and humor I felt better.

That afternoon I took a photo of my face from an arm's length away with the river in the background. The area Momma had smacked was red, my eyes swollen and lonely from the tears I'd shed hoping she would love me one day. I stared at that photo for days. I still have it. I started to get interested in shooting not rivers and waterfalls and flowers, but people in pain. People like me.

Which led me to a major in journalism in college and a minor in photography, which led me to newspapers and documentaries, which led me to war zones.

Which led me to so many thousands of images of utter, abject, hideous suffering in my head that eventually my mind, on top of what was already there, split open and electrocuted itself.

And that's when that other thing happened last year.

I shook my head, my braids swaying off my shoulders as I cleared out the memories.

And now I was back, headed toward a bakery I'd hated working in.

"I can't believe I'm here," Janie whimpered.

Bommarito's Bakery is a two-story brick building between the pharmacy and a bookstore on the main street of Trillium River.

Momma had "revived" it two years ago after she closed it a year after Janie left for college. "The people of Trillium River begged for my desserts, desserts made my way. The River way," she had told me, arching her brows.

The bells jangled as I opened the door and we stepped inside.

"Now, this isn't gonna be fun," I groaned.

"Not good, not good, not good," Janie moaned.

There were five red booths and seven tables. They needed a scrub down. The floor was black and white checked and scratched and dirty. It needed a mopping.

The red canopy outside was dusty and sagging, the lettering on the windows washed out, the window treatments boring beige. There were two long display cases for the cookies, cakes, sweets, and breads.

They needed to be replaced.

This was in direct contrast to how the bakery shined when we worked here. Momma had handed us toothbrushes, sponges, brushes, and mops and made us work 'til that place was so clean you could lick the floor.

"I knew it." I had known it. Cecilia hadn't wanted to tell me.

"The bakery is dead. It's like there's ghosts wandering around," Janie whispered as we stood in a ray of sunlight, dust bunnies dancing around our heads.

"Ghosts?" I sputtered. "You're not into ghosts."

"Yes, I am. I am researching them for my next book. I think they're fascinating."

"They think you're fascinating, too. In fact, they have elected you to be president of their Ghosts in Oregon Society. There's a national convention in June. 'Ghosts Beware' is the headliner followed by 'Multicultural Ghost Awareness Night' and 'Sensuous Ghosts: How Not to Disappear.' "

"Stop it. I can hear the ghosts."

I froze to hear the ghosts. "Boo!" I shouted.

She jumped.

I laughed. "There's a ghost in the booth. Gasp. He's naked! He's gorgeous!"

"Then maybe you can sleep with him, Isabelle. For one night, not two. That might constitute a relationship."

"It'll be ghostly sex. I'll burn another bra and thong. My white ones." I slung an arm around her shoulder. "Come on. I'll cook, you sell."

"We're both cooking. You sell. I don't want to talk to all those people, and you know I don't do raisins. When I touch them I feel like they have to be counted."

"I know you don't do raisins."

"They're too small."

"Yes, I know, Janie. Their smallness unnerves you."

"They're not tasty."

"Right. Raisins are not tasty."

"They're tight and wrinkled and shriveled. Yuck."

"I know. Tight, wrinkled, and shriveled is a no."

"Right. And they crunch sometimes. They're rough in my mouth." She smacked her lips.

"You sound positively sexual, do you know that? Do you have a hidden thing for raisins?"

"That's disgusting."

"Yep. So is being unnerved by a raisin."

Her face set. "I'm not embarrassed to tell you that I also don't handle hazelnuts anymore."

"No hazelnuts?"

"Too thin. Poor taste." She scrunched up her nose.

I rolled my eyes. "Got it. I will be the raisin and hazelnut woman in this bakery."

"Don't make fun of me."

"I'm not. You can still work with icing, right?"

She threw up her hands in frustration. "Icing is smooth."

"Smooth?"

"Yes. Plus its initial color is white."

"White and smooth." I didn't even try to put that together. "Come on, icing woman, let's get to work."

At six thirty we opened our doors. Based on the shabbiness here, I did not expect a rush of people, as had happened when we were high schoolers. Back then people came by before work for coffee and treats. They came by during the day for streusel or orange bran muffins or brownies with white chocolate chips.

The card-playing ladies came in on Tuesday night and the quilters came on Thursday. We had a Sunday church crowd and the Saturday afternoon train of people who needed treats for that night's potlucks.

I was surprised to see *no* customers, though. Zero. Nada.

Janie turned on her east Indian music and hung up the photo of her therapist.

We propped open the old cookbooks, most from our dad, a man who loved cooking when the demons weren't prodding him with pitchforks, and kept baking.

I ignored the loss I felt. I ignored the memories that swirled around and about those early dawn hours, wretchedly painful and hilariously funny, soul crushing and radiant. I did not want to dive into those memories.

So, we baked.

At ten o'clock, an older woman shuffled in. She left her shopping cart, piled with filled black garbage bags, outside the door. She wore a blue flowered hat, three sweatshirts, saggy jeans, and one black shoe and one brown shoe.

"Good morning," I said.

She grinned. She was missing teeth.

I brought over a menu as she sank down in a red booth.

"Breakfast today?" I asked. I had put a white apron around my waist and my braids were back in a ponytail. I knew there was flour in them already. Wouldn't surprise me if I had purple marzipan icing on my cheek, either.

She shrugged her shoulders.

"Coffee?"

She smelled like honeysuckle and mint. I learned later that she somehow always had a plastic bottle of scented lotion with her.

"Juice?"

I saw a flash of confusion in her eyes, then she opened a sugar packet and tipped it into her mouth. She did it with a second one, too.

I thought I'd leave her to her sugar. "I'll come back in a minute."

I returned to icing about two dozen blue, pink, and green whale cookies.

Ten minutes later I headed back out. "Decided yet? I have cookies in whale shapes."

No answer. A smile.

About three seconds later, she leaned over and curled up on the red bench. She made a gurgling sound in her throat.

She slept.

"Ma'am?" I shook her shoulder softly. "Ma'am? No whale cookies?"

A snore escaped her nose.

We learned later her name was Belinda.

Life had not been a whale of fun for her.

At three o'clock, we'd been mass cooking all day, and we were still empty. Belinda had woken up, snuffled, snorted, and left after using the bathroom. I could tell she'd used our sink to take a minishower, though the bathroom was perfectly cleaned up when I checked.

I had dug through the trash where Janie and I had tossed pies and cookies and bread. Now, to be fair, these goodies were several days old and wouldn't taste fresh.

Still. The bread tasted like sand and water mixed with a dead scorpion thrown in. The doughnuts tasted like soggy sugar and the cookies tasted like corrugated cardboard laced with paper. I gave a bite to Janie. She spit it out.

"Good. That helps me with my book. I needed to know what dead flesh would taste like."

"It wasn't dead flesh."

"I know. But I needed a way to describe it."

What do you say to things like that?

People ambled on by outside, some carrying windsurfing boards, others pushing strollers. Two women with briefcases. A man wearing a blue apron. Three teenage girls giggling, followed by three strutting teenage boys.

Now why weren't they all in here? Spending money?

Easy. The food sucked.

⧸ 8 ⧹

That night we went to see Momma in the ICU. Janie drove her Porsche, which means we got there only slightly ahead of a turtle traveling backward.

Eventually our turtle made it to the hospital.

On the way my brain had a fight with my emotions over Momma. I loved her, but sometimes I hated her. I did.

Nothing I had ever done was good enough for her and I had stopped trying to get approval or kindness from her long ago. Cecilia had never stopped, and Momma still scared the intestines out of Janie.

Momma would never think I was anything more than a wandering, difficult, loose daughter she couldn't possibly relate to. Not having Momma's approval about ripped my heart out for years, but somewhere along the way, probably about the time I went home to visit her in my late twenties after being shot in Afghanistan and still had a bandage wrapped around my upper arm and she told me I was a "slut" and a "disappointment" as a child, I had let it go.

I had to. It was let it go or die emotionally. I was already half dead emotionally anyhow, and survival instincts kicked in.

But I wanted Momma to recover. I did.

I'm not that vengeful. Vengeful, but not that bad. Bad, but not murderously so.

But, man, she was a damn terror.

We met with the doctor on call first. Dr. Gordon was about fifty, short, African-American, and had studious glasses and big green-gray eyes.

"How's our momma?"

The doctor tensed a bit.

"She's not bouncing back like we'd like. No energy. Physically lethargic. Complains of pain. So you can go in and see her for a few minutes, but her recovery time is going to be lengthened. She'll need to stay here longer than we expected."

"Oh!" Janie whispered. "Tranquility. Serenity."

"Hmm," I said. "Bummer."

"That's hellaciously good news," Cecilia mused.

"Why good?" the doctor asked, tilting his head.

Cecilia cackled. "Ah. I see. You have not spoken with our momma much, have you?"

"I had the pleasure of making your mother's acquaintance." The doctor stared at the ceiling and stroked his chin. "She could hardly speak, but I heard something about how I was too young and too short and was I really black? As in black black? Were my great-grandparents slaves?"

Janie leaned against a wall. I exhaled, slumped. So tactful, our momma. So sweet.

"I believe she also said that I was not, under any circumstances, to burst into any rap songs or play rap music at any time. I had to reassure her I have never belonged to a gang nor did I carry a gun."

"That would be our momma," I sang out. "Cheerful and filled with goodwill and love for all."

Janie and Cecilia and I then apologized at one time. How many times had we had to do that? A thousand? Eighty god-zillion?

The doctor smiled. "Hey, it's no problem unless I want to join a gang here at the hospital. Come on in. I'll walk you there." He politely held the door open for us.

Even I was shocked to see her.

She was white white white, like crinkled paper, her mouth a crooked slash, her eyes sunken. Our tough, Scarlett O'Hara, perfectly made-up momma (when she wasn't drowning in one of her tarlike depressions) was one step away from a corpse.

"Momma," we all said together. "Momma."

There was no response.

I leaned over her and felt her breath on my cheek. "She's still breathing."

Janie put a hand on Momma's chest over her heart.

"Her heart is still beating."

"Good God!" Cecilia said. "She's shrunk. Shrunk and shriveled."

"Shhh," said Janie, wringing her hands together. "She can still hear you!"

"How can she hear me?" Cecilia said, flicking her blond hair back. "She's not even fully conscious. She's whacked out."

"Do you have to say whacked out?" I asked, my tone mild. I felt like having a Kahlúa snack.

"Yeah, I do have to say whacked out. Because that's what she is. Watch this." She leaned in close. "Momma! Momma!" No response. "See? She's whacked out. For once she's not nagging. Or criticizing. Or telling me I'm fat, and 'enlarging' each day. *For once.*"

"You shouldn't . . ." Janie said.

"Shouldn't what, Janie?" Cecilia stage whispered. "Shouldn't raise my voice? Shouldn't be honest? Maybe I should be like you. Over there with your hair in a bun and those brown shoes you always wear. Always quiet, cringing around Momma, scared to death, not sticking up for yourself. Don't you ever want to scream, Janie? Scream because you had a lousy childhood and your momma tells you, to your face, that you're insane and that you drive her insane? Don't you?"

"Stop it, Cecilia," I said, moving in front of Janie. "This isn't the place for you to slash and dash Janie."

Janie swallowed hard. "You're making me nervous."

"I'm making you nervous?" Cecilia said. "*Too bad*. I make myself nervous. My life makes me nervous. Momma makes me nervous. My kids make me nervous. I'm nervous all the time. I want to kill Parker, but at least I don't hide, don't cower, don't mutter to myself."

"Why are you so mad at me, Cecilia?" Janie said, her eyes filling up, her fists clenched. "Why are you attacking me? I have done nothing to you. Nothing."

That stopped Cecilia up short.

I pushed my braids back. "Well? What, specifically, has Janie done to you to make you so mad at her?"

"I'm not mad at her," Cecilia spat out.

"Then you hate me. *You hate me*. And that's fine." Janie's voice was ragged. She stepped in front of me. "You always have. I don't care."

"*You don't care?* I do."

I could tell that Cecilia was pretty miffed about not hating Janie.

"And I don't hate you, Janie."

"Must we hammer out our hatred now?" I asked. "Momma is pale and ghastly in that bed. Surely there's a better time for this?"

"Why not now?" Janie demanded, those tears spilling out. "Momma can't hear and I want to know. I'm sick of this! Sick of you, Cecilia! Sick of your condescension, your criticisms. Nothing I do is right. You think I'm a head case, a loser. *I am not a loser*."

I could tell that Janie, who was definitely not a loser, was losing it. I reached out to pat her arm. I hurt for Janie. "Janie, chill."

"No, I won't! Tell me, Cecilia!" She spoke through clenched teeth, tears pouring down those perfectly carved cheeks of hers. "Tell me. *Why do you hate me?* Why?"

Cecilia's anger seemed to deflate as fast as it flared up in the face of Janie's ragged anguish.

"Why do you hate me?"

Janie's words were bordering on a scream. "Janie, get ahold of yourself," I said. "We're in a hospital."

"I know we're in a hospital!" She yanked her arm away from me and swiped at a few stray hairs, her voice pitched and shaky. "And I want to know why that mean, fat bitch hates me!"

Cecilia and I froze. Janie rarely swore. It wasn't in her nature. Though she might torpedo people with flying saws for her books, she preferred speaking in the same civilized manner as English women in the 1800s.

"Janie, I—" Cecilia started, cupping her face with her hands.

"What?" Janie hissed, charging toward her. She compacted her emotions right into a box of obsessions and checking. I had never seen her this mad. *"You what?* Tell me. Do you hate me because I'm obsessive? Compulsive? Odd? Ugly? Frumpy? Which is it? Or is it all of them, Cecilia?" Her nose ran, but she didn't bother to wipe it. "Because I am sick of not knowing. I am sick of being attacked by you. I am sick of it and sick of you!"

Cecilia sank into a chair.

I should have gone to Cecilia, but I couldn't. Part of me was glad that Janie had drawn on the war paint. Cecilia deserved it.

"Janie . . ." Cecilia started, then patted her chest where her heart was. "Janie."

Some machine blipped, which caught my attention. Why can't family arguments ever occur at the right moments, the right places? Why do they always explode exactly when an explosion is not needed?

"I'm jealous of you, Janie," Cecilia said, voice weak.

"Oh, now there's a revelation," I murmured. "I'm floored. Shocked."

"You're jealous?" Janie sputtered, red and mottled in the face. "Jealous? How can you be? You've told me yourself that I'm the biggest head case you've ever met."

"I'm jealous," Cecilia whispered, finally meeting Janie's gaze. "You left Trillium River."

"Not that again," I complained. I was so sick of that jealousy. We'd been around and through it ad nauseum.

Janie clasped her hands over her ears. "Cecilia, I can't hear you whine for one more minute about being stuck here. I've heard it until I want to throw my pink-and-white china off my back deck at passing boats in groups of four! Please, shut up about that, shut up shut up shut up!"

"Can you let me finish?" Cecilia said, her anger flashing, as she kept patting her chest. "I'm jealous because you left and made something of yourself. You're a best-selling writer. You're thin. You have a cool houseboat and cool things. You're only frumpy because you don't want attention from men. You play down how naturally beautiful you are. You hide. You try to disappear. I'm frumpy because I'm the size of a cow."

"I worked to get what I have, Cecilia," Janie shrieked, her body shaking. "*I worked hard. I still work hard. I'm a workaholic.* Do you think it's fun to have murderers running through your head? Do you think it's fun to have all these crime scenes lurching about on the pages in front of you and you have to study all the sick, tiny details? Do you think it's fun to watch people get strangled in your mind? Or bludgeoned with hammers? It's not, Cecilia, it's not! I write because I have to write. I can't not write. You get that? *I can't not write.*"

"But, Janie, your obsession with writing has gotten your skinny ass famous. You being a recluse only makes you more famous. I'm a kindergarten teacher. That's it. I teach kids how to count. How to read. We sing clean-up songs and songs about love and flowers and a whale who yodels. I teach the boys how to pee in the toilet without spraying the walls. The other day I got peed on."

Cecilia tried to lasso in her emotions. "I'm so damn fat. I hate myself. I can hardly move some days. I can hardly get up. I put my fat face in the mirror and all I see is fat. I will probably die young because of it, but I can't stop myself. Yesterday I had eight tacos. The night before I made myself a stuffed turkey!"

If Cecilia thought her confession was going to soften up Janie, she had another thing coming. "Cecilia, your weight is your issue," Janie roared, fists clenched. "It's you who have chosen to stuff your mouth full of food until your guts are gonna explode. You got that? It's you. It's your fault you're fat and I have zero pity for you. You have no right to chip away at me, to find my weak spots and attack, all because you don't like yourself and the way your life turned out. You're responsible for yourself and you are a miserable, miserable person and you make me miserable, too. Miserable! Sometimes when I'm with you I want to take a shovel to my own head after digging a grave for myself to fall into!"

Janie did shriek that last part, then sunk into a chair on the opposite side of the room and pulled her body into a tight ball.

Cecilia leaned over her knees and sobbed.

I hardly knew which sister to go to first. I was smack in the middle of a fight. That's the worst. If either sister thought I was siding with the other, I'd get jumped. I'd be pulled in as sure as a tsunami's gonna take out the palm trees when it barrels on through. Sisters do that to each other. Neutral doesn't work.

But then Momma took care of the problem.

"For God's sakes, Cecilia, stop that infernal snuffling," she said, eyes still shut. "Janie's right, you are a terrible bitch to her. She can't help it that she's thin and you're fat and she's a writer and you're a kindergarten teacher. What was she supposed to do? Become a gas station attendant so you wouldn't feel bad? And what's to feel bad about anyhow? Those little brats love you. God, I cannot stand small children. They make me ill. And, Janie, Cecilia's right. You are so meek and so odd it makes me feel like smashing my colored-bottle collection. Get it together before we all jump over a cliff." She sighed. "I've raised a fat girl, a slut, and a wacko."

I snorted through my nose. Now you might think this was insensitive of me, but with Momma you have to either laugh or move to Baghdad to get a little peace.

And if you can't laugh, then you'll fall into this black pit infested with horrible thoughts and agonizing aloneness and hopelessness and fear. I should know. I've been there.

"And you, Isabelle," Momma croaked from the bed. "Please don't make a slut of yourself in Trillium River again. The last time you did, it ruined my reputation as a mother. Ruined it. I was ruined. *Ruined.*"

I snorted again. See what I mean about laughing?

"I'll try, Momma. But I feel some sluttiness overtaking me right now and who knows what your reputation will be like when you get home."

"I won't tolerate it, Isabelle," she wheezed out. "Get out of here, girls. *Get out. Out.*"

We needed no further prodding.

We were outta there.

We drove back to Trillium River in silence.

It's the silence that only simmering sisters can produce together. That rigid, tight, resentful silence that is about as bad as if we started blasting cannonballs at each other's brains.

Sometimes the silence lasts minutes. Hours. Days. Weeks. It can last years.

Depends on the sisters.

The problem I see with fights between sisters is that the fights can degenerate to scorching meanness so quick, the words cutting right to the marrow, because sisters know how to hurt each other with pinpoint accuracy. They have history and hurts and slights and jealousies and resentment and they don't know how to rein it in, filter, or how not to be brutally honest with one another.

Sometimes it's a lovely relationship.

Sometimes it's a disastrous relationship.

Sometimes it's both.

* * *

Cecilia dropped us off.

None of us said good night.

The silent treatment, I am sure, was engineered and developed by cavewomen fighting with their sisters over who got to spear the mastodon.

The next day we worked at the bakery starting in those wee hours again. It was the weekend, so Cecilia was there, too. She had hired a sitter to spend the night.

The atmosphere was frigid. Like the back of a polar bear's butt if he'd been sitting on the ice for six years straight. Janie turned on sad classical music and kept looking wistfully at her therapist's face.

We worked perfectly together, as if we were teenagers again, our steps choreographed, our movements fast but never in the way of anyone else, efficient and quick and good.

We were so good.

Until I heard Janie's whimper.

Cecilia heard it, too.

Janie went into the freezer and shut the door.

Cecilia and I followed her into the freezer.

"Honey," Cecilia said, "I'm sorry."

Janie nodded her head, up and down, like a bobble head. "Me-Me-Me-too. I'm sorry."

"I love you, Janie."

"I love-lo-lov-you, too, Cecilia. And Is. Love you, Is."

We hugged. We were tearful messes, trembling and carrying on with great drama.

Sisters are the worst. And they are the best. A sister can be awful and complicated and loving and protective and petty and competitive, and when you die she is the person you want beside you holding your hand.

Somebody's gotta organize the potluck after the service and you know your husband's not gonna be up to the job.

This I know.

I drank my latte with a squirt of Kahlúa in it by the Columbia River the next morning around five o'clock.

The sun was making its usual breathtaking appearance and the sky was golden and clean and soft.

I watched the windsurfer with the purple and red sail glide and fly over the water. It was the same man I'd seen when we drove to the hospital. If I was still a photographer, which I'm not (I ignored that shooting spasm of loss in my gut), I'd snap the shot.

I used to come down to this exact spot with friends and boys during school. I'd had sex in the Columbia River many times, starting in high school.

I hadn't been a virgin when I arrived. I lost my virginity in a shed with rakes. He was the older brother of an acquaintance. Later he was jailed for raping a hitchhiker. He invited me into a shed and kissed me. That was kind of fun. He was an older boy, a tough guy sort that all naïve girls are attracted to, and he was paying attention to me. *Me!*

The fun stopped when his hands wandered. I pushed them away, he shoved them back, and shoved me against some fertilizer and told me I'd "like it hard."

I hadn't liked it.

It felt as if my body were splitting in half; I could hardly breathe. I was petrified, ashamed, in agony, and trapped because he held my wrists above my head. I struggled; he grabbed my neck and held me down.

"Relax," he bit out, as he yanked up my skirt, ripped my underwear, and started pumping, my tight body rejecting his, even though he shoved one of my legs to the side to open me up. "Are you frigid or something? A priss?"

I watched his face get redder through a haze of sheer pain, his pumping increasing in speed, his grunting piglike, until his spit sprayed my face one last time and he collapsed over me, his chest heaving. When he could move he squeezed my boobs like you would two sponges, got off, peed in a corner, zipped up, and left. I heard him whistling.

All I remembered seeing was a row of rakes. Rakes for leaves, rakes for gardens, big ones, small ones, tiny ones.

I lost my virginity, through rape, against a sack of fertilizer.

I was almost fourteen. It is a miracle I did not become pregnant.

I didn't tell Momma about the rake incident because I knew she would blame me. I told Cecilia. She knew something had happened anyhow because her vagina hurt for days and she kept getting in the shower. She felt dirty and thought she smelled.

It was probably the fertilizer. I later dumped the clothes I was wearing, including my bra, which was held together by a safety pin.

Promiscuity followed me after that. Why not? I remembered feeling dirty and damaged, as if I was nothing anyhow. At home there was no dad, no stability, no love, and a momma who sank into a morass of hopelessness on a regular basis. I flirted with boys because I got attention, which I craved. Very unfortunately, I was skinny and sexy, which brought more boys, and amoral men, my way. Things went speeding downhill from there.

I grew to know other girls who were promiscuous in the various towns we'd lived in and we had one thing in common: an absent or abusive father or abuse by other men in our lives.

It was a sad, reckless, damaging commonality to have. We were regarded with disdain, nice boys' mothers didn't want us around, and "nice" girls whispered horrible things behind cupped hands and moved away when we came near. We were labeled "sluts," such a calamitous, hideous burden for a girl to bear.

And yet we were searching, endlessly searching, for the most innocent of all emotions, the purest of feelings, and what the heart longs for above all else: Love.

Only love.

We found rakes instead.

✺ 9 ✺

Our dad became an absent dad the morning after he held a cocked gun to Momma's head.

She was screaming, begging, weeping.

I was screaming, as were Janie and Cecilia, who later told me she heard my bloodcurdling screams in her chest. Henry was hollering in his crib. He was four, but he refused to sleep in a bed. Me and Cecilia were about eight, Janie was seven.

My dad believed, at least for the length of the flashback he was fighting through, that he was in mortal hand-to-hand combat with the Viet Cong. That was why his arm was snaked around Momma's neck, his gun-holding hand shaking, his eyes wide and gone, gone like our fun dad wasn't there anymore, gone and lost somewhere in the perilous jungles thousands of miles away.

This episode had followed other nightmares where our dad would leap out of bed and scream, "I'm fuckin' gonna kill ya, ya got that, you slant-eyed gook?" Or he'd grab Momma and yank her off the bed and whisper, "Get down! They're coming! *They're coming!*"

That dad scared me so bad that on several occasions I wet my pants.

As soon as the urine dribbled to the floor, Cecilia would wet her pants, too, and she would glare at me as if it were my fault. "I felt you peeing your pants. That was stupid, Isabelle. We're not babies!"

"Shut up, Cecilia." I was too scared to be humiliated. "Shut up!"

Dad had done two tours in Vietnam. On the second tour the Vietnamese invited him to live in a cage where they alternately beat, whipped, and starved him. He gathered rainwater to drink by sticking a hand through the bars. By the time he escaped, he weighed about one hundred pounds; had permanent scars on his back from a whip; was missing two fingers on his left hand, which had been chopped off; had a scar shooting through his right cheek, from a knife fight (he lost, it was six Vietnamese against him); and was partially deaf in one ear from the guns and a particularly bad beating.

His left knee had been broken twice while cage living, and he walked with a limp. He was on painkillers for his body but nothing for his mind.

Our government, so surprisingly, pretended these issues did not exist, and the response of people here in the States when they knew my dad been in Vietnam was less than complimentary.

I remember him telling Momma, his voice edgy, raw, "I've been called a baby killer and rapist more times than I can count. I never killed a baby and I never raped a woman. How is that I was drafted into a war I didn't want to go to, didn't want to fight, didn't believe in fighting, my buddies are killed, I get beat to shit, I'm a prisoner of war, and when I come home, I'm the bad guy? I'm the rapist? I'm the baby killer? How does that happen? *How the fuck does that happen?*"

Momma's response was to hug my dad all the time. She told me once, her eyes black with exhaustion, "I don't know what else to do. *I don't know what to do.* His monsters are bigger than we are."

After one visit he refused to see a psychiatrist again. The psychiatrist had asked him, "How did living in Vietnam make you *feel?* Angry? Sad? Tell me your *feelings.*"

I heard him tell Momma that he had told the psychiatrist it had made him feel like killing the psychiatrist.

It hadn't gone over well.

He had, however, managed to hold a job as a foreman in a factory. His anger was sometimes a problem at work, as were his reactions to any abrupt noise. He ducked and took cover, flying over anything in his way. To his credit, on a number of occasions, he also took down to the floor anyone who was by him, intending to save their lives, which paradoxically endeared him to many of his coworkers.

As his boss said to Momma after Dad had tackled him, "No one, and I mean no one, River, has ever tried to save my life. I like that man of yours."

But Dad was also gentle and loving and told us stories, built us a tree fort, and said he loved his "Beautiful Bommarito Bambinos." He sang songs and paid special attention to Henry.

And the man cooked. I think creating beauty in the kitchen, filling our meals with spices and flavorings and richness, was a haven for him. There was no hopeless war, no ricochet of bullets, no prisoner starving to death next to him, no swampy jungle hiding a lethal enemy. It was him, his kids, his kitchen—something he could control, a gift he could give to his family.

"Food is art, girls, don't forget it," he'd tell us.

We didn't just eat, we dined. He minced, diced, sliced, stewed, sautéed, bubbled, rolled, and marinated. Sauces were drizzled, vegetables scalloped, breads twisted into golden yum.

His desserts were legendary. Nothing was too difficult for his family. He'd bring out his cookbooks, we girls would choose a dessert and, together, we'd whip it up. It *always* looked like the picture in the book.

But the night my dad held a loaded gun to Momma's head, he knew it was over. He was done. If we were going to be safe, he could not live with us one more day.

He left the next morning, early. I heard him with Momma. I hid in a closet and cracked the door. "You'll be fine, River. I know you will be. I love you. I will always love you. Not a day will go by when I won't think of you, sugar."

Momma had cried and they had kissed, long and with such passion I averted my gaze and studied a lamp, before he'd quietly shut the door and Momma collapsed on our white linoleum kitchen floor, her body shaking.

The sad part was that even though we had a dad who had diabolical flashbacks, swore at nonexistent Vietnamese people, fought against his nightmares, dragged Momma to safety at two o'clock in the morning, had rages and furies, was obviously hanging on to sanity by a fingernail, and came within a hair of shooting Momma's brains out, we missed him terribly.

Though there were no Viet Cong chasing us down a muddied river or through a dirt tunnel, no helicopters picking up partially blown-up buddies, no eardrum-shattering bombs, no burning villages or Agent Orange, our own nightmare had only just begun.

The bakery was clearly a failure.

Like Janie said, Momma's treats tasted like kidneys, her pies like guts, and her bread like a carcass. Momma had never learned how to cook like Dad.

I needed to do some advertising so the town would know that, at least temporarily, we had new management. I needed to get people in here and excited about what we baked. I needed help.

"Hey hey!" Henry yelled, dangling the bell on the door of the bakery. "I here to say, 'Hi, Is!' "

I eyed him. He was wearing a red and blue beanie and a green shirt with a gold cat on it. It said "Nice Kitty."

Yep. Henry would do nicely.

I put a striped apron on Henry, sliced up a chocolate cake into little pieces, and put them on doilies.

"You're going to be the chief advertiser for Bommarito's Bakery!" I told him.

"Ha!" He laughed. "Ha! I the chief! Big chief!"

"Yep. You're in charge of the outside treats."

"Okay dokay. I do that!" He grinned, adjusted his beanie. "What I do, Is?"

"Henry, you give people a little cake on a doily."

"I do it! I give them cake!"

"For free. No charge."

"Ha! Free cake to all the peoples and I tell them Jesus loves you, I do it!"

We set up a table outside and covered it with a red-and-white flowered tablecloth and set Henry to work.

I watched him for a second, that protective instinct I have for him in full force.

It was unnecessary.

That man knew almost everyone walking by and he greeted them by name or said, "Hello to the man behind the counter at the pharmacy with the funny glasses!" or "It the lady at the hair salon with black nails!" or "You drive blue truck. It growl like a bear! Grrrr!" He was always excited to see people and they stopped to chat and hug him.

"Jesus loves you!" he informed them. When no one was in front, he sang songs to himself.

In the end we sold out of all of our cakes, including a chocolate cheesecake with crumbled cookie crust, apple coffee cake with cinnamon, and carrot cake with thick cream cheese icing and an iced pink bunny holding a giant carrot.

At five o'clock we closed and cleaned up.

"Well, not a bad day at the bakery," I said to Janie, so exhausted even my teeth hurt.

"Not bad at all. Feel this, Isabelle." She ran her hands through a bag of oats "I think this is what dried, crushed people bones would feel like. What do you think?"

* * *

We worked like our hair was on fire the next few days at the bakery. I whipped up a cake shaped like a snake with crossed eyes, a pink zebra, and a giraffe with a long, long neck. If the kids love it, the parents'll buy it. That's my motto.

Janie baked a wedding cake that she decorated with light pink icing and this flowing, cascading ring of flowers out of marzipan icing. It was stunning. I saw people line up outside to stare at that cake.

The perfection of that cake reminded me of my dad and the sheer beauty of the cakes he baked with us. I turned away.

Belinda came in, same time as always, laid down on a bench in the booth, and went to sleep. Today she smelled like roses. Through the window I saw her shopping cart and the black bags. A little face appeared and I blinked.

Belinda had a black cat. It was wearing a pink bow.

Janie and I exchanged a glance.

What were we supposed to do about Belinda, anyhow?

One time I'd woken up by myself on a park bench. That would not be so unusual, but I had no idea what park I was in and was further confused about which state. I knew I was in America because I saw the flag.

Our grandma believes she's Amelia Earhart, our brother informs everyone that Jesus loves them, and our momma, elegant and well dressed, could slice and dice anyone who got in her way like an expert swordsman and has done so many times. Momma and Grandma once had a screaming match in church because Momma wouldn't hold Grandma's hand during the Our Father prayer. The blessing had been given over their shrieks.

Cecilia swears like a fishwife when not teaching kindergarten and weighs close to three hundred pounds and Janie has to chill in the freezer a few times a day to cool her head off and break up her counting regimens. I have a man problem and have battled depression problems so all-encompassing I felt my toes dangling over the pit of hell. Our dad took off because he mentally time travelled back to Vietnam.

Now, come on. Who are Janie and I to judge anyone for their odd behaviors?

We let Belinda sleep.

On Wednesday Janie and I drove Henry to the church for his volunteer work with the high school group.

I stared at the carved church doors, the cross on top of the roof, and the statue of Mary.

I had spent many hours there as a high schooler. Momma had insisted. I had gone to church on Sundays, no matter how hung over I was from the night before or what had transpired six short hours before church in the back of some guy's car.

I had attended the classes on Wednesday nights and confessed nefarious numerous sins to Father Mike and the following day went back out and committed the same ones.

I had had sex with three guys in the basement and two on the altar. We even stole the communion wafers to eat with the stolen wine. I had told Cecilia and Janie that now we could eat a ton of the body of Christ and gallons of his blood. We thought that was hilarious.

I wanted to see Father Mike, but I couldn't. I couldn't go into that church. I had done too much. I could not forget what I had done, or forgive myself. There probably was not a commandment I hadn't broken. Except for coveting thy neighbor's wife. I had never coveted a wife.

Henry gave me a kiss on the cheek and a smile.

"Bye, Henry, have fun."

"Okay dokay, Isabelle. You have fun, too. You going home make spaghetti now?" On Wednesday night, Henry came home and had spaghetti."

"Yes, I'm going to make spaghetti."

"Meatballs?" He grinned at me.

"Meatballs, too. I promise."

"Stringy cheese?"

He meant parmesan cheese. "Yes, stringy cheese, too."

Henry grinned again and clapped his hands. "I love you, Janie and Isabelle, my sisters. Yeah, yeah, I do. My sisters."

"I love you, too, Henry."

"Love ya, Henry." Janie blew a kiss.

And I did love Henry. I watched him amble up the church steps, those brown curls silky and smooth. A group of teenagers turned the corner when Henry reached the bottom and I instantly cringed. Janie sucked in her breath.

My hand clenched the handle of the car, as did Janie's, ready to race out and protect Henry, as we'd done as kids, to protect him from one fist-punching freak or another.

One time, while we were living in some backwater, mosquito-infested town in South Carolina, three kids chased Henry all the way home through a field when he was in fourth grade. They hit him with their backpacks, yelled at him, held him down in the mud, and swore.

Now for anyone, being chased by a gang of rowdy kids is terrorizing. But if you are a specially abled person, like Henry, the fear is magnified. It's like you're being attacked by a sword-wielding army, with a siren ringing in your ears, and you're stuck in a dripping tunnel with hissing, biting snakes and can't figure the way out or why this disaster is here in the first place.

He burst in our front door bruised and bloodied and screaming. He didn't stop screaming for an hour. His screaming woke Momma up, who was in the midst of another black bout, and she started wailing. They clung to each other. Eventually we got Henry's hands unpried from Momma and got him cleaned and bandaged up as he told us what happened between tears and hiccups and a spell of hyperventilating.

The next day, after school, Cecelia, Janie, and I waited for our prey. We watched Henry leave school and head home wearing his favorite green baseball hat with a frog on it and a shirt that said "Boo!" We had told him we would get the bad guys and protect him, but he was so nervous he was shaking, his walk an odd gait.

That same gang of shits started following him. "Hey, retard! Retard! REEEEE TARD! Stupid head! Yeah, you!"

Henry started running, frantic, his frog hat flying off.

We sisters started running, too, toward the shits, only we kept it quiet, like we were executing an ambush. We had experience in these matters.

"One . . ." Cecilia panted when we were close to the three boys who were running after Henry. She was big then, but fast. "Two . . ." The kids didn't even hear us over the roar of their own feet and laughter and taunts of "Hey, fuckface. Hey, dummy! You're retarded! Dumb shit!"

"Three!" Cecilia screamed. Her fury had runneth over.

On three we each dove for one of those shits.

We smashed them to the sidewalk, the air rushing out of their bodies with the force of our landing. I heard a *crack* from the body of my boy. We weren't screwing around. We never did. Plus, we were pissed. Pissed off at those guys for torturing poor, sweet Henry, pissed off that Momma was in bed again, pissed off there was no food in the house, pissed off we had no dad, pissed off the phone was cut off again, pissed off at our dingy bras. It was endless what the Bommarito girls were pissed off about.

We hammered those kids with our fists, the recipients of our hate, while Henry ran home, as instructed, after he got his frog hat back on his head. Cecilia jammed her boy's head into the sidewalk. I brought my knee up in one movement and shoved my fist into my guy's nose at the same time.

Blood. All over his face.

Janie counted, "One, two, three, four, one, two, three, four, one, two—" Each time she hit a number she hit the guy. Janie had brass knuckles so we'd let her tackle the biggest guy.

They struggled, but it was of no use.

After I'd punched my jerk in the gut, I whipped out a small

knife. Cecilia and Janie yanked on their boys' hair until they were forced to watch me sticking the tip of the knife into my guy's neck.

"Do. Not. Ever. Ever," I shouted, my face two inches from that petrified shit's face, "come near our brother again. Do you get that? Do you get that, you shits? If you do, I will kill you. Got that, you, shits?"

Janie's kid tried to get up. Smash. "One. Two. Three. Four." Smash. Blood.

Cecilia's prey tried to wrestle her off. "Get off of me, fat ass!"

Her anger went a-flamin' away at that remark. He was crumpled in a ball by the time she was done with him, sobbing for his mother.

My guy didn't move. I smiled at him sweetly, my knife still pricking. "Care to go to the prom together?"

He paled.

"I could show you my other knives." I smiled again. Then I leaned down and whispered, "I will make you into a woman if you come near my brother again, you got that?" I dropped the knife to his crotch.

He whimpered. "Okay. I wanna go home . . . home . . ." Tears started streaming out of his eyes. He spit out a tooth.

"One, two, three, four, let 'em go," Janie said. We all stood up, and Cecilia and Janie and I moved shoulder to shoulder. Janie fisted her brass knuckles; I held the knife out and smiled.

"That date to the prom?" I taunted.

"That was fun!" Janie declared. "I had a good time!"

The next morning we were sitting right across from those three bullies in the principal's office.

The bullies were bruised and beaten. I snickered and flipped up my middle fingers at them. Janie counted out loud and Cecilia wrapped both hands around her neck, pretended to strangle herself, then pointed at them.

The principal, Mr. Wong, who had apples on his tie and wore huge glasses, said, "These young men said that the three of you beat them up." He cocked an eyebrow at us.

The vice principal, a woman named Ms. Drake, was sitting beside him. Both of them had satisfied expressions on their faces.

"These boys have been in here before. *Many times*," Ms. Drake drawled. She had white hair in a braid wrapped around her head. "We are quite familiar with them, but it's always because they beat up somebody else. What's happened here, girls?"

Janie exhaled and drummed up a few tears. We had all worn dresses and clean white socks that day, and had even shined up our shoes with toilet paper. We had practiced our responses. "We *had* to, ma'am."

"You had to?" Ms. Drake asked. She chuckled, then coughed to cover it.

"Yes, we had to. For protection. For safety." Janie dabbed at her eyes with a lace handkerchief of Momma's. I thought she appeared small and fragile. I tried not to giggle when I thought of how expertly she had wielded her brass knuckles.

"What do you mean, for protection? They said you beat them up for no reason," Mr. Wong said, fingering the apples. "None. Zero. Out of the blue."

The boys squirmed. I stared at the crotch of my guy and made a scissor-cutting motion with my hands. He flushed.

"We beat them up because they're assholes," Cecilia interjected. She had not paid much attention to me and Janie when we had practiced our victim-like responses last night.

I side kicked Cecilia.

"Young lady—" the principal started.

"I'm sorry, sir, ma'am," Cecilia said, contrite momentarily. "I won't say the assholes are assholes again."

"Cecilia—" Ms. Drake warned.

"I'm so sorry, ma'am, for my . . . my *impertinence*," She glared at the boys and mouthed, "Assholes."

They squirmed in their chairs again.

"Let's start over here," Mr. Wong insisted. "These boys are missing teeth, Shaw's mouth is swollen up, and Damien's got a bump on his head the size of Kansas. Their parents called and they want answers. What happened?"

"We defended our brother, sir," I said, tilting my chin up. "They attacked Henry yesterday. They did it the day before, too. When we found out about it, we followed Henry on his way home from school to keep him safe and that's when those three attacked him again. Twice. In two days they jumped him."

The boys stared at the floor. I hummed a little song to freak them out.

"You what?" Mr. Wong turned toward the boys. He was usually mild-mannered, but his son had special needs, too, and he and Henry played checkers together. When Henry didn't come to school, the son threw fits.

"You attacked Henry? Henry Bommarito?" Mr. Wong was aghast. That'd be the word for it, *aghast.*

Ms. Drake lost her secret smile.

The boys started to stammer and stutter.

"Damien did it. It was his idea—"

"Dirk started it—"

"I didn't want to, but Shaw said if I didn't help that he'd kick me out of the club—"

"It's only Henry anyhow," Shaw muttered through his swollen lips. "He's okay. He's a stupid person, you know. He don't got no brain like us."

Well now, that did it.

"It's only Henry?" Mr. Wong bit out. He turned purplish red and got up and whacked each of them on the head with a sheaf of papers. *"He's a human being."*

"But—" Damien interrupted. "He ain't like us. He ain't normal."

"He is normal, you're the ones who aren't normal!" Mr. Wong

yelled. "What kind of animal beats up on Henry? How sick." He thunked them each on the head again. "Sick. Sick. Sick. *Are you animals?*"

"He made funny faces at us!" one of the boys shouted.

"Yeah, he's always smiling and saying, Jesus loves you!"

"He's a retard!" the third boy said. "Retard!"

Oh boy.

Chaos.

We Bommarito girls *hate* that word.

That was one ugly scene. Cecilia, Janie, and I leaped at the three boys at one time. I landed on the middle one so hard I knocked him over.

The principal managed to catch Janie in midair as she flew at one of the other boys. She screamed and kicked and got one kick in right on Shaw's swollen lips.

Cecilia torpedoed herself at the other kid and karate kicked him in the chest before the vice principal restrained her. We both noted later that Cecilia was allowed to get off one more banging good karate kick before the vice principal actually used some muscle to pull her off.

We were carried out of the principal's office by force, our feet flailing in the air as we struggled, and tossed into chairs in the outer office.

Those bullying, creepy boys were expelled.

The principal and vice principal summoned us back to the office and we braced ourselves.

At first there was dead silence, then Mr. Wong sighed heavily. He nodded at Ms. Drake.

"I hear you girls bake a tasty German chocolate cake," Ms. Drake said, sitting up straight, smiling sweetly as if the melee that morning had never occurred. "And apple pies. I'd like one of each. I've had a hankering for apple pie for weeks now."

What to say, what to say? No punishment?

"My secretary said that you also bake a four-layer chocolate cake that tastes like heaven. My wife would like two for a family dinner we're having," Mr. Wong said. He fingered the apples on his tie.

We were speechless. Speech. Less.

Mr. Wong swiveled in his chair. "If you'd like, girls, you can put an advertisement up in the staff room and an order sheet for your desserts . . ."

I about quivered I was so excited. No expulsion *and* a job opportunity.

"Ha! The assholes are out and we're in," Cecilia said, swinging her fists in the air.

Ms. Drake hid her smile.

"Yes!" Janie leaped out of her chair. "Yes! We'll do it! One, two, three, four!"

We did it.

And, for a while, we Bommarito girls had enough money for food and the electric bill.

There were other kids, in many other schools, and our knife, our brass knuckles, and our fists unfortunately were used many times to protect Henry. Henry, our sweet, innocent Henry, with the frog hat and a shirt that said, "Boo!"

So when Henry and the teenagers met up in front of the church, I could feel my blood pumping. Janie and I were ready to go, ready to rip. I heard her start counting beside me.

"Hello!" Henry said, smiling, waving to the teenagers. "Coming to church? We got doughnuts!"

One kid gave him a gentle pat on the back. He was dressed all in black and had two chains hanging from his belt. Another one had spiked green hair. He said, "Hey dude. What's shakin'?" which made Henry laugh.

"I not shakin'," he said, his face lighting up. "You funny, Connor. Hey, Jesus loves you! He love you."

We watched them walk up the steps together.

I loved Henry.

"I love Henry," Janie sighed. "He reminds me of Vivaldi and Yo-Yo Ma. Blended."

I couldn't speak. I swear, the light that Henry has brought to my life has sometimes been the only light I had at all.

❧ 10 ❧

"Come over."

"What?" I leaned back against the white wicker couch on the porch, my hand loosely holding the phone. Janie was stretched out on the floor. "Now, Cecilia?"

"I can't move," Janie said. "My bones are sticks, my muscles jelly."

We hadn't had a day off in well over a week. Word had gotten out about Bommarito's Bakery and we were seeing a steady stream of people. We were baking like fiends, and even though Cecilia helped afternoons and on the weekends, we would probably have to hire workers. We couldn't continue at this pace or my bones would shatter and dry up and be taken off by the wind to Holland.

"Yes! Come over!" Cecilia said, her voice gleeful. "The girls are in bed. I have to show you two something."

"What, specifically?" I pictured my exhausted kidney on a stretcher, an IV line running through it, oxygen mask over the kidney's face. Do kidneys have faces?

Janie whispered, "My body doesn't work anymore. I am left with flesh and capillaries, a few arteries, no working bones."

But Cecilia had splendiferous news: "I got the private investigator's report back on Parker."

I felt a few brain cells ping and pong.

"And?"

She almost cock-a-doodle-doodled. "It's a doozer. It's a blast! It's an explosion! A happy explosion!"

Ping-pong ping-pong! I sat up.

"Oh, I am dancing, yodeling, tootling!" Cecilia sang. "It's a glorious, victorious, vengeful night!"

Suddenly, I wasn't much tired at all.

I relayed Cecilia's message to the semicomatose Janie.

We flew out of that house like we had falcon wings attached to our asses.

Cecilia sat up straight and folded her hands neatly across the thick blue folder in front of her at the table. The candles she lit to celebrate flickered under her chandelier.

Cecilia's home is cozy, filled with bright colors, lush fabrics, thick rugs, and soft furniture. It sits on three acres, partially surrounded by apple orchards, and I swear you can smell those juicy apples in the house all year long.

"Your home feels so much better without the varmint in it," I said.

"Thank you. It's unfortunate I didn't poison the varmint before he left." Cecilia's blond hair was back in a ponytail and her eyes gleamed with satisfaction, I mean, they *gleamed*. Like there was a layer of olive oil over them, in a good way.

I could barely contain myself.

Janie *giggled*. She didn't even count anything.

"I have a kick-ass investigator," Cecilia intoned, all professional-like, after pouring champagne for each of us. "This is his report."

I laughed. Janie's giggle soared around that room, light and triumphant. Oh, she hated Parker even more than me. In fact, a man exactly like Parker was the killer in one of her books. The killer's last name was Pakrer. She'd even described Parker's cocky strut, how he used "big" words to impress people, how he carried an old copy of Proust around to seem smart, and how he discussed opera but clearly didn't have a clue about it.

Parker had been furious.

Janie had pled innocence.

Pakrer the murderer in the end had gotten his buttocks sliced off with a meat cleaver. Not realistic, but hey, Janie's fans loved it.

Cecilia cleared her throat, signifying the importance of this grand moment. "I now know about Parker's new girlfriend. Constance Lodge, whose real name is Bianca Landon Bach, was born in 1982 in Los Angeles. She has a slight criminal record, let's see here, where is it? Ah. Here." She raised her eyebrows as she read the rap sheet: Shoplifting, third-degree assault, credit card fraud, bank fraud, check-writing arrests, her own mother sued her for stealing from her, as had a number of other businesses and individuals.

"A splendid girl to bring home to Parker's momma!" I declared. "Splendid! A perfect example of unblemished and pure womanhood!"

Cecilia hated Parker's mother. The woman was tiny and creepy and rich and thought Parker was perfect and Cecilia a lame-duck wife. She'd told her that, too. "A lame-duck wife, that's what Cecilia is, Parker sweetie. Look at her!"

"In 2002, Bianca was charged with pros—" Cecilia sputtered and giggled before getting a hold of herself. "*Prostitution*, how I love to say that word! And, in 2005, our capitalistic, opportunistic business buddy Bianca was charged with running her very own prostitution ring."

I could barely get the words around my tongue I was so ecstatically befuddled. "So Parker is dating an ex-*madam?*"

Janie snorted.

"Apparently," Cecilia gurgled, "Constance ran a ragingly successful business in San Francisco. When she was busted, she gave her little black book to the papers and no less than five local politicians, one U.S. Senator, two U.S. representatives, six sports stars, university professors, and executives were publicly embarrassed at their own indisputable indiscretions."

"So she's clever!" I exalted. "Parker's mother will love her ingenuity and shrewdness! I shall rejoice in telling her myself *after* the wedding!"

"My private investigator has enclosed a few articles." She thunked a sheaf of papers on the table and we pored over those newspaper articles as one might pore over winning lottery tickets.

"Does he know she's an ex-madam?" Janie asked.

"I am sure that he doesn't," Cecilia said. "He's having a roll in the hay and can't see past his dick. So what we know is a secret."

"It's a spectacular, incredible secret!" Janie picked up another article. "His karma has caught up with him. I relish his downfall."

"She's also been married three times previously. My guy met up with one of the exes at the bar and, without revealing who he was, got the first ex to spill the beans. Look at this."

"Bianca stole me blind," we read, printed from the recorded conversation. "All I had. Gone. Poof. She told me she was a student. I thought she was sweet. Can you believe that? *Sweet.* Damn. She racked up my credit cards and took loans out on my house until I might as well have been living in a tent. I tried to keep her happy and she still cheated on me. Stupid bitch. You know how guys come home and catch their wives in bed with another guy? I caught her with another woman. But they weren't even in bed. They were naked in my boat—the boat she insisted I buy her— doin' it against the wheel. God, that's sick. Totally sick. I was married to a lesbo."

"Cheers to Constance!" Cecilia boomed, holding up a glass of champagne. "May she enjoy a new boat, bought with Parker's credit card, and may she and her sexy girlfriend enjoy it, naked, against the wheel as Parker watches!"

"Cheers to Constance!" I echoed.

Sometimes life is so blissful, so jittery with justice, it makes one want to sing. "La, la la!"

* * *

We paid the price for our late-night visit to Cecilia the next day, but it was totally worth it. After we rejoiced in the report, we had too many Kahlúa and creams (it's the family drink), and I laughed so hard I wet my pants and had to borrow a pair of sweats from Cecilia.

"My tinkle smells like a Long Island Iced Tea!" I shrieked.

"Pee Tea!" Cecilia declared.

"Tea Tinkle!" Janie said.

We laughed so hard we had to lie on the kitchen floor.

"Get divorced as soon as you can, Cecilia," Janie said, as she waltzed herself around the room. "The sooner you do, the sooner his demise begins, his karma will crash, his aura will blacken."

"But I want to hang him—" she protested. She wrapped her hands around her own neck and made a strangling face.

"You've hung him," I said. "Let him hang himself."

"The esophagus is crushed when a person's hanged, it—" Janie started.

"Please, Janie," I said. "Don't add to my nightmares."

Needless to say, we slept at Cecilia's.

Thanks heavens for Velvet.

"I can barely see, I'm so tired. I think my eyeballs are still in bed," Janie said as we left the house and I drove Janie's Porsche through the darkened streets of Trillium River to the bakery at 4:30 the next morning. I reminded myself to go and get my own Porsche in Portland. We'd hobbled out of Cecilia's house, gone home, showered, changed, and headed out.

"I feel like squished oatmeal has taken the place of my brains," Janie whispered. "And I didn't get to embroider last night . . ."

"I feel like death has a seat in my head," I said. "And he's kicking my cranium."

When we got to the corner, Janie looked imploringly at me.

"No," I told her.

She made a little squeaking sound in her throat.

"You have got to get a grip."

"I'm trying."

"Not trying hard enough. Say yes to drugs."

"I won't be able to concentrate," she whined. "All day, I'll be unfocused. I'll probably burn the orange-lemon muffins and the chocolate roll-up crepes with the skinny shavings and cream."

"For God and hell's sakes," I spat out. I did a U-turn in the middle of the street. I had to give in. This would go on all day.

Janie sighed with relief.

We drove back up the hill to Grandma's house. I parked in the driveway. Janie scampered out, her skirt flying behind her. She checked the door. She had locked it.

"Eureka! What a surprise!" I sang out to myself. She opened the door, ran into the house. I knew she was rechecking the stove and oven, the upstairs iron (which no one had turned on). I know she would tap the iron four times—on the side that could get hot, to make sure it wasn't hot. She would tap the dials on the stove and oven, too, four times, to assure herself the house would not burn down.

I saw her dart out the front door. I saw her lock it.

She ran to the car.

"You exhaust me," I told her.

She leaned her head back. "I exhaust myself. Give me a hug, Is."

"Oh, for heaven's sakes." I gave her a hug and we breathed together, head to head. In and out. Quiet. Peaceful. The wind outside windy-ing around. "We're pathetic."

Problems can be so overwhelming. So huge. So unfixable. I believe that the human mind is a labyrinth of guilt and regrets and pleasure and passion and memories. But if you have someone to put your head together with, temple to temple, their heat sharing your heat, their pulse beating in time with yours, their warmth your warmth, life is better. Not perfect, it can't ever be. But it's better.

*   *   *

The next day a small Asian man limped into the bakery.

He was about five feet, three inches tall but hunched, as if he'd lived his life with pain in his back and the pain had permanently pushed him partway over.

Hard grooves were carved on both sides of his face, but what stood out to me was his neck. Curling over the perfectly clean, buttoned-up collar of his shirt was a scar, thick and wide and pink and shiny, scrawling halfway around his neck.

His eyes were black and gentle, but I felt like I was staring into two tunnels of pain.

"Hello, welcome to Bommarito's. Can I help you?"

"Yes, thank you," he said, his voice quiet, accent heavy. "Please, sandwich bread."

"Allrighty, I'll get it for you." I smiled, packaging up his bread. Janie had made garlic cheese bread this morning because she "felt like garlic. Ominous and hard and breakable."

I eyed him again. I figured he was in his sixties. At least. He was staring at the cookies.

He was boney thin. Like a sad skeleton with a face.

I added two cookies in the shapes of seahorses in a separate little bag. I'd painted one seahorse pink with green dots and the other green with pink dots.

"Oh no. I no order cookies," he said. "Bread. Thank you, I thank you."

I handed him the bread and the cookies. "It's a treat for you. A gift."

"A gift?" His eyebrows shot up.

"Yes."

"A gift," he said, so quietly. His face showed surprise, then a flush of pleasure. He bowed to me. I bowed to him. "Thank you," he said, his tone serious.

"You're welcome." I put an arm out to direct him to a window seat. I could tell he needed a rest. He reminded me of so many of the bedraggled, desperate people I'd met in war zones. "Please sit down."

He didn't move for long seconds. Hesitating. Unsure.

I smiled. "Please rest."

"Yes. I like that. I rest."

He moved slowly, that limp making his right hip rise several inches each time he took a step. Settling into his seat took some time even though I helped him. I heard him sigh when he got settled.

"I thank you."

"You're welcome." I handed him the cookies. He took them gently, with his right hand, his left hand still.

When he was settled, I went back to work. I was going to make a super-tall three-layer cake. Each layer would resemble a wrapped present. The bottom layer would be pink-and-white striped, the middle purple with simple flowers, and the top a beautiful blue box with a huge white ribbon on top.

I surreptitiously watched my customer while I worked. He was staring out the window, nibbling at the cookie. After each bite, he closed his eyes, as if in ecstasy. I smiled to myself. Well, our cookies were darn good!

He was so thin, fragile thin.

I learned later that his name was Bao. He had immigrated from Vietnam.

I learned that he lived a life of almost complete solitude, but not by choice.

And I learned that hunched-over, gentle Bao lived with the haunting memories that snaked a scar around his throat, caused him to limp, and snuffed the light of life right out of his eyes.

Henry and I baked sixty cupcakes for church on Wednesday night. He insisted we use blue icing and each one had to have a white cross, "for Jesus."

I didn't want to go into the church, but packing sixty cupcakes up the steps without help would have been impossible, so there I was in jeans and a T-shirt with blue icing on it, trudging up the steps.

God must have been busy, for he did not send a smack of lightning into my kidneys when I entered the doors of the church, nor did the roof become engulfed with flames.

A priest stood in the doorway of the vestibule. He smiled when he saw me, then as recognition dawned, he spread his arms out wide like a black eagle, his hair whiter than white.

I could hardly move. It was Father Mike.

I got all choked up. The man had practically saved my life.

"Isabelle, Isabelle, Isabelle! You dear girl!" he said, hobbling over to me, his hip in bad shape from where he'd taken shrapnel in the Korean War. "I've missed you!"

I put the cupcakes down and gave him a hug, and it was like hugging safety and comfort and friendship all in one, but dear God, if this man only knew the multitude of sins I had engaged in since I left Trillium River, I didn't think he'd be hugging me now.

What would Father Mike think of my bra burning and the events that led up to it? What would he think of the men? The selfishness?

He wiped the tears off his cheeks with both hands, then boomed, "Dear girl, I need you in the choir immediately."

Now that was Father Mike. Hey, how you doin', come on in to the church and help me. All within two seconds. "Hello! I need someone to lead Sunday school for the fourth graders and I hear you're a former teacher! How about starting next week?" Or "I hear you moved to Trillium River! What instrument do you play? The trumpet! Wonderful! Well, go and get it, you're playing solo today between communion and the offering!"

Funny thing was, I could tell you at least thirty families who were still here after that initial invitation from Father Mike.

"Oh, no, Father Mike. I don't sing anymore."

"Isabelle Bommarito! Raise the melody of your voice to God once again and say Hallelujah! You were such an addition to our choir when you lived here! Such! An! Addition!"

I had sung in the choir because Father Mike made me. He

told Momma I could "sing like a nightingale, fifty nightingales," and she made me, too. Ironic, but the Wednesday night's church choir had been led by a gal (moi) who was an Expert Sinner.

"It's only for thirty minutes," Father Mike said. "Thirty minutes! The kids all sing together. Rock songs. Christian rock. We get the drums going." He imitated playing the drums, his age-spotted hands surprisingly limber. "The electric and acoustic guitars rolling." He imitated playing the guitars, rocking his hips back and forth. "I need you! Janice! Janice!" He waved over a plump, smiling, gray-haired woman who appeared harried and rushed. "Here's a blessed lady for your choir. She sings! Like a nightingale, like fifty nightingales!"

"But I can't—"

Janice fell all over me, she was so relieved. "Perfect. Outstanding. So outstanding! We definitely need someone who can sing." She patted her hair and spoke with no pauses. "The kids will be coming in seconds they sound like a herd of charging buffalo so watch out dear now most of the band is made up of the high schoolers, but our guitarist got sick and the two girls who sing well . . ." She fluttered and flustered as she shoved me up toward the altar, where teenagers were milling around with their instruments.

"Let's say they're beginning singers and leave it at that. There's a little stage here where you'll be with the others dear, come along."

"But I don't—"

"We'll give you the sheet music. Joshua, here's your new singer."

Josh was a young boy with a pierced nose and a pierced ear. "Cool. Hey, how are ya?" He stuck out one hand for me to shake and handed me sheet music with the other. "Let's rock."

"Rock and roll," I told him.

"Dig the braids," he told me, nodding in approval.

"Thank you." I flipped them back. "Dig the pierced nose."

He gave me a three fingers up, two down sign.

"God in heaven, calm my nerves and thank you for this singer," Janice said, still fluttering, flittering.

Father Mike grinned at me, mimicked playing the guitar, and wiggled his eyebrows. This wasn't going to happen. No way. No. I got off the stage.

"Oh, dear, dear," Janie said, following me, tut-tutting. "We have only minutes, *minutes* honey don't you want to study the music?"

"Father Mike," I said, trying not to pant. "Father Mike!"

"What is it, Isabelle? Are you troubled?" He smiled at me. So dear, so innocent. But he knew what he was up to. He was a sneaky priest, I thought. *Sneaky.* Trying to get me up there to sing Christian rock.

"Father Mike." How to put this into words? How could I? I choked. Janice patted my arm.

"You can do it, love, Father Mike has faith in your voice and so do I," she cheered, her face flushed.

I pulled the two of them to a quieter corner as the teenagers rushed in like a herd of charging buffalo in heat.

"I'm not fit," I whispered.

They were both utterly baffled.

I tried again. *"I'm not fit."*

Janice eyed my body. "Well, dear. You could have fooled me! You're thin." She squeezed my upper arms. "And you have muscles but don't worry about that at all you don't have to be in shape to sing here at church!" She yanked my arm. She was surprisingly strong.

"No, no." I stood still, dug my heels in. Getting up on that stage in high school to sing was one thing. I was a kid. I was messing around, but I was a kid. The sins had grown deeper and wider since then and the sins had been deliberately made by a fully responsible and turbo-charged, whacked-out adult.

"I mean, I'm not fit . . . I'm not fit to be up there."

Understanding dawned in Father Mike's eyes.

"What? Ooo . . . ah . . . ohhhh . . ." Understanding dawned in Janice's eyes.

"I can't. I'm not a practicing Catholic. I don't even go to church anymore. I can't imagine God wants to see me here. If I went to confession, Father Mike, we would be there for hours. I mean hours. I'd be saying Hail Marys 'til I was eighty, and that would only cover what I've done in the last few years. I can't—"

Father Mike smiled, spread his arms. "Jesus loves all of us, Isabelle. We're all sinners. Who am I to judge you or anyone else?"

I felt this tiny warmth in my heart. I always felt that way when I was around Father Mike.

"Oh, he's faithfully right!" Janice flutter-flittered. "There's no judging going on here please, dear, I don't care what you've done I personally used to be a drug addict before God came and got me I even sold drugs to get drugs it was a terrible life and terrible deeds!" I felt my mouth drop open to my ankles. Janice was a drug dealer?

Father Mike beamed at Janice, his hands outstretched upward. "Praise God! You see! Janice is here now in the church! God loved her so much he pulled her out of her own hell and brought her here! She runs the music program! She handles the seniors' choir, kids' choir, teenagers' choir. She organizes the choir for Sunday, too, and we have eighty people! An eighty-person choir, all because of Janice! She knows how to reach people's hearts through music. God gave her a difficult path to follow so she could later use her own experience to help lead people away from the sins of drugs and alcohol, bless his name! *Bless his name!*"

"Oh!" Janice squeaked, pulling a handkerchief from the pocket of her dress and swishing it about. "Oh! When I hear you say those words, Father Mike, I . . ." She sniffled. *"I have to cry!"*

"Tears of joy!" Father Mike thundered. "Tears of joy! Utter joy for God's great works! We walk through the fires of hell and come out on the other side with a bucket full of holy water to pour on others who are sinning to make them new again and join all of us in our love for our Father!"

Janice sniffled in her handkerchief, waving a hand in the air. "Praise God," she squeaked, blew her nose. "Praise God!"

"Janice opens the door with her music so the words of Christ that I speak on Sunday can fall into people's hearts!"

"God saves the worst of us, Isabelle," Janice said, fanning herself with her handkerchief. "I'm living proof of that. Now, up you go heavens! The teenagers are coming in!" She caught her breath. The tears gone, purpose behind those eyes. She got behind me and—I am not kidding you—she pushed me until I was up on that stage in a not-so-Christian way.

And that's how I started singing Christian rock again. I was rough at first, but by the end of it, well, I was rockin'.

At the end of the worship music, the kids were cheering and we had not been struck by lightning, swarms of locusts, or flooding, and there were no reports of the Red Sea parting again.

"You sing good, Is," Henry told me, rocking back and forth. "Jesus loves you!"

I rolled my eyes.

Father Mike clapped.

He's a sneaky priest.

৩ 11 ৶

Momma had come down with an infection and was staying at the hospital.

Janie and I baked like fiends; Cecilia taught school, then baked, while often swearing. Kayla and Riley helped. Kayla wore a toga (studying Greek religion) and Riley lectured all of us on recent scientific discoveries.

But we could not have functioned without Velvet. She kept an eye on Grandma and Henry while we worked and visited The Viper in the hospital.

Late one night, after drinking her homemade lemonade, lemonade so tart it could have made a bull drop his balls, we got on the subject of men.

"Isabelle, darlin'," Velvet drawled honey-thick while she rocked on the wicker rocker on the porch, "I was so sick of fakin' orgasms I could not bring myself to marry again for the fourth time. It astonishes the heck out of me how old, fat, white men can *believe* they're so good in bed they can actually get a woman to scream."

Her voice was so soft, so melodious, and clashed so dramatically with what she was saying, I blew ball-dropping lemonade straight out of my nose.

"How can they think they're so suave? So skilled? Beer bellies are not sexy. Sweating men are not a turn-on, darlin', you know this. The only man who could ever turn my ticker and rev me up was Robert Redford, and he has consistently ignored my letters and calls."

"You faked all of them?" I asked.

"For years I did, sugar. Menopause hit me hard. Like a desert sandstorm come to settle in my nether regions. Before that, I was a she-devil." She fanned herself.

"Once those hot flashes and night sweats came they carried off my sex drive. I sweated out all my desires. I was reduced to fakin' it then. Pantin', moanin', gnashin' of my teeth, a tremble here and there, my head way back in supposed ecstasy, holdin' onto their backs as if I thought my head would explode, the pleasure so, so intense." She clucked. "Honey, I sure as a hanging possum should have been given an award for my efforts!"

"You should have. I'll give you the I Faked More Orgasms Than Anyone Award." I tilted my head. If I was still a photographer, I could shoot her. Her face was craggy and mysterious . . . but I'm not a photographer anymore, so I won't. I smashed down the feelings of utter loss that assailed me.

"I have earned it, darlin', I have. But now I've got myself a huge house by the prettiest river in the west, a Cadillac, and a trust fund over two million dollars thanks to Jonathon, Earl, Mack. I call it the JEM Fund. Do you get that, love? Each husband's name is a letter." She laughed.

"You are so clever, Velvet."

"All of us southern women are clever, we have to be. But here's what I learned from my mother: If you give a man a couple of drinks before you start up, his engine is softened and he'll get done in the time it would take to pull a skunk's tail. Quick as a wink you can go about your business." She snapped her fingers. "Quick as a wink!"

"I'll remember the skunk tail–pulling trick, Velvet, thank you."

I had another sip of lemonade, endeavoring not to blow it out of my nose, leaned my head back against the chair, and let the wind soften up my stress as I thought about Velvet's advice.

Here's what I know: Never underestimate what you can learn from women older than you, especially the ones with white hair.

Those gals know everything.

Bao came in with his chess set and played by himself with his one good hand. I brought him coffee and a slice of my fresh pumpkin bread. He smiled a little, lips turning up, creakily, as if they hadn't had much practice in that department for several decades.

His scar peeked at me.

His aloneness peeked at me.

His pain peeked at my pain, I was sure of it.

And that's why I liked and related to Bao. Pain. We had that in common.

"She's pulling her hair out."

"What?"

Cecilia and I were in a booth at Bommarito's Bakery. It was four o'clock and Cecilia had brought the girls in. They were in the back icing cookies with Janie. "She's pulling her hair out." Cecilia ate a bite of the pecan pie I'd made. "This is melt-in-the-mouth delicious, Isabelle. Incredible."

I nodded. Pecan pies were my specialty. My dad had taught me the secret. "Who's pulling her hair out?"

"Riley is."

I slumped in my seat. "Riley is pulling her hair out? *What are you talking about?*"

"Haven't you noticed? Do you have one eye shut or something? She's wearing a headband, which covers some of it, but she's going bald right down the middle of her head because she's yanking her hair out one by one."

I felt sick. *"Why?"*

"Because she's got the Bommarito Family Trait of Disasters

and Discomforts." Cecilia's lips tightened into a hard line, and I knew she was trying not to cry. She dropped the fork and lowered her voice. "She has a disease named trichotillomania. I couldn't figure out what the heck was going on. Her hair kept getting thinner until I saw this bald area. I didn't want to make her feel bad, feel ugly, like I have felt my entire fat life, but I started watching her and I noticed how much she plays with her hair. One time she was watching TV and I watched her yank a hair out."

"She pulled it out deliberately? Maybe she hadn't meant to pull it." *Why would Riley pull her hair out?*

"I kept watching, and she did it again. I wasn't even positive she knew she was doing it. She was feeling around on the top of her head, the sides, the back, as if she was trying to find the perfect hair, and when she did, she wound it around her finger and pulled. Then she stuck it in her mouth—"

"Her mouth?"

Cecilia slapped her hands over her face. "Yes, and she played with it in her mouth. Then she put that hair on her leg and found another one."

"Did you say anything to her?" *Sheesh.*

"Yes, after about four hairs. I wanted to be nice about it so I said, 'Riley, what are you doing? Do you want to be bald like an alien?' She jumped as if I'd shot off a cannon. I went over to her and picked up the hairs on her legs and showed them to her and she came apart. Her whole face crumpled and I held her and rocked her back and forth. It was terrible. Shit! Pulling out her own hair!"

"Did you tell her to stop?"

"No, I told her to pull more out. Gee. What do you think I did, Einstein? Told her to make a nest for the birds? Maybe some hair macramé? She promised she'd stop."

I watched Cecilia's face as it crumpled.

"She didn't stop," I said.

Cecilia shook her head. "I've begged and pleaded and threatened her. She keeps pulling and pulling like a hair vulture. The kid's gonna go bald. Her part is about an inch wide now and the kids are teasing her. I took her to the doctor and I studied her symptoms online. I even joined some cheesy parent support group, and you know what I think of a bunch of people getting together and whining about their problems."

"Yes. I believe you said that was for weak-boned spiders."

"Yep. That's right."

I nodded.

When I hear about an adult having a problem, whether it's mental or physical or emotional, well that's a sad thing. But it's life. We all get hit in the face. We all get brought to our knees. Buck up and take it.

But kids. That's a whole 'nother bucket.

And a kid that I know and love.

Riley, our brilliant Riley, lover of physics and family, pulling her hair out.

"I'm sorry, Cecilia."

"I'm damn shit sorry, too." She dropped her head to her hands.

I slung an arm around her, kissed her temple.

Why can't life be easy?

Grandma, Henry, Janie, Cecilia and the girls, and I sat down and had homemade pesto and tomato pizza together the next night at the wood table in the kitchen, the French doors open to a drifting breeze. Velvet was playing poker with a coed group in town. (A woman always won. "Now that puts a stingin' bee in those boys' bonnets!" she'd tell me. "A stick in their overalls!")

Grandma did not take off her goggles the entire meal and made an airplane engine humming sound.

Riley pulled on her hair and flicked two hairs to the ground as she slurped her strawberry shake.

Kayla wore a white toga and a gold necklace over her head with a half-moon hanging almost to her nose.

"I am studying alternate, ancient religions," she told us in an airy monotone. "I am going back in time, into the recesses of my mind, to reach our ancestors."

"Oh, that's not a good idea," Janie protested. "What if some of our stranger relatives pop out and start telling you to do crazy things? Grandma's mother had agoraphobia, remember? She would stare at people on the street through her lace curtains. And Grandma's sister, you know, Helen, she had so much stuff hoarded in her house that Great Aunt Tildy had to bring in three giant trash containers when she died." Janie smoothed her hair back into her messy bun. "She had newspapers from four decades before! And Aunt Tildy talked to voices. Friendly voices. They were friendly."

Kayla held her hands out to the side, yoga-style. "I'm not afraid of our ancestors. Their lives are my legacy, the memories hiding in the deepest caves of my brain. I am using those memories to form a spiritual basis from which I can do further religious exploration. This necklace is helping me to be celestial in my thinking."

"I think it's helping her to be strange and weird," her sister helpfully added. "She's a toga-ghost with a moon between her eyes. What's so spiritual about that? Give me a break." She yanked out a hair and dropped it to the ground.

I saw Cecilia's lips tighten.

"Don't worry, Riley," Kayla said, back to the airy voice. "I'm going to go way back in time and ask for the powers from all of our ancestors to come forth and rid you of this gruesome habit."

"You're gruesome," Riley told her. "Totally gruesome."

"I'm going to use my incense to pull the demons out of your body," Kayla told her, wriggling her fingers. "The evil one is making you a hair puller."

"You're a demon, Kayla," Riley said, squinting her eyes. "Definitely a demon."

"Hey, if you could pull the demons out of my body, I'm on," I told her. "I'm *so* on."

Kayla sighed in the way only disgusted young girls can sigh.

"You choose your demon, Aunt Isabelle. You like her. That's why she stays."

Whoa.

"How philosophical!" Janie breathed.

"My demon is sure stubborn!" I said. "Always following me around and around, making me frolic about on the demonish side."

Grandma farted, then spread her arms out and flew around the table. "There's gas in the tank!"

Henry told us about the brown dog with big teeth that bites at the animal shelter. "He wears a yellow collar. That mean, watch out! He bites!"

"You got a lot of furry friends, Henry," Janie told him.

Henry thought that was hysterical. "Yeah yeah! Furry friends." He made a meowing sound, then he barked. "If animal shelter bigger, we take more doggies in. We need more room, Paula Jay says. More room for furry friends! I love pizza."

Grandma leaped up on her chair, hand shielding her eyes from the sun. "I see a ship! We're saved!" she shouted.

I waved my napkin. "Hooray!"

Everybody else waved their napkins, too. We have to do this or Grandma gets upset.

It was pathetic how easily I was falling into the Bommarito family insanity.

The sun rose over the mountain, golden and pink, purples and blues. I sat on a rock and stared at the Columbia River, the wind flipping my brown braids all around me.

The windsurfer glided toward shore. I wondered what that was like, windsurfing in the early morning hours, before the sun was much awake, before work, before my emotional instabilities got a fierce grip on my neck and shook it.

He turned and smiled at me and waved.

I waved back.

*   *   *

"The Jell-O tastes like embalming fluid."

"Have you ever tasted embalming fluid?" I asked Momma, taking the seat farthest from her bed in the hospital room. Cecilia sat down next to her bed, glaring at me for taking the seat I did, and Janie hid behind me as best she could.

"Don't be disgusting, young lady." Momma patted her bell-shaped, ash-blond hair and straightened her pink robe. "The food is terrible. The service is terrible. So many nurses and doctors coming in all the time like rats, I can barely think. See? Here's one now."

She sniffled as Dr. Janns entered.

"Mrs. Bommarito, how are ya today?" He smiled cheerily at her. "Givin' all the nurses a bad time, I hear."

"You have the smile of a Cheshire cat," she told him.

Dr. Janns grinned widely, showing her all his teeth. "You can call me Cheshire, ma'am. Are you in any pain? Achin' anywhere?"

"I couldn't be in more pain if I were strung up on a wall by my ankles being whipped by a midget."

"A midget?" I asked.

Beside me, Janie whimpered and whispered her self-help talk. "I cannot control what comes out of her mouth. She can't hurt me. Other people can defend themselves."

"Yes, a midget."

"Why a midget, Momma?" Cecilia asked. She is always so much nicer to Momma than the rest of us. It's that desperate "One Day Momma Will Love Me" syndrome.

"Because he reminds me of one."

I rolled my eyes. The doctor was actually almost six feet tall. "I apologize again for my momma. She is rude."

"Do not apologize for me, Isabelle Bommarito. It is not necessary. I am in grave pain." She plucked at her pink robe and examined her fingernails.

"Well, it's good to see you sittin' up today, Mrs. Bommarito," Dr. Janns soldiered on. "Spry and ready to face the day with good cheer."

"After you ripped open my rib cage and poked at my heart with your handy dandy carpenter tools it's amazing I still have a heart left. With you being so young, I'm surprised you didn't mistakenly operate on my uterus." She arched her eyebrow at him.

He laughed. "Mrs. Bommarito, as you are not in possession of the ol' uterus anymore, that would have been a challenge. I was tempted, however, to operate on a kidney for fun. Give myself the jollies. I also thought about closing my eyes while doing so to create more challenge for myself."

I laughed. Janie gasped, then snickered and covered her mouth. Cecilia hid a smile.

"I'm surprised you didn't. You surgeons think you're God and can do anything."

"Not God, ma'am, but we are the ones with the sharp knives. It kind of makes us like the boss. You know. *The boss.* You're out cold, I'm wielding a weapon. You're totally at my mercy." He grinned again. "So, I take it you are feeling better than yesterday?"

"Yesterday I felt like my lungs had been sliced open. Today I feel like my heart has been stabbed. Which is worse, doctor?" She eyed him up and down.

"Sliced and diced!" the doctor said cheerily. "But I personally think you look terrific, Mrs. Bommarito. I wish all my patients came out of their operations as well as you."

Momma's chin lifted and a weak "Is that so?" dropped from those red-lipsticked lips.

"Most assuredly!" Dr. Janns went on. "Your coloring is rosier than it was yesterday, your vitals are vital! You don't seem tired. You're rockin', Mrs. Bommarito. Rockin.' Fantastic and beautiful, if I can say so."

My mouth fell open. I couldn't believe it. Momma tried to hide her smile. "I'm a strong woman."

"Yep, you are," the doctor agreed. "Strong as an ox, as soft and gentle as a lamb, as flamboyant as a peacock, as cuddly as a kitten."

I sucked in my breath, waiting for the snip snip from Momma.

She glanced out the window. "Perhaps you did a *fairly* good job on my heart, I'm not sure. I can't tell yet. I'll let you know. If you didn't, you'll be sure to hear from me."

The doctor was still smiling. "It would be a pleasure to hear from you at any time, Mrs. Bommarito. Any day, all day."

"All right, then I'll tell you your hair is unbrushed. Untidy."

"Momma, please—" Cecilia started.

I sat back in my chair and pulled on a braid.

"Oh maaaan," the doctor pretended to whine. "You don't like my hair? Yesterday you didn't like my tie."

"I don't like your tie today, either. It makes me dizzy." She huffed. "Do you want to make your patients dizzy, young man? Do you?"

I sighed. Janie whimpered. Cecilia shushed her.

The doctor was buzzed and checked the number on his beeper. "Mrs. Bommarito," he said, leaning over her, "I think you're going to be one of my favorite patients ever."

At those truly shocking words, that momma of mine did something surprising. She took that doctor's hand in hers and patted it. "Have a good day, Dr. Janns," she told him. "I'll see you this afternoon, as usual. Do not be late. Tardiness is not acceptable."

He grasped her hand in his. "I wouldn't miss it."

The doctor grinned at us and left.

"These doctors are incompetent," she said as he left, the scowl back in place. "Completely, utterly incompetent."

Two days later, Janie and I locked up the bakery and drove to Cecilia's. We were going to melt some of Parker's tools down with a blowtorch as a sisterly bonding activity.

We drove up the hill toward Cecilia's house in my Porsche, which we'd snagged after a visit to Momma. I have spent a fair amount of time trying to decide if I like my motorcycle or my Porsche better. I cannot decide.

As we were getting out a brand-new red Corvette roared up the drive.

"Speak of the King of the Devils," I said. "Our blowtorch sisterly meltdown will have to wait."

"I see he's brought his motorized pitchfork," Janie drawled. "Already I feel bleakness swirling through my gentle karma."

The man driving the Corvette, Parker, Cecilia's soon to be dung-faced ex, if this infernal divorce would ever end, was a prime example of an MMMMM. Translation: Major Male Menopause Moment Man.

"Good thing the girls aren't here," I said. "He's come to harangue Cecilia. Bully her up. She says he does this in the hopes that she'll get so battered down, she'll give in." I laughed. "As if our Cecilia would ever get battered down."

"Ladies!" Parker spread his arms out wide, as if he thought we would race to him for a hug.

I spread my arms out wide, too. "Adulterer! Slime-Man! Mold and scum!"

Janie spread her arms out. "If it isn't the devil! Where's your pitchfork? Come on, now, show me that pitchfork!"

Parker dropped his arms, the sleazy smile disappearing.

"Forgive us for not jumping into your arms," I said. "We've restrained ourselves with great effort."

"Hello, vermin," Janie said. "Did I tell you that my hatred for you makes me a better crime writer? I think of you when I'm killing someone."

He cringed, paled a bit, then got his footing back. "How are your one-night stands going, Isabelle?"

"They're going well, thank you. Plenty of them." My skin crawled as Parker took me in from head to foot. He is a shortish sort of man with vampire-like teeth.

Cecilia married him because he was the first guy who expressed serious interest in her. She was bowled off her feet, her usually smart brain going to mush in a handbasket because her self-esteem at that time was about as low as a beetle's groin. He gave her attention, and she licked it up. Grateful.

Sad.

"Janie," Parker said. "How's the houseboat? Able to leave it without counting all the cracks in the sidewalk, I see. Maybe you'll be able to go to the store by yourself soon."

I wandered over to his car and took out my lipstick. I twisted it upward, then jammed the entire thing into the sheepskin liner on the driver's side, smearing it as I went.

"What the—" Parker ran over to me, flushed and furious. He dipped his head in the car. "Isabelle, you're gonna pay for that!"

"I sure will, snake oil man. I have some Monopoly money in the house. How about pink?"

He spit out a bad word that started with a *b*, but I have been called worse. I threw my lipstick at his lips. I noticed that his bottom was bigger than last time. "I notice your bottom is bigger than last time!"

"By the way, Parker," Janie said, hand to cheek, "what's your middle name? I'm trying to name the gambler in my next book who has no morals, cheats anyone he can get his hands on, and ends up in a grave alive. He suffocates slowly. What is it again? Deadbeat? Hairy Chest Man Loser? Gopher Face? I can't remember. Help me out, Isabelle."

"I think his middle name is: I Come In My Hand A Lot," I said. It's good to be helpful.

"You are so smart, Is," Janie gushed. "I knew I could rely on you. For a second I thought it might be Masturbating Monster, but no. You've got it."

Parker used that *b* word again. Pluralized.

We laughed, both of us. As if that word would throw us one whit.

As soon as he was in the house I accidentally let the air out of a tire.

I was told later by Cecilia that Parker had gotten stuck on a back country road with Constance and they'd had to hike back. Five miles.

"Parker said you have to pay Constance for her heels," Cecilia had said. "They're designer. Six hundred dollars."

We had laughed so hard at the thought of me paying Constance back we had to cross our legs.

"Isabelle, forgive me," Janie said, touching my arm. "But I think that Parker's car is in need of literary help." She took out her black permanent marker and wrote, "Tengo un pequeño pene" (I have a small penis).

Four times.

The trunk, side doors, and hood.

There was that number four again!

We Bommarito girls are masters at vengeance.

"I'll settle this divorce, Parker, but first I need you to drive up your attorneys' fees higher," Cecilia said, smirking.

Me and Janie sat on either side of Cecilia at the kitchen table. We sisters were all eating lemon cake and drinking tea.

We had offered Parker nothing.

Well, that wasn't true.

Janie had placed a dead piece of asparagus in front of him on a newspaper. "Bon appétit, perverted porn man."

"The three musketeers." Parker sneered. "The three sickos, more like it."

"I'm not sick," Janie said. "One. Two. Three. Four. You. Are. A. Dick. One. Two. Three. Four. You. Have. Walnuts. For. Balls."

"I'm not sick, either," I said, surprise in my voice at his misconception. "Healthy as a horse. How are you feeling, though, Parker? Any new Web site adventures for unhappy but married people? How's the porn going? What, exactly, does a gigantic fake boob feel like anyhow? I've always wondered."

He got all red and flustered and angry and gross and pointed at Cecilia.

"You tell your sister to settle this thing on the double. I am not—you hear this, Cecilia—I am not going to spend any more of my life battling this out. I am not giving you a cent. Just because no one's ever gonna be dumb enough to marry this fat bitch again, I'm not takin' the heat."

Dear us.

Janie had a knife in her hand *from her purse* lickety-split, and I had both of my hands around Parker's chicken neck and jammed him against the kitchen counters.

We have to work so hard, we Bommarito sisters.

Together we marched a struggling, swearing Parker to the porch and shoved him up against the rail and made him bend far, far, far back and Cecilia shoved his legs over. He's a little guy, so it wasn't hard.

He took off, and we laughed when we heard his howl upon entering his midlife crisis car. He obviously could read a little Spanish.

I glanced out the window of the bakery before I closed up around nine o'clock the next night and caught the eye of an older gentleman across the street under a street light. He was tall with white hair.

Our eyes held for a second. I thought I saw him smile.

The phone rang and I turned to grab it.

When I turned back, he was gone.

Amelia Earhart stood at attention on our front porch, her legs wide. "I am here to inform you that I have been named the Queen of the Air for my outstanding flying contributions to America!"

Velvet swung on the porch swing, her hands busy crocheting. "She's been a peach today! A southern Carolina peach!"

"Hello, Amelia! Congratulations."

"I am flying to Honolulu shortly, and I can take you with me! You have to fill out this form first, though. It asks your name, address, hair color, Yosemite, waffles, if you own flight goggles and diapers. Are there any flatulence problems? How is your bottom?"

She handed me a piece of pink paper with a smiley face in the center of it.

"I'll fill it out immediately, Mrs. Earhart."

"You do that. I'll have my assistant get back to you."

Henry came out, smiling at me. "Hi, Isabelle! You pretty!" he shouted, waving his hand. He was in a flight outfit that Momma had bought for him so he could play airplane with Grandma.

He snapped his goggles over his face. "Ready for takeoff!" he shouted. He pulled a pink baseball hat over his brown curls.

"Ready for takeoff!" Grandma shouted. They both leaped off the front steps and onto the grass. Grandma crouched in front of Henry. They both bopped up and down while making engine noises, then Grandma started running and Henry followed. Both spread their arms way out like wings as they sped across the grass.

It was likely, I thought, as I watched their flying maneuvers, that I would get dementia. Momma, too.

I laughed. Who knew. Maybe Momma would believe she was Mary Poppins and start carrying an umbrella.

Nah. It was more likely Momma would morph into Attila the Hun. Or Dracula.

Henry and Grandma skipped under the willow trees.

Heck, if dementia transformed me into someone with purpose and happiness like Grandma, I wouldn't complain.

Not at all.

But I would want a copilot exactly like Henry.

"Cupcakes," I said.

"Cupcakes?" Janie and Cecilia said.

"Yep. The cupcakes will be Bommarito's Bakery's signature treat," I told them.

It was six o'clock in the morning on a Sunday and we were having a Bommarito Sisters Meeting.

"We already make cupcakes," Cecilia said, taking another gulp of coffee and a doughnut hole.

"I don't mean your regular, run-of-the-mill cupcakes," I said. "They'll be different. They'll be huge. Like small cakes, only we'll call them cupcakes."

Cecilia and Janie blinked at me.

"We'll decorate them so the tops will be 3-D-like. I'm thinking mermaids and monsters, lizards and spiders, ghosts and vampires. Creatively decorated, huge cupcakes. Special. Yummy. Bommarito's Heavenly Cupcakes."

I waited. Cecilia and Janie stared at me.

I opened my eyes up wide, spread my hands. "Hello? Are we still here together on planet Earth or has a dwarf alien slipped inside your mouths and tied your tongue to your teeth?"

More silence.

Finally, Janie said, "I'm thinking of all the ways I could ice big cupcakes. We could pile on chocolate shavings like a chocolate sculpture or alternate meringue and strawberry filling in a swirl."

Cecilia said, her voice misty, "We could do tiny scenes on the cupcakes. Like two girls in a garden. Or a forest scene with a raccoon staring at a fish in the pond."

We sat in our own cupcake heaven for a second.

"Cheers," I said to my sisters.

"Cheers! To Bommarito's Heavenly Cupcakes!" Cecilia said.

"One, two, three, four," Janie said. "I'm not out the door."

I rolled my eyes.

We all raised our coffee mugs and clinked them together. Cecilia's broke, coffee spilling to the table.

So typical for the Bommarito girls.

12

To launch our cupcakes, we bought an ad in the local paper with photos of five of our different types of decorated cupcakes.

At three o'clock on Thursday, the time when we said we'd be selling those cupcakes, a line snaked out the door.

We ran out in fifteen minutes.

People were not happy.

"I waited for an hour for the cupcake with the giant squirrel."

"I told my daughter I'd get her the cupcake with the octopus on it and the blue candy bubbles . . ."

"It's my parents' anniversary, those cupcakes with motorcycles are perfect because they ride bikes . . ."

"My garden club is meeting tonight and I need those cupcakes with the smiling flowers . . ."

"Come on. Make some more. Please?"

We shut the bakery at six o'clock. For the next week our working hours expanded once again. We were working sixteen-hour days and flopping into bed, exhausted.

I knew we couldn't go on like this for long, but I had goals. I had plans. We'd work to make Momma some money, hire people who knew how to bake and manage a bakery, and I would move back to Portland, and my life, but not my photography because I'd had to give that up, and I'd check out of this town and back into reality.

That's what I would do.

And maybe, for once, Momma would appreciate what we'd done.

I laughed.

Nah. Ain't happenin'.

Bao continued to come in. Each day he smiled at me, shuffled over to the counter, and ordered. I think he was the most gentle man I'd ever encountered.

On Friday I served him and he sat down and set up his chess set. I brought him a free cookie. He smiled. "Thank you, Isabelle. You kind woman."

Janie and I were baking and I was serving customers. The phone was ringing and we were trying to take orders. A shipment of pans had not been delivered, we were trying to unload food that had recently arrived, we had cakes and cupcakes on order that we had to bake, and we were wiped out.

I watched Bao playing chess by himself for a second, pushing my braids out of my sweaty face. Now there would be nothing to indicate my next decision was going to be a good one. The man limped, moved slow, and only one hand worked well. I went by gut instinct, the same gut instinct I'd used when deciding not to stay at a certain hotel in Baghdad that was obliterated two nights later.

"Bao," I said to him. "Think you'd be any good at icing cupcakes and cakes?"

Bao was a gift.

Janie had taken a few seconds to show him how to ice a couple of cakes and cupcakes, and he'd gone to work. First he was simply doing the background icing job. By the end of the second day he graduated to full cake decorating.

He was brilliant. He wielded those icing tubes like a professional artist.

A few days later I showed him how to make lemon and pumpkin breads and the recipe we followed for our cinnamon rolls and tiramisu. No problem.

No problem with the tarts, either.

He did all his bakery work perfectly, with such care.

At the end of the first day, we'd hugged him. He hugged us back, his eyes teary.

I handed him an employment application.

He bowed.

"No, I work here for you, when you need Bao. As favor. A gift."

"Thank you, Bao. I appreciate that, but no can do. Your first day was today and we'll pay you for it. Fill out the forms. We're all Americans. We like forms. You'll come in tomorrow? And the next day? Forever and ever?"

Bao smiled and it transformed his face.

"Please, Bao," Janie begged. "We need help."

He raised his eyebrows and said quietly, almost to himself, "I have job. First time long time. I have job." He grinned again and his face lit up. "I have job. I be here tomorrow. Early."

In the midst of waiting for another batch of giant cupcakes to bake, I got a break. I decided I should take a lookie at the books. Get the numbers on how Momma was doing.

It didn't take long to read it. I sat down heavily.

I tapped my fingers. Leaned back in a chair. Steepled my hands. It was worse than I thought. Momma had undoubtedly used some of the money she received from the settlement to re-open the bakery. But she couldn't bake. She was impatient and bored with the whole process. The bakery had worked because of us three, not her.

Reopening the bakery was a nice pipe dream of hers. She said she'd done it because the people of Trillium River loved her baked goods and insisted on it. My guess was that she was worried she would need more money for Grandma down the road if she was unable to care for her—and possibly long-term care for herself if she inherited the same disease.

Nice dream, nice thought, but here was the reality: The income from Momma's bakery would not have supported a family of squirrels.

In fact, it would not have supported even one squirrel on a lifetime fast.

She was broke.

I may have mentioned that we are no strangers, as a family, to being broke.

It's how we lived our whole life after our dad left.

During one winter, when Momma was stripping, and she fell into yet another black, sticky, morass of depression, we hit a new level of despair. Her depression lasted two months. She lost her job and would not get out of bed, her hair eventually sticking to her head like glue.

We baked and baked, as we'd done for years by then, using our dad's cookbooks, his recipe changes noted and followed in the margins.

I could almost feel my dad as I sifted, chopped, melted, iced, and stirred, could hear him directing me, encouraging me to make it perfect. "Life isn't perfect, girls, but everything you bake in a kitchen can be. It's a moment of order and edible art in a life of disorder and chaos."

We made layered lemon cakes, peppermint bars, pumpkin cheesecakes, you name it, as our dad taught us, but it wasn't enough to pay the bills.

We were evicted for the fifth time on a rainy day. Our new home was our car. It was an old Ford, a long black-green car. All our belongings went in the trunk with room to spare.

"We're going to get a trailer," Momma told us one evening,

her voice wobbling, as we ate popcorn for dinner in the backseat behind a hardware store.

A trailer didn't sound too bad. Maybe there would be a bathroom in it. We were cleaning up at gas stations in the morning before school, but it's hard to wash your hair in a gas station sink. Our clothes were getting dirtier and we had no dimes for the Laundromat.

Janie had lost a shoe so was wearing mismatched. Henry was fussing, throwing temper tantrums, and occasionally wetting his pants.

Janie's migraines kicked up, Cecilia's rashes flared up, and Henry's general health problems ballooned up.

"We need a trailer for the winter," Momma told us. "It's going to be cold. We'll put it out in the woods and pretend we're a pioneer family without the oxen. It'll be fun."

"That not fun," Henry said. "Woods dark. Scary."

I held his hand.

"Ghosts in wood. Scary ghosts," he said.

We drove way out into the thickest of woods the night Momma went to get us our trailer. It grew darker and darker, as if we were spiraling into a melting black crayon, the trees a tangled, gnarly mass, the moon disappearing, too scared to stay with us. The road disintegrated into gravel, then dirt, becoming bumpier as we rode.

Momma was scared down to her fingernails. I could tell by the way she gripped the steering wheel, her lips tight, but I could also feel her near-paralytic fear swirling around us.

"Where are we going?" I asked, fear making my body tingle.

"We're going to the home of a man I know from work, now be quiet." She exhaled, inhaled, **exhaled.** "That's all you need to know."

Henry whimpered, "What wrong Momma what wrong? I scared."

Janie started to count and Cecilia gurgled down a pop we'd stolen from the five-and-dime that night. We had been reduced to stealing food from the supermarkets. The stealing made Janie cry and hyperventilate, so Cecilia and I did it. We only cried and hyperventilated on the inside.

"Nothing's wrong, Henry," she snapped.

"When are we going back to the hardware store to sleep?" Janie whimpered.

"Hush up, quit asking questions," Momma said, her fear slinking around that black car like oil, slick and greasy. She pulled around a corner, our tires skidding, and stopped about twenty feet away from a run-down shack.

A man immediately appeared on the porch. I could see him under the yellowy porch light. He was short and squat and had a few hairs pulled over a bald spot. His facial features seemed to be all mashed together. He was smiling a sick, manipulative smile and I felt, *I felt*, his depravity.

"You kids stay here. Do not come in that house, do you understand?" Momma's voice pitched up and down. "I'm going to talk to this man about his trailer. Do you understand? *Do not move.*"

"Who that?" Henry asked after Momma got out of the car, her walk unbalanced.

"We don't know," Janie whimpered, clicking her tongue.

Henry pulled a blanket over his head and his stuffed dragon to his chest. He later vomited on them.

The man slyly grinned at Momma as she tottered up on her heels. I saw him brush her arm with his hand. She pulled her arm away and glared. The door shut behind them.

We waited and waited out in the wickedness of that inky, sinister night, the crickets making the only noise. To this day, I cannot bear to hear crickets.

Finally, I got so scared for Momma I could hardly breathe and got out of the car. So did Cecilia. We both climbed the porch steps, trembling. I held Cecilia's hand. I could feel her terror in my whole body, like she was in me. The second we got to that rickety porch and had our hands up to knock on the door, Momma darted out, straightening her dress.

Her expression changed from sheer self-hating despair to boiling anger. "I told you two to stay in the car! Did you not hear your momma? Are you deaf? Get in the car this minute!"

"Well now, hold on, River darlin'," the wrinkled man said from behind her. "I didn't know you brought your girls, didn't know you had your fillies with you."

He reached out and stroked my cheek. Momma moved so fast, I didn't even see it coming. She whacked that man's arm with both her fists so hard he said, "Fuck."

"Get your hands off my girls." She stood in front of us and pushed us toward the car. "Go girls, now. Run."

We wanted to run. I knew Cecilia wanted to run, because I could feel how she was having trouble breathing, but neither one of us moved. We were not going to leave Momma with this sweaty guy with a hard, bowling ball stomach and smashed-up face. No way.

In the yellowy light I noticed a bruise across Momma's cheek. She had high, swooping cheekbones and the bruise was red and purple, swollen. A little blood was caked in the corner of her mouth.

"Now that was fun, River. Howdy doody fun. You come on back whenever you want and we'll bargain again." The man laughed. He smelled like smoke and sweat and pure evil. "I didn't know you liked it rough. You're a wild horse, woman."

I heard Cecilia growl like an animal before she rushed him. I followed her and we had him on the ground, pummeling him with our fists, our anger our backup. He swore and Momma tried to yank us off him.

He was quick, he was violent, and he punched Cecilia in the face, her head flinging back like a beach ball, then punched me. My blood spilled onto my shirt, my back smashing into the rail of the deck.

I heard a high-pitched squeal right before Henry jumped from the rail and landed smack on that guy's back, pulling his hair with both hands and screaming. "You no hurt sisters! You no hurt Momma! No hurt Momma!"

Henry wrapped his legs around that dirty creep, then got off two slugs before the man shoved him off, Henry's head hitting the deck with a thud.

Janie appeared from out of nowhere wielding part of a tree branch and she cracked him in the face. He stumbled back woozily, then charged her. She clipped him again in the chin and that stopped him, but only for a second. He grunted and flung her off the deck stairs where she landed right on her back.

Momma was kicking him, pounding him on the chest, and I stood up woozily, grabbed a chair, and swung it at his back, feeling truly murderous, but seconds later dizziness hit me like a Mack truck. I heard him laugh after he socked me in the gut, and soon the deck was gone and all I could see was black.

When I woke up, Momma was carrying me off the porch, yelling, "Get the fuck away from us, Reg," and Janie was dragging a bleeding Cecilia. Henry was hysterical and screaming, "You no hurt Momma! I hate you! You no hurt Momma!" and holding his head.

"Shut up, retard!" He laughed at Henry. "Nice tits!" he yelled after Cecilia. "River, honey, you bring the whole family back next time and, hell, I'll give ya two trailers. We'll buck together!" He wiped at the blood on his face with his sleeve. "But not the retard. Leave the retard at home."

"I not retard," Henry said. "You retard. You fat retard. You fat and ugly retard. No hurt Momma! No hurt sisters! You retard!" He picked up a handful of gravel and threw it at him.

I still wanted to kill "Reg" and was coherent enough to drop to my knees and grab a rock to hurl at his head. He was glaring at Henry so it smacked him in the eye. I pelted another one at him and it hit its mark, too.

He swore again, picked the rock back up, and sent it flying in my direction. He missed by about four feet.

"Fucker!" Cecilia said. "Fat fucker!"

"Now that's ripe, missy," he yelled back. "Coming from a pig. A pig with big tits!"

"You retard!" Henry yelled, tears streaming down his cheeks.

Janie hobbled back to him, and I followed her, my vision blurry, even though Momma was shrieking at us to get in the car this "damn minute" and dragging a struggling Henry.

"You are an old, dirty, ugly man and you will always be an old, dirty, ugly man," she said, her voice rough. "But we won't be." She tilted her chin up. "We're poor now, but we won't always be. We're going to be somebody. We're not going to live in a shack with one yellow light in the woods. You will always be a loser who took advantage of a poor mom and beat up her kids. You're a loser. You lost. I hope you die a painful death with lots of blood and your guts burst and I hope it takes you a long time to die."

She turned away slowly, and I knew by the way she moved that her whole body was killing her. Stunned, I couldn't move, but I finally did, and stumbled after her, the man's dropped jaw and shocked expression going with me.

Momma grabbed us and shoved us in the car, backing around the house toward a camper trailer, screaming at us, "I told you to stay in the car! I told you to stay in the car!"

The trailer was rickety, beat up. I got out of the car, my face and back splitting, and helped Momma attach it to our hitch and we drove off. We went back the way we came, the trailer swaying like a group of bats from the devil's own cage.

Cecilia was moaning, mopping up blood; Momma was shaking and yelling at us; Henry was hyperventilating and wheezing out, "Blood, oh there blood, Isabelle!"; and Janie and I were silent, shocked to the core, the pain in my head splitting my brain in half.

Cecilia reached for my hand. "Your head. Are you okay?" she whispered. She put a hand to her head in the exact same spot my head was pounding.

My breasts ached so badly I could hardly breathe. But the man hadn't touched them. He'd grabbed Cecilia. It was the twin thing again. "How are your boobs?"

"I hate him, I do." She wrapped her arms around her chest. I felt her hurt and fury and disgust. My breasts throbbed. "I hate him."

After a bumpy half-hour ride, Momma pulled onto a dirt road in the woods near a creek. It was pitch black outside but Momma told us to get in the trailer, her voice whipped, beyond despair.

Inside was a cooler with ice and on the ice was venison. That was Momma's payment: an old trailer and deer meat.

That night we made a fire and cooked the meat. We were silent while we ate because Momma was making pitiful gasping sounds, her hands wobbling like they had currents of electric shocks running through them.

After dinner she screamed between the swaying trees.

Who knows how long we would have been camping out there had the lice not come.

Our hair started to itch on the third day. On the seventh day we all discovered lice in abundance.

Those lice sent Momma straight over the edge as surely as if she'd leaped off a cliff that never ended. She was in free fall.

She had no job. Her four kids all had lice. One was disabled. She had no husband. No food. We were living in a trailer in the woods that she'd had to sell her soul for, with no toilet or running water. We had eaten through the meat and were down to eating berries. Momma had to put Henry in diapers because his bladder control withered.

She found a louse in her mouth one night and that was it. She started screaming.

We couldn't get her to calm down.

Soon Henry was wailing, too.

A woman who owned a sprawling cabin up the road heard them and not only called the police but came down to help us.

She held Momma close to her and rocked her until the paramedics came and gave Momma a shot to calm her down.

By then, Henry had slipped into hysteria. He was keening,

clinging to the dragon, which he'd vomited on. Janie was holding herself with her eyes shut and periodically patting Henry. Cecilia was kicking a tree. I was trying to help all of them while I itched my hair.

The police took one stunned look at us, studying in particular our dirty clothes and the bruises on our faces, and contacted social services.

We were in foster care for six weeks.

You would have thought Momma would have called Grandma then for help.

No way.

Then Grandma would have won, the evidence irrefutable that her daughter couldn't care for herself and her family. Momma had refused to go to college, refused to get training like Grandma had told her to, just ran off with some guy (our dad) who ran off on her, what could Momma expect? She'd warned her! She'd known it would happen! She should have listened!

Momma's pride wouldn't let her admit that anything was less than perfect to a woman who had criticized her her whole life.

Unfortunately, that meant we had to deal with things like lice, trailers, hunger, and Momma's life slipping out of her a few weeks later.

Once I got rid of my lice and left starvation behind, I loved foster care.

Janie, Cecilia, Henry, and I were the only kids in Miss Nancy's house. She had a home in the suburbs with a big lawn and a stream in back we played in. Cecilia and I shared a big yellow bedroom, and Janie and Henry each had their own.

Miss Nancy hugged us when we arrived at her clean and cheerful home. She got medication for Janie's migraines, Cecilia's multitude of rashes, Henry's breathing/asthma/sickly problems, and bought us clothes, put us back into school, helped with our homework, and held us when the tears threatened to drown us alive. We did not have to bake to keep the lights on.

She put on classical music and taught Janie how to embroider.

She was a Sunday school teacher and Cecilia became her aide.

She signed me up for the church choir because she said I had the voice of the head angel of God's choir.

She had dogs and cats and Henry loved them, as they loved him.

As you can see, Miss Nancy's effect on our future adult lives was profound.

She packed us a sack lunch to take to bed each night because she knew we were panicked about food. "If you're hungry in the middle of the night, eat," she told us. Cecilia took that to heart and ate her lunch and mine.

When Momma came to get us, we clung to Miss Nancy and sobbed. Momma was not pleased.

"Stop blubbering," Momma told us. "Go to the car."

Momma was wearing a green blouse and black slacks with heels. Her hair was brushed, her makeup on. She was gorgeous. She should have been in a magazine.

I learned later that they had committed her to a nice, soft, mental health place. Momma finally got some care.

Some rest and sleep and time to think.

And she finally said yes to a few medications that balanced her out.

Things went along fine for a while. Momma had secured an apartment with help from the government, we got food stamps, and she had a job in an upscale women's clothing store that paid commission.

The owner gave Momma three chic outfits to wear to work to advertise the clothes. She made good money because she was beautiful and could convince a turtle he should give up his shell and wear a silk cape. On the outside, it appeared we were an odd family, but definitely okay.

On the inside things were not well. Not well at all. They were rotting.

And on the horizon yet another disaster was looming for the Bommarito family. This one was a bloody mess.

Cecilia had roped me into volunteering in her classroom when a parent volunteer backed out because she had menstrual cramps.

The question I was to ask each of Cecilia's kindergarteners after they'd finished their paintings of giant Easter bunnies was simple: How does the Easter Bunny get all the decorated eggs hidden all over the world in one night?

It was not as easy as it sounds.

Gary was a gangly kid. He reminded me of a spaghetti noodle with glasses. He said to me, "Are you married?"

"No, not married."

"How come?"

"Because I don't want to have a husband."

Gary pondered that. "Why?"

"Because I'm too cool."

"Oh." He took me seriously. "My mom says she's not married right now because all men are shitheads."

"Well. Your mother is super smart, clearly. Now about this Easter Bunny. How do you think he delivers all these eggs?"

"First off, the Easter Bunny is a she, not a he. That's what my mom says. She says men couldn't find their asses if they weren't attached to their bodies so how could the Easter Bunny find all the houses that need eggs if he was a boy? So, the Easter Bunny's a girl."

"How old are you, kid?" I asked.

"Five years, three months, fourteen days, eight hours and"—he eyed the school clock—"four minutes. Are you a hippie?"

* * *

A girl with a braid to her butt told me she was magic.

"Bibbity boo! Can you see me now?"

I assured her I could.

"You cannot."

"I can."

"You can't. Whenever I do this for my mom and dad they don't know where I've gone! I'm invisible! You're stupid!" She stomped on both of my feet and stalked away.

One kid drew a bunny with a green Mohawk and a tattoo of a knife. Another refused to write about the bunny; he insisted on writing about Slime Man.

Even my liver was exhausted when I left Cecilia's classroom.

⚗ 13 ⚗

"I spoke with Dr. Silverton today," I told Cecilia that afternoon at the bakery.

Her hands stopped over the black bottom cake she was mixing. "Oh yes," she breathed. "He told me. We had a short meeting in his office this afternoon. He is such a nice man."

"Yes, kindly nice."

"He told me I'm one of the best teachers he's ever come across, that's what he told me." Her face flushed.

"Well, you are one of the best, if not the best." That was the truth. I knew it and so did all of Trillium River, whose parents got extremely upset if their little sweetheart wasn't in Cecilia's kindergarten class. Four had threatened to sue. Three had gone to the school board.

"He is so polite, Isabelle, so gentle."

I noted that Cecilia's voice was gentle, too. I hid my smile.

"During my evaluation—well, we got busy chatting, so we didn't actually get to the evaluation part—but we shared our favorite vacation spots and the Little League team he coaches and the bakery and Momma, he met Momma, and said she's a 'fine lady.' " She snorted.

"So it was a good conversation?"

"Yes, I told him a little bit about my divorce and he was so kind, Isabelle . . . so kind . . . it was like—" She stared in the air. "Like my anger poofed away when I was telling him about it. I didn't feel like strangling Parker."

"Well, that's good. Murder is bad. I'm glad you like Dr. Silverton."

"I do! I do like him," she said.

I tried not to laugh. "I'm glad you really like him."

"Oh, I do! I really like him."

I laughed.

That snapped her out of her daze. She threw a piece of pie crust at my face.

Janie and I decided to invite ourselves to Cecilia's next divorce powwow in Portland. We thought it would be entertaining. Stimulating. A vengeful activity we sisters could bond at.

To celebrate Cecilia's emancipation, Janie had agreed to let me dress her. She wore sleek jeans and borrowed a pair of my four-inch heels with a green-and-beige shiny patina and a greenish silk blouse. I flat-ironed her reddish hair, shoved some bangles on her wrists and dangly earrings on her ears, and with those luminescent eyes of hers she was downright vogue.

"Janie, I'll never know why you dress like a frump," Cecilia had snapped. "When you brush your hair and refrain from wearing those brown boats on your feet, farm-wife aprons, and lace collars, you're gorgeous."

"I don't dress like a frump. I dress so my body feels like it's smoothly flowing, ethereal, connected to my spirituality. I'm uncomfortable with these heels on. They hurt my feet, and this shirt—" She picked at it. "If I lean the wrong way, my bra will show."

"Please don't," I told her. "Don't lean the wrong way. No one wants to see your beige bra."

"What's wrong with my bra? It's sturdy. I've had it for years."

"Yes, I am aware of that," I told her. "I can tell. Anyone could tell."

Cecilia had put on a jean skirt and pink shirt and hoop earrings. She'd grimaced at the mirror and snarled, "I'm almost the size of a rhino. Where the fuck are my horns?"

I wore jeans, a gemstone-studded belt, a chocolate brown low-cut blouse, and chunky jewelry. I thought my outfit went well with my braids.

"We've got our war paint on, ladies," I said. "Now let's go get Parker's scalp and put it on a spike."

We went to school with Cherie Poitras, Cecilia's lawyer.

Cherie was a tough, wild girl who became a tough, highly paid attorney in Portland who now owned her own firm. She was an only child of a man who believed that to spare the rod was to spoil the child.

Cherie got herself declared an emancipated minor at fifteen, the old and new scars on her back from a belt smoothing her case along. The law saved her and she fell in love with it. In her spare time, she advocated in the courts for abused children and had adopted four of them.

We became friends with her after a painting incident. A teacher continually made her feel like an idiot in math class, even telling her "girls don't have the brains for math." So one Sunday she'd snuck into the gym and, using spray paint, made a mural that stretched across an *entire* wall. The mural depicted the math teacher naked with three nipples, a hot dog for a penis, a unicorn horn, and fish feet.

We knew she did it. We never told. We were friends for life.

The three of us were in her elegant conference room in a high-rise in Portland. The Willamette River sparkled below, various ships leaving white froth in their wake as they swooshed past the bridges.

"I miss my houseboat," Janie whimpered, staring down the river.

"I miss my loft," I whimpered, staring up the river.

We sighed with a high-octane dose of self-pity.

"And I miss having my sanity, but you don't hear me whining on and on, do you?" Cecilia barked.

"I stopped missing my sanity a long time ago, Cecilia," I told her. "Maybe you should pipe down about it."

"Sanity is tenuous," Janie mused. "Tenuous. Comes and goes. Many of the brightest people floating about this planet have only a finger's grip on sanity, if that."

"Okay, ladies," Cherie interrupted, her voice like a drill sergeant's as she burst through the door. "My secretary told me the rebels are on their way down the hallway. Cecilia, keep a lid on it."

Cherie was wearing a black leather skirt, a white silk blouse with a wide collar, and four-inch black heels. That made her about six feet one inches tall. "Janie and Isabelle, I don't need any fighting, yelling, or throwing of anything right now."

"I can't think of a single thing about Parker that would lead me to fight, yell, or throw," I said.

We heard their footsteps. I winked at Cherie. She lifted her chin. She still loved a good fight.

And she was a hell of a fighter.

Parker and three lawyers—all billing out for stupendous sums, no doubt—filled the doorway.

Parker had a smirk on his face, but his eyes widened like a startled turtle and he stopped dead in his tracks when he noticed me and Janie standing in front of the windows.

The three lawyer-stooges stopped behind Parker, the one right behind Parker colliding into him as he caught my eye.

One of the lawyers, the one I immediately knew was "the boss," blinked rapidly and flushed when he saw Janie. Even Parker was shocked at her appearance. But only for a second.

"What are you two doing here?" Parker barked out.

"We came to enjoy the circus," I said. "We're hoping you get eaten by a lion!"

Parker turned red and flushy.

"We came because we simply can't bear to miss out on any opportunity to be with you in an earthy, cosmic way," Janie said, smiling sweetly. "Your company being so pleasant, your personality so soothing."

One of his lawyers coughed into his hand.

"I don't like it," Parker seethed. "You two don't belong here. It's between me and Cecilia. You both owe me money to fix my car and, Isabelle, you still gotta pay *my fiancée* for her heels."

"Send the bill again," I drawled. "I know exactly where to shove it. It's a hot, smelly place . . ."

Cherie interrupted. "Gentlemen, the ladies aren't leaving. Please, have a seat. Let's remember to keep this civil and calm."

Cherie and Parker's lead attorney sat across from one another. Parker's lead attorney, the one who flushed like a fire engine when he saw Janie, was about forty-five. He was white and balding, at least six feet two inches tall, and wore glasses. He was kind of handsome. The other two attorneys were in their thirties, stuffed into suits, one stocky like a water tower, the other gangly like Abe Lincoln.

Cecilia and I were on Cherie's left, Janie on her right. Parker sat right across from Cecilia and glowered. All of a sudden, he laughed. "I can't believe I stayed married to you as long as I did."

One of his lawyers, the Water Tower, turned to him and said, "Parker, not now."

"I can't believe I stayed married to you, either," Cecilia said, smiling. "Momma said you were a man with a small dick, physically and mentally. She warned me. So many times. I ignored her. She was right. My momma is always right."

Now, the part about Momma being right was a lie. But the part about Momma thinking that Parker had a small dick physically and mentally was dead-on. Momma had said, "Parker will always think like a man with a small dick. Petty. Jealous. Mean. Close minded. He's got short man's complex on his groin, don't forget it. I'm warning you, Cecilia, he'll bring you grief."

"You've bemoaned Parker's small penis throughout your marriage, Cecilia," Janie said, clasping her hands together, her voice curious. "And the unsturdiness that brought to your marriage bed, but I thought that Parker was on Viagra? No?"

Parker was not happy. "I don't need Viagra. You can ask Constance about that."

"Parker!" the Abe Lincoln attorney snapped. "Settle down."

Now that made me raise my eyebrows. His own lawyer snapping at him?

Parker settled back down, like a killer fish retreating into its shadowy cave.

"All right, let's get started," Cherie said. "Both of you, back off. Let's leave less blood at this meeting than the last one. Cecilia is ready to settle. She wants the house."

"I already said that's fine," Parker said, hitting his palms on the table. "No problem. She can buy out my half."

"No, she's not going to buy out your half," Cherie said as if he were an unruly, bratty child. "The house is almost paid off and she wants it in its entirety. She will, however, agree to let you have your retirement account."

I heard the loaded pause in the conference room. The house was worth about $650,000. The retirement account that Parker had built up as a cheesy and slick but successful computer salesman was about $450,000.

"That's still an unfair split," Parker's lead attorney, Bob, said. Bob was the balding guy. He was The Man in Charge. I had the distinct impression that poor Bob had been handling these messy matters for a long, long time.

"Like hell it is," Cherie said. "Parker has his brand-new Corvette, he says he wants his other older model Corvette, which is still at the house, his tools, and other toys, including a big-screen TV. Plus, Cecilia is the main caregiver for the children. Surely, Parker, you want the kids to be able to stay in their childhood home?"

Parker made some grumbling noises. Like a bear who has a blackberry bush stuck up his bottom.

"In addition, Parker must agree to take all of his credit card debt with him. That includes the total amounts he built up on his cards while married to Cecilia and all the charges he's billed since they separated."

"No way," Parker spit out between clenched teeth.

"All of the charges were for you and Constance," Cecilia said. "I *refuse* to settle this divorce if I have to pay for your mai tais in Mexico and the Bahamas. We have separate cards. You take yours, I'll take mine, fucker."

The balding attorney sighed. Cherie kicked Cecilia under the table. Cecilia did not object to the kick.

"Also, there is the matter of child support and of Parker reimbursing Cecilia $30,000 for her to go back to school to get her master's degree," Cherie said. "Cecilia took out a student loan and Parker needs to pay for that. If Parker agrees to pay for Cecilia's master's, she'll drop the alimony."

Parker again protested, like a whining snake. "I am not paying for her to get a master's degree. Ya got that? She's a kindergarten teacher! You don't need even half a brain for that. All she needs to know how to do is write the alphabet and sing a few goddamn songs, for goddamn's sakes!"

Bob The Man in Charge said, "Shut up, Parker."

"Do not say 'goddamn' again, Parker," Abe Lincoln told him. "We've told you how we feel about that word."

Parker slapped his palms on the table.

"Anything else?" Bob The Man in Charge asked.

"Yes. Parker will pay my legal fees and will put $1,000 each month into each girl's college fund. In addition, he will pay $3,000 a month in child support."

The Man in Charge nodded. I noticed he was fiddling with his pen in a weird way, forward a few circles, back a few circles, forward a few times, back. Odd. The rhythm was so like Janie's. "Can you give us a minute?"

"Sure can."

We ladies all stood up and left the conference room, but not before Cecilia whispered loudly, "Having sex with Parker was like having sex with a pencil. Thin and pokey." And Janie said to Parker, "Remember when you made a pass at me at my houseboat? I couldn't leave my home for days because as soon as I thought of your face I got diarrhea. Yuck."

I didn't do anything until I saw Parker smiling crudely at me, his eyes staring right at my boobs. I sidled right up to him as he leaned back in his swivel chair and smirked. When I was eye to boob with him I moved zippity quick and tipped his chair right over.

Parker somersaulted out backward, like a rag doll wearing a pimp suit, swearing as he went, and landed facedown.

I smiled sweetly at the surprised attorneys and left.

Bob The Man in Charge tried hard not to smile before he went back to his rhythmic circles.

We headed down the hallway to Cherie's office. She opened a little door behind a stack of books and flicked a switch.

"Don't ever tell anyone about this or I'll get disbarred," she muttered.

Like we would do something heinous like that, sneaky lady.

Ah. Beautiful. We could hear every word the lawyers and Parker were saying. Every word.

"Take the deal, Parker," The Man in Charge said. "You're done. We're done."

"You're not going to get better than that." I knew it was Abe Lincoln speaking. "She gets the house, you get the retirement money. You got your cars and the TV. You make a lot of money. You'll be fine."

"Hell, no!" I heard him slap the table again. "I'm getting ripped off! Ripped off! And I sure as hell am not going to pay for that fat ass's student loan."

I saw Cecilia flush. I wanted to kill Parker.

"You won't get better than this and all you'll end up doing is dragging out the inevitable. I've been doing this for twenty years. Trust me," Bob The Man in Charge said.

"But what about the credit cards?" Parker's voice sounded like a weak-willed weasel's.

I heard Bob The Man in Charge grunt. "Hey, Parker, you ran those up, they're your cards, you signed each slip, I've seen 'em. She's not going to agree to take on your and Constance's Botox, lip plumpers, and colon flushings. Ever. A judge isn't going to make her pay for them, either. They're not generally sympathetic to people who cheat, go to Mexico with their girlfriends, and try to get the wife to split the cost."

Cherie's eyebrows flew up.

Parker swore. Always the tough guy. "But the child support! God! $3,000? Each month? It doesn't take that much to raise kids."

"Yes, it does," The Water Tower said. "I have five kids. I handle the money in our house because my wife is too busy to do it. Your payment is based on a formula that the state of Oregon uses according to your income. You're not going to wriggle out of that one, Parker, so give it up."

Parker swore again. "She's like an albatross around my neck. She's jealous. She's a sick, manipulative, fat—"

"We counseled you to settle more than nine months ago," Bob The Man in Charge said. "You have already paid us $35,000 in fees. You're on the hook for another $10,000. You're gonna pay Cherie's fees, too. You can't afford to not settle this. You got that, buddy? You can't afford it. Get the divorce done, then go out and marry that woman. What's her name again?"

"Constance."

"Constance. Marry her."

"Yes, do go and marry Constance the colon flusher," Cecilia whispered. "Please do. Immediately."

"You've overcharged me—"

"All charges deserved," Bob The Man in Charge drawled.

"What's that supposed to mean?" We could hear Parker breathing heavily.

"It means that you're an asshole. You cheat on your wife with some bimbo—"

"Don't call her a bimbo," Cecilia whispered. "Don't put any ideas in his head. He needs to marry the bimbo!"

"Constance is not a bimbo," Parker said, but his voice wasn't too convinced.

"Constance is—" Bob The Man in Charge laughed. "Okay, Parker. We're done."

"Cut my fees or I sue you, Bob. I'll sue you for . . . for . . ."

"For?" Bob paused.

I decided I liked Bob.

"I'll sue you. I'm not paying you a dime more."

"There isn't an attorney in town who will take your case, Parker. Not a one. If you don't have that money on my desk in thirty days I'll attach your paycheck at that fancy business you work at so fast snot will fly out of your nose. Think your boss will like that?"

Parker's hands slapped against the table again. They had to be hurtin'.

We were summoned in and tried not to laugh upon entry, although Cecilia was still boiling at the fat comments.

I subtly raised my middle finger at Parker and waved it. Janie grinned, her face serene, amused.

When we sat down, I saw her smiling at Parker, her fingers tapping the table, one, two, three, four. When he caught her gaze he said, "What?" in this accusatory tone.

"What?" Janie said, pleasantly. She bit her lip. I knew her. She was already killing Parker again in her head for another book.

"Why are you even here, Janie?" Parker said. "Don't you have someone to kill?"

His lawyers tensed.

"No, no, don't worry," I said, with reassurance. I kicked Janie. She was gazing at Parker as if she adored him. She detests the guy as most of us would detest a tarantula attached to our nipple, but when she gets a plot going in her head, there's no stopping her rampant, free-flowing joy.

"Janie's a crime fiction writer," I said.

The face of Bob The Man in Charge settled into perplexed lines, but then his face cleared and he sat straight up. "Well, I'll be darned!"

I was surprised by his exclamation. *Well, I'll be darned?*

"You're *Janie Bommarito*, aren't you?" He was delighted. A treasure had been found! "I can't believe I didn't put it together!"

"Janie Bommarito!" The Water Tower laughed. "We read your book *Devon's Scars* for our office book club. It scared me so much I could only read it during the day. I even took a day off work to stay home and—"

He clamped his mouth shut tight and lickety-split pleaded his case to Bob. "I mean, I was *sick*. I was bed-ridden sick. It was that day after the trial with the Mallorys—"

Bob The Man in Charge hardly noticed, his excitement at the grand privilege of meeting Janie making him wriggle with unrestrained joy in his seat.

"I've read all of your books. *All of them*. Some twice. I've already preordered your next one, *Melody's Slashing*, online. It's a pleasure to meet you in person, Ms. Bommarito. You are the only crime writer I read. I tend more toward reading the classics. *Pride and Prejudice. Jane Eyre. Wuthering Heights.*"

Now that stopped us all up a bit. This huge man loved *Wuthering Heights*? I would have thought he would be reading books on sharks.

"You're a classics lover!" Janie breathed. "One of my hobbies is to collect early editions by the Brontë sisters!"

"Are you serious?" The Man in Charge gasped. "I do the same! Collector's editions! I've created an English-style garden, too!"

I thought Janie was going to faint. She put a hand to her chest. "You didn't!"

"I did!" Bob's smile reached ear to ear. "I've built stone walls, paths, fountains, a pond, a bridge, all to the period!"

Janie gasped again. "Oh my goodness! My goodness!" She leaned forward, eyes shining. "Can I come and see it?"

"It would be my deepest pleasure. I would be delighted. It would be my privilege." He inhaled, his fingers continuing the forward circle motion with his pen, only faster. "Could you bring part of your collection? It would be an honor—"

"Yes, absolutely! We can look at them in the garden! It will be so authentic, so historical, so literary! I'll bring my favorite teas!"

My mouth dropped open. I tried to shut it. Was that *Janie* agreeing to go to a man's house with her books and teas and tapping?

The Man in Charge slid his card across the table, grinning, eyes twinkling like strobes. "I love tea! I'll get the scones!"

Now I thought Janie was going to keel over. A man who loved tea! Next we'd find out he loved Yo-Yo Ma.

"Shit, Bob, shit!" Parker protested. "Can we end the lovefest on the classics now? Could we? This is about my long-overdue divorce from the fat cow sitting over there who wants to suck me dry because she's a jealous, vindictive, vengeful bitch!"

Oh, I couldn't help myself.

I was up and out of my chair before I knew it and Parker was sprawled again on his face.

"I apologize for helping to create a tense environment," I said, so polite, to the attorneys.

"Apology accepted!" Bob The Man in Charge grinned.

No one helped Parker up.

◖ 14 ◗

Thinking we would kill two bloodsucking birds with one stone, we went to see Momma. She was soon to be discharged. She had battled an infection, then another one, but was getting better.

She wasn't pleased with life at the hospital.

The doctors had the educations of water rats.

One of the nurses was "the blackest person she'd ever seen. Never stops smiling." That nurse had brought her a crocheted shawl she'd made herself. I figured the woman was a saint to reach out to our grouchy momma like that. "I wear it to make her feel good." She sniffed. We pretended not to see the sheen in her eyes as she fingered that beautiful, colorful shawl.

Momma would not take it off for weeks.

She did not like the food. "It was made with dog food, probably, dead horses . . ."

We kissed her, left.

Sighed when we got in the car.

We burned Cecilia's wedding dress in a bonfire on the back lawn after a typical Bommarito family dinner that night.

We'd set the kitchen table with Grandma's china and silverware and all the candles we had to celebrate Cecilia's freedom. We put flowers in the colored bottles from Momma's collection and scattered them across the table. Cecilia brought over a huge pan of steaming lasagna, melted cheese layering the top. "Parker loved this lasagna. He said it was the only thing I did right. Too bad I never put arsenic in it."

I brought Bommarito's Heavenly Cupcakes from the bakery designed in an Alice in Wonderland sort of way with colorful purple mushrooms and wildflowers.

Velvet wore a green velvet dress and a pink flowered hat. "Remember, Cecilia, sugar, men are only for dessert, not the main course. Think: Treat. Not: Meat. You have that, child?"

Kayla wore a Jewish beanie and carried the Old Testament. Riley wore a bright red headband over her hair and discussed all she understood about quantum physics while plucking a few hairs out.

Henry wore a shirt with a picture of a basset hound on it, a Batman cape, and a black mask. "Ta da!" he yelled when he jumped into the kitchen, holding the cape to his nose. "I Bat Man! Yeah, yeah! I save you, Is! I am hero!"

Grandma prayed, "Dear God, this is Amelia. Planes should be piloted by women. Men will crash them. They have pea brains. Except my copilot. You screwed up on them. Amen. Dear God."

Our conversation at the table was eclectic as usual: the finding of human poop in a cave in southern Oregon that dates back 15,000 years, Neptune (Why is it blue?), Riley's use of "excessive force" in dodgeball at school and how she was suspended for two days.

Janie got up twice and checked to make sure the stove and oven were off, and seemed distracted. I figured it was Bob The Man in Charge.

"Are you going to call him?"

"No. Yes. No. Too scared." She tapped her fingers together.

I remembered that rhythmic circling Bob did with the pencil.

"I think you should." I handed her the cranberry nut salad. "Take a dare."

"Oh! Oh! Oh!" She steepled her fingers. "I'm so strange. He'll think I'm strange. A nut-head, nutcase. What would Emily Brontë do?"

Baffled me, it did. "I'll ask her," I drawled. "I think the Ouija board is still in the attic."

Grandma interrupted our conversation by lifting her middle fingers in the air. "Amelia Earhart does not have time for sexual frivolity. I will not be a servant to what a man with a pea brain wants. That's no way for a woman to live her life, by golly! Who cares what men want?"

We all held up our wineglasses—we always use wineglasses even when there's milk in them—and cheered Amelia Earhart.

"I will abstain from intercourse until I am married for religious reasons," Kayla said. She put her hand on the Old Testament.

We quieted down a bit.

"That's the best thing I've heard come out of your mouth for ten years," Cecilia growled.

Kayla glowered at her.

"To abstaining!" Janie shouted. We cheered and clinked glasses again.

"And cheers to physics," Riley said. "Especially quantum."

"I Bat Man!" Henry announced, climbing on his chair and swirling the cape. "I got a cape."

Grandma farted, middle fingers pointed upward. "Gas in the tank!"

"Remember," Velvet intoned, adjusting her pink flowered hat. "Men are treats, not meat."

After the girls were in bed, Cecilia, Janie, Henry, and I danced around the bonfire, twirling and spinning. Henry insisted that we do the hokey pokey. He loves the hokey pokey. "Put your whole self in, Is!" he encouraged me. "Put your whole self in!"

I thought that was rather philosophical, but Henry really gets it. Gets life.

The tears streamed down Cecilia's face, but she didn't stop hokey pokey-ing.

Henry saw this and said, "I kiss you! I love you, Cecilia! You my sister!" He kissed her on the cheek.

See? He gets it.

We hugged in a mob as the ashes of the wedding dress drifted toward the night sky on a spiral of wind, the stars sprinkled above, Henry's laughter bopping all around us like peace.

Later we put Henry to bed with a heating pad. His stomach was hurting, and we have learned over the years that this is the way to handle it. He said he ate too much Alice in Wonderland cupcake.

The three of us sisters collapsed in my bed. I woke up the next morning hugging Cecilia's backside, Janie hugging me.

I felt better.

The darkness on the edges of my brain matter was back in its cave again. I knew it was waiting for me, waiting for a weak moment, but at least I had it contained, controlled, if only for a little while.

"Your mother, Ms. Merry Sunshine, is ready to go, ladies," Dr. Janns announced with great gusto. "The ship is leaving the port. The shuttle is ready for takeoff. The quarterback has thrown the ball."

I raised an eyebrow at Dr. Janns. Janie giggled. Cecilia sighed.

He shot his arm across the air in front of him, signaling a shuttle blasting off.

"He always does things like that," Momma complained from the bed, her pink robe wrapped around her, as she fiddled with her crotcheted shawl. "He's a midget."

"A bit out of the midget range, I'd say," Cecilia said, tilting her head up at Dr. Janns.

"He's a midget," Momma insisted. "A midget in his head. Dr.

Janns, you have a spot on your coat that reminds me of blood and I am uncomfortable with your hygiene."

Such a genteel lady, our momma.

"And I'm uncomfortable because you won't get up and dance with me, Mrs. Bommarito." He bowed. "I have been craving a dance with you since the second you told me I reminded you of a bad crossword puzzle."

I had no idea why she said that.

Momma waved her hand in the air. I could tell she was trying to hide a smile. "I'm not going to dance with you. You would crush my feet. Your shoes are the size of canoes. Dear me."

The doctor leaned way, way over to gape sorrowfully at his canoes. "Big and healthy. Please, relieve me of my broken heart. Dance with me down this hallway."

"Never," she said. The smile curved up again before she forced it right back down.

"A tiny waltz? A tango? A fox-trot? I take dance, you know, at a studio right around the corner from here."

"You've told me, midget," Momma said.

"My happy days at this hospital are numbered, Mrs. Bommarito. You're leaving me."

"These girls are insisting that I go to a retirement center to rest up. I don't need to rest. I'm fine. Fit as a fiddle. They're forcing me against my will to go and live with old people. Old people. How boring."

"They're smart daughters."

Momma was still weak and there was no way she could handle Grandma and Henry and the business.

Mostly we bad daughters were not prepared to handle Momma.

We had discussed the 'movin' and groovin' retirement center again with Dr. Janns. It cost an arm and a leg, but Janie and I were going to pay for it.

"She'll love it!" Dr. Janns had told us. "It'll groove her out. It's not for old, sick people, it's for old people who wanna live, rock out, go on trips, meet people. My aunt was there for twenty years. She lived to be 106."

Spare us, I thought. Oh, *spare us.*

In the end Momma waltzed with Dr. Janns, gently, gingerly, elegantly, down the corridor of the hospital, doctors and nurses clapping.

Momma smiled, her beautiful shawl swirling around her.

She cried and cried when she hugged the nurse who gave it to her.

It was a long afternoon, but we got Momma settled in Brickstone Retirement Center in Portland.

She hated it. ("It's a prison. You're putting me in a prison.") She hated all the other residents. ("Old people. They're all old, creaky old. I am not old.") She hated her room. ("Too small. The view is of the city skyscrapers. All that crime!") She hated the dining room. ("Big enough to hide a molester.") She hated the location. ("Portland! Liberal freak town. Earth lovers and savers. Bicyclists who don't pay attention to road signs. Hippies with dreadlocks. Women with no makeup.") She hated us. ("Ungrateful daughters. After all the years I spent caring for you all . . .")

We were so exhausted on the way home to Trillium River, we didn't even speak.

I spent a long time laying on the grass studying the stars that night, wondering if other aliens on other planets had mommas as difficult as mine.

Did they have to go on drugs?

The Man in Charge called Janie. For a manly man, and a tough-ass attorney at that, I could tell the poor guy was nervous.

I took the call—Janie was at the bakery at the time—and relayed the message.

"Oh, I can't call back!" she said, tap-tap-tapping her fingers on the kitchen counter that night.

"Yes, you can," I said gently.

"I can't. I'm odd. Weird. Then he'll know I'm odd. Weird."

We argued.

She couldn't. She didn't.

"She's gone!" Janie yelled as she burst into the bakery, the door smashing into the jamb. "She's gone!"

I jumped in my seat in the booth, as did Bao, who actually leaped out and got in a crouched position. I gaped at him, baffled for a second, but then threw my attention back to Janie. Half her hair was out of her bun and she clapped her hands together four times, paused, clapped them together again.

"What? Who's gone?"

"I've been trying to call you on your cell!" she said, trying to catch her breath. "I called and called. I left the house without checking the stove and the oven and the door and came here right away because she's gone. I have to go back and check—"

"Who is gone?" I shouted. Momma? Henry? I fought down panic.

"Grandma. *Grandma's gone.*"

Grandma? Gone? Grandma should never go "gone." I felt my stomach dive-bomb to my toes.

Janie grabbed me and shoved me toward the door.

"Velvet called a few minutes ago," she puffed. "One, two, three, four. Grandma was taking a nap on the couch, so she darted out to drop Henry off at his art class and when she got home, Grandma wasn't there. Velvet searched for about a half hour and couldn't find her."

"Oh *shit*," I said. I took off after Janie, then stopped. There were ten people in the bakery and we were closing soon. "Bao? Bao?"

Bao was up from his crouch. I saw a line of sweat on his brow. The man did not like sudden noises. It had to have something to do with that scar, but I didn't have time to think of it.

"Go, go, Isabelle," he said, his voice strangled. "I take care of bakery. Go. I help find Grandma when I done. I help find Grandma."

Belinda sat up in her booth and burst into tears. She gets scared easy, too.

"Help Belinda, Bao," I said. We were off and running.

"We're going to check the river again first thing in the morning, Ms. Bommarito," the police chief said to me. She nodded at Janie. "Ms. Bommarito. First thing."

Lyla Luchenko was about fifty-five years old. Her white hair was in a ponytail and she had a youngish face. "It's midnight. We can't search it any more now."

The two other detectives in our grandma's parlor were almost ashen. The entire police force and hundreds of volunteers had been searching for hours.

I had called Father Mike and he immediately put out the call to the congregation for help. They had responded in force, as had our neighbors, Cecilia's teacher friends and students' parents, and almost all the other people I'd ever even seen in Trillium River. "My prayers for Stella's safety begin now!" he boomed.

Headquarters for the search was our house. There were people in our home I'd never met working the phone and handing out stacks of fliers for other people I didn't know to take and hang up in stores, bus stations, truck stops, and restaurants.

Police and other searchers were studying maps and ordering people to different areas to search for Grandma, including a state park, logging roads, and smaller towns.

I stumbled out onto the deck and put my head on the rail. *Oh, Grandma,* I thought, devastated. Grandma. All alone. Maybe outside. Cold. Scared. So confused.

The wind whipped up my hair, back and forth, back and forth.

I heard the police giving orders to drag the river.

Please. *Not the river.*

* * *

We didn't sleep. We were out the door by four thirty. By five o'clock, a mass of boats were out searching the Columbia River. Cecilia, Janie, and I stood huddled at the river's edge as the sun rose, without much color, without fanfare. We had left Henry with Velvet, quivering with fear over Grandma, clutching the pilot's hat she'd given him.

Under that sun, and the wind that never quit, we waited, grim and deathly afraid.

I felt myself age about ten years standing on the side of that river. We watched search boats scour the sides. We wanted them to find Grandma, but on the banks of the river, not in the river, bloated full of water and nibbled on by fish.

The media was there and we tried to avoid the cameras and the reporters. We asked that they not take photos of us. Having Janie there made it all the more newsworthy. All I wanted to do was smash their cameras.

At one point, we got in Cecilia's van and drove down the river to another spot to avoid the cameras.

"Stop it," Cecilia hissed at me.

"Stop what?"

"Your stomach. It's lurching all over the place and it's making me feel sick."

She was right. It was lurching. "Okay, sure, dandy, Cecilia. Hang on a sec, I'll bend over and tell my stomach to be calm and serene. Zenlike. But if your breath would stop coming in gasps, like a drowning rat, I could breathe better, you high and mighty—"

"Me, high and mighty?" she screeched.

"Yes, you high and mighty drama queen, bossy—"

"Me, bossy? You're the worst, you control maniac, you self-destructive—"

"Me? You're the one who is self-destructive, always angry, you've got the personality of a bulldozer—"

"And you live like you're on a roller coaster with no damn seat belts, Isabelle, hands up in the air like a maniac—"

"Stop fighting, please," Janie begged. "Stop."

We glared at each other.

"Your stomach is disgusting, Isabelle."

"Yeah? Well, I can't breathe, Cecilia."

We glared again, then glared at the river.

"She's not there," Cecilia said after a while, brushing her blond hair out of her eyes as the wind sailed on past. "We won't find her in the river."

"How do you know?" I asked.

She ran her hands over her face. "She's not that interested in it. Never has been. She told me when she was still relatively sane that the only thing she did by the river was to make River. But, damn, where would Grandma go? Where would that skinny, demented woman head to?"

"I can't imagine anyone would kidnap an old woman," Janie said. "Did I lock the door when I left the house?"

"Who cares?" I said. "Velvet's there."

"Oh, right. Did I turn off the stove?" she fretted.

"Nobody would kidnap Grandma," I said. We'd gone over this, but we had to reassure ourselves. No one would have done that, would they? An old woman?

A lone plane flew over the gorge, a little plane, white with black letters underneath it. It wasn't moving quick, as if it wanted to fly through the rays of the sun, enjoy the sparkle of the river, take in the cliffs lining the gorge and the waterfalls shooting from the ledges.

It made that grinding sound those small motors make, and it cut through our silence like a machete cuts through bamboo.

The conversation between us came to a shuttering halt, the quiet changing, the tension a quaking, shuddering movement.

"She wouldn't have," I said, denying it.

"She couldn't get there," Cecilia said, in wonder.

"Oh no no no," Janie moaned. "Oh no no no."

As one, we hurtled toward Cecilia's van, cranked out an illegal U-turn, and sped toward Portland International Airport.

* * *

Portland International Airport is not a huge airport. It's manageable, modern, very Oregon. There's a long drive into the parking garage, which we bypassed and went around to the back side where the planes take off.

Years ago, when I was a kid, you could watch the planes taking off from pretty darn close. Since 9/11 they've erected a fence, so it keeps terrorists and other homegrown vampires away from the runway. In fact, there are places where you're not allowed to park.

We parked there anyhow, got out, and started searching the perimeter. We had told Lyla where we were going and she had radioed ahead to airport security and Portland police, who soon joined us.

We trudged along the fence as one plane after another took off and landed. The sun was now up and it was hot. We were all sweating, but Cecilia was awash in it, the sweat dripping off her nose, her hair sticking to her face in long strands.

"Sit down, Cecilia," Janie begged her. "Sit down. Or get a ride with one of the police officers."

"Shut the fuck up, you skinny Gumby doll," Cecilia said, not breaking stride.

Now that roiled my blood. I shoved Cecilia with my hand. "Don't talk to her like that. It's abusive. You got that, Cecilia? I know you're scared, but you can't take it out on us."

"Okay, braid-woman, I won't, but don't pander to me because of my weight," she huffed. She shoved me.

"That hurts my feelings, Cecilia," Janie said, standing right in front of Cecilia, legs spread to fight, which surprised me. "It's okay for you to tell me I'm a skinny Gumby doll, but if I said you're a fat-assed water buffalo and told you to shut the fuck up, you'd be screaming at me."

Whew! Now I was shocked.

Cecilia tried to punch Janie, but Janie skittered away.

Cecilia huffed, sweated. She tried a punch again. Janie skittered.

That ticked Cecilia off even more. "Stop running, Gumby!" She swung, Janie ducked.

"Stop being mean!" Janie said.

"Knock it off, you two," I said, coming physically between them. "Cecilia, shut your mean mouth."

Cecilia swore.

Janie counted planes, then started listing her favorite teas, in order.

The sun burned hotter and hotter and Cecilia panted and heaved. I insisted we sit down and said I was hot and tired and needed to rest.

"Give me a shitty break," the kindergarten teacher said. "I know you want to sit down because you think I need a rest."

"I'm doing it because I'm afraid your heart's going to explode and that may kill me." I put my hand to my chest. It was pounding like a drum.

"Plan your funeral," she muttered, trudging on.

After what seemed like hours, we finally saw a little army-green lump, curled up tight, right by the fence. The lump had white curly hair and was wearing goggles.

We'd found her.

We sank into the ground beside her.

She was breathing.

Amelia Earhart was alive.

We got Amelia into bed after we took her to the hospital, by ambulance, for a checkup. The hospital visit did not go well. She was confused and angry. And angry about being confused. And confused about being angry.

Near as we could determine Grandma had spent the night outside by the planes.

I asked her how she had gotten to the airport.

"By plane, you silly girl!" she'd admonished me, shaking a finger. "I flew my plane." She glared at the doctors. "Modern medicine is full of quacks," she told them.

I rolled my eyes. Must Momma and Grandma be so disrespectful to doctors? Must they be?

"In 1935 I was the first person to fly all by myself from Los Angeles, the city of angels," she shouted, "to Mexico City, land of piñatas and burritos and banjos! That's how I got my bottom bullet wounds!"

When the nurse brought in a tray of food, Grandma gobbled it up, then declared, "The pygmies know how to make someone feel welcome on their island!"

When the doctors wanted to examine her, she hit one in the chin and kicked the other. "Savages! All of you! Run to the plane!" she instructed us.

When the nurse adjusted the IV line, Grandma yelled, "I won't be injected with your tribal poison!"

There were no cuts or bruises on her body, but she was pretty seriously dehydrated.

For days it remained a mystery how Grandma got to the airport.

Finally, a teenager from a neighboring town confessed. "I sees this old lady on the road, you knows? She's wavin' and salutin' me and I stop. So she tells me, like, to take her to the airport because she's going to fly her autogiro. I dunno what an autogiro is. Sounds like a sandwich to me, maybe turkey, but she's already in my car and I gotta go to work in Portland at the dock sos I take her. So why not? Like, she's a nice lady but I think somethin's wrong with her, you knows? She kept tellin' me she flew across the Atlantic twice by herself and she could fly at fourteen thousand feet. But she never said her name, said she was on a secret mission and she was a secret agent. Sos she tells me to drop her off near the runway so I did. Am I gonna, like, be arrested? Hey, I'm sorry, dude."

We took Grandma home and put her to bed. She told me she had to go and "check on her secrets in the tower," I assured her she could do it tomorrow. She woke up only once during the night. I was sleeping on the floor next to her bed.

"Fly!" she sat up and yelled, "Fly! Fly away!" She pointed at the closets. "Fly high!" She lay straight back down in bed and didn't wake up for sixteen hours.

The next morning I headed to the river to throw rocks before going to the bakery. Janie would stay with Grandma for a while today so the rattled Velvet could "gather her bearings unto her rattled bones and rest."

The windsurfer was out there again.

I watched him for a while, but mostly I let the sun do its work on me as it scooted above the horizon. I was breathing hard, exhausted, my heart pounding. My heart always pounds when I, or Cecilia, is superstressed.

I was overwhelmed with . . . what was it? Bitterness? Anger? Pain? Recognition of defeat? I tossed a rock.

I tried to figure it out and gave up. Why are emotions so hard to name? Shouldn't we be able to put a finger on one and say, "Today what I'm feeling is . . . drum roll . . . shame!" And, voilà, we could tackle it down, shake it up. Handle it.

But no. Trying to pull through the mass of your own emotions is like trying to pull a piece of yarn through a ball that's all tangled up. It gets stuck, knotted, twisted, frayed, and the harder you pull it the harder the knot sticks.

So I could hardly figure out what I was thinking, but it basically went like this: I was emotionally whipped from trying to find Grandma.

But what to do? Move her out? Grandma would hate not living in the home she'd lived in for sixty-four years around people who loved and cared about her.

Henry needed attention and care.

Momma could not handle a mother with dementia and a special-needs son alone anymore. She wasn't as weak as she pretended, but she wasn't as strong as she'd like to think herself, either. The bakery was a whole other issue, too.

Cecilia had shouldered Momma and Grandma and Henry too

long. She had more crap coming down the pike with Parker. Her kids were screwed up and needed her.

Janie had her books and her compulsions and obsessions and could help some, but eventually she'd probably go back to her houseboat and shut the door.

And that left me.

It left me. I threw another rock in the water. The sun inched up over the river, the gold splashing onto the waves.

I did not want this role. Imagining myself living with, or near, Momma again made this rush of anger and hurt come at me like a tsunami. I could not become a caregiver to two people and a target for the third. I also could not live in this small town again, especially with my sterling ex-slut reputation.

I couldn't do it.

I can't do it.

No.

But that niggling question kept hitting me in the cranium: *If you won't do it, who will?*

Several nights later, after I'd made a baby shower cake in stork shape, a batch of butterscotch cubes, three Marion berry pies, a wedding cake with a blue icing waterfall (the couple had met at a local state park under a waterfall), and countless other sugary delights, I headed home.

As I rounded a corner, I saw the same man with white hair staring at our bakery across the street from under a trellis at our local park. I pulled over and watched him watching our bakery until he turned and left.

⚬ 15 ⚬

I headed to the cool grass and the willow tree late the next night and found the dippers and the North Star.

The constant trips to the hospital for Momma and Grandma had tripped me up. It was the smells that triggered the memories. The antiseptic, soapy, sterile smell of the hospitals that did it.

I had tried to get rid of those breath-sucking memories, pushing them into a mental box and nailing the lid on, but it hadn't worked, no surprise there. I have learned that sometimes you have to let your breath-sucking memories have their way with you if only so they will go back into your brain caves and you can continue on your merry life. I braced myself, and the memories slithered out of my brain caves like sea snakes.

There was so much blood that afternoon. Blood soaking the mattress, dripping to the floor, seeping from Momma, then clinging to us, hot and sticky.

I didn't say anything at first when I saw it, a hot, sticky red river. I couldn't speak. My shock sent my nerve endings hollering in disbelief and my brain shut down.

But even though I didn't speak, in another room, Cecilia felt me, felt my terror, my frozen horror. She screamed. Her scream exploded in me, as if she were in my body, howling, frantic, terrorized.

My scream joined hers, a room apart, one twisting, keening, horrific howl of pain.

It was about six weeks after Momma had returned from the hospital after the lice incident with the trailer in the thick of the woods.

She was doing well at the women's clothing store. No one would ever guess that behind the perfect face and the bell-shaped hair lurked a woman who could dive into a black pit so windingly deep, you'd figure you could find worms squiggling away at the bottom of it.

She refused to sign the papers we brought home from school that would have given us free breakfast and lunch, saying she could provide for us now. She tossed the papers in the garbage. "They think we're poor, don't they? We're not. We're not white trash. We don't need charity."

Janie forged her signature.

That fateful day Janie and Cecilia and I picked up Henry from his special classroom at his school. No one had harassed Cecilia for being plump, Janie for being nerdy weird, me for being a supersmart loner, or Henry for being Henry, and there'd been pizza for lunch, so the Bommarito kids were fairly happy.

We were headed to a neighboring school, about a mile away, where our principal told us they were giving out free clothes. "Have your mom drive you on over, Isabelle," he'd whispered to me, and handed me four passes to get in. Well, there was no way our momma, "We don't take charity," was gonna take us, so we went on foot and came home with a huge bag of clothes each and cookies in our stomachs that the smiling ladies handed out.

I had found two pairs of cool, bell-bottomed pants, one with purple butterflies on them; a pair of jeans; four T-shirts; and a couple of sweatshirts, no stains or rips. I had even found a pair of tennis shoes with pink laces that weren't beaten up, a red jacket, knitted gloves, and a package of new underwear with pink flowers.

I had started wearing a bra and had found one at a garage sale, but the straps had broken and I was hooking them together with safety pins. My other bra had to be taped together by Cecilia each morning. I found a soft pink one and a white, lacy one that day and felt like I was wearing gold.

It was the start of my fetish with bras.

Henry shared one of the two bedrooms in our dimly lit apartment with Momma, so when we got home, I took his bag in, intending on putting the clothes in his drawers. I figured Momma was still at work.

So I dragged the bag into the room Henry shared with Momma, and that's when I saw the pool of blood.

Momma was in the middle of that pool, in the middle of the bed, in the middle of the carnage.

It was like her entire life had bled right out of her. I thought she was dead. She was ghastly white, her mouth open only slightly, her head bent at almost ninety degrees, her legs splayed out like a chicken's.

That's when Cecilia screamed even though she hadn't seen what I was seeing.

By the time Cecilia, Janie, and Henry rushed in, I was patting Momma's face, blood sticking to my fingers. She didn't move. She didn't blink. I yelled her name, but she didn't respond.

"Call an ambulance!" I screamed, putting my head to her chest. Her heart was beating. I put my cheek to her mouth. She was still breathing, God only knew how.

Janie immediately passed out on the floor. I saw her slump and grab the corner of a dresser, her body and face hitting the bloody mattress, before slipping to the floor. Cecilia vomited.

"Call an ambulance, Cecilia! Hurry! Hurry!"

Cecilia crawled to the phone, flicking the vomit away from her face, not caring that her knees were carving right through it. I heard her screaming into the phone, her words hardly coherent.

A primal roar ripped out of Henry's throat. He rushed for Momma, hugging her close to him, Momma's head lolling to the side.

"Henry!" I yelled, grabbing at him. "Put her down! Put her down!"

"Oh, Momma! Momma!" He cradled her to him, his body now covered in her blood. "Momma!"

"Let go!" I screamed at Henry as more blood seeped out of Momma, my knees sinking into the blood on the mattress.

"No! I hug Momma! I make her better!" Henry insisted.

"Henry, stop it, stop it!" He gripped her harder.

It was the only time I hit Henry, my fist cracking hard against his forehead. He fell off the bed, tumbled flat to the floor, then huddled in a ball and wailed. I grabbed for Momma.

I could do nothing about him. Nothing. As I could do nothing about Janie breathing shallowly on the other side of the bed, her body crumpled up.

I laid Momma down and yanked up her dress.

I could hardly comprehend what I was seeing. The blood was new, it was caked, it was seeping out, it was dry. I stripped off a pillowcase, wadded it up, and put pressure on Momma's vagina so her life wouldn't slip out of her.

"Momma!" I shouted, frantic, shaking her shoulder. "Momma!"

Cecilia crawled back in and I yelled at her to get a towel because the pillow slip was soaked.

She wretched again on her way to the bathroom and I felt my stomach heave. She grabbed a white towel, then got on the bed with me. We pressed the towel in tight. I pushed back my hair and felt Momma's blood on my face.

"Are they coming?" I yelled at Cecilia over the din of Henry's pathetic wailing.

"Yes, they're coming. Momma! Momma!" No response. There was nothing coming out of Momma except blood. "God, is she dead?"

I put my bloody, trembling hand on her neck. "No, there's still a pulse."

"I hug Momma I hug Momma," Henry pleaded. "I make her better."

Janie, white as snow, struggled up and pulled herself to Momma's face, ignoring the blood from the mattress that soaked her T-shirt. She cupped Momma's face with her hands. "Don't die!" she begged. "Don't die, don't die, don't die."

I will never forget that begging, that wretched begging, as Janie beseeched Momma to stay with us.

The white towel was now red and I grabbed another one, pressing my hands on top of Cecilia's, all four covered in blood, our heads together over Momma's still body, tears mixing.

Henry continued pleading, his voice raw; Janie kept begging Momma to live; Cecilia swore and panted; and we held that towel tight.

Seconds later I heard the scream of the ambulance, the pounding of feet up to our apartment, the staccato knocking on the door.

The doorbell rang and Henry let loose with a primal roar. Another gush of blood spewed from Momma, and Janie screamed. Later I heard that the paramedics and police heard those spine-tingling sounds and didn't wait. The door was almost instantly kicked down, the hinges splitting, the wood crashing to the floor.

Paramedics and policemen rushed in and they'd hardly known where to start. Cecilia and I had blood on our faces, hands, and arms. Janie had passed out again and collapsed to the floor, blood covering her T-shirt, her body curled up.

Henry was in a corner, hysterical, seconds ago passing into a place where no one could reach him. The room smelled like impending death, vomit, and free-ranging fear.

"Oh God! Help us!" Cecilia screamed, "Help us!"

Within nanoseconds, those guys were on their radios screaming for backup, and soon the sirens were ripping through the neighborhood, men filling our apartment in suits and uniforms.

Later I was told they thought we'd all been attacked by some knife-wielding psycho.

Cecilia and I were forcibly carried from the room, struggling, not wanting to leave Momma, and shoved into an ambulance. Janie was strapped onto a gurney, an IV poked up her arm as her pale face wobbled side to side. Henry, bloody Henry, was picked up by three firefighters, all holding him as he slugged them in sheer panic.

When we left, we saw the paramedics and firefighters surrounding Momma, quick hands working to save her life, radios squawking, men yelling, and one paramedic slumped in the corner, passed out.

Momma stayed in the hospital for two weeks. We kids stayed overnight. The police came and asked us questions, the doctors and nurses never leaving us alone, patting us when we couldn't hold back the tears, our arms around each other as we rocked back and forth. We insisted on sleeping in the same room, so they shoved beds together.

Henry did not speak, not one word, his eyes vague, spacey, not with us. Janie started to count out loud, something she'd been doing softly for a long time, but now she didn't bother to cover it up. Cecilia ate. Packages of cookies, whole pies, red Jell-O and pudding, entire pepperoni pizzas. I slipped into the darkness of my head.

Miss Nancy came to get us in the morning.

For the next two weeks, we all woke up with night terrors. More than once I woke up pulling on my own hair, dreaming blood was stuck in it. Cecilia had nightmares, too, and she'd whisper, "Stop the blood, stop the blood."

I don't think Nancy slept.

She never said a word of complaint, only came in with hugs and assurance, her cool hands stroking sweating foreheads, holding shaking hands, cupping lonely, lost faces.

She helped Janie with her embroidery and put on more classical music.

She tried to get Henry to talk, but he wouldn't. Henry's speech wasn't superarticulate, and he regressed after that night. It took him about two years to get back up to where he was. He spent a lot of time petting the animals.

She had Cecilia working with her at Sunday school and put me back in the church choir.

We played in the stream behind her house again. Caught bugs. Watched a snake slither away. Spied on a possum we named Superman and a raccoon we named Grass.

We didn't know initially what happened to Momma. No one wanted to share anything with three young girls. We wouldn't have known, except that Cecilia is an expert spy. When Nancy went outside to talk on the phone, we figured that was the conversation we needed to hear.

It didn't take long to hear the word *abortion*. It didn't take us long to do a little sleuthing.

So, that's what it was.

An abortion.

An abortion gone hideously wrong.

Pregnant by the violent trailer creep who called her darlin' and hit her and her children. Pregnant by the trailer creep who sold us that white piece of trash for a piece of Momma's soul that gave us lice and took her to a place where no one could reach her. Pregnant because she'd wanted something to keep us warm in the winter and it was all she could do.

Not pregnant anymore.

All that blood. I still remembered it.

But Momma didn't give up, even then. We didn't move home to Trillium River and Grandma and her "I told you so." It took one more cruelty, one more perverse crime, to finally break her back and send her, one fingernail clinging to reality, back to Oregon.

* * *

I wanted to go home and crash after a twelve-hour day at the bakery, but I couldn't. It was Wednesday night, which meant I was singing at the church. As usual, we had rehearsal for an hour ahead of time.

We had a guest musician that night. His name was Samuel Griffin. He was eighty-five and played the bongos. No kidding. The bongos.

Right before church the teenage drummer and electric guitar players came up to me.

"You're the coolest mom ever," one said, enthused. He gave me a fist bump.

"Yeah, I wish my mom was as awesome as you," the other said. "You're awesome." Fist bump.

Awesome. Cool.

But I was not a mother.

I buried that one, deep and hard. I buried that.

I begged my brain caves not to let that memory out again. I couldn't do anything about it, so why think about it?

Samuel Griffin bonged it hard that night.

Father Mike jammed.

I sang.

Like a nightingale who had no kids and never would.

The familiar blackness edged up on me over the next ten days. I could feel it in my chest, my head, in the air I shakily sucked in. Depression, at least with me, comes in one of two ways: It sneaks up on me, bit by bit, until I'm enshrouded in it, or it arrives like a hurricane, blowing in all sorts of nasty feelings, mood swings, sad and terrible thoughts, followed by a spiraling sensation downward and, eventually, a shutdown on my end, where functioning like a human is iffy.

I had been working seventy-to-eighty-hour weeks since I arrived in Trillium River. I was often sleeping on the floor of Grandma's room because she kept trying to leave in the middle of the night. As she grunts in her sleep and yells, "Turbulence!" it is difficult to get much sleep.

I was spending time with Henry, too, and the girls, who needed both me and Janie, clearly, in their lives, along with their mother, who was still a volcano of exploding emotions.

I was exhausted and trying to fight the black, but I could tell the black was winning.

On Sunday morning Cecilia told me I resembled beige shit and I should go home to Portland for a couple of days.

I argued.

Janie told me I was pale and sickly and offered me her Indian music tapes, *Jane Eyre*, incense, and the peaceful photo of her therapist. "Get some rest in your loft, Is. We'll be fine."

I argued. They argued.

I lost. I got in my Porsche and headed back to Portland.

I drove along the Columbia River. The more miles I put between me and Trillium River, the more uncomfortable I felt, the more alone. The more lonely. I am used to those alone and lonely feelings but hadn't experienced them so much since arriving in town.

I tried not to think about that wrench. Missing Trillium River, or my life there, was not in the plan.

But neither was getting strangled or having my face pummeled.

Good thing we don't know what's coming down the pike for us or we'd never get out of bed.

We agreed that I would check in on Momma at the retirement center in Portland on my way to my loft. I made an appointment ahead of time. She was wearing her pink robe and shawl, her head on the pillow, when I arrived. She moaned like a champ and I heard the same complaints.

"I'm getting sicker."

"There's something wrong with me."

"I can hardly move. I ache like I'm being eaten."

"I feel like I'm dying. I am dying."

Now these comments initially alarmed me, somewhat. So I met with the director, Sinda Phillips. Sinda is half Mexican and half Asian. She's six feet tall.

When Momma first met her, she said to Sinda, "You're a brown giant with cat eyes."

Sinda had laughed.

I had nearly died.

"I'm going to hate it here." Momma swung her bell-shaped hair. "I don't want to be here. I feel like a prisoner. My daughters are forcing this on me. *Forcing it on me.*" She sniffed.

"I'm sorry you feel that way, Mrs. Bommarito," Sinda said, sweetly, her voice almost music in itself. "I think you may come to like it here."

"That will never happen, young lady."

The conversation sped downhill from there, as Momma listed her complaints, much like a go-cart zooms brakeless down a hill.

"So how is my dear momma?" I had asked Sinda after she'd been there about ten days.

"Your mother is . . . how shall I say it?" Sinda mused, cupping her face with her hands.

"Don't bother gussing it up. Spit it out."

Sinda laughed. "She doesn't like her room. Too small."

"Too small, too dirty, too bright . . ." I held my hands palms up.

"She doesn't like all this talking and laughing."

"Yes, that would be a problem. Laughing especially."

"She hates to eat with the other people in the dining room. Too noisy."

"Noise, noise, noise." I sighed.

"But the biggest problem was that people were coming up to her and asking her to go on the outings. To the waterfalls. To the shopping center. An overnight at the beach. A picnic. A museum. Too many invitations."

"How sad for her," I droned.

"But a miracle occurred," Sinda said, pointing both pointer fingers up in victory.

"A miracle?"

"Your momma tried one of the trips to the shopping centers. She bought two blouses. One white, one blue."

"Good."

"She went on the picnic the next day. She became slightly inebriated on the vodka that old Mr. Ricker snuck in in Thermoses."

I tried to imagine The Viper inebriated. Couldn't do it.

"She did a dance for the residents."

I cringed. "What kind of dance?"

"She made them all get up and get a partner and waltz around. They loved it. She had more vodka. Other people shared Mr. Ricker's bounty."

I laughed.

"She also decided that she would join Wily Women's book group and chess club." Sinda looked proud. "Your mother is an outstanding chess player."

Momma's father had taught her how to play chess before he'd toddled off the cliff, but I'd rarely seen her play. "Play like you want to kill your opponent," she'd told me her father told her.

"She joined the Wednesday afternoon activity group and the Saturday Evening Out and About group. We take them to plays, concerts, things like that."

"Ah." I got it.

"I believe she is fitting in perfectly, though the youngest person here."

"She would like that. Being the youngest." I thought for a second. "So when we come to visit and find her in bed, complaining, in grave pain, saying she's so sick we should put her out of her misery?"

Sinda coughed. "I believe that your mother is sometimes suddenly uh . . ." She coughed again. "Uh, suddenly *stricken* with sickness when she knows you girls are coming to visit. Her sickness causes her to scramble into her robe and into bed and become, well, *ill*. Quite ill."

I blinked.

"Rest is good, though," Sinda said, pretending to be stern. "Especially with her schedule. Yesterday she did the Mt. Hood Timberline lunch. Afterward, the ladies all went to see Keanu Reeves's latest movie. They think he's sexy."

"Ah." Okay I got it. "Keanu Reeves is wicked sexy. I'm in love with him myself. I think I understand the situation."

"Yes," Sinda told me, smiling. "She's a clever one, your mother."

She was that, indeed.

"Remember to send me the bills."

"Your sister, Janie, told me to send her the bills."

I laughed. "We'll take care of it."

Some mothers drive their daughters to drink with their behavior. Momma drove me, often, to my favorite spa. It smells like vanilla, it's classy and elegant, and I love it.

The gal who always does my massages did a double take. "You look like shit," she told me. Graciella is half French, half Chinese, and totally gorgeous. She was wearing a blue kimono with a gold dragon on it.

"Did Cecilia tell you to say that?"

"Who's Cecilia and no she didn't I thought of it all by myself what's been going on why haven't you been taking care of yourself you're too skinny and your skin needs help have you not slept in, like two years or something? You need the full treatment especially on your face what the heck is wrong with your nails you been sharpening them with a knife I'll help you."

First I hid myself in a hot steam room that smelled like roses. Then I had an hour and a half hot-rock massage with Graciella.

Next came a European facial with orange citrus, a pedicure with foot rub, a manicure, and the salon fixed up my braids.

I went home and went to bed. I slept seventeen hours straight through. Ladies, do this.

Life is too rough and tough and sucky to go through it without taking yourself to a spa. Trust me. You deserve it.

✿ 16 ✿

I didn't feel like I fit in my loft anymore.

It was as if I were in someone else's home and I was a gawking stranger. It was stark and modern, stuck between the high-rises, with my photos of people with despairing, haunted eyes hanging floor to ceiling.

I saw that cushy bed of mine and remembered the men and that's when my depression took another whirlwind and started moving in on me like black clouds. I could feel my mood dip, as if it were on a roller coaster ride.

I headed to a bar around the corner from my loft, which was my first gargantuan mistake. It was as if the darkness was reaching for me again and my own lurking darkness reached back, and together we created a colossal disaster and a strangulation.

Before I left I slipped on my new white bra with black swirls and matching underwear. I wriggled into a short black skirt, sexy heels, and a slinky red tank top. I hated myself.

I pulled my braids back into a ponytail and matched my lipstick to my shirt. I hated myself more.

I attract men. This is not a bragging statement. It is a fact. I've got good bones via Grandma and I'm thin. I know how to wear clothes and I have long braids, biggish lips, and cat eyes. Men come swirling around me. They have no idea what a head case I am.

I hate that head case part of me. I hate myself, the head case.

I found my man that night.

He was a head case, too.

It is a wonder that I have lived to write the rest of this.

"Nice taste in food," he said to me.

The bar was expensive, high up in a pink building, and classy. I was having chicken wings, crab cakes, clams with butter and garlic, and my second vodka.

I glanced up. I'd been sitting at the bar for eight minutes and here he was. This was not quick for me. Usually it takes less time to get a man on a stool next to me than it does for a chicken to squawk.

"Thanks," I said. I held my braids away from the butter/garlic sauce.

He reached over and did it for me.

That was a little surprising, but not much.

I pulled my braids back, kept eating.

"Here by yourself?" he asked.

"Spare me," I snapped. "Can't you think of a better line? One that might require a larger and more creative vocabulary?"

He wasn't taken aback by that. "Sure. I'd like to hold your braids in my hands all night and stroke them."

I stared at him through the mirror over the bar. He stared back.

I knew by the next day I would hardly remember the color of his hair. They're all a blur.

But this one was white, brownish curly hair, skinny. Had an intense face, as if he spent much of his time sucking on a lemon. Eyes closer together than normal, biggish nose, high cheekbones, a scar on the left one.

I turned to face him, our knees touching. His eyes . . . there was something funny about them, I noticed. They were too bright . . . too intense . . . too off. Something.

"So. Can I?"

"Can you what?" I asked.

"Can I hold your braids all night?"

I turned around and started eating again, signaled the barman to bring me another vodka. "You're not entertaining me," I told him.

"I can."

He said this suggestively.

I made a disgusted sound. "I've heard that before."

"But I'm telling you the truth."

"I've heard that, too. Men are mostly talk, you know. Show-offs. Macho-maniacs. They puff out their chests and then . . . nothing." I wasn't kidding with him or trying to be argumentative. I was stating a fact. I drank the vodka.

"Can I have dinner with you?" He ordered what I was eating. He tried to make small talk. I mainly ignored him and continued my drinking.

The darkness swirled, helped by the vodka, into a moving mass.

"Let's go," I told him when I was done eating. I didn't know how much time had passed. I'd lost count of my vodkas. I grabbed my purse, threw some money on the bar to cover my meal and a generous tip. "Pay for your own dinner," I told him. He took out his wallet and slapped some bills down.

He put a heavy arm around me when we were almost at my loft. I shrugged it off. I felt nauseated and exhausted. I stumbled a bit and almost fell to the ground. He hauled me back up from behind and tried to kiss my neck.

"Gross. Wait, will you?" I said, pushing his pointy lemon-face away with my hand as we neared the entrance.

He moved in and kissed me again, superaggressively, like a machine that wouldn't stop a certain function no matter how much you pushed the Stop button. I wrestled out of his spindly arms and pushed on his chest twice, but dizziness hit me again and I ended up leaning against him for balance. "Wait," I snapped, but my voice sounded thick, foggy.

In the elevator up to my loft, he pressed me against the corner and tried to stick a sticky, sweaty hand up my skirt.

I pushed his hand away with both of mine, my head fuzzy and swirling. "Damn it, I said stop." I picked my men carefully. I liked the cheerful, loud, funny guys with kind eyes and big smiles.

I clearly had not done so good tonight. Too much vodka.

The elevator swooshed on up. I was familiar with the feelings of self-hatred that assailed me. I was familiar with the feelings of degradation that wrapped around me, tight, so tight. I was familiar with feelings of dread, too, like death flying in on a cape to settle on my shoulders.

I tried to ignore these feelings, as usual, but they were stronger this time, more insistent, louder than they'd ever been. Plus warning bells were clanging through the fog, and the weird light in this guy's eyes was making my nerve endings screech.

When he tried to hug me again, hard groin grinding into my stomach, I shoved him away. He lounged at the other side of the elevator, staring at me. I met his stare. He had eyes like a ferret's, lips like barbed wire, and a skinny body like a tightrope walker without the amusing pole.

I stumbled down the hall to my loft and he put both arms around me and manhandled me up against the wall, his barbed-wire lips trying to find mine. I fought him off. He panted and grinned. He tried it again and I fought him off again.

I bent my head in front of my door, my braids falling toward my face, my keys in my hand.

The word *no* came from a distance, as if it were swooping

down a tunnel through the vodka-sponginess of my brain. I heard it, and for the first time, I listened to it.

"No," I said. I turned toward him. "No." I said it louder.

"Yes," he whispered in my ear. "Yes." The whisper sent shivers zigzagging over my spine.

I wriggled away. "No!" Through the fog a rational voice. "No!"

He moved so quick, I couldn't even respond. He grabbed my braids, whipped me around, and smashed me face-first into my door, pain splintering through my entire head. I dropped the keys, he grabbed them, unlocked the door, lifted me through, and slammed the door.

I sprawled in my entry, my balance weak, blood gushing from my nose. He dropped his whole weight on my back and I heard something crack. My breath rushed out and the edges of my vision blurred.

He yanked my braids until I imagined the roots being torn out of their tiny sockets, then giggled, high-pitched, a giggle right out of one of Janie's books. "You said I could come home with you and stroke your braids all night long," he said in a singsong voice. "That's what I'm gonna do."

"Get out!" I said, trying to scream, but my voice came out a wheezy whisper. "Get out!" I struggled but he twisted my hair harder, leaning his weight against my back, his knee forcing my legs apart.

"See here, bitch. You invited me up here. You want it. I'm here. Take your clothes off."

Ever feel terrified? I mean, bloodsuckingly terrified? This is what it's like: You can feel your body draining of blood, as if your blood is too scared to be there anymore. Your kidneys and liver feel like they're origamically folding up. Your mouth goes approximately as dry as the Sahara desert. Your eyes feel as if they're going to bug right out of your head and drop to the ground because panic is pushing them out of your skull.

Oh, and you can't breathe and your heart wants to leave your body it's so panicked.

That's only the start of it. Because you know the worst is yet to come.

"Off go your clothes . . ." He sang these words so melodiously, like he was a member of a church choir. He hauled me up by my braids to my knees with two hands, twisted me around, and smashed my face to his dick.

"Eat it," he sang, loud and high. My insides were shaking with fear, my whole body rocking.

He giggled. He let go of a fistful of braids and pulled on his belt.

I tried to get up and he lifted up his knee and smashed me in the chin. I heard another crack and my head went flying back. Instantly my neck ached. He tossed my head like a ball, and it crashed into a corner of my wall. I could actually see white stars, green stars, black stars, all these stars colliding together before my eyes. Blood gushed hot and sticky over my shoulders, joining the blood from my nose.

He yanked his belt open and the button of his pants with one hand, then dragged me back up to the kneeling position again so through dizzy, rolling eyes I was staring at that bulge again. I tried to breathe, and couldn't.

"Here we go, Isabelle." He yanked his pants to his knees, his boxers still on, then reached in and pulled that log out. Through crackling, vibrating pain, and my own internal, frantic screams, I could smell the urine, the sweat, and a rotting scent. It brushed my cheek on its way out, hot and throbbing. I would have fought, but I could hardly see straight.

"Taste that, cunt."

I hate that word. *I hate it.*

The log was sticking straight out, and while he sung a high-pitched song, he swung my head back and forth, like a Ping-Pong ball, from one hand to the other.

I tried to get up and he slammed me back down, his fist in my gut. My body shook in agony.

"Here's your dinner," he sang. "Dinner's ready! Come and get it! Din-din!"

And that was it. I knew where my mouth was gonna be in about one second and I would rather die than do that. And somewhere in that rampaging pain, the fog of my throbbing head, I knew I would be raped after that and probably dismembered.

A vision of my family flitted through my head. Momma declaring the doctor a midget, Grandma saluting in her flight uniform, Janie smiling across the conference table at that weasel Parker, Cecilia teaching her kindergarteners, Kayla and her burka, Riley and her current devotion to alpha particles and atomic masses.

And Henry.

Henry's crooked grin seemed to reach down the river and into the city and right into my heart. I loved Henry.

And that did it for me.

Henry did it. I would not leave my brother.

I would fight.

I would not die.

I raised both of my hands up, grabbed that log, and yanked down as hard as I could. He fell against me, hit me with his fist across the jaw, then sang a high note. "Laaaa!"

I vaguely felt blood running into my mouth.

I pulled on his log harder and stood up. He cracked his head against mine, and I saw black edging the corners of my vision as I went down again.

Still fighting, I raised my foot up, clad in a pointy, high heel, and jammed his dick. He stopped singing and shouted, "Cunt bitch." He kicked at my shin, and pain zoomed from my toes to my head.

He was heaving and panting and had this creepy, creepy smile on his face, like he enjoyed the challenge. "Fight, girl, fight!" he whispered, then sang "Laaaa!"

I shook my head to clear the mess out of it as he yanked the belt out of his pants and whipped it in the air. Clearly things were going to get bloody ugly.

The belt hit me on the shoulder, a thousand needles spiking through to the bone, but I rushed him anyhow, my legs shaking, grabbing his wrist and bringing my fist up as hard as I could into his chin. When he jerked, I kicked him in the groin with the point of my heel.

That dropped him to the floor, but he dragged me down with him. I reached for his eyes and poked them hard, digging straight in. He shouted through clenched teeth, obviously not wanting attention to come to the attack that was happening in my loft, and clenched both hands around my neck.

Terror became a living, breathing thing, swooping and swirling around as if the death vultures were circling. I grasped his hands and struggled, then pulled my legs up and got an ankle around his neck. This was a maneuver you do not ever want to have to do. It put pressure on my spine and my bashed head that almost made me pass out. I kicked with my other leg. This loosened his grip and I flipped him off me, then karate-chopped him in his own esophagus.

He was finally down for a second and I stumbled to the knife rack in my kitchen, brandishing the biggest one in front of me.

"Get out!" I spit blood out of my mouth in a great gob as I slashed the knife through the air. *"Get out."*

He was sweating and red and panting and furious. He swore at me, his language vile. Then, with an abrupt personality change, he giggled and sang out, "I'm going to kill you, kill you, kill you."

I grabbed the phone on my counter and hit 911. I flipped it up and grabbed another knife.

When I heard the operator I yelled, "I need the police. A man is trying to kill me." I gave them my address, even though I knew they'd be able to trace the call.

He chuckled again, pointed at me, and straightened up awkwardly. I knew I'd hurt him. "I'm coming for you again, sweetheart," he said, reaching down for his pants. "That was fun! We'll do it again."

"I need help right now," I shouted. "Now!" I limped around my counter, frantic, shaking off death, my body sinking into a morass of sheer pain.

"I will come for you, my darling!" he sang. "I will be your dar-rrling!"

"Get out of here, you sick fuck," I said, my voice low. I spit more blood and a tooth out of my mouth.

He turned and ran out of the apartment into the hallway. I followed him, limping, and threw a knife at his back. Miraculously, it stuck, his back arching in the air. He turned around and grinned at me, then pulled the knife out of his back as if it didn't even hurt, wielding it in front of his face. "This is for you the next time we rendezvous!"

He turned and ran, blood pooling onto his shirt.

I slammed my door, locked it, and picked up the phone with a bloody hand. I told the operator exactly what the guy was wearing, down to the type of designer shoe I recognized and the blood congealing on his shirt.

She kept having to interrupt, "Ma'am, I'm sorry, I can't understand you . . ."

I had to spit blood out of my mouth. I tried again and tried to speak clearly. For some reason my tongue wasn't working. I could feel blood dripping down my back.

I limped over to my French doors, fumbled them open, and leaned over the balcony. At eleven floors up, it'd take that psychopath a minute to get down. My balcony overlooked the entrance.

I saw him run out. For a second he turned and stared up at me as I stared down at him, feeling sick, half-dead, petrified. He waved cheerily, blew me a kiss.

I heard a siren in the distance, and he started running. I watched him as far as I could, then gave the operator exact directions, twice, because she couldn't understand me through my mouthful of blood.

I stumbled back into my loft and laid down on the floor because my legs gave out. The police officers announced themselves by yelling, "Police! Open the door!" I heard them but my own dizziness was swirling my brain around like a yo-yo. I tried to open my mouth to speak, but I couldn't. It was like my jaw had been hammered shut with railroad spikes.

Because I couldn't speak and, I was later told, the only thing the dispatcher heard was silence, those policemen smashed my door down, exactly like the afternoon Momma was bleeding to death. The parallel was not lost on me.

Two officers came right for me, my blood rushing out of my head and various other places like a faucet. Three more came after that, guns drawn, as they went through my loft, not trusting he wasn't still there.

Their radios squawked and I heard one of them from a far-off, distant land order the dispatcher to send the medics up *right now!*

A police officer with a crew cut knelt by me. "Hello, ma'am, I'm Lieutenant Sherm Walsh."

I couldn't speak. I thought I was dying.

"What hurts?" I could only groan. He and the other police officers around me were spinning in and out of focus, like ghosts dressed as policemen.

His next question undid me. "Who did this to you?"

Who did this to you? I didn't know. *I didn't know his name.* The tears filled like lakes in my eyes. I didn't know any of their names. I had never, ever wanted to know. I couldn't have cared less if their names were Tom or Chad or Robot Man or Scotty Beam Me Up.

The policeman took out a handkerchief and held it to my head while he eyed my injuries. The policewoman on the other side of me patted my hand. The third policeman, holding my head still, leaned over and said, "You're gonna be okay, honey. You're gonna be okay."

I was not okay.

I did not believe, at that moment, that being okay was part of my future.

I had a "heck of a concussion," according to my doctor. I had severe bruising on my neck, stomach, and back, and my esophagus had taken a beating. The back of my head was so swollen I figured I was growing another head, and my nose was broken. I had two cracked ribs and a cracked bone in my chin, not to mention a bruise the size of Texas on my shin and a whip mark cutting through my shoulder.

Later the nurses told me that approximately ten minutes after the police arrived at my loft, my attacker had been caught hiding in a Dumpster. Based on a fingerprint test, I had barely escaped a man who was wanted in three states for multiple rapes and one state for a rape and murder.

"They said you got him good," a policewoman told me triumphantly, helpfully holding an ice pack to my face. "You brought that son of a bitch dooown. His dick is bruised and off at some weird angle and his balls are swelled up like bowling balls, that's what I hear. He's gonna be squeakin' for life. Plus, he's got a bad injury to his eye and they can't find an eye doctor. Too bad. Hopefully he'll go blind. Then he'll never be able to identify his boyfriends in jail."

Another policeman said, "You can testify against him, ma'am, make sure he pays for what he did to you. He's going to jail forever, though. That guy's gonna die there if the chair doesn't get him first."

"I'll testify," I said through my squished, bruised lips. Sure as hell I'd be there.

No woman deserved what had happened to me. None.

Even slutty head-case women who had one-night stands like myself.

I was repeatedly asked by the police and hospital staff which family members and friends should be contacted. I repeatedly told them not to contact anyone. I felt like dying when I thought of the pain I would cause my family, the tears dripping over my bruises and bumps and dried blood and puddling in that little hollow in my neck where the life had almost been strangled right out of me.

Two Portland police detectives knocked and came into my hospital room, smiling gently. I felt like a mummy. My head was wrapped, my ribs were wrapped. I had bandages all over my face.

There was also a doctor and a nurse and a rep from the rape crisis center whom I'd met when I was still spitting up blood. She was African-American, about fifty, and wore a colorful turban on her head. I have never seen such compassionate, warm eyes in my entire life. I wanted to pull myself into a ball and climb into them.

The doctor stood next to me with a hand on my shoulder. She was from India and wore her black hair in a ponytail. Her gold bangles jingled when she moved.

The nurse stood next to her. She was Russian, weighed about 250 pounds, and had the face of a wrinkled man.

One of the police officers was Asian and seemed barely old enough to be out of high school. I was taller than him. Later, he would tell me that he was twenty-four and had a black belt. The night before he'd persuaded a meth addict out of committing suicide with a .45 on a boat in the Willamette River.

The police officer who questioned me was African American, about six feet six inches tall, with a military-type haircut.

We were a regular United Nations Group.

"I'm Detective Walter Carrington. I'm from the Portland Police Department."

I tried to nod. Tried to swallow, too. The nurses had been feeding me through a straw.

"First, I would like to say that I'm sorry this happened to you, Ms. Bommarito." He reached out and cradled my hand. I wanted this man to come home with me so I could feel safe forever.

The doctor patted my shoulder, and the rep for the rape group massaged my leg gently.

Oh no. Kindness. More tears were coming.

The tears came in earnest, the sobs followed, the moaning and hiccupping later. I was patted and hugged.

God, I was a mess.

We started again after forty-five minutes. No one seemed to be in a hurry here. The detective's questions were direct but compassionate.

I felt like dying. I did.

"Ms. Bommarito, how do you know Russ Bington?" Detective Carrington asked.

I didn't even want to answer the question. I knew what they would think of me when I did.

He asked it again, patting my hand.

I couldn't answer. I was decimated, humiliated.

"Can you tell me where you met?"

I swallowed, but swallowing didn't feel normal because part of my throat was zigzagging in the wrong direction. "We met at Hal's. Downtown."

He nodded. "Was that the first time you met?"

"Yes." My voice was scratchy from my near strangulation.

He paused. "Ms. Bommarito, was it a one-night stand?"

I caught a sob.

The detective gave me a delicate way out. "Ms. Bommarito, we've all made mistakes. Not a person in this room is free of them."

"Yes," I said, ashamed. So ashamed. "It was supposed to be a one-night stand."

Should I also admit: I had one-night stands to forget that I had one-night stands and to tease my depression, and I had had them since I was a teenager, after the incident with the rakes, because I felt like nothing, and had no dad, and each time I lost a little more of myself even though I always searched for something more but the "more" was invisible and I never found it?

"This is not your fault," the detective told me. "*Not* your fault, young lady."

I let the tears flow.

✌ 17 ✍

I telephoned Janie on her cell to tell her I would not be back until Wednesday or Thursday. I figured I'd be able to hobble about by then, if my shin stopped splitting like a matchstick.

"Thank God it's you, Isabelle!" Janie gushed. "Cecilia's not here. Last night she woke up and her whole body was throbbing—especially her jaw and her shin—and she was having trouble breathing. Her nose bled! She called me, and I drove right over and told her we should go to the hospital, but she refused to go *because it was you causing it.*" I heard her panting, her nerves jangled and jittering. "You! It's the twin thing again!"

I put my hand to my bandaged head and the tears rolled out, blinding me. *Oh, Cecilia, I'm so sorry.* "How is she now? How is she?" *I made my own twin hurt. She couldn't breathe.*

"We dialed your cell phone a million times but you didn't answer. She's almost hysterical worried about you. At one point I thought she was dying. She kept holding her ribs and her head. You're okay, right?"

I heard her burst into tears and I turned the phone so she wouldn't hear my smothered sobs.

"I had to embroider for hours with Vivaldi!"

"How is Cecilia?" *I did that to her. I did that to my sister.*

"She's in bed and she's in a panic about you and the back of her head is pounding and she can't move her jaw right and her shoulder is burning. Her nose bled again. How are you?"

"I'm fine." *I felt so guilty I wanted to die.*

"What's wrong with your voice?" she shrieked.

"I'll tell you later." *Could guilt kill a person?*

"What's wrong? I know something's wrong!"

"Nothing." *Except I will never forgive myself for what I did to my family last night.*

"You're making me nervous, Isabelle," she squeaked.

"Janie, I love you and I'll tell you later." *I'm sorry. I'm so sorry. I choked on my grief. Cecilia, I'm sorry.*

"No, tell me now. I don't like when you say you'll tell me something later. I know you're alive, but are you hurt? You're hurt, aren't you? Cecilia's right!" She started a round of heavy breathing. "You're hurt!"

My heart hurt the most. *How would sweet Henry react? Not well, I knew it.* "I'm okay, Janie. I'll see you soon."

"Are you bleeding? Was it a multicar accident on a bridge? A freak explosion? A fire started by an iron? Did someone else hurt you? Oh nooooo."

I collapsed into my guilt. She had it, I knew she did.

"You had a one-night stand, didn't you?" Her voice pitched to a high operatic note. "I have told you not to do those things. How many times have I told you that, Isabelle? He hurt you, didn't he? I'm coming to Portland. I'll be at your loft in an hour."

"I'm not at my loft." *I'm in hell.*

She screeched. "Whose house are you at? Where are you? Oh my God. You're at the hospital, aren't you?"

"Oh, sheesh." You can't hide anything from Janie.

"Which hospital?"

"Janie, stay in Trillium River—" *I can't stand to see your pain when you see mine.*

"Let's see." She paused and I knew she was thinking. "You're either at the University or Saint Eileen's. I'll bet it's Saint

Eileen's. You have insurance. We're coming right now, oh, Is, I love you. I love you so much. We're coming!" She hung up.

I turned off my cell phone.

I had hurt my sisters. I had hurt my family.

I curled into a ball, curled into my misery.

Cecilia and Janie arrived shortly.

It wasn't pretty. They took one horrified look at what had been my face and dissolved. Janie started keening and crying at the same time, hands waving periodically in the air.

Cecilia hit the wall, then decided it needed to be kicked. Janie moaned. Cecilia raged. Janie counted.

We're a mess, all three of us. We have no idea how to rein in emotions and when something bad happens to one of us, we're all the messier.

We hugged and our tears melded our hot faces together until we didn't know whose tears were whose.

Several days later, as Cecilia drove me along the highway next to the Columbia River, the wind so strong our car swerved a couple of times and my whole body still aching as I dealt with a monstrous amount of lingering terror, I had a sweet blaze of clarity. I knew with every single swimming cell in my wracked body that that was the end of my one-night stands.

The sex had destroyed my soul and almost killed me.

Worse, I had hurt Cecilia and Janie. This would hurt Henry and Grandma and Momma. This would hurt the girls.

Forever and ever, I was done.

I had told Cecilia and Janie that I shouldn't go back to Trillium River, that I should stay at a hotel in Portland so that my new face and mummy wrap would not upset Henry and Grandma, but they wouldn't hear of it. They had all sorts of reasons: I needed medical attention, they wanted to care for me, what if this guy was let out of jail, and so on.

"I've got two guns," Cecilia told me. "Momma has three. I'll move one pistol to your top dresser drawer, Isabelle, and the other to the pink box in the hall closet on the top shelf."

"I brought my knives. Fourteen of them," Janie said. "We'll hide them all over the house . . ."

Cecilia and I gaped at her. *Fourteen knives?*

"And my collection of brass knuckles and whips. I have my noose, too."

We gaped again.

"If you need a rope, let me know. I brought two."

Whoa.

When we got home, Grandma's and Henry's unbridled anguish about brought me to my knees.

Grandma whipped off her goggles, grabbed my upper arms, and said, her voice wobbling, "You've had a crash landing! A crash landing!" She hugged me for about five minutes, then zipped off and got a pink piece of paper and told me to go to the hospital right away. She had drawn a sad face on the paper. I thanked her and she hugged me again, then went behind the couch, crouched down, and sobbed.

Henry burst through the door after volunteering at the animal shelter, came to an abrupt halt, and started wailing, "What happen Is? What happen Is?" He held his arms way out to hug me, his face flushed and scrunched in pain, but Cecilia and Janie had to hold him tight so he wouldn't squeeze me in a viselike hug, possibly undoing what little was holding my ribs together.

"A bad guy get you? I get him!" he yelled. "I get him!" He tried to get away from Cecilia and Janie, but they held him tight, his inherited Bommarito rage growing rapidly.

"Henry, calm down!" Cecilia yelled, but it didn't reach him, the tears dripping down his red face.

"I get him, Is! I get him!" He pretended he was punching someone.

Grandma popped up over the couch and started shouting, "SOS! SOS!" through her tears.

Velvet ran in the room and, though momentarily startled by my face, instantly went to help Henry, who had started howling, the sobs coming from his scared, dear soul.

"SOS! SOS!" Grandma said, voice hoarse, before pulling into her tight ball again.

"Oh, Is!" Henry yelled, collapsing to the floor. "Oh, Is! My sister!"

I went to hug him.

"Easy, Henry, be gentle," Cecilia said.

"Soft hug, Henry," I said.

"I know, I know. Soft Henry hug," he croaked out.

I got down on the floor and he reached for me, Cecilia and Janie and Velvet ready to jump in if he couldn't resist a tight hug.

But Henry was gentle, so gentle, his sweet face next to mine as he melted down into his meltdown.

Janie ran to Grandma.

"SOS! SOS!" she yelled. "Help us, help us!"

Being naked after a beating is not a pretty sight. Janie and Cecilia both lost it when they saw me. For once there was no anger from Cecilia, no swearing, but I could feel her misery choking me. "Cecilia," I whispered.

"Don't . . . say . . . anything . . ." Cecilia sobbed. "Nothing . . . I can't handle . . . anymore . . ."

Janie's hot tears fell on my shoulders, her fingers cool, as she helped me with my clothes. I could hear her chanting to herself as she lightly touched my wounds and cuts and bruises.

When I was in a pink flannel nightdress and lying in bed, my sisters crawled in with me and we emotionally unraveled together, holding hands.

I had done this.

I had brought this grief to my sisters.

I brought their hands up to my mouth and kissed them.

Under a moonbeam slanting through my window, my guilt

converged from all corners of my body into my stomach and became a writhing, burning mass.

I had done this.

Oh, how I hated myself.

The next few days did not go well in the Bommarito house. Henry refused to leave for any of his volunteer responsibilities at the church, the animal shelter, Cecilia's school, or the senior center. He refused to go to the bakery. He would not let me out of his sight.

When I took a nap in my bedroom, he stayed with me and quietly played with his marbles or his stamp collection, or he read his comic books.

I would wake up with him anxiously examining my face for any signs of life from about five inches away.

"You okay, Is?" As soon as I said I was, he'd burst into tears and I'd have to hug him and pat his back until his tears stopped running down my neck. "Your face! Your face! That bad man! I get him!" He pounded the air. "I get him!"

During the day when I rested on the porch, he sat next to me and we read his animal magazines together. When I limped around the property, he came with me. We talked about animals and our favorites: favorite color (green), favorite state (Florida), favorite ice cream (chocolate mint).

At night I would pretend to go to sleep as he sang me songs. When he thought I was asleep, he would go to bed, but only after making sure that Cecilia or Janie was with me.

"I love you, my sister, Is," he told me a thousand times, his chin quivering.

"I love you, my brother, Henry."

This was pure Henry: the man simply loved. He loved people wholly, innocently, sweetly. There were no strings, no manipulations, no qualifiers, no arguing, no games, no competitiveness. It was pure, it was everlasting.

He was complaining more about his stomach hurting and I knew it was because he was upset.

I had done that to him. I had done that to my brother.

Grandma's natural courage and pluck and fury boiled over the third day. "I'm going to kill the motherfucker with my plane!" she shouted at me on a regular basis. "Yes, I am!"

She handed me sheets of pink paper about five times a day. "This is the knife I'm going to use!"

There was an extremely unhappy face on it.

"Thank you, Amelia."

"This is the gun!"

Another unhappy face.

"He deserves to die!" she yelled. "The motherfucker. He made you crash-land!"

For a millisecond, her expression sometimes changed, and her old self shone through. "I love you. I love you. I love you." She lightly cupped my pounded face with her hands. "I love you."

I hugged her, her little body so tiny in my arms.

"I must go now!" she announced. "I'm taking off at first light to find the motherfucker!" She ran up to the tower.

I drank a glass of Velvet's lemonade, which she regularly brought me.

"Remember, it's my mother's recipe, sugar peach. When she was poor they sometimes had to eat possum and they always had to have lemonade with it, family tradition. Strong stuff, but it'd hide the possum taste."

Once again, Velvet's lemonade had enough tart in it to blow the ears off a peacock.

The bone-chilling nightmares came at night and during my naps. I even had bone-chilling nightmares when I was awake. Russ Bington was chasing me, giggling, laughing. He put his belt around my neck and pulled. A bat flew out of my mouth and a snake slithered in.

He giggled.

In my dreams I couldn't breathe. He grabbed the mermaid table that Cassandra gave me before she'd jumped off the building downtown and he smashed it on my head. The mermaids tried to protect me, but he still bit me on the neck.

When I felt myself dying, I would wake up, sweating, paralyzed, yelling.

Janie slept with me at night, after she embroidered for about an hour. My yelling woke her up and she'd start yelling, which woke up Grandma, who would start to bellow, "My engine's on fire! My engine's on fire!" and Henry, who would babble, "Momma, Momma, Momma," then hide in the closet.

Velvet would sprint into my bedroom, her flannel nightgown flying behind her. "Gracious me . . . gracious me . . ."

We'd stumble to Grandma's and Henry's room and comfort them. A few times one or both of them wet the bed in fear, so we'd have to change out the sheets, clean them up, put new sheets down and, with Henry, start his good-night routine again, which consisted of milk, a story, a back rub, a hug, and bed.

We were all exhausted.

One morning I found Henry tucked in bed beside me, an orange juice glass on the nightstand, his hand clutching mine. Henry never drank orange juice. That he would even touch a glass with orange juice in it was a first in twenty years.

Henry had good reason for never drinking orange juice. The last time he'd had orange juice he'd been drugged up to his eyeballs and had ended up hiding in a tree from two juvenile delinquents.

I stared at his sweet face, his brown lashes curling on his cheeks. I brushed my fingers through his brown curls.

He had survived many, many traumas. He had learned to laugh again, to be joyful, to trust, to live with gusto and courage. Would I?

I ran my hands through his curls again.

Would I?

She was dressed like a nun.

Kayla held her head high as she reverently touched the giant wood cross laying flat on her chest. She had on a black, long-sleeved shirt and ankle-length black skirt and had somehow created a black veil with a white band across her forehead. When the bells on the bakery door jingled and she, Riley, and Cecilia noisily entered, I had to do a double take.

"Peace be with you," Kayla said to me. She reached out to shake my hand. We shook, my own hand speckled with flour and cinnamon from my cinnamon loaves.

She crossed herself and said, "In the name of the Father, the Son, and the Holy Ghost."

"Peace be with you, you odd child." I turned to Riley, who was wearing a purple headband with rhinestones. "How ya doing?"

"I'm doing well except for I'm going to be bald like a chicken soon." She said this in a funny way, but I saw that broken, quaking hurt swimming in her eyes.

"I like chickens," I told her, hugging her.

"Me, too, but I don't wanna look like one."

When the girls had seen my battered body and my mushed-up face, which by then resembled a beaten-up blowfish, they had been rocked to their cores, which ramped my guilt-o-meter up ten notches.

I told the girls I'd had a bad date.

I believe I've scared them off dating for good.

They cried and cried, cried more, and I felt like the worst aunt who had ever scuttled about the planet Earth.

Janie came out from behind the counter to say hello. She had flour in her hair and a green streak of icing on her cheek.

"Peace be with you," Kayla said, shaking Janie's hand.

"Peace be with you, honey, why are you dressed like a nun?"

"Because I'm thinking that's what God is telling me to be, and I want to make sure that I'm hearing God's voice and not the devil's. He's tricky."

Cecilia groaned and went behind the counter. "I'm going to go and smash challah bread between my hands for a while. You two handle them." She disappeared into the back.

Riley plucked a hair out.

"Do you want a cupcake, Riley?" I asked.

She pulled out another hair.

"I told you not to do that in here, Miss Dreadlock."

She shrugged her shoulders.

"Are you planning on plucking out all your hair?"

"No," she said, her face crumpling. "It's not like I want to do it, Aunt Isabelle. *I have to.* My fingers . . . they're always going up to my hair. I have to feel it and I have to pull it out and I feel better right after I've done it but then I feel like I'm gross, you know, and I know I'm ugly. I am so ugly."

"Honey!" Janie said, reaching out to hug her close. "You need some Yo-Yo Ma and mediation time!"

"You are not ugly, Riley, not at all," I hugged her, too. "You have the Bommarito Family Trait of Disasters and Discomforts. It's a family curse. I get depressed, so does your grandma. Janie counts and obsesses about stuff. Your mother eats. Kayla is trying out religions and is dressed like a nun."

"But I'm a sicko," Riley said, running her hands over her face. "I'll sit in front of my mirror at night and I'll promise myself that I'll pull out only one hair, maybe two, but hours go by fast and I'm still pulling! I can't go to sleep 'til I'm done."

There was silence for a bit.

"Why do you do it?" I asked, gentle, so gentle.

"It relaxes me. If I'm all nervous, by the time I'm done pulling I feel better. But in the morning I feel like an ape, picking away at myself like they pick away at each other's lice, and I'm balding in spots!"

I wanted to cry.

Riley's face crumpled. "All the kids say I'm a freak! A bald freak!"

Kids are so nice.

Kayla stepped up close to her. "I'm gonna pray for you."

"Pray all you want, Kayla," she said, angry. "It's not gonna help. I can't even go to sleep at night unless I pull out my hair."

Then Janie said, "We Bommarito women are all . . . celestially unique, effervescent, flowing . . ."

"We've got a screw loose somewhere," I said, pulling Riley in closer. "And that loose screw keeps screwing us down the generations. So, be weird. Accept your weirdness. Be one with it. And chat with your shrink."

"I don't like my shrink," Riley said, miserable. "Her head is shaped like a cone and her nostrils are the size of the Grand Canyon."

Janie tilted her head to the side. "One of my shrinks spoke to spirits she said were sitting around us. Another believed in reincarnation and she was in her fourth life. I still went."

Riley had refused to speak to two shrinks and had run away from the third. Cecilia had not been able to find her for four hours. That run-and-hide thing ran in the family, too, just like hiding in closets.

"Why did you go, Aunt Janie?" she asked.

"Because I thought I would drive myself insane if I didn't. I love my therapist now. She's soothing and serene, like waterfalls and rainbows, and she doesn't make me feel like I'm an object to be studied. I'm a person to her, not a caseload. I've got issues, she's trying to help me with the issues, but basically she's trying to help me like myself."

"Don't you like yourself, Aunt Janie?" Kayla asked. "God almighty has blessed you. You're a best-selling author and you got a cool Porsche and a houseboat."

Janie thought about that and said, "That's all stuff, Kayla. Stuff doesn't make you happy, but I'm liking myself better since we came to Trillium River. I've actually left my houseboat. It's not easy for me being out of my houseboat, and sometimes I feel like I can't breathe, and I have to hide in the back of the bakery, or count or tap, but I'm doing it. I believe I'm coming into some cosmic peace. Plus I have you two. I love you girls so much."

"Maybe your shrink can give me some of that cosmic peace?" Riley asked.

Janie smiled at her. "I'll call her! Hey! We can shrink-out together!"

"And I'll get you a cupcake," I told her, kissing her cheek. "Chocolate, right? With the shavings?"

Riley nodded, wiped a tear from her eye. "Yeah. Cool."

"Praise the Lord. I'll have the cupcake with the cats," Kayla said. "And don't worry, Riley. I've already beaten up six girls who made fun of you, and I'm good for more."

"Yeah, I know, Kayla." Riley ran a fist over her eyes. "Thanks."

"No problem. I like to get in fights. I'm good at punching. God made me a fighter. Peace be with you all," Kayla said.

Peace be with you two girls, I thought. Bommarito women never live easy lives.

Bao had not responded well when he'd seen my mangled face.

He had brought me dinner several times while I was at home, but we had not seen each other. The dinners were Asian works of art. He constructed a little house made out of noodles for one of my dinners and had created a 3-D design with chopped vegetables for another. I could hardly eat them they were so beautiful.

I watched as his expression morphed from delight at seeing me back at the bakery to devastation.

"I no understand . . ." he said, his voice hoarse. "Your face . . . Ah, Isabelle, Isabelle . . ."

"I'm okay, Bao, I'm okay. Please don't worry."

"Ah, Isabelle . . ." Tears sprang to his eyes before his whole face froze, not a muscle moving. It was as if he was moving to another part of his mind. "You been shot?"

"Bao?" I said.

His eyes didn't blink. His mouth opened a little and he seemed suddenly petrified, as if he were in the midst of his own horror movie. "You been shot."

"Bao!" I said, louder now. "Bao!"

"Attack. Attack." He didn't move, but his mouth closed, then opened and he made low, moaning sounds as his eyes skittered back and forth.

I grabbed his arm when he started muttering in Vietnamese.

Grabbing Bao's arm was the wrong thing to do. He instantly crouched, arms out at the elbow, hands in a karate-like position. He spoke again but the words were chopped and fast, as if he was giving orders. He hunched down.

I instantly let go and threw up both hands up in the I'm-not-going-to-mess-with-you position.

He made a few sharp commands, still in Vietnamese, then got on his stomach.

"Bao," I said, so gentle. "It's Isabelle. You're not in Vietnam. Bao . . ."

One tear trickled from his eye. It dribbled past his nose and off his chin. When it hit the floor, he suddenly lurched up, hands in a defensive position, and limped out.

I saw his profile as he hobbled by the window, mouth open, eyes wide, his expression encased in fear. I took off after him, as fast as I could, which wasn't fast at all because my shin felt like it was splitting again, my ribs, I was sure, were recracking, and my split chin sent jolts of pain to my ears.

Two giant trucks had to rumble out of nowhere, so I had to wait to avoid being turned into a human pancake. For a short, skinny, scared man, he was moving right along.

When the trucks finally moved, I limped down the sidewalk but lost him when he left the main street and shuffled up a hill lined with houses.

When I rounded the corner I caught a glimpse of Bao opening

and shutting a white garden gate. The gate was attached to the side of a triplex in truly stunning disrepair.

On the front lawn of two of the three dwellings, there was trash, a beat-up trailer, an old car with no windows, broken kids' toys, and a creepy guy out front who barely noticed me through the haze of the pot smoke encircling his head.

Bao's side was different. It was the lush gardens of Eden compared to the burning dry desert. His home had a curving rock pathway to the front door. Both sides of the path were covered in flowers and shrubs with two flowering pink trees spreading majestically over the tiny lawn. A white, curving arbor led to the front door.

I limped across the road and opened the white garden gate, my body almost splintering from my venture. I saw Bao crouched behind a tulip tree in his little garden.

"Bao?" I said, coming closer.

He spoke, but it was still in Vietnamese. I could tell he wasn't with me yet, still in his own terrified world. I crouched in front of him and he kicked his feet out at me and put his arms up in that karate style again.

"It's okay," I whispered to him, wiping the sweat off my brow and pushing my braids back. "It's okay." I shivered because this whole thing reminded me of my dad and that calamitous last night when he held a gun to Momma's head, panting just like Bao, crying just like Bao, sweating just like Bao.

And Bao was Vietnamese, so it didn't take a rocket scientist to figure that Bao may have well fought in the same war and fought the same war-demons that had eaten away at my father until my father was too eaten away to father anymore.

Bao spoke again, his body rocking back and forth, back and forth, his eyes frozen in front of him, his hands angled in a fighting position.

The same word kept coming up again and again until it was the only word he spoke.

The word was *run*.

Run, run, run.

"They coming!" he shouted. "Guns! Guns!"

"There's no guns, Bao. We're in your garden. You're safe."

"No!" he screamed. "Hide! Hide!" He yanked me toward him, pushed me to the ground, and shielded my body with his, his body shaking, his eyes gone, his mind back in Vietnam and the bombs and the killings and the blood and the starvation and the attacks that had been made on him, and to the gruesome hell that his innocent life had become.

❦ 18 ❧

I did the best I could at the bakery in the upcoming days, but my body still felt like it had swords sticking through it. I was wiped out from the torture chamber my sleep had become, emotionally shredded by how I'd hurt so many people, and upset about Bao.

Belinda had come in, her mouth squirming around in distress when she saw my face, and refused to take her nap.

She started weeping and wailing and trudged out, shaking her head. Janie ran after Belinda, but she took a swing at Janie, cuffing her in the cheek. That she hit Janie upset Belinda even more and she threw her hands up in the air and dropped a black plastic bag she was carrying. A bottle of jasmine-scented lotion thunked to the ground.

Janie tried to hug her, but she struggled away and ran off, pushing her creaking shopping cart ahead of her, her coat flapping, her boots making squishy sounds, her cat's head with the dirty pink bow bopping above the black trash bags.

It was terrible to watch that scene with poor Belinda, but what I found out inside Bao's little home—and I mean little—had about killed me.

Bao's tiny garden, separated from the others by that white

picket fence, was the same sort of garden an angel would have, I was sure of it.

There was a white trellis overhanging about half of it with pots of flowers hanging from hooks. A glass table and one white chair sat in the middle of a minute green lawn, with two flowering cherry trees and the tulip tree bordering the grass. Flowers and shrubs of all shades and colors bloomed along the border, not a weed to be seen.

He had constructed several little arbors for various vines, their purple and white blossoms half the size of my face. A collection of old watering cans on one fence and a collection of birdhouses on another seemed so . . . artful. Wind chimes hung from hooks and birdhouses from the trees. In a sunny corner, down a teeny gravel path, he had a beautiful rose garden.

But where beauty bloomed outside, inside was dreary, although perfectly clean and orderly.

Bao lived in one room. There was a tiny kitchen, a bed, perfectly made with a blue blanket, and a wood table and two wood chairs.

That was it. Except for three frames hanging on the wall. This was where we sat together, after he'd tackled me, when his eyes finally focused and he returned from the war in his head.

"Is this your family?" I asked Bao, as he drank the tea I poured him, his face drawn. The photo was of Bao and a woman and four children, all smiling, in front of a pretty house with jungle foliage framing the sides.

"Yes, that my wife. My children. My little children. Sweet children. Sweet smiles." His face was bleak, but blank, too, as if agony had sucked out his emotions on this topic.

"They killed in our village. All of them. I in forest when happen. When I come back, our home on fire. No family left." He sighed again. "No family left. Me."

"Oh, Bao."

"They burn the house. They come and burn the village. Whole village. People screaming. People can't find their children. Their mothers. Their wives. My friend, he go in his home through flames to save family. He not come out. I no see my friend again."

I reached for his hand.

"I go to well and get pail and throw water on house to save my family. I can't get in door. It all—" He put his hands in the air. "Fire. No house. All in fire but I use bucket until neighbor come and hold my arms. He said the water not work now. Water not work."

I couldn't even fathom it. What would I have done without Cecilia and Janie and Henry? Grandma and even Momma?

"So many little children in our village. Gone. The soldiers come back and we run into jungle, but I so angry, they kill my family . . . I come out and they . . ." He made a slashing motion against his neck. "They beat me with guns, they break my leg, my hand, they think they kill me, but my neighbor, when they gone, he take care of me."

Although my body already felt crammed with pain, apparently there was room for more, because I felt it then for Bao.

"I help American army. Then I come here. Americans say I live here now because I help save Americans. I come alone. No family left. See my family? So beautiful." He sighed. "My wife beautiful and smart. My little children. Beautiful."

I stayed with Bao for another hour. We went back to the garden after having tea and sat side by side on two rocking chairs painted yellow. We didn't talk, we rocked; we were together, that was enough. What words could comfort anyhow?

The wind breezed through, not in a hurry.

The wind chimes tingled.

The birds sang.

Bao wiped a tear from his cheek.

"I miss my wife."

Another tear rolled down his cheek.

"I miss my children. My little children. I miss them."

I reached over and we held hands.

We rocked as the wind chimes tinkled and the birds sang.

The wind never stopped.

As soon as I joined my sisters on the porch on a sunny, breezy afternoon, they abruptly stopped talking as if they'd been gagged with an invisible rag.

This is never a good sign, folks.

"Morning," I said, my antennae bouncing about like a Slinky.

"Good morning, Isabelle," Janie said. "How are you?" Her face was red and puffy from crying.

"Janie, what's wrong?"

"Isabelle, we're sick of this," Cecilia bit out.

Janie whimpered a little. "Say it nicely, Cecilia. How about if we put on Yo-Yo Ma?"

"No. No Yo-Yo Ma and I'm not going to say it nicely."

"She was beaten up only ten days ago!"

"That's because she invited a strange man to her home, a man she didn't know, wasn't dating, a man whose name she didn't even ask, isn't that right, Isabelle?" Cecilia slammed both hands on a wicker table. "And he nearly killed her. And me."

I had apologized to Cecilia after the attack, until she'd put a tired hand up and said, "Do not say one more word, I can't take it." I had apologized to Janie until she'd said, "No more, no more. Let's have tea. And scones to drink. And eat some Vivaldi. Please."

"Janie and I have always been worried sick about your one-night stands. How could you put us through this?"

"I'm scared for you, Isabelle," Janie whispered. "I'm scared I'll lose you! I'm scared that you'll die next time!"

"And I'm scared that I'm going to kill you myself if you do this again!" Cecilia nearly shouted. "*We need you.* I need you for myself, for my girls, for help with Momma and Grandma and Henry. Janie needs you. She's nuts, and you and I are her only friends. You can't run around risking your life when all these people need you. That pisses me off. You piss me off."

"Cecilia—"

"I don't think I can live without you, Isabelle," Janie whimpered. "You're my light. My positive earth flow and the sister of my being."

"Janie," I whimpered back.

Cecilia was not finished. "You're not on Neptune by yourself and you have a moral obligation to the rest of us to stay alive and well. Is it too much to ask that you curb your sluttiness?"

"You said you would be nice, Cecilia!" Janie accused, wringing her hands. "How about some orange tea?"

"This is nice, dammit! I'm being nice! I haven't thrown anything at her, have I? I haven't said she's selfish, reckless, wild, immoral, always has been—"

"You're being mean!" Janie protested. "Negative karma!"

"It's mean that my nose bleeds twice in one night and my head feels like it's been kicked and my shoulder is burning because she's invited a murderer up to her loft!" Cecilia shouted. "Now that's mean!"

"Hey!"

We all whipped around to see Henry smiling at us from the doorway, his hair messed up from sleeping. He was wearing his favorite railroad pajamas. "Hey!" he said again. "Hey, hey!"

"Good morning, Henry." Cecilia's anger started to evaporate. It always did in the face of Henry. Henry was like Cecilia's hot-water bottle, cozy cup of hot chocolate, and live teddy bear all in one. "How did you sleep?"

"I sleep good. I have a dream!"

"What was your dream about, Henry?" I was going to be saved by Henry. I sank back into a chair with my guilt and my anguish nestled around me tight.

"A frog hop hop." He hopped.

"A frog?" I had to smile. I saw Janie smile, too. Even the corners of Cecilia's mouth turned up. Henry does that to us.

"Yeah, yeah. A big frog. We went to a lake. We went swimming." He mimicked swimming, froglike. "Hey Hey! Janie sad!

Cecilia mad! You sad, Is? 'Bout that bad man? Let's do a Bommarito hug!"

I didn't feel like hugging Cecilia.

She crossed her arms. She didn't feel like hugging me.

"Come on! A Bommarito hug!" Henry laughed, arms out. "Yeah, yeah! Hug!"

Cecilia glared at me. I didn't blame her. I hated me, too.

"Give me a hug!" Henry encouraged. I could tell he was getting hurt feelings. "You no want to give Henry a hug?"

My sisters and I joined the hug, Cecilia scowling at me. Janie smelled like peppermint. Cecilia smelled like chocolate. Henry smelled like hope. He had always been our hope.

We hugged, then Henry started jumping. "We're a frog family. Frog sisters, frog brother!"

I took a deep breath. "I'm done," I told my sisters as we jumped like frogs. "I'm sorry, truly sorry, and I'm done. Never again will I have a one-night stand."

"Good. It's a damn shame it took this long to get your damn act together, dammit," Cecilia said, jumping about. She fisted a tear from her face. Scowled.

"Thank you, Isabelle," Janie said, her ponytail bopping around. "Thank you. My soul is at peace now, my spirit soothed."

So there we were. Three crazy people and one normal person, jumping like frogs.

The normal one being, obviously, Henry.

I was finally brave enough to lay in the grass near the willow tree at night alone again.

The shadowed branches reminded me of all the photos I'd taken of cool trees before I'd quit photography. I'd always had a thing for trees, their symmetry, their shapes, their personality. (Yes, trees have personalities. Look close.) I took a swipe at my eyes and crushed the sadness that bubbled up as I thought of my ex-career that I would not go back to because of what happened.

I rubbed the shoulder that had been hit with a belt. I had been in contact with Detective Walter Carrington and several other detectives and attorneys about Russ Bington. Detective Walter had reassured me that Russ would never see daylight again without wearing an orange INMATE shirt on his back, and if the state of Texas had their way he'd soon be frying in a chair like a scrambled egg in a pan.

He had asked how I was in that gravelly, calm voice of his, and I had told him I was grasping for my sanity but was okay.

Though my bruises were fading and my bones were healing, I was devastated, guilt-ridden, and still scared out of my mind. But, strangely, I was not depressed. I waited for it, waited for the blackness of doom I was so familiar with, but for the most inexplicable reason it didn't come for me.

I was, however, *grateful*.

Profoundly, utterly grateful that I was not buried six feet under the ground. That gratefulness stayed with me pretty much all day long. Although I would not recommend this route for anyone, I had finally realized how much I liked life.

My mirror and I were not on speaking terms for weeks after my attack, but one morning I woke up and stared at myself, particularly my braids. I had lost weight, my face was the color of Silly Putty and purple-green mixed, and my jaw was still swollen as if I'd gained ten pounds in my chin.

But I was still standing. Still alive. That surely counted for something.

I had my hair braided during a particularly grueling assignment photographing the people in a medical clinic in the Congo for a documentary.

Our documentary was on fistula. Fistula is basically when a hole forms between the bladder and the vagina or the rectum and the vagina. This results in a constant leaking of urine and fecal material for the poor woman. In the United States, it's a simple operation and the woman can take herself out and buy a new pair of high heels pretty quick after she leaves the hospital.

Not in the Congo. A lack of medical care means they're stuck with it. Most of the women and young girls at the clinic suffering from fistula had been violently gang-raped, some with foreign objects.

Other women were at the clinic because a long and terrible childbirth caused blood to stop flowing and the tissues to die, poorly done abortions by some witch doctor, and gynecological cancer. In addition, there were girls there who already had several children because they were child brides to some fifty-year-old great-grandfather.

Here, it's rape, punishable by a long jail sentence. There, they call it marriage, celebrated with a party.

The women who had been raped or who had fistula were ostracized from their villages. They were often left by their spouses and families, destitute, crawling in poverty, and forced to sell themselves.

We were there to photograph what was going on at the clinic where doctors and nurses from around the world were performing operations to fix the fistula and helping hundreds of women. The crew was there for weeks, I stayed on for more than a year to help out.

I had my hair braided by one of my best friends there, a nurse named Eshe Mwizi. She had escaped from an abusive husband with her three daughters and now worked at the clinic. I still send large chunks of money monthly to the clinic, and I will for the rest of my life.

My depression, however, lurking throughout my life, grew to this huge monster when I returned from Africa. It shook me around and made me think terrible thoughts until I sunk so far down into an endless, churning tunnel I couldn't get myself out.

I could almost feel my mind snapping, too many horrible stories whispered in my ear in Africa, too many months facing the results of evil and depravity and war, too many memories of my own past to grapple with. My genetic leaning toward depression also did not help.

I was unable, and still am unable, to talk to Cecilia or Janie about it.

My shrink told me to willingly check myself into the hospital for a few days followed by a stint in a restful and expensive mental health place out in the country or he would commit me. He said this pleasantly, but I knew he was one step short of shoving a straitjacket over my head.

And somewhere in the thick murkiness of my depression I knew it was go, head to the hospital, or head to a mortuary, and buy my own coffin.

So I went. I had lots of counseling sessions with groups of people in the same snake pit as me. We made crafts and painted pictures of flowers and strolled along garden paths.

I made friends with an obsessive-compulsive who made Janie seem like she had slight idiosyncrasies, a paranoid schizophrenic who used to be a NASA engineer and gave detailed lectures on the development of the space shuttle, and a bipolar artist named Cassandra, who gave me the mermaid table and later jumped, as I mentioned.

A blond doctor named Brenda Bernard saved my life, and I came out feeling like I was no longer going to follow Cassandra's lead.

I wasn't excited about being hospitalized for depression. The mental illness stigma sticks like tar and feathers to people, which is patently ridiculous. You get help for diabetes, no problem, poor thing. You get help for cancer, what can I do to help you, dear?

You get help for a mental illness? People start to steer clear. They are blockheaded, insensitive, narrow-minded morons who will never get past their own flaming ignorance, but they peg you in a hole, treat you with annoying kid gloves, condescension, and/or like they think you're a weak, perhaps dangerous, eternally sick whack job, unsafe or unhealthy to be around. It's beyond their minuscule minds to accept that people with mental illnesses get better all the time. *All the time.*

My hospitalization had to be done to save my own sorry life.

So I did it.
And I'm still here because of it.
Somebody doesn't like that?
Fuck 'em.

On my way to the bakery the next week, I stopped by a styling salon. I told the gal inside to cut all my braids off. She argued with me because she was young and hip and had a pink Mohawk and a ring in her nose like a bull. "They're awesome . . . so cool . . . like, are you sure?"

I told her to chop 'em off.

She wasn't happy, but she did it.

When I emerged from the salon, my brown hair was short and fluffy and light and curly. I felt like I'd lost ten pounds.

My new haircut didn't do anything for my swollen jaw or my greenish-purplish appearance, but I felt like a new person.

I loved it.

Loved it.

Janie didn't recognize me at first as I stood at the counter, chin down. "I'll be right with you," she said cheerily as she iced a wedding cake that she'd shaped into Mt. Hood because the couple had met on Mt. Hood, in a snow cave, on a group hike, when a blizzard hit. All made it out alive, two fell in love.

"Allrighty, what can I get you?" She smiled as she picked up an order pad. Such a change for Janie, who used to like talking to people about as much as she'd like to take off a toenail with a shoehorn.

I smiled back.

Her mouth dropped and her eyes bugged out like a ladybug.

"Oh my gosh!" she screamed. *"I love it!"*

Henry loved my haircut, too. He hugged me tight and long. "No braids! You still pretty, Isabelle!" He pushed my nose with his finger, lightly. He fluffed my hair.

I have perhaps mentioned that Henry loves. He loves the world. (Except the "bad man" who squished my face.)

He loves butterflies and dandelions. He loves watching geese fly overhead and spiders making their webs. He loves eating cookies and spaghetti and he loves Saturday morning cartoons. He loves the sun and he loves rainy days when he gets to wear his yellow galoshes.

He loves handing out dessert samples and saying, "Jesus loves you."

He loves.

I made an appointment to see Momma and rode my motorcycle to Portland. Part of me was scared to be that exposed after getting attacked, but that's why I did it. To fight the fear so the fear wouldn't twist me into someone else. Someone I could not live with.

Momma was in bed when I saw her, wearing the pink robe and the shawl.

I had previously told her I was sick so I couldn't visit her. She told me my illness was because I was a "poor eater . . . skinny like a scarecrow . . . lazy in my personal health habits," and so on.

"Get over here, Isabelle," she snapped, pulling my face down close. I sat on the edge of her bed. I pretended not to see the ruffled blouse under the robe.

"For God's sakes, what did you do this time?"

I was too tired to lie. She was too smart to believe a lie, even if I wrapped it up in cotton candy. "Bad date, Momma."

She studied me for long seconds, turning my face this way and that, her green eyes missing nothing. "You've cut off your braids. Good. You're not black, you know. This haircut is better. Choppy, a mess of a job, but it's better."

I nodded, exhausted, worn-through, running from my flashbacks of my attack.

A remarkable thing happened then: Something crumpled in Momma's eyes, her face softened, her lips trembled, her chin wobbled, tears sprung out, and she hugged me close. She did not let go for long, long minutes, rocking me back and forth.

I cried into her shawl and she patted my back. "You're going to be okay, Isabelle Marie Bommarito, you're strong, baby, and you're going to make it. By God, you are."

Momma hugged me so rarely and now, with my rainbow face, it made me cry harder, my lungs gasping for air.

One of the times she hugged me tight was after the abortion. She had hugged me because she was falling, in free fall, her pinky fingers slipping from the edge.

She cupped my face with her hands, not bothering to hide a hundred tears. "I'm going to kill the bastard that did this to you."

Bob, The Man in Charge, called Janie and left a sweet message about scones, tea, English gardens. He sounded so nervous. She did not return the call. Too scary.

Each time Father Mike saw me on Wednesday nights, he gave me a hug.

"I knew God would open the door and you'd burst right through it and bring peace to my soul!" he'd declare. Or, "Lord, I thank you for this girl."

Something must have flashed across my face one Wednesday night because Father Mike said, "Isabelle, child, What is it?" Still having the nightmares? The flashbacks?"

Where to start?

Those kind eyes stared into mine.

Waiting.

Not judging.

Kindness swimming around in them.

He saw my hesitation and led me to a pew. The kids were already in their classes, so we had the sanctuary to ourselves. We made small talk, but Father Mike is impatient with that, he likes to get to people's "spiritual essences," so he said, "Share with me, dear girl. Let's talk as the Lord wishes us to talk, with honesty and trust."

And it all came out.

"I hate what I've done in my past, Father Mike. I'm so . . ." I took a deep breath. "I'm so . . . I'm so ashamed. I feel so dirty, like I'll never be clean, never be normal. I wished I'd never done what I've done and now I can't get it out of my head. I hate myself for doing it. I do, I hate myself."

"You hate what you've done in the past? You hate yourself? Lovely girl, lovely girl!" He clasped my hands in both of his. "Lay your shame and the past you hate on the feet of Christ and know this, dear child: God loves you. He understands you. He forgives you."

"No, I don't think so."

Father Mike spread his arms like the wings of an eagle. Or an angel. "Ask and you will receive forgiveness. And then, Isabelle, forgive yourself. Do not hate yourself, do not spend time regretting what you cannot change. No sins are too great for Christ's light."

"Hell, yeah. They are, Father Mike. Mine are."

"Christ is bigger than the sins. God's love is eternal and everlasting. They are the light. Embrace the light, Isabelle. Embrace it."

I bent my head again as so many shameful, demoralizing memories flooded it.

"If Christ had wanted us to wallow in regret, he would have said so. If Christ had wanted us to let guilt rule our past and future, he would have told us. He did not." Father Mike clasped my hands again. "If Christ felt we were unforgiveable, he would not have offered forgiveness. God would not have sacrificed his son for us."

He smiled at me, pure, sure.

"Isabelle Bommarito, I see Christ's light in you shining bright. I see it in the way you bring God's music to the hearts of teenagers. I see it in the way you left your own life to care for your mother, for Henry, for Stella. I see it in the love you have for your sisters. I see Christ's light emanating from you, dear child. *Emanating.*"

I bent my head to our hands and let my hot tears slip through our fingers.

"Isabelle, God is proud of you. Your walk took you away from him, and now, by your own choosing, you are back. The angels of heaven are singing, glorifying in your return. Christ is rejoicing."

I did not resist when Father Mike hugged me, his hand patting my back.

"Welcome back, dearest Isabelle. Welcome back to God's house. We are delighted you are here."

Tears gushed out of my eyes, but in the wash of water, I think, I hope, I believe . . . I saw a tiny glimmer of light.

ᔥ 19 ᔣ

Momma's abortion—dangerous, dirty, cheap—was done by a doctor who'd had his license shredded for molesting women patients when they were under sedation and for a number of botched operations on Long Island millionaires. It not only almost killed Momma physically, it about killed her emotionally.

She hadn't wanted to be pregnant, but then she hadn't wanted to have sex with that rattlesnake at his shack, either. She did it for a trailer so her kids wouldn't freeze.

Not the street many people would have taken, but it's easy to judge someone else when you're not battling a raging depression, single motherhood with a disabled and often unhealthy son, three daughters, no roof over your head, no job, an empty wallet, and you think you may well freeze in winter.

Six months after we came back to live with Momma after the blood-soaking mattress incident, the woman who owned the clothes store Momma worked at divorced her husband because she decided she'd been stuck in a rut for "one decade too many." She skipped off to Italy, deciding to stay " 'til I run out of money."

Momma was out of a job again. Henry had a major allergy attack, followed by pneumonia, which landed him in the hospital. His stomachaches worsened with stress. The medical bills piled on. We had government-sponsored housing and food stamps, but we weren't making it. Momma waitressed during the day, and nights she did second shifts, but Henry's health problems lost her the jobs.

Momma headed to bed again for two weeks and we baked and baked and baked, selling chocolate silk pies, pumpkin pies, and pink frilly cakes on the corner. We started adding our own notes in the margins of the cookbooks next to Dad's. Oddly, it brought me a little comfort. If a recipe could be further perfected, it should be. I had gotten that from him.

On the last day of the second week, Momma got up, brushed her hair, and put on a tight dress. She tried to cover it up under her fraying coat, but I saw it.

I knew what Momma was going to do.

I begged her not to.

She hugged me tight, that hug I remembered.

She wrote us a pink note of what to have for dinner and house-keeping chores we were to do.

I told her I didn't want a stripper for a momma.

She slapped me, that slap I remembered.

It was love and fury, which defined my relationship with Momma.

The slap about knocked my teeth out.

The money started coming in again. The more it came in, the more Momma slipped emotionally. Henry continued to have medical problems: bronchitis, asthma attacks, weird skin rashes, stomach upsets. Cecilia's rash came back; Janie had her migraines.

Momma danced at night and took care of Henry during the day when he wasn't at his own school, unless she couldn't get out of bed, which meant that Cecilia or Janie or I stayed home and missed school.

One night Momma passed out at work, right onstage, and she was carted into an ambulance. She was hospitalized for six days with exhaustion and pneumonia. By the time she got out, a fellow dancer suggested that Henry go into a group foster home.

Momma resisted at first.

But she passed out a few nights later, to the frustration of her boss, a mole-slug of a man, and was transported to the hospital. She finally gave in.

At that point, I believe Momma was an inch from taking her own life. Earlier in the month I'd seen her staring at Drano with a fixed expression. Another time she was leaning a little too far out from our third-floor apartment window.

I caught her as she tilted and hugged her to me. She moaned in my arms for an hour, deep and guttural, done with life.

On several miserable, mind-crushing occasions, wild with depression and remorse, she rasped, "I killed my own baby. I killed him. Do you think it was a boy, Isabelle? Or do you think it was a girl? I told them I didn't want to know, but I do!" She gasped and gasped, like there was no air left in the room. "I couldn't have another child, *I couldn't*. But now I can't bear it that I killed my own baby. Killed it. Killed it. I killed my baby."

I held her and rocked her, then Cecilia would take over, then Janie, who rocked Momma while repetitively counting the objects in any given room we were in.

"A little baby . . . a sweet baby . . ." Momma muttered before we carried her into bed. "There is no more baby . . . no more baby . . ."

I could not imagine Momma having one more child. We, as a family, could not have handled it. But that abortion made mishmash of Momma.

Momma decided shortly after that that Henry was going to a group foster home. We argued with her, but she was resolute in a "I'm about to completely lose it" sort of way.

We gave up fighting with her.

So Henry, at age eleven, went into a group foster home for kids. We were told that he would love it.

It did not go well.
Momma never forgave herself.

The home was officially run by the state and Momma quali-fied financially for help. Then it was considered a modern, new way of handling the disabled and/or "disenfranchised" boys and girls.

We thought that the woman, Thelma, and her husband, Trent, ran it out of their personal home. We thought they lived there full time. We thought they slept there. That was incorrect.

Thelma looked like a man dressed like a woman and the man was grizzled and ugly. Trent reminded me of a molding tank. He smelled like dead sweat and rotten meat.

The day we dropped him off, Henry tried to get back in the car with us.

"No, Henry," Momma said, her bright eyes filling with tears. She was skinnier than I'd ever seen her, she'd aged ten years in two weeks, and her body hadn't stopped trembling for months. There was no life left in her eyes. "Baby, I love you, love you so much." She held his face close to hers. "Love you."

I stifled down the pain that arose like a bubbling volcano at her words. Momma rarely told us girls she loved us, which is why a dozen alarm bells clanged in my brain. I finally grasped the truth: Momma was dropping Henry off at a foster home because she was searching for a place Henry could live in when she was gone, knowing we wouldn't be allowed to care for him ourselves.

Momma hugged Henry long and tight, her tears making her whole face wet and splotchy. She was on the way out the door, speaking from a heavenly perspective.

"You stay here, Henry," I told him, hugging him close. I knew, even as a troubled teenager, that it was going to take all we sisters had to get Momma back on track. "We'll be back in a few days."

"No. No, Momma," Henry said, shaking his head, fluttering his hands. He was wearing his favorite shirt. It had a smiley face on it. It said, "Smile!"

"I go with you. I stay with Momma and Henry's sisters."

"Henry," I said, my voice breaking. "You can still go on your trips. They're going to take you to the doctor's for your appointments and the yellow bus is coming to take you to school. It's only for nine days, Henry. You'll come home weekend after next."

Henry burst into tears.

Janie burst, too.

"Henry," Cecilia said gently. Henry was the only person she was gentle with, the only person she's always, always been gentle with. "It'll be an adventure. You'll like it."

"I no like it here!" he shouted, his face red. "I no like it here. I go home. I go home with Momma! I go with sisters!"

I thought Momma was going to dissolve into the sidewalk, and I held her up on one side. When she sagged further, her eyes checking out even more, Janie grabbed the other side.

Thelma and Trent took charge. They grabbed Henry by the arms as he made a clumsy run for the car.

"He'll calm down," Thelma snapped, her fat underarms swaying like white wings. "He'll get used to it. Don't baby him like this."

"We're not babying him," Cecilia retorted. "It's his first time—"

Henry wailed, then shouted. "I no stay here! I love you, Momma! I love you, sisters. I stay with you!"

Momma sagged further, like her legs were made of oatmeal.

"He's manipulating you," Thelma informed us, her face lined with disapproval.

"Henry never manipulates anyone," I protested. "Never." I hated Thelma and Trent on sight. Stern. Forbidding. I heaved Momma up again.

That Momma didn't fillet Thelma with her words convinced me further that she was almost beyond help. Momma could eviscerate anyone at any time. That her head only wobbled in defeat scared me well beyond one of her raging rants.

I saw two skinny boys hanging around the porch. They both had black hair and brown eyes. There was something eerie and gross about their grins, something weird about the way their fingers never stopped moving, the way their heads jerked back and forth. One of them made a slashing movement across his neck when he saw me staring at him.

"He's manipulating you by throwing a fit," Thelma snapped, wrestling Henry into the house with her husband as he hollered and kicked. "These people need rules and boundaries like normal humans and I can see he hasn't had any."

Momma moaned in my arms as Henry's high-octave scream torpedoed us straight in the heart.

"Oh, shut up!" Cecilia yelled. "He's had discipline. He's scared, can't you see that?"

"Be nice to my brother or I'll kill you!" Janie shouted, her fists clenched.

My head swiveled to her. Janie was so gentle. Later she told me she went home and started thinking violent thoughts that exact day.

"Good-bye, Miss Bommarito," Thelma said with nauseating authority. "I have spoken extensively with the state about your . . . *special situation* . . . and I can handle Henry. I'm taking over. You go home now."

"Momma!" Henry wailed. "Cecilia! Janie! Help me! Help Henry! Help Henry! Is! Is! You help Henry!"

"Pull yourself together, young man. Don't be a big baby," Trent ordered, heaving Henry up the porch stairs. "Dammit," he said as Henry kicked him in his wobbly stomach.

Thelma and Trent hauled Henry in, their grim faces flushed, the boys on the porch laughing and giggling, fingers twisting, while Momma died a slow, terrible emotional death.

We had to keep Momma from killing herself, so we drove her straight to the hospital. I drove. I hardly knew how to drive, but we didn't have far to go. The doctors sized her up, sized up her chart, and admitted her. We told them we were going to our aunt Caroline's. They were too busy to check on that.

On the seventh day we went to get her. I drove home slow. Momma was slightly better, more rested, and had new medicine in hand. She still had that hollow, blank expression plastered on her face, as if she had gone on to somewhere else. How she turned it on for her job, I don't know. But the men weren't there to see Momma's eyes anyhow.

"Hello, Momma," we said.

"Take me home," she rasped out. "How is Henry?"

We tried to stifle the hurt we felt that she didn't ask how we were.

It was one of many stifled hurts.

On Friday we went over to the foster home right at 5:00. Henry tumbled into Momma's arms and they hugged. He hugged each one of us, crying in a way I'd never heard him cry, pathetic, weepy sounds gurgling from his mouth.

"What happened, Thelma?" Momma asked, clutching Henry. She was still trembling, but not as much.

"Nothing happened," Thelma snapped. She crossed her fleshy, age-spotted arms over her cannonball stomach.

"Now, Henry, tell your mother what you did."

Henry's eyes flew open wide. He flung back his head and howled, a howl from the bottom of that poor boy's soul. "I no tell I no tell I no tell!"

Momma's face registered her shock, as did Thelma's and Trent's.

To the side of the house, I saw that those two bony boys with the maniacal grins had their hands over their mouths so they wouldn't laugh.

Henry whipped around to the boys. "I no tell I no tell I no tell!" he shouted at them. "I noooo tell!"

I knew something was going on, but I didn't know what. People didn't talk back then about that type of secret, plus I never even knew that crime existed. It was beyond my imagination.

"I wanted him to tell you, Ms. Bommarito"—Thelma's upper lip arched in disgust—"that Henry went to the zoo with us."

"I no tell! I no tell!" Henry sobbed, clinging to me, eyes squished shut.

"I think we're done here," Thelma said, her disapproval dripping and sticky. "I would like to inform you that we will be imposing discipline on Henry. He may not like it, but he needs it. We can't have him out of control like this. Emotional. Needy. Even *these* people can learn new tricks. They can be trained." She made to shut the door. "Like pets."

"He needs a man's hand, River," Trent said. "A man's hand. Not a woman's weakness, and I aim to give Henry the discipline he needs. Women alone can't raise boys to be men."

"You big fuck—" Cecilia started.

"You watch your mouth, missy," Trent roared. "I can see you're going to take after your mother in your behavior. A husband's gonna have to take a firm hand to you—"

"I'd like to take a firm hand to your face," I said. "Maybe I could slap it back into shape."

"Shut your mouth—"

"Shut yours or I'll nail it shut," Janie whispered. (That line went in her first book years later.)

Trent's eyes popped.

"That's enough," Thelma snapped. "See you on Sunday."

"I don't know if you'll see us on Sunday," Momma yelled over the din of Henry's screams.

"Well, dear, I don't think you have a choice. You have a night job, right?"

Thelma's husband smirked. I saw the way he stared at Momma and I wanted to smack him. "Yes, you're busy nights, aren't you?"

Momma turned red. "Come on, Henry. We're going home."

"I no tell I no tell!" Henry howled, his arms locked around my waist as I tried to reassure him, comfort him.

Impossible.

We went home.

As soon as we got there, Henry started throwing glasses. We

had to duck. We had to hide behind the couch. We had to hide under the table.

Calm, sweet, loving Henry was enraged.

One glass cracked and somehow split Momma's hand open. Blood gushed.

"Blood! Blood! Blood!" Henry screeched, cowering in a ball and covering his head. "Oh no! Blood! *Blood! I sorry Momma! I sorry!*"

To get Henry to go back to the group home on Sunday night, we had to drug him.

"Should we keep him home?" Cecilia whispered Sunday afternoon, before the drugging, while inhaling her fourth ice cream bar.

"He hates the foster home," Janie said, rocking back and forth as she embroidered. "One . . . two . . . three . . . four . . ."

"I know he hates it," I said, clenching my teeth. My nerves were fried, my head ringing from stress. "But what about Momma? I think she's about ready to jump off a roof." I wasn't kidding.

"She still wants to die," Janie sobbed.

"We need to send Henry back," I insisted. "Maybe this week will be better. Momma needs time to sleep during the day and not worry about anything. We may have to take her back to the hospital to stay while we're in school." I paused. "Henry's going to be hysterical or Momma's going to go over the edge. Which is it?"

We drugged him.

Momma put two of her sedatives in his orange juice. When he was asleep, we hauled him out the door and to the car.

Momma's hands were white, trembling doves on that steering wheel and she did not speak.

The weekend had been fraught with Henry's hysteria. He seesawed from tears to rage and back again. We lost five more teacups, and one green and one red beveled bottle to the wall. He clung to us, weeping.

He barely made it to the toilet to defecate. Janie and I had to yank his pants down for him and shove him to the toilet. He screamed, as if it hurt, and told us to "Get out get out get out! Privacy! Privacy!"

We got out.

Later he had diarrhea and told us his bottom "ouched." We kept asking him what was wrong, but he yelled, "I no tell, I no tell!" and we couldn't get anything from him.

We took the sleeping Henry from the car and into his bed at the group home.

Thelma watched disapprovingly from the doorway of his bedroom as Momma limped out, head held up. She did not acknowledge Trent standing there, who we were later to discover went to watch Momma all the time at work.

"Your momma's got good tits," he told us, smirking, when Momma was out of earshot.

"And you have a small dick," I told him. "Flaccid. Weak."

"And a fat ass," Janie added. "Like blubber cannons. I'd like to chop them off with a hatchet." (Line in her second book.)

"Are you related to a pig? Your nose, it's amazing," Cecilia said. "Piglike. Snort for me, would you, you ugly pig?"

Over the next week, Momma relapsed.

She spent all day in bed, dragging herself out to strip at night. She was seeping away from us, minute by minute. I had found a large stash of sleeping pills under her mattress and when I held them in front of her, she moaned again, not speaking, not arguing, moaning.

She told us that she loved us on a Thursday afternoon. We'd gone to the church in town after school and she'd clutched her rosary on the altar as she said her prayers.

It was sad that the love declaration had to come pre-suicide attempt. "You are the only good things I've done with my life besides Henry."

We knew then she was done. Done. She'd given up.

"Momma," Janie said. "Please don't do this. Please don't. What would happen to us? To Henry?"

Momma shook her head and left for stripping, though we begged her to go back to the hospital. We waited at home, wide awake in bed, hoping to hear her key in the lock, panicked that Momma would drive down some curving lane and go to sleep forever.

We found a pink note on the counter. It said, in a shaky scrawl, "I love you."

We drove a weak, almost stumbling Momma to the hospital the next morning, skipping school again. We hauled her in to her doctor. The appointment lasted two hours and she came out clutching two new bottles of pills.

We got the call from Thelma the ugly man-woman at eight o'clock on a Thursday night.

"Henry has run away, young lady. We can't find him." Her voice teetered and I could tell that even she was upset.

My mouth went dry. "What do you mean he's run away?" I yelled. Cecilia and Janie came running in from the kitchen and picked up the other phone to listen in.

"He tried . . ." She stopped.

"He tried what?"

"He wasn't happy when he woke up here on Monday morning and he's been trying to run away since. We had to put him in . . ." She coughed. "We had to put him in . . . in restraints."

"Restraints?"

"What the hell is a restraint?" Cecilia shouted.

"It's a . . ." Thelma faltered. "They're leather straps that go on the wrists and the ankles—"

"What?" We all wailed like banshees.

"You tied Henry down?"

"You put leather straps *on Henry?*"

"I'm calling the police!"

"We already did," Thelma said. "They're looking for him." She muttered, "God help me."

I turned to the window. It had rained all day. It was still raining. Shadows swished and shifted. And Henry was out there by himself. Soaked. Scared right out of his sweet mind.

"How long has he been gone?"

"I'm not . . . we think hours . . . we're not sure . . . Someone took the straps off him, they must have. It wasn't me."

"What do you mean you don't know? He's in your house! Weren't you watching him at all?" Cecilia shrieked. "What if he had to pee? What if he had to shit? What if he was scared to death? Dammit, you fat cow, how long was he in restraints for?"

There was silence on the other end.

"How long?" I yelled.

"We have to restrain these retarded people sometimes so they don't hurt themselves, they can be animalistic in their behaviors . . ."

"How long?" Janie demanded. "Tell me or I'll come over and slash your face with my pocketknife." (Line from her third book.)

"We can't let retarded people have the same freedoms as normal people, they're not normal, they need to be handled . . ."

"I am going to handle you, you stupid bitch." I could hardly suck in air. "Now how long was it?"

Thelma sighed. "He was in restraints twice. Once for ten hours because he wouldn't calm down, then a break. He had a temper tantrum about two o'clock in the morning on Wednesday, so we had to put him in restraints again."

My head swam. "But you checked on him at night—you stayed with him, right?"

A long pause. "Well, no. My husband and I say good night to the boys and then we go to our home next door to sleep."

"You don't sleep in the same house?" I said, fighting a wave of nausea. "Henry was left alone, *tied down to a bed with leather straps?* Is that right?"

There was no answer.

I felt sick.

"You're going to regret this," I told her. "You are so, so going to regret this."

I hung up. Cecilia slammed a fist into the cupboard and cracked it. My hand instantly ached. Janie folded in on herself and fell to the ground, fingers twitching.

I called the police because I didn't trust that Thelma had actually done it.

Miraculously, they already knew about the case and were organized and searching for Henry.

Our next call was going to be much, much worse.

One minute later I had the strip club on the line. Cecilia hit the cupboard again, the fake wood split, and the bones in my hand felt like they'd cracked. "Stop it, Cecilia!" I told her, holding my fingers. "Stop it!"

A man picked up on the twentieth ring. "I need to speak to River Bommarito."

"She's dancin', can't talk now."

"I *have* to talk to her."

"Call back later."

"I can't, it's an emerg—"

"She ain't comin' off that stage."

The dial tone zinged in my ear.

Janie groggily sat up with Cecilia's arm bracing her back.

"Momma's not home for another six hours. We have to go and tell her," I said. "She needs to know."

We breathed deep.

"On the count of three," Janie moaned. "One . . . two . . . three . . ."

We all turned at the same second, grabbed our coats, and stumbled through that front door as if we were being chased by a band of Satan's terrorists.

* * *

We ran through all the shifting shadows of the night to the strip joint, the rain drenching us straight through. In the distance I could hear thunder, with lightning forking through the electrified blackness.

It was named "The Gentleman's Club." The doorway had a hint of an Asian influence with a semi-elaborate arch and two fake trees in front. Obviously, there were no windows.

But, as always in these places, there were not any gentlemen inside. Not that I'd been in one, but I knew it, even as a kid: Gentlemen do not go to strip clubs.

We panted as we raced to the back of the building, knowing there was no way anyone would let us in the front. We tried one door and the next, but they were locked.

I bit my mouth until I tasted blood. I was so furious I cried.

"Stop crying, Isabelle!" Cecilia hissed at me, even though tears were running down her own cheeks. "You baby."

"Shut up, Cecilia."

"No, you shut up."

"Both of you shut up," Janie told us.

We waited for a back door to open, and the second it did we slid into the shadows, then slipped into the building like ghosts.

The door clicked behind us, the corridor lit by a single bulb. We heard women chattering in a room to our right, and I edged myself around the corner. It was the dressing room. I saw three women, all in various states of undress, their hair teased out, makeup heavy, cheap perfume wafting out, but no Momma.

We sneaked along the cement walls, the smell of decades of smoke and alcohol and hopelessness and moral depravity clinging to them.

Maybe there was another place Momma would be? Another dressing room?

We rounded another corner and landed about four feet from the stage. The spotlight shone down, some silver ball spun on the ceiling, men hooted and hollered, the music pounded, and there was Momma, made up, a long blond wig on, swinging around a pole, almost completely naked, only a sparkly sash wrapped around her body in strategic places, with a ton of money stuffed in a tiny G-string.

Janie burst into tears.

Cecilia made a gagging sound.

I wrapped my arms around myself, suddenly freezing cold. And sick. I felt sick. Disgusted. Humiliated.

A ball of blackness ping-ponged through my brain. Even then I recognized my depression, roarin' on in.

❧ 20 ❧

Momma slithered down the pole for a grand finale, tossed off the sparkly scarf, stood with her shoulders back, and bent to bow.

I turned away and bent over double. I felt like I'd been hit in the gut with a two-by-four. Cecilia motioned me to grab the other side of Janie because Janie's eyes were shutting, eyeballs rolling back, her knees giving out. I knew she was shifting into faint mode.

We caught Janie and propped her up against a smoke-infused wall down another creepy corridor. She made weak panting sounds, as if she were drowning in shock.

Once I had her propped, I laid my forehead against the rough wall of that smoky hallway, too.

I wanted to kill those men.

I wanted to die.

And, for a flash, I'll tell you this: I hated my momma. I had hated her many times, especially for the stripping, but seeing it was another thing altogether.

But along with the hatred and the searing anger, I recognized another emotion, one she would hate knowing I harbored: pity. I pitied my own momma for the gritty, dirty nightmare her life had become.

And, in one corner of my selfish teenage brain, I knew this: She was doing it for us.

When Janie was woozily standing upright again by herself and Cecilia had quit swearing and hitting the wall with her fist, and I didn't feel shock cruising through me like liquid bile, we scuttled back into the dimness of the hall and hid in a tiny alcove about four feet down from the dressing room, closest to the outside door. Momma would kill us when she saw us, but at least she would never, ever know that we had seen her up on that smoky stage.

Momma grabbed me by the ear and hauled me out of the Gentleman's Club. I stumbled along behind her, worried my ear was going to be ripped right off my head, as she hollered at the three of us at once.

"I am going to tan your hides!" she shrieked. "You have done some stupid things, but this is the stupidest! I am so angry at all of you I could spit! In fact I think I will spit! Dammit! This was your idea, wasn't it, Isabelle!"

She unlocked the door of our old, beat-up car and shoved me in before I could utter a word. She had taken one stricken look at us in the hallway of that strip club and had started yelling, throwing a sweatshirt and jeans on, but not before I saw the abject horror, the searing shame in her expression.

I hit the top of my head on the way into the car but scrambled over the seat as quick as I could. Cecilia and Janie dove into the back. Janie was hiccupping she was so upset, and Cecilia was muttering swear words.

Momma's hands shook as she tried to turn the key of our old clunker. The engine didn't turn over, not once, but twice.

"Shit shit shit!" She wiped the tears rolling out of her eyes with both hands. "Shit!"

"Momma . . . Momma," I waved my hands and shouted. "Momma!"

"You shut up! I am taking you home and we will discuss this later! I have to be back in twenty minutes or I'll lose my job!"

"Momma! Momma!"

She closed her mouth for a millisecond at my high-pitched scream. I took a deep breath. This was going to level Momma, I knew it. Level her flat. "Henry's gone."

"Wh-What?" Even in the dim light, rain pouring down the windshield, I could see her face. It drooped, her mouth going slack. "What do you mean Henry's gone? He's not gone! He's at the home."

"Yeah, Momma, he is, he is gone," Cecilia said. "The police have been called. He ran away."

I swear to this day that twice we took corners on two wheels on the way to Thelma's as Momma yelled and swore. Her depression still enveloped her like an avenging spirit, but her instinct to save her child overrode it.

Thelma, the man-woman, met us at the door, snuffling, her nose running, her blue robe stained. Trent stood behind her, tanklike, stale smelling and pale. About six policemen were also there, the blue and red lights flashing over their cars.

"What the hell happened, Thelma!" Momma spat out, ignoring the policemen. "Isabelle said you had my boy in leather restraints and that you tied him to the bed! Is that true, *you bitch*, is that true?"

Thelma put her chubby hands over her face.

"Is it, ma'am?" the policemen asked, perplexed. "Was the boy in restraints? You never mentioned that. Neither did you," he accused Trent. The officer glared at them.

"We had to put him in . . ." Thelma cleared her throat. Trent poked his wife in the shoulder. I didn't miss that, nor did anyone else.

I wanted to shoot them. Kind, loving Henry, in leather restraints, held down to a bed, alone. It about blew my mind.

"Answer my question!" Momma barked out. "Did you have my boy in restraints?"

She nodded. "I had to!"

Trent roughly shook his wife's shoulder. "Close your mouth. Keep it closed. We're gonna need a lawyer."

Momma can move fast when she wants to, and she had that woman on the floor, her fist pounding that woman's nose before you could say, "That woman's gonna get beat to a pulp."

Cecilia and Janie and I let her do her thing. When the police officers jumped in to pull Momma off, we girls waited only a flash before Cecilia took on Thelma and Janie and I took on Trent.

Within minutes the entry was filled with cops who were pulling livid, pounding, kicking Bommarito women off those two scummy, worthless, abusive losers.

I knew those two boys had something to do with this, and I told the policemen, who then questioned those rats.

"He was hollerin' 'cause he was in the leathers," one of them said, that weird gleam in his eye. "He was noisy, but we didn't do nothin' 'cept our homework, that's it. Then we played Ping-Pong downstairs."

I did not miss their snickers, or the smirks they exchanged.

"He's retarded, okay? He's a stupid shit. All he did was cry while he was here and say weird stuff."

Two policemen grabbed me in midleap when I tried to get at that psycho-jerk.

"Did you take the restraints off," the police asked.

The boys were cagey, giggly.

"No," the younger one said. "The retard got out. Maybe he retarded himself out, you know? He's like an animal. I had a dog smarter than him." They wriggled their fingers again.

"Stop talking about Henry like that," a tall policeman with a grizzled face ordered.

"Why? He ain't got any brains. He ain't normal. Shouldn't have ever been born. Should have been killed, you know, when it was still in the mommy's stomach. Like, with a knife."

That produced another chaotic scene. Even Momma tried to get at him, her rage an unstoppable force, the boy's comments hitting too close to home in more ways than one.

Cecilia succeeded in wrapping her fingers around one of their necks, and Janie, skillful Janie, got on the ground and crawled through the mayhem, then kicked at his crotch. He doubled over.

I did not mean to hit the police officer in the chin; I was aiming for one of the psycho-jerks who seemed to find my rage funny as he laughed and laughed. When he choked on the tooth I knocked out of his jaw he stopped laughing.

As I was manhandled out of the room none too gently, the other creep made a slashing movement across his neck toward me.

I flipped up my middle fingers. "You will die!" I shouted. "You will die."

When Momma, bordering on complete hysteria, was pleading with the police to "find her boy, please, find him," we snuck off into the night. We were soaked again, in minutes, the lightning flashing, thunder booming, shadows threatening.

I then understood the meaning of, "It was a dark and stormy night."

But no one had ever mentioned the white-hot fear that went along with it.

We searched for hours, my sisters and I, in the rain, our figures outlined by the forking lightning, the thunder splitting the earth.

We turned away from the foster home, the police cars and ambulances and searchers, and from Momma, who was getting a shot from a medic.

It was three o'clock in the morning.

"Where would he have gone? Which way?" Janie moaned, asking the same question we'd asked again and again.

"We have to be Henry," I insisted. "The second he was free from those restraints, he would have run," I said.

"He might have run out the front door, but the back door was a possibility, too."

We stood at the back door, the wind howling through the trees.

"And if he had run out the back door, he would have been running into blackness."

"Henry doesn't like nighttime, but if he was trying to hide, he would have run toward it anyhow."

"And he would have run straight until he couldn't run anymore."

We started to jog, yelling back and forth through the cacophony of the weather.

"He would have run 'til he fell . . ."

"And he probably would have curled up and fallen asleep."

"He does that when he's scared or upset."

"Yeah, he takes a nap."

We ran about ten feet apart from each other, our feet sloshing through the mud.

We crossed a field behind the home, hopped a fence, and ran through columns of fruit trees. We shouted his name and our names, so he would know who we were. We kept running until we were a little bit tired because that's when Henry would have stopped running.

"This is about as far as he could have gone until he couldn't run anymore."

The wind wrapped around us; the rain poured down.

We had stopped in the middle of a farmer's yard and we yelled again, our voices seeming to carry on the wind, blending with the howl. A lightning bolt split a tree and we all jumped, then hit the ground.

When we could breathe again, Janie yelled at me, "Where would he go from here?"

We searched the blurry horizon.

There were lights on in the houses lining the field, and a farm-house in the distance.

"He wouldn't go to one of those homes."

"No, they're strangers."

"The strangers he was with had tied him down."

I felt my stomach boil with liquefied fury.

"He would be tired now."

"He wouldn't even be thinking."

In the distance, I could see a tree. It was one of those big, leafy trees. "Henry loved trees," I said.

"He loves the tree in front of our apartment. He's there all the time," Janie said.

"At night, since he's scared, and running, he might have thought it was the same tree," Cecilia said.

We took off at a dead run, straight across the fields. The ground grew muddier and soggier, the rain pounding down in sheets, soaking every inch of us, and we still ran.

When we got to the tree we screamed his name, so hopeful that he would be under those sweeping branches, somewhat safe, curled up, sleeping.

There was no Henry.

We collapsed against the rough trunk of the tree, defeated. I beat down the panic that kept rising and rising in my chest.

We had to find Henry.

I could not live without Henry.

I don't think any of us could.

"Henry!" Cecilia screamed, her head back. "Henry! Henry!" Her screams got coarser, the screech of some wild thing, only the wild thing was my twin sister, and her raw pain wrapped itself around my heart and squeezed. I put my hands over my ears to shut her out.

No, we could not live without Henry.

"Henry!" My shout was as primal, bare, and lost as Cecilia's

In the silence we heard the raindrops on the leaves, Janie's incoherent pleas, Cecilia's choppy panting.

But then . . .

A small noise.

Low and deep.

I froze, sure an animal was above us in the branches.

Cecilia and Janie heard it, too, and we all grasped hands and backed away.

It moved.

But it was wearing a brown sock and jeans and a black T-shirt with a picture of a white cartoon cat on it.

It was Henry. Way up in the tree, between two crossing branches.

"Henry go home," he said, his voice broken, crackling with misery. "Henry go home."

The three of us propped Henry up between us and carried him across the field.

He wouldn't speak, his tears mixing with the rain, an occasional lightning bolt highlighting the field.

When he saw Momma, at first he wouldn't hug her, wouldn't let her hug him. I could feel my heart thudding, watching that scene. I so wanted Momma to hug me, and here Henry was, rejecting her hugs.

"I mad at you, Momma. I no like that place. Henry go home."

"Henry," she choked, "Henry, you're going home. You're not going back. Not ever. You're coming home."

"Okay, Momma. Okay."

He let her hug him. "Bommarito hug," he said, weakly, pathetic. "Come on, sisters. Bommarito hug. I love yous."

We stood together and hugged.

It was only the beginning of yet another tragedy.

"He was repeatedly raped."

The white walls of the hospital seemed to squish in on me at the doctor's words.

"He has old wounds, and new ones. I'm sorry."

The police officers and the doctors and nurses in the conference room with me, Cecilia, Janie, and Momma all disappeared in my mind as the walls squished and squished until I could barely breathe, until I could see the doctor's mouth moving, opening and closing, but I couldn't hear any other words.

I couldn't hear anything at all, actually. Nothing. It was as if I were in a white, soundless box with people moving frantically all around me and I was disappearing into the white along with all the noise.

I saw Momma clench her fists and she opened her mouth and her head fell back and I was sure she was screaming, but I couldn't hear anything. I saw two nurses hold her as she slumped to the floor, her face a twisted mask of grief and fury. The nurses and the doctor picked Momma up off that white floor, her head thrown back, her fists clenched to her eyes.

Two nurses sprinted in with a stretcher and lifted Momma onto it. She struggled, her arms out toward Henry's room, and I watched her mouth form the words, "Henry, Henry," but in my mind, she was doing it in silence, the white walls sucking up all of the noise as if everything she said and did and screamed and banged was being sucked out through a funnel.

I saw Janie fall backward, the police officer behind her lifting her up, two doctors rushing to her. Their mouths were open, flapping, I knew they were shouting, but I couldn't hear a thing.

I saw Cecilia whip around and slam her forehead against a wall. A hollow ache immediately formed in my head. A police officer and a doctor manhandled Cecilia away from the wall. She arched her back and whipped her head around to me and her tears and the blood from her forehead hit me in the face.

They took her away, too.

Soon I was left alone with the squishing white walls.

It was silent.

* * *

Henry never went into a foster care situation again.

He wouldn't talk to us or to the police about what happened.

It was only when I told the police, in front of Henry, about the two snarky, demented boys at the foster home and Henry started chanting repetitively, continually, "I no tell I no tell I no tell no kill sisters no kill sisters, no kill Momma, no please, no please, no kill Henry's sisters!" that Cecilia, Janie, and I knew we had our rapists for sure.

The policemen shared a glance and headed out.

Momma did not leave Henry's side for a week. We stayed home from school. When it was pretty clear that Momma was going to lose her job at the club, we baked and baked, selling our cookies, pies, and cakes door to door, to teachers at school, outside a church on Sunday mornings, in front of the library.

We remembered to sift flour twice, to drizzle with a light hand, and to never, ever overcook, like our dad had taught us.

We did okay moneywise, not great, and we didn't even attempt to pay any of Henry's hospital bills, but we did okay.

As for the boys who we knew had raped Henry?

They caved within minutes. When I was older, I read the transcripts. They said they raped Henry themselves and with pencils and one time with a screwdriver. "He drove me to do it because he wouldn't shut up," one said. "He kept begging for his mommy and his sisters. What a baby. I had to put two socks in his mouth to keep him quiet. *Two socks! Not one, two!*"

"We were having fun with him," the other said. "He's a retard, okay? What does he know about what's going on? His face was in the pillow. He liked it. I'm telling you, he liked it. Plus, who's ever going to have sex with him? We did him a favor. Now he's not a virgin. He's a fag."

Momma got herself an ambitious, young female lawyer, eager to prove herself in what was then a man's world, and she sued the foster home and the state. Henry was unable to testify, but the doctors did. The police did. And a fourth boy who was in the foster home testified, too, as he had also been attacked by the boys.

Trent's record as a child molester didn't help the state's case, nor did the fact that he and Thelma always slept in the home next door to get a good night's sleep, despite their assurances that was not the case.

Add in the boys' candid confessions, repeated as if they were proud of themselves, and it was a done deal. The boys went to a residential center for young male criminals until they were twenty-one, then were transferred to a prison for five more years.

About twenty years later a book was written on the horrid conditions of that residential center for boys, and the author, who had been there the same time as Henry's rapists, made tons of money.

Momma won a huge settlement against the foster home and the state. All Henry's past medical bills were paid for by the state and the Veterans who were finally brought in. The young attorney started her own firm and continues, to this day, to prosecute the worst, most dangerous criminals.

So we got victory, financially, but the whole incident had eviscerated any emotional strength Momma had left. She was done.

Completely, utterly done.

"We're going home," she told us one night, her checks in her trembling hand, her body frail and worn down, her mind shot. "We're going home to Grandma. Pack up, girls."

Packing up took about twenty minutes, because that's all we had left of our lives. Our car broke down halfway to Trillium River, and Momma wrote a check for an only slightly used van that started the first time Momma turned the key. The engine purred. We thought it was the most beautiful thing we'd ever seen. We were so comfortable in the padded seats, I remember thinking it would be just fine to live in if we had to.

On the way there we stayed in hotels with pools and went out for hamburgers and shakes twice. Momma bought us new clothes.

She bought Janie an embroidery set, Cecilia books, Henry a new checker set, and me a camera. We felt we were in heaven.

Grandma's Queen Anne house was a safe palace. She instantly proved to be a stable—if cranky—force. We went to school; Grandma helped with Henry, who had stopped speaking completely; and Momma went to bed.

When Momma got up two months later, she used part of the settlement money to open the bakery.

It was rape money in my mind, but we had to use it.

⤙ 21 ⤚

I hopped on my motorcycle and went to visit Momma one afternoon later in the week. My nightmares continued, my fear continued, my depression continued to slither around the corners of my mind like black ink, but I was functioning. I was proud of that. Sometimes, I think, we have to praise ourselves for simply functioning. Simply getting up to try out another day.

I called ahead to schedule with Momma. I knew from Sinda that she'd been at Bunco Club that morning before her girl gang went out to lunch.

"Well, I'm weak," she told me over the phone, her voice teeny, tiny, tiny. "Bone weary. I haven't been out of bed for days. *Days!* I have called the doctor and discussed my health with him and my lack of progress."

I tried not to laugh.

When I arrived she was in bed, her robe on, lights dimmed, the curtains pulled against the bright sun.

"Momma?" I said. "Momma?"

Her eyes were closed. Slowly, she opened her lids.

"Isabelle," she croaked out.

"Hello, Momma." I bent down to kiss her forehead and stifled my laughter.

"Be careful with me. I ache all over. I've hardly been able to move."

"I am so sorry to hear that, Momma."

She opened one eye. "Your face is not as bad as it was, Isabelle." She actually reached out and held my hand.

I was touched.

"Every time I think of what that man did to you I want to kill him, and every morning when I wake up and I know he'll be electrocuted soon, I'm glad. Damn glad." She cleared her throat. "You're a pretty woman, Isabelle. A good woman."

"Thank you, Momma." We sat there for a minute together, and I basked in such rare mother love.

"You're too skinny, though." She speared me with those emeralds of hers. "Stickish. Scarecrowish. Put on some weight. Cecilia's still fat, I've told her she needs to reduce, and when Janie was here—oh—that *tapping!*" She rolled her eyes. "And that counting! Not from my side of the family, I'll tell you that!"

Well, that did it. I had to stick it to Momma a wee bit. I am such a *bad* daughter. I cleared my throat. "Momma, there's something I've been needing to talk to you about." I breathed in deep. "We need you to come back and work at the bakery—"

Momma's eyes flipped open and she sat up in bed as if a spring had binged her back. "That is out of the question!" she huffed. "Haven't you heard a thing I've said? Have you gone deaf, Isabelle Bommarito? Deaf? Have you?" She coughed a couple of times, squeezed her eyes shut as if fighting a tsunami of pain, and fell straight back to her pillows.

I bit my lip.

"I'm sick!" she rasped. "The doctor will never release me from this boring rat hole in my condition. Never."

"But we *need* you."

"You'll have to stick it out, Isabelle. You and your sisters. I've worked hard for years." She flushed with anger. "Surely you three can do the work of only me? Can't you girls do that?"

"It's hard, Momma—"

"Life is hard, suck it up!"

Me oh my, how I almost laughed out loud.

"Momma, I can tell this visit is tiring you out. Go to sleep. I'll sit right here by your bed until you're asleep."

"Oh God, no!" she barked, eyes flying open again. "You are *not* going to stay here."

I shoved down the laughter comin' on up in my throat. I knew that in minutes she was leaving to see *Phantom of the Opera* in Portland after dinner downtown. Momma had always, *always* wanted to see *Phantom*. As long as I could remember. She knew all the words to all the songs.

"Oh sure, Momma. Sleep. I'll sit right here. I have nothing else to do."

She pierced me with those bright eyes. I tried to pretend I did not see her red silk blouse below her pajamas. Poor woman. She'd probably had to throw that nightgown over her head in such a rush when she heard I'd arrived.

"You are *not* staying. I will not have my daughter staring at me while I sleep. Go home, Isabelle. I can manage here by myself. All alone."

She flopped back down on the bed, sighing, her eyes shut. She cleared her throat. She coughed.

"Okay, Momma." I paused. Oh, how I loved to torture her. "Are you sure, though? I would like to stay. I'll be so quiet—"

"Young lady, you leave right this minute. Right this minute. Do you hear me?"

I sighed. "Okay, Momma." I bent down and gave her a kiss and said good-bye.

I left the room, then opened the door in the hallway to a linen closet and stepped in. I cracked the door a tiny bit. About three minutes later I saw a group of older people laughing and chatting as they trooped down the hallway. They were dressed up in suits and sparkles and stopped in front of Momma's door and knocked.

The door whooshed opened and Momma stepped out, resplendent in a lovely, shining, purple dress and lace shawl that I had never seen before. Sinda said she had been shopping . . .

"Beautiful, River, beautiful!"

"Bravo!" one of the men shouted. "Bravo!"

Momma smiled. It made my heart ache. I had so seldomly seen Momma smile with such abandon and joy.

"Ready?" she asked. She gave each person a sheet of paper. "I have the CD for *Phantom* in my purse and we can all sing along in the car . . ."

"Oh, wonderful idea, River!"

"Perfect! I am the Phantom . . ." one man sang, baritone. "The phantom of the operrrra!"

I clamped my hand over my mouth. When I was sure Momma was gone, I let my laughter roll.

I wondered if we'd ever get her back to Trillium River.

Several days later Henry had to go and lie down because he said he was sleepy and had a "tummy ache."

"When I goes like this," he told us, leaning a little forward, "it hurts. But when I goes like this," he leaned back, "I feels better."

He was upset because he had planned to go to the animal shelter but we couldn't let him go.

"The dogs needs my love!" he protested.

"Yeah? And so do I, big guy. Come on, I'll read to you. We'll read your favorite books."

"Okay! Dokay!" He smiled and we went upstairs. "You pretty, Is."

I thanked him. I noticed he wasn't moving with his usual pluck. I telephoned the shelter and told them Henry wasn't coming in.

"Well, that's a shame," Paula Jay, the supervisor, said. She is an ex-prosecuting attorney, about sixty-five years old, and the angel of all animals.

"We love Henry! Why, last week we had two pit bulls dropped off that had been used for fighting. They were scarred and scared and jumpy. Why do men make dogs fight? We should lock those men up in a pen and make them attack each other, horrid, horrid people. Anyhow, where was I?"

"The pit bulls."

"Oh, yes. So these pit bulls' teeth had been filed down so they could be used as bait for other pit bulls. Do you understand what I mean, dear? Other pit bulls would go and attack these two, but they couldn't fight back because their teeth were filed down to almost nothing. Those poor, poor dogs, I would like to take a hammer to those men's teeth! Oh! Where was I?"

"The pit bulls."

"Yes, so we thought we were going to have to put them down but then Henry, your Henry, he came in and sat at the edge of their cage. Those two dogs backed right into the corner, barking and whimpering. But Henry, oh my stars, your Henry, he kept talking and singing and on the third day Henry got down on his stomach and the dogs came over and they went nose to nose. Now, when Henry comes in, glory be, those dogs jump up and down, they're so happy to see him. In fact, we're not going to put the dogs down now because we know we can place them in a home someday, oh my stars! Why do men make dogs fight? I wish I could sterilize all of them like we do to the dogs, only without anesthesia, that would calm them down. Now where was I?"

"Henry."

"Yes, a dear boy and we'll miss him today. Give him my love, will you? We'll see him soon."

I assured her I would and we clicked off.

Everyone loves Henry.

"Stay, Isabelle?"

"Sure, Henry. I'll always stay with you."

I kissed his forehead.

I waited until he was asleep before I put another blanket over him. I watched him, his mouth open, his slanted eyes shut.

"I love you, Henry, my brother," I whispered.

* * *

Baking birthday cakes was another forte of the Bommarito Sisters.

For a kid who wanted a normal cake, he could skip on down the street to the local grocery store. But if he desired a cake to end all cakes, with some jazz and a little raz-a-daz, we were the bakery for them.

We made yellow-and-orange gecko cakes and panda bears in pink aprons and ladybug cakes with licorice antennas.

A man with spiked hair wanted a cake in the shape of a guitar for his bandmate, and a lady needed a special cake for a girls' weekend away so we'd made a giant cake in the shape of a wine bottle. The name of the wine was "Women Rule."

A local newspaper ran photos and we were overrun with orders.

School got out and Cecilia came to work full time. If she hadn't, we would have had to hire two more people.

Bommarito's Bakery was booming.

Momma would undoubtedly give birth to a bleating cow when she saw the changes we'd made.

"Who is that?" Janie asked, peering out the window of the bakery. "I saw him yesterday and the day before."

"I don't know," I said.

The booths and tables in the bakery were filled. Saturday mornings had turned into a small mob scene. All we'd done is offer free coffee with the purchase of a treat. Any treat. Momma would have a bleating cow over this, too.

Bao was in the back making lemon bars with powdered sugar with Belinda. We had given her simple, repetitive tasks, and she did them well. Bao treated her gently, kindly, and Belinda loved him. She'd been scared at first at the thought of a job, but then had calmed down. She muttered here and there, took a nap at ten o'clock on the dot, but was actually a steady, smiley worker.

We had a largish room above the store with two windows and a bathroom we'd given to Belinda once we got our acts together and took a second to lift our heads out of the sand and help someone besides our own sorry selves.

We brought in a refrigerator, a comfy couch, two padded chairs, a TV, rugs, pillows, a few lights, a table and four chairs, and we shoved a twin bed in the corner with a red-and-yellow bedspread. We did not buy a stove or a microwave—sounds callous, but we were afraid that Belinda would burn the building down.

We brought her upstairs one day after she finished icing eighty cupcakes for a company party.

"Would you like to live here, Belinda?" Janie asked.

Belinda's mouth dropped open. "Here?"

"Yes, here."

Her face lit up. "It beautiful!" Her face sagged. "I don't have no money."

"Yes, you do," I told her. "You have a job now. You work for us and you can live here and we'll give you extra money, too, for food and clothes and cat food."

"Joe can come, too?" she asked hopefully.

"Joe can come."

Joe the mangy, ragged cat with the dirty pink bow, who Janie sneaked off to a pet boutique for a wash when Belinda was working. I reminded myself to get another bow for the cat.

Janie and I prodded her into the shower that day. When she got out, we handed her a new pair of jeans, a T-shirt and sweatshirt, new shoes, and socks. We put her other new clothes—jeans and pants, shirts, two sweaters, socks and undies, tennis shoes, and a jacket—in a chest of drawers. We took her old clothes with us and threw them out.

She had her shopping cart, so we helped her sort through that and threw it all out when she turned around. She never missed it. We left her holding Joe, watching a soap opera.

Her face told me all I wanted to see: She had found peace.

So Belinda and Bao worked and we stared at the man.

"I've seen him before," Janie said. "The White-Haired Dove."

That's how I think of him because of that thick white hair. I saw him staring at the house a couple of times . . ."

"Let's go meet the White-Haired Dove," I said.

But it wasn't necessary for us to go to him.

He was a tall, lean man, and he came to us, limping.

It turned out that he was our history, on feet, with the gentlest of gentle smiles on his face.

I remembered that gentle smile.

Lines fanned out from the corners of his eyes below a grooved forehead. The scar cut through the right side of his face. Life had beaten him up and spit him back out, that was for certain. He was still a handsome man in a toughened-up, roughened-up way, and when those brown eyes filled up with tears, I knew instantly who he was.

My heart stopped. "Daddy?"

"Would you like a sugar cookie?" Janie asked our dad, nervous, twitchy, as we settled into a booth. "We have sharks with braces on their teeth, mermaids with peace signs, and men's boxer shorts. You know, like underwear. Red or blue. The underwear. You can choose the color. Isabelle made jock strap cookies, too, in purple. And bras. Pink. Striped. You probably don't want a bra cookie. Do you? Want a bra?" She slapped both hands to her face in embarrassment. "A bra cookie, I mean. I didn't make the bras. Isabelle did it. Not me."

Janie prattled on. I was speechless.

I have to say that if the Columbia River had suddenly been run over by a tsunami sweeping up the hill, and had that tsunami deposited a pirate ship on our roof, I would still not have been as shocked as I was now to be sitting in a booth across from our dad.

He had so gently asked about my gnarled-up face. (He did not refer to it as "gnarled-up.") When I told him I had a bad date, I saw a muscle throb in his temple as he stared out the window. He choked out an "I'm sorry," then couldn't speak for several minutes. I saw his hand move toward mine before he withdrew it, but the pain in his bleak expression never withdrew. "I'm sorry, Isabelle."

"Or, I can bring you a plate of garlic cheese bread," Janie prattled on. "Or a wedding cake? Those are good. I could grab a wedding cake for us to eat. Or a blue spider cake? We don't serve wine. The moms sneak it in on Wednesday mornings. We don't. Have it. No wine."

I tapped her on the knee.

"We also have giant cupcakes," she rambled. "We've named them Bommarito's Heavenly Cupcakes." She leaped up and grabbed eight—eight—of the cupcakes and plonked them on the table. "The flowers almost look alive, it's sort of freaky, but we weren't trying to scare anyone, it's how they turned out, all wiggling and squiggling, like they could talk. The flowers, I mean. Not that I think flowers can talk. I don't. They don't talk."

"Janie."

Her head snapped to me. I put a hand on her arm.

She took a deep breath.

"I'm sorry," she said, breathless. "Sorry."

"Please." Our dad held up a hand. "Please don't be sorry. I can see you have a thriving business here." He cleared his throat. He blinked rapidly. Blinking didn't help. Tears dribbled out of his eyes.

"He's crying," Janie murmured. "Those are tears."

I raised my eyebrows when she stuck her finger through a nontalking flowery cupcake. She stared at her finger, seemingly surprised at the action it had taken, then raised hurt, green eyes to our dad. "Where were you, Dad?" she said, her voice breaking into little glass shards. "Why did you leave us? Why didn't you come back?"

The silence was so noisy, I could almost feel the nerves in my head cracking.

Janie reached for my hand under the table and pulsed it in sets of four. "Where were you?" The icing squished between us.

Yes, Dad, where were you? Where were you when we fell apart? When things collapsed for our family and then got worse?

"I have . . ." He started, cleared his throat, started again. "I have thought for years, forever . . . about what I would tell you girls if I ever saw you again. How I would explain my unforgiveable absence." He tipped his chin up. "I have never veered from my first answer to myself: I would tell you the truth."

"Truth is good," I told him. "We deserve it."

"So where were you?" Janie asked. She tapped the table, then reached for the sugar packets. I knew she would sort them into groups of four.

"I was in jail for fifteen years."

The words hung between us, like an exploding emotional grenade. Fiery, smoky, heavy, dangerous.

"J . . ." Janie couldn't get the word out. She sorted quicker. "Jail?"

He nodded. "Yes, jail."

Jail? Jail! "What . . . what did you do?" I asked, not sure I wanted to hear this any more than I wanted to hear the details about a human gutting.

"You committed a crime?" Janie asked.

I breathed then. Thank God for Janie and her inane questions. "No. He made the cotton candy at the carnival too pink."

"Well . . . uh . . . um . . . um . . . um! Um! I thought he would say that he was innocent!"

Janie actually hates crime. It fascinates her to write about it, but when she reads about people committing crimes and innocent people hurt, she gets upset. We have to be careful around her. Crime pays, for Janie, but only in her books. The rest of the time she prefers to believe the world outside is a nice, fuzzy, yellowish-pink place filled with Jane Austen and Little Women that she doesn't have to interact with too much and our childhood was simply a nightmare.

"I wasn't innocent."

We both sagged at the same time against the booth, my stomach slipping down my insides and heading south for my feet.

"I was guilty. I accepted it from the start," he stopped. "I will never get over what I did. Not a day goes by that I don't regret it a hundred times."

"What did you . . ." Janie started in on a napkin, ripping each one into four pieces, then reached for another one.

"What did I do?" His gaze did not waver. "I killed a man."

"You kill—" Janie stuttered, then ripped another napkin.

My stomach kept sliding. I wanted to get on that pirate ship and take off.

Our dad was a killer. *"Hello, this is my dad. He's a murderer."*

"I did. I had left you all about three years before and was having . . ." He stopped, his voice barely above a whisper. "I was having a bad time of it."

He was having a bad time? Bits of my childhood shot to my mind, quite unpleasantly. *"You* were having a bad time so you killed someone? Should I feel sorry for you?"

The gentleness in that familiar face was almost my undoing. How could he have taken that gentleness from us? I remembered my dad laughing. I remembered how he'd taught us to make omelets and how we'd watch Saturday morning cartoons and lay all over him. I remembered how we rode on wagons to get pumpkins for Halloween.

And then, in a flash, he was gone.

We were children. Our entire world crashed.

"You should not feel sorry for me, Isabelle. I'm not asking for that." His voice was warm and humble and low.

"Do you know—" I stopped because the rush of emotion about drowned me and I decided to put the murdering my dad did aside for a second. "Do you know what happened to us after you left? Do you have any idea?"

Janie patted my arm. Pat pat, pat pat. Four times. Pat pat, pat pat.

He bent his head for a second, then lifted it back up. Through my mist of anger and anguish, I had the impression he was a man who was willing to take it on the chin. "No," he said. "I don't. The hurt I caused you has haunted me daily. Nightly. Always."

"And that excuses it?" The mist bubbled in me, bubbled in the kid I used to be, lonely and lost and thrust headfirst into a scary, relentlessly cold world.

"No." Firm, resolute tone. "What I did is inexcusable."

"We lost the house. The sheriff actually came and kicked us out. It was devastating." I remembered a neighbor helping Momma out. She was bent over with grief, clutching her wedding album and her wedding veil. We had sold anything of even remote value, so there wasn't much to pack.

"We went through homelessness in different states." There. I'd said it. We'd never said it when we were kids. That word was *not allowed*. Janie had said it once and Momma had slapped her. "We're not homeless," Momma had seethed. "We're not losers. We're not white trash. We are temporarily spending the night in our car until I can figure out what to do, but we are not homeless. Do you have that?"

I could tell he was dumbfounded, then horrified.

"We went through times when we were starving, especially during the summer when the school wasn't providing us with free meals."

He paled further.

"Henry had health problems, but you knew that when you left, didn't you?" I could feel my anger building.

"Yes. I knew that Henry . . . there was almost always something wrong . . . I knew that."

"But you left anyhow. *You left*. One time Momma had bronchitis for a year because we couldn't afford the medication. Cecilia kept getting rashes we couldn't treat. Janie had migraines and the over-the-counter medication didn't work."

I saw that jawline clenching. Not in anger, though. Not in anger. *In shock*.

But I was angry. "We were broke. Momma couldn't pay the

bills. She often couldn't find a normal job because she couldn't get someone to watch Henry while she worked because he was so often sick. She didn't have an education, didn't have work skills. Kids made fun of us because we were so poor." And because we were the daughters of The River of Love. "They picked on Henry. *We had nothing.*"

He put a shaky hand to his face and rubbed it.

"That wasn't the worst of it. You know Momma suffers from depression? She'd take to her bed for weeks at a time, so Janie and Cecilia and I took care of Henry and baked desserts for money. We fought for each damn thing we had. We were always scared, always moving, always striving to survive. And Momma," I paused, inhaled. "Momma was not often in a good mood."

The understatement about undid me. As an adult, I could understand Momma's moods, the swings, the unbelievable stress, and the depression better. She was suffering more than any of us. But knowing what caused parents to act as they did in childhood does not make childhood better. It doesn't make it sweeter or pinker or more rainbowlike. The scars are still there, the hurts ongoing, those brittle, searing moments still raw.

Janie patted me. Pat pat, pat pat.

"You abandoned us. To this day, do you understand, *to this day*, I do not trust men. I do not trust relationships. I hardly trust myself. Cecilia eats all the time and is constantly flipping her lid about something, and Janie, well, look at her."

Janie had destroyed six napkins. She had piled the pieces up in four different piles. The pieces crisscrossed each other. "I've got some mental issues," she whispered. "A few. Here and there. A couple of habits and counting problems and I check things. I don't like to leave my houseboat. People make me nervous . . ." she driveled off. "I tap. Check. Tap."

I saw nothing but compassion on my dad's face, but I ignored it.

"Want to know what your wife ended up doing?" I demanded, sitting forward in my seat and leaning toward him.

Our dad exhaled. "Yes, I do."

"Stripping. Stripping her clothes off."

We did not miss that strangled sound in his throat or the way his face turned into a tight mask.

"And don't you dare judge her. *She* hated it. It about killed her, but she did it because we didn't have money for food or rent or Henry's medical bills, and waitressing and our desserts weren't cutting it. That's what you did to us, *Daddy*, and we're only touching on a few surface problems."

I took a deep breath. I felt my tears, wrapped up in a tight ball in my throat, expand and grow.

My daddy was now about the same color as the napkins Janie was shredding. "I don't understand—" he rasped out, as if he could hardly get his words between his vocal cords. "Your mother never should have—"

"Would you like to say that to her face, *Daddy? 'You never should have stripped, River.'* Trust me, it wouldn't go over well. She did what she had to do." And that was the truth. River Bommarito had done what she had to do. She was backed in a corner and she was fighting for four kids, all on her own.

I rolled those words around in my head and felt a little love seep in for Momma. *She'd done what she'd had to do.*

Our dad sank back against the booth, as if the bones in his body had collapsed.

"It's nice to see you, Dad," I snapped. "But forgive me for not being more gracious. Momma, right now, is refusing to leave a retirement center after heart surgery, even though she's perfectly healthy, because she's getting the first vacation of her life. *Of her life.*"

I thought of Momma going out on the town, to shows and restaurants, bowling and book group, bridge tournaments and chess games. *For the first time in forever.*

"I don't think you understand the situation we were in when you left," Janie started, gentle as always, shred shred, shred.

"No, I'm not understanding that situation," Dad said, completely confused, palms up. "I'm not understanding your financial struggles, at least. Why didn't your mother use the money I left her? Why didn't she?"

Janie stopped shredding and gasped.

I'm sure my arteries stopped pumping blood. The pirate ship on the roof came to a dead halt.

"What are you talking about?" I whispered, shoving the words out of my constricted throat. "There was no money. None."

"Yes." Dad leaned forward. "Yes, there was! The money from the government, from my years in the military. I authorized my monthly check to be mailed to your mother, as it was mailed to her the whole time I was in the army. Plus, I left her the inheritance I received from my parents after they died when I was in 'Nam. What happened to that money? That was enough to pay off the house. It was enough for savings. It was enough for college for you girls. River should not have had to work a day in her life. Not one day."

I was stunned. It felt like someone had lassoed that pirate ship that had landed on our bakery and bashed me in the head. Janie made squeaking sounds. She clung to my hand and pulsed.

"I have no idea what you're talking about," I told him. *"None."*

"There wasn't any money," Janie squeaked. "Except for what we made from the lemon meringue pies you taught us to make, the chocolate cookies with peppermint were popular, I think the cherry pies did well . . ." Her voice trailed off weakly. She went back to shredding.

"Oh my God," our dad groaned, putting both hands to the sides of his head. *"Oh my God."*

❦ 22 ❧

Icalled Cecilia and asked if she could come over to Grandma's for dinner. I figured it would be better there, then Cecilia could run, major temper tantrum flaming, if she wanted. I was uncertain of Cecilia's reaction.

No, strike that.

The only uncertainty I had was how extreme Cecilia's reaction would be and if she would start throwing items of value out the windows as she eviscerated our dad.

We decided that Dad—how odd it was to say that word— would follow me behind my motorcycle up to the house in his blue SUV, and Janie would follow him in her Porsche. I think we all needed a moment alone on the drive.

It was all a bit much. A dad appearing—the shock, the tears, the initial rush of love, then the fury. The white, burning fury.

A fury that had flared up and settled back down, then flared up and settled. I could feel it flaring up again.

How dare he. How could he? Waltzing back into our lives after ruining our childhoods? After leaving us with Momma? After all we went through that could have been prevented, or at least mitigated, by his presence?

We had made him Christmas presents for three years. We didn't even leave our apartments on our birthdays in the hopes that he'd call. It shattered us to lose our dad. It would have been easier if we'd lost a leg and half our brain.

And here he was.

I turned out of town, breathed in, breathed out, following the rushing Columbia River part of the way, before turning up the hill.

I couldn't deny my other emotions, though: Part of me was so glad to see my dad again I could cry.

So I did.

Cry, that is.

My dad held my gaze on the front porch and those big brown eyes teared up and I had the distinct impression he wanted to hug me.

I turned away.

He held the screen door for me and Janie.

"Thank you, thank you," Janie fluttered. "This is Grandma's house. There's a sunroom. A pergola. It's a house. It's Grandma's. She hides her secrets in the towers," Janie babbled. "We'll sit in the sunroom."

Dad just nodded, smiling, tearing up.

Janie grinned with her teeth when she went through the doorway. "You didn't smile," she whispered to me. I ignored her.

"I'll make coffee," I disappeared into the kitchen. The sun was slanting through Momma's bottle collection, sending a prism of color to the countertop. I sighed.

I heard Grandma marching down the stairs. She was singing a patriotic song at the top of her lungs. "It's a grand old flag, it's a high-flying flag . . . It's the emblem of the land Amelia loves . . ."

She came to an abrupt halt when she saw me. She had found a cane somewhere and thumped it on the wood floor.

"I can see I have company," she announced. "I'm giving my autobiography on the front porch tonight and I'm expecting a crowd. Please make pretzels for them."

"I'll do that, Amelia, and I'll eagerly anticipate your autobiography."

"You should. The United States is dying to know the secrets of Amelia Earhart." She thumped her cane again. "I am a flying genius."

I heard Janie's voice in the other room. So did Grandma.

"The crowds must be forming already." She spun on her heel and headed to the sunroom.

I grabbed her arm. "Uh, Amelia."

"Yes, dear?" She snapped her goggles over her eyes. When I did not respond, she put them back up on her flight helmet. "Speak now or forever hold your peace. Speak."

What to say? Your son-in-law is here? You only met him a few times after Momma ran off and married him. Remember that man? He went to Vietnam? Lived in a cage for a while . . . that one?

But, no, she wouldn't remember. Her memory was shriveled and hiding somewhere in a cavern in her mind, door shut.

"I'm happy to see you, Amelia."

She tapped my foot with her cane. "And I, you, young lady." She strutted toward the family room.

I put sugar and cream on a tray. Should I prepare Dad? I stopped. Why should I prepare him? Had he been here when Grandma started going downhill, forgetting everything, getting lost, getting angry, talking nonsense, her behavior erratic? No. Had he been around to make sure that Momma didn't become exhausted taking care of a mother with dementia and a mentally disabled son? No. Had he been able to provide a home? No. Grandma had provided that.

Grandma marched into the sunroom. "It's a grand old flag . . ."

"Mrs. Howe," I heard Dad say, so polite.

"Young man!" Grandma protested, arms rigid at her sides. "Watch your manners!"

I followed her in.

She marched past Dad. "My name is Amelia Earhart. I've got

a crowd today to speak to, and I have no time for more interviews by pot-smoking, crackpot journalists. Out of the way."

Dad got out of the way.

"Let me give you some advice, young man." She ogled him, leaning toward him, then adjusted her goggles over her head. "Do I know you?"

"Yes," Dad said. "I believe you do."

"What is your name then?"

"I'm Carl Bommarito. I married your daughter, River."

"Hmm," Grandma said, fiddling with her goggles. "River River. That is not correct. You are confused. Confounded." She grabbed a piece of paper and pen from her antique rollback desk.

I knew what she was doing. I wondered how Dad would react.

She turned around and gave the paper to Dad.

"That's a map of Hawaii. You'll need that in order to land. I use it myself. No need to thank me. I must go now."

I watched Grandma march out the door. She made the sound of an engine, then yelled, "Get me my copilot!" She farted. "Bottom bullet wounds!"

Velvet followed behind after nodding at Dad.

Dad opened up the paper. There was a smiley face on it.

His face was unutterably sad as he rubbed his eyes.

"She believes she's Amelia Earhart," I told him.

I thought he might cry again.

She pushed him as hard as she could.

She screamed at him, "Get out, get out, get out!"

Then she let him have it.

Janie and I physically held Cecilia back.

"Asshole!" she snapped. "You jerk! You leave us, you leave *four* kids, and now, after we're all grown, you come back? What are you thinking? I have two kids. *Two of them,* and I would never, ever abandon my children. Get out. *Get out!*"

"I understand, Cecilia," our dad said. "I do." He stood up, his face grave, pained, exhausted.

I still held the raging Cecilia; so did Janie. We were a clump of writhing Bommarito sisters.

"Oh my God," Cecilia accused, shaking her head in disgust. "You deserted us, we were instantly broke—"

"Uh, Cecilia," I said.

Dad's left eye started to twitch.

"Momma had to sell her wedding ring the first month. She cried over that ring. *She cried over it.* She held it in her hands and kissed it right before she went to the pawnshop."

Dad's pale face became ashen. He swayed.

"Cecilia, um, can we chat for a sec?" I said.

"We moved from one slummy, scary apartment to another with slummy, scary people."

Dad dropped his head, hand to neck.

"Don't let go," I whispered to Janie over Cecilia's head.

"Why are you here? Why the hell did you come back? Want to play Dad? It's too late. It is too late for you. *We don't need a dad.* We got by without you and we don't need you in our lives."

I held her tight and grunted out, "There's one thing you should know, Cecilia—"

Janie whimpered.

"You flattened Momma, you screwed all of us up—"

Cecilia continued on her enraged tirade until it was cut short by Henry's sweet, innocent voice.

"Hiya, sisters! Hiya!"

Our heads whipped around, but I did not release the struggling Cecilia.

"I been petting the dogs," Henry said. He was wearing a brown T-shirt with a fluffy white dog on the front of it. It said, "Bark!" He likes to wear dog or cat shirts when he works at the shelter.

"I pet Al. His name Al." Henry grinned. "He a big black dog. No biting, Al! And I pets Sherman. A dog named Sherman!" He snickered. "He a white little dog. He sat in my lap. He sleepy. And I pets Emily."

What to do?

How should we tell Henry? Should we tell him? Did he need to know? How long was Dad going to stay around, anyhow? Wouldn't it be more devastating for Henry to meet his dad and lose him again when Dad took off?

How would Dad treat Henry? I remembered Dad dancing around with Henry on his shoulders, laughing, but would Henry make him uncomfortable now? So many people were.

But the decision to tell or not tell Henry was taken clean out of our hands.

Henry tipped his head to the left side, then the right as he stared at Dad. He smiled in wonder.

"I think that my dad," he said, leaning forward at the waist. He circled his hands and put them up to his eyes, like glasses. "Yep. I think that my dad. I got a picture of Dad in my Bible. You my dad, right? You my dad. Hi to my dad."

The three of us sisters stood there, like Silly Putty, stunned. We had all seen Henry staring at Dad's photo. He had always told us that Dad would come back.

"Hi to my dad!" Henry smiled. "Hey! Hi to my dad!"

This was too much for Dad. One kid, finally, being kind to him.

Henry put his arms out. "I give my dad a hug. I glad to see my dad."

"I'm glad to see you, too, Henry," Dad said, his shoulders slumping, face reddening. "I am so glad to see you." He hugged him. It was a long, long hug. Dad's tears ran right down those cheeks, right down that scar.

Janie made a sound like this, "Ohhhh. Isn't that sweet?"

Cecilia said, "Shit. Hell and shit."

When they pulled away, Henry said, "Now I got my dad. I been wanting my dad back. Hey, Cecilia and Isabelle and Janie. Dad back." He grinned. "Dad back."

It was Henry who had all of us outside on the porch eating cupcakes and drinking grape juice minutes later.

"We go and have treat!" Henry announced. He grabbed Dad, an arm slung around his shoulders. "You sit by me. You my dad. Two guys. We sit together."

"I think Daaaad"—Cecilia dragged out the word—"has to go, Henry. He has things to do."

Dad stood there, dignified, quiet. I am not a beast and I knew he was hurting, too. Hurting all over.

"No!" Henry shrieked. "No!" He put another arm around Dad. "He no go. He stay and visit. Dad's back. Dad, you stay!"

Dad turned and hugged him again, wiped his eyes. "I'd like to visit with you all, Henry. I'd like that."

"Good!" Henry clapped his hands together. "Good." He ran into the kitchen, and I knew he was getting the Bommarito's Heavenly Cupcakes I'd brought home earlier.

"You're going to hurt him again," Cecilia spat out. "He's had your picture forever. Now you're here and he doesn't get what's going on. He probably thinks you're moving back in. He has a dad, the dad's back. What'll we tell him when you leave again?" Cecilia burst into tears, then bit her lip.

"How dare you hurt Henry again? We can take it, but he's . . . *he's Henry,*" I said. "When you go, it will be months before he's the same. When you left the first time he stopped talking and had to start wearing diapers at night."

Henry had thrown fits and thrown things and thrown Momma for a loop. Henry's reaction was pure Bommarito—we don't know how to feel things halfway, and his grief was insidious and long-lasting.

I ran my hands through my shortened hair, exhausted. Drained. Blown away.

Henry darted in and yelled with great joy, "I come one minute! I be there one minute say hi Dad." He clapped his hands and ran back into the kitchen. "Hi to my dad!"

"You're in his life and you leave—"

"Cecilia, I'm not leaving this time," Dad said. "I'm not leaving."

"Yes, you are. You will."

"I have a job at TechEx, the new plant being built in Dulles, down the road. I've come here a few times in the last months and I've bought a home. I'm staying."

Silence. *He was staying?* Henry burst into a song about a bear in the kitchen. He made the growling sounds.

"What?" Janie said. "I don't get it. You're moving to Trillium River?"

"I've moved to Trillium River," he said, "from Los Angeles."

"Why?" I asked. "Why?"

"Because of you all," he said, his voice breaking. "Never in my life will I be able to make up to you what I did. Never. I can tell you that I have always loved you. Not a day, not an hour, has gone by when I haven't loved you all and thought of you. Not a day has gone by that I didn't regret . . ." He stopped, gathered up those rampaging, raw emotions. "That I didn't regret my actions, what's happened. I thought about staying away . . ."

"You should have!" Cecilia assured him. "You should have."

"I struggled with that, Cecilia. I did. My selfishness told me to come back, to be with you all. The other side of me said that I would be an intrusion, that coming back would hurt you all over again, cause you upheaval and pain—"

"Our dad left years ago," Cecilia said. "We don't have one. We don't need one."

"Don't be so mean, Cecilia," Janie whispered.

"Ha!" Henry darted back in. "Ha! My dad here! I knew it!" He clapped his hands, then ran back to the kitchen.

"I don't want to cause you any more pain than I have," Dad said again. "I have no right to come back. I have no right to think of myself as your dad. I have not earned it, and I can never tell you how sorry I am for what I did." He teared up, coughed. "I am sorry beyond sorry. To the depths of my soul, I am sorry."

Cecilia's mouth dropped open. I leaned against a wall. Janie sank into a chair.

"Please, I'm asking only for a chance," our dad said. "One chance to get to know you, to help you in any way that I can—"

"No, God, no," Cecilia said, emphatic.

"A chance?" Janie asked, hope in her voice.

"We needed help when we were kids, Dad—" I said.

"Okay sisters and my dad! I got the cupcakes. I make grape juice," Henry announced. "Dad back! Dad back! I sit by Dad. Two guys. Me and my dad."

We went out to the porch for mongo-sized cupcakes and grape juice.

Why is family life so intricately, exasperatingly, exhaustingly . . . complicated?

"I wore my burka at Dad's wedding," Kayla announced. "I'm exploring being a Muslim."

My fork fell from my hands to my plate. *She'd done it!* I high-fived her over the table.

Janie, beside me, choked on her peppermint tea, and I had to pound her on the back.

It was three days after Dad's miraculous appearance and we Bommarito sisters were still recovering from the surprise. We had agreed that The Subject of Dad was off-limits for the night.

"What's a burka?" Henry asked, taking another bite of spaghetti. It was, again, Spaghetti Night for the Bommarito family. We had dimmed the lights, lit the candles, and passed the noodles. And the wine.

I exchanged a glance with Cecilia and tried not to cackle with glee. Her whole body was trembling with suppressed laughter as she studied her cranberry-and-feta-cheese salad.

"I'm going out on a night flight!" Grandma announced as she wielded garlic bread. "The weather's perfect. I'm making a trip to the equator. I haven't seen the inhabitants there for a while and I am their conquering heroess." She growled like an engine.

"My goodness sakes, souls alive and dead," Velvet murmured. "A burka, Kayla? You mean you were covered head to foot in black? Even a black veil over your eyes? Like the Saudi women wear?"

"How did your father like your burka, Kayla?" I asked. I let some of my cackles out. Couldn't help it.

"He didn't," Kayla said.

Riley swirled a hair around her finger. She was wearing a wide red band. "He hated it. He hated it even more than he hates discussing molecules and molecular dynamics. Things he doesn't understand trigger that temper of his. Short man's complex. He's got it."

"Did you ask your father beforehand if he would mind?" I could barely contain myself. I wanted to stand up and cheer. *Kayla. In a burka at her father's wedding.* She was a true Bommarito!

"No. Do I look that dumb, Aunt Isabelle?" Kayla said. "He wasn't supportive when I became an evangelical Christian and told him he was going to hell for not accepting the Lord Jesus Christ as his savior. He wasn't supportive when I turned Jewish and educated him about Job and Exodus. He didn't like hearing about Revelations 'cause he knows he's gonna burn. He also wasn't too nice when I was Hindu and told him he would be reincarnated into a slug based on this lifetime's behavior. I mean, it's not like the guy's open-minded to anything but cheating on Mom."

Cecilia blew air out of her mouth rather noisily, then stabbed the butter cube with her knife.

Henry dropped a noodle into his mouth. He was wearing his Superman shirt. "Noodle woodles. I love 'em."

"Constance is a bouncy-boobed bitch," Kayla mused.

"Don't swear at the table, Kayla," Cecilia said.

"Give me a break, Mom. You've said that word before yourself."

"You also said she's a sl—" I put my hand over Riley's mouth.

"If it's raining, I may have a hard time taking off tonight," Grandma mused, tapping her goggles. "Weather can be a problem. It can blind you without warning, make you feel like you're upside down when you're right side up."

"Upside down, right side up," Henry sang. "Upside down, right side up, topsy-turvy, topsy-turvy." He ate another noodle by slinging his head back and wrapping it into his mouth in circles.

"So you wore your burka to the wedding, Kayla?" Janie prodded. She pulled on the lace collar around her neck and had a sip of tea.

"Jeez, Aunt Janie, give me a break." Riley sniffed. "Kayla wore the fluffy red dress to the wedding that Constance said we had to wear to be bridesmaids. We looked like Valentines on drugs. But right before Kayla was supposed to *gracefully* walk down the aisle in the red dress she ducks quick into a bathroom that's right there in the atrium and as soon as she hears the music for us bridesmaids she, like, runs on out and heads up the aisle in her black burka in front of all the people."

I bit my tongue. I mustn't cackle again!

I sneaked a glance at Janie. She was covering her face with her napkin. Cecilia's body was shaking from her laughter, her jaw clenched tight.

Kayla looked proud as her sister continued the riveting story, starring Kayla.

"I was right behind Kayla," Riley said, "and I thought Daddy was going to have a coronary and die right there, you know. He was standing up at the front of the aisle with this minister guy with a long black braid, I mean he didn't even seem like a minister because his T-shirt was New Wave and black with a skull on it." She stabbed her fork into her spaghetti and twirled it around.

"Then what happened?" Janie asked.

Velvet murmured, "Land sakes, child."

Grandma made the sound of a plane humming. Henry giggled. Spaghetti makes him laugh.

"Well, so Kayla is dressed all in black, you know that burka thing," Riley explained, "and all you can see is her eyes in a slit and she's supposed to hook elbows with one of Constance's guy friends who was wearing a white tuxedo with a pink tie, how weird is that, plus his shoes were pink, how weird is that, but she doesn't want to. Kayla walks up that aisle herself and when she gets to the top she climbs up the steps and stands right by Daddy."

Some days one is more blissfully glad to be alive than others. This was one of those days. I sighed with pleasure.

"Daddy's almost got his tongue hanging out he's so shocked at first but then I can tell he's bloody ripped," Riley said. "I mean, Mom, he is about ready to lose his head. He is, like, *raging* sick. I think he wants to yank Kayla on out of the building—did you know that Constance and Daddy had a hard time getting married in a church?" She tilted her head. "No one would let them do it. Daddy asked Father Mike to be the priest dude and Father Mike told him that as soon as the devil was running heaven he would marry him and Constance. They went to a couple of other churches, but the ministers wanted them to do counseling and Daddy said, 'I can't wait that long to marry my bride,' so the ministers said no. One woman minister said she wouldn't feel 'ethical' marrying them. Whatever."

I raised my eyebrows. Ah. Justice in the world.

"So, anyhow, Kayla's walking down in that black thing and Dad's almost purple he's so ticked. Mom, I didn't know anybody at the wedding. No one. I mean, didn't Dad have friends in town? What about the Guzinskys? What about the Shores? What about the Chins and Kuchenkos? None of them came. Did he not invite them?"

"He invited them, Riley," Cecilia drawled.

"Well, whatever. I didn't know anybody except Weird Grandma." (Parker's mother) "There's only Constance's friends and family, but not a lot of people, you know? And they were all, weird. Like, Daddy says that Constance's brother was there straight out of the can. You know, like jail. For drugs or something. So Kayla's standing by Dad in her black burka and I follow Kayla up the aisle in that Valentine red dress on drugs that Constance told me to wear. I looked like a walking red vein. She made me wear a hat, too, 'cause she said I'm going bald and that's embarrassing for her because she sells hair products."

I breathed in deep. Oh, how I hated Constance.

"So—"

"I'll tell it now," Kayla interrupted Riley. "So I'm standing, like, next to Daddy at the altar. I know he's about ready to shit bricks so I stare down the aisle and up comes Riley and she's right, Mom. She did look like a walking red vein wearing a hat."

Riley wasn't offended. "Yep. I did."

"Anyhow, Constance is suddenly there and they start pounding out that boring bride music." Kayla took a bite of spaghetti, chewing slowly. I was on the edge of my seat.

"Constance is wearing this light pink dress and her boobs are almost popping out and her makeup. I mean, come on, I mean. She's all gooped up, but I see Dad—it's hard to see in a burka but there's the slit thing—and he's all happy and he's got this goofy expression on his face, it was gross—"

She stopped. "Sorry, Mom."

Cecilia sniffed. "Who cares about that repulsive, son of a—" She closed her mouth, stabbed the butter.

"Constance comes down the aisle and right before she gets to Dad she stares straight at me." Kayla shook her head sorrowfully, takin' her time with the story. "It's like she hadn't even noticed me in my burka before she got up close. What am I, invisible in one of those things? So she sees me and she sort of jumps and does a little scream thing and Daddy puts his hands out and whispers, 'It's okay, it's Kayla.' And Constance has a hand on her mongo boobs like her heart's beating too freakin' fast and she says, '*It's who?*'"

Kayla rolled her eyes. "She's so damn dumb and right in front of all those people she says, 'What are you doing in that? I bought you a dress.' And I told her the truth, that I was exploring being a Muslim and she's all red in the face now and said, 'You're not exploring being a Muslim at my wedding.'"

Laughter is so hard to smother when it wants to come out. So hard. I slapped both hands over my mouth.

Janie made another choking sound.

"Takeoff is soon!" Grandma yelled. "I'll need my flying papers."

"Hey! I made a mouse with my noodles!" Henry announced. "A mouse!"

"Constance is so mad her boobs are about ready to pop out all by themselves," Kayla said. She had a bite of garlic bread.

"And?" I prodded.

"And she goes, 'Get that black thing off or get off the damn altar.' And Dad says to me, 'Kayla, take off the burka or you can't be in the wedding. Take it off right now.' "

Kayla ate a bite of spaghetti, wriggled around.

She was killing me. "What did you say?"

Kayla took her time swallowing and had some milk. "Well, first thing, Aunt Isabelle, you were right when you told me before the wedding that Dad had to respect my religious choices even on his wedding day. That was so cool."

Cecilia raised an eyebrow at me.

Janie studied the table, then took a wee sip of tea. Janie had been there when I had encouraged Kayla to "defend your freedoms, in particular your religious freedoms, at all costs, even in the face of opposition from others, in particular, your father. Be true to yourself and your beliefs, especially if someone, your father, is trying to squash them!"

Kayla took another slow bite. She knew how to pause for drama! "So, yeah, then I told my dad, okay, I'll take the burka off."

"So you changed?" I asked. I was crushed. I struggled with my disappointment at Kayla's easy acquiescence. Where was her fortitude? What happened to the rebel? Where was her Bommarito fighting spirit?

Kayla took another bite of spaghetti. "I'm an obedient child. So, yes. I changed."

She took another gulp of milk.

"And?" Janie breathed.

"I first took off the black veil thing right there on the altar and then I took off my burka."

Riley started to giggle. "That was *the best* part. *The best.*"

"What were you wearing underneath?" Janie asked, her tea cup frozen in midair. "The red dress?"

"What was I wearing?" Kayla asked. She took her time chewing some garlic bread. Swallowed. "I was wearing my favorite outfit."

"And that outfit would be?" I prodded.

She dabbed her mouth with a napkin. "I was wearing my pink T-shirt that says 'Fuck Off' and my short-short jean shorts."

Velvet started the laughter first, Southern style. "Oh me, oh my. Oh me." She fanned herself. "That's funnier than a skunk on the loose!"

Cecilia laughed so hard she sounded like a donkey. Janie and I eventually had to lean on each other to stay propped up.

Henry laughed because we were laughing. "Noodles!"

"Then I jumped off the altar and the walking red vein girl followed me—sorry, Riley—and we went right to the reception, where there was a bunch of food."

"So neither one of you saw your dad get married?" I garbled out.

"Nope. I got right back into my burka at the reception when Constance boomed on in," Kayla said. "Dad was so mad. He said I ruined the ceremony. Constance was so mad one of her boobs almost came out and I said, 'Constance, stick your right boob back in, it's out and about,' and that made her throw her flowers at my face. Whatever. After they left for the honeymoon, I didn't feel like being a Muslim anymore, so I threw off the burka and me and Riley danced for about two hours and had more wedding cake. The guy with the pink tie danced awesome cool. He taught us some new moves."

"Weddings are stupid," Riley said.

"Yeah," Kayla agreed.

A burka.

At Parker's wedding.

She was a true Bommarito. So was her sister. I was so proud!

I damn near fell out of my chair I laughed so hard.

"Hold on, passengers!" Grandma screamed suddenly. "Hold on!" She leaped on the table, grabbing the controls of her imaginary plane.

We turned our chairs, threw our napkins on our heads, and braced for a crash.

"Don't worry!" Grandma reassured us. "We'll get through this weather!"

Indeed we would.

❦ 23 ❧

Not surprisingly, the murdering our dad did weighed on our minds, so we had to clear up the wee issue of the killing before we let him back into our lives even an inch.

He invited me, Janie, and the still angry/reluctant Cecilia to a classy French restaurant in town. Over white linens and wine, for me and Cecilia, chamomile tea for Janie, and water for our dad—he doesn't drink alcohol—we got the full story.

"So, who did you kill and why did you kill him?" I asked, after our orders were taken. I believe in being blunt.

"I had had too much to drink in a bar in Sausalito," he said, the candlelight softening his scar. "Drinking was the way I numbed much of my life. It was cowardly and stupid. I hated myself and what I'd done in 'Nam and what I'd seen done. Alcohol smoothed the edges, but it was a weak excuse for a weak man."

I leaned back in the booth. He certainly did not try to soften things up.

Janie took sugar packets out and started to sort.

Cecilia humphed in her seat and crossed her arms.

"I had a disagreement with a man because he was hitting on a woman next to me and the woman was trying to get rid of him. He reached and grabbed her and I reacted. I was always angry, always looking for a fight back then, and I'd had many. I hit him first and we fought knuckle to knuckle. All of a sudden I saw a Vietnamese soldier in front of me instead of that guy. In my head, I was back in 'Nam and apparently started whaling on him. I should have stopped, but I didn't. I hardly remember. He was in critical condition, then died. I was sent to jail for fifteen years. Rightly so."

"Great!" Cecilia said. "Now we can worry that you're going to come after us. Super! A murdering dad."

"Cecilia," I said. "Stop."

"Why? Why should I stop?" She sounded tough, our ol' Cecilia, but she was fighting back another round of sobs, I knew it.

My heart was thumping because hers was, and I patted my chest. "Stop because my heart's pounding and I can't take it."

She wrinkled her nose up at me, but she started deep breathing, eyes closed.

Janie shook the sugar packets. "Then what happened?"

"In jail I obviously had a lot of time to think."

"Obviously," Cecilia drawled, eyes still closed.

"I had killed a man and thought the guilt would drive me out of my mind. I had killed who knows how many Vietnamese soldiers during the war who probably had no more desire to be there than me. That guilt ground its way into all the waking moments of my life. I felt guilty because I lived and so many of my buddies there didn't, and I felt I didn't deserve to be alive. I felt guilty about the innocent civilians who were caught in the cross fire. I felt guilty about leaving you all and River. I loved you." He paused. "I still love you. My guilt about killed me."

He stared out the window, his temples thumping, and it was at that mini-second that I related to my dad. I related to the guilt.

"I could not bring back the man I killed in the bar. I could not bring back the men and other civilians I killed in 'Nam. I could not bring back my buddies. I could, however, try to be a part of my family's life again, when I thought I had something to offer."

"What did you do after you got out of jail? Why didn't you come home right away?" I asked.

"I worked on getting my act together. I earned two degrees while I was in jail, and when I got out I became an accountant."

"A murdering accountant," Janie muttered.

"Does TechEx know you murdered a man?" I asked.

"Yes. They know. The man who owns TechEx, Tony Hallicon, fought in 'Nam. My ex-boss, the man I've worked for since I left jail, also called Tony and recommended me."

"Why didn't you come home sooner?" I asked.

"Because I didn't believe that I had a right to. I didn't believe I was good enough. You all had gotten on with your lives."

"What changed that?" I asked him.

My dad put his chin up and blinked rapidly. "Love," he said. "Love changed it."

"What do you mean?" Janie asked.

"I mean that I have always loved you all. Always. I missed you all." His voice broke. "And your mother. I missed your mother. River was . . ." He shook his head. "We were soul mates. I met her, and I was done. I knew that I would be in love with that woman the rest of my life. And I have been. I have never stopped loving your mother."

By agreement, we had decided not to say anything to "the soul mate" about Dad's return. I couldn't have him traipsing in, then traipsing out again on Momma. The "soul mate" did not deserve that.

"I have missed you all. I have worried incessantly about you. I have never, ever felt whole, since the day I left, and I couldn't fight wanting to show you that I still love you, have always loved you, anymore. Maybe it's selfish, and wrong. But I had to try. Had to show you that love. Love brought me home," he said.

Not even Cecilia knew what to say to that.

How can you argue with love?

"Love brought you home?" Janie squeaked.

Our dad wiped his eyes with his napkins. "Love brought me to you all. You are my home."

I sniffled.

Cecilia said, "Hell and shit!" and covered her flushed face with her napkin.

Janie said, "That's beautiful, serene, refreshing, oh!" She waved her hands.

"It's the truth," Dad said, his voice rough and scratchy. "You are my home. You have always been my home. You will always be my home."

Two days later, after baking jelly rolls and strawberry tarts in the shape of hearts, Janie and I came home from the bakery on my motorcycle to a white picket fence Dad was building around the house.

"He says he has three more weeks off before he starts work," Janie whispered to me as we spied on Dad through her bedroom window. She had hung new pink curtains to invite "rosy peace" in. I noticed her latest embroidery project—pink flowers in yet another wicker basket—on her dresser. "I was surprised when he told us that Momma had always wanted a white picket fence."

"Me, too."

Momma had never mentioned it. Probably because she was as likely to own a house with a white picket fence as she was to own Venus when we were younger. He had asked if he could build it and we said yes.

When Dad needed to kneel down, he struggled a bit with his bum leg, but he did it.

He had a gentle dignity about him. It squared with some of the memories I had of him, the happy ones. I could see that the raging, delusional man that Vietnam had thrown home was long gone now. The war had done its damage, had eaten him from the inside out, but he had wrestled with his demons and flattened them down to the mat.

"It's a nice white picket fence," Janie whispered.

"Yes, it is. It's nice." My heart warmed a tad.

We watched him through the rosy peace.

On Friday, after Dad had spent the afternoon with Henry petting the dogs, he asked to take all of us out to dinner. Cecilia refused to come, although I could tell she was weakening. "He's trying to weasel his way in and I'm not having it."

Dad came into the bakery, and I couldn't deny the hope in that man's eyes when he politely issued his invitation.

So we'd gone out to dinner. Grandma was lovely in her black flight outfit. She fastened a pink bow to her helmet. Dad didn't even blink. Velvet wore a green velvet dress and a yellow flowered hat. I wore jeans and heels. Janie defrumped and put on a skirt with a clean blue T-shirt. Henry had on beige slacks and tucked in his shirt. "I go to fancy dinner with my dad," he kept saying. "I all fancy."

I did not miss the way the hostess, who was about forty-five, flirted with Dad on the way to our table.

He was polite but he did not flirt back.

We actually had a good time after Grandma's prayer, which was: "Dear God, this is Amelia. Thanks for the food and the handsome man at this table. He seems stable. Good teeth. Clean gums. Hair. No weapons. Amen."

I would have envisioned conversation to be difficult. Forced. Lots of undercurrents.

There was none of that.

You know how you're out with people sometimes and there's one person who controls the conversation?

He wasn't like that.

Or, you know how there's often one person who *must* have the focus on them?

He wasn't like that.

Or, there's a guy in your group who brags or a woman who preens or someone who doesn't pay any attention to more than one person?

He wasn't like that at all, either.

He was friendly and interesting and entertaining. There was not an awkward moment.

We talked about the white picket fence that Henry was helping to build, Florida, Henry's stamps, Janie's scary new book, why I like photography (it shows truth, human nature, human emotion, disaster, joy, and I tried not to get all emotional about my lost career), my travels, Velvet's mother's recipe for possum, and Amelia's plan for her new luggage line.

He told us how impressed he was with the bakery, not only with how it looked, and all of our customers, but in the perfection of our desserts. "Outstanding." He'd nodded. "Every detail attended to in your presentation. Each dessert a testament to your skill and knowledge of the food arts and your understanding that food should be enjoyed and appreciated, not just eaten."

I tried not to blush. I tried not to show how pleased I was at this compliment. I tried not to gush out my thanks. It was hard.

We did not talk about all the time we'd spent baking in the kitchen with him as children. I think we all knew that would be one raw ache more than we could handle.

It was a warm and fuzzy and scrumptious dinner.

I actually felt myself relax, as if honey had been poured through my veins and marshmallows had taken the place of my rigid muscles.

I've always liked honey and marshmallows.

"Tell me about your childhood after I left."

"Definitely no, we couldn't. Let's not go there," Janie said to our dad after the dinner, as we settled onto the couches in front of our fireplace with coconut orange cake and coffee. "Poor karma. Bad memories. Negative flow."

"I think we should skip that," I said, glad that Henry, Grandma, and Velvet were tucked in bed. "Dinner was great. Let's not mess it up."

Dad put his coffee down, the firelight dancing across his cheeks, softening them, softening his scar. "Janie, Isabelle, I want you to tell me about what happened after I left. You deserve the chance to place blame where it should be placed. You deserve the chance to unload on my shoulders all of the problems you had, right where it belongs."

"Our childhood belongs in a tightly locked trunk," I said.

"Our childhood is best left to the universe," Janie said. "Out by the asteroids, in its own galaxy."

"Please," Dad said. "When you're ready, I'd like to know what happened. From the day I left. Maybe not today, not next week, maybe not even this year, but when you're comfortable with it, I want to listen."

"Well. We missed you. We always, always missed you." Janie tried to take a sip of chamomile tea but her hand shook. She put the teacup down. "But all right." I could hear some anger tinging her words amidst the grief. "If it will open up the mysteries for you, I'll tell you."

We were there with the firelight until four in the morning, new logs adding sparks as we piled them on.

We did not tell him all the gory details. We had secrets; some of them involved Momma, and she was the only one who should choose to share, or not, those secrets.

By the end of it, I'm sure he felt like he'd been bombed. He looked like he'd been bombed.

"This was all, completely, my fault," he said, voice ragged with regret. "I take the blame and responsibility. I know you won't forget it. No one could. But I hope that you will forgive me." He paused. "I will never forgive myself. Not a day has gone by that I don't feel the weight of my desertion, and if I live to be one hundred years old, I will still never forgive myself."

I thought about that.

Forgiveness.

My world had been so completely shaken when my dad left, I'd never even thought about it. We'd been cast into a swirling mass of despair and confusion and poverty almost instantly. It wasn't long before it got worse and we'd fallen into a swamp of tragedies.

From the porch I studied the black outlines of the waving trees, the wind whipping up the short curls of my hair.

Forgiveness. Could I? Could I get rid of the perpetual, incessant anger that had lived within me for decades? *Could I forgive him?*

I had never fought in a war. Could I judge someone who had been through years of combat and imprisonment? Could I judge my dad's desertion of his family? And, if I did, would it be fair?

I, for one, had never been shot at while hiding in a swampy ditch, the jungle swaying overhead with the enemy, unshowered for weeks, my feet rotting, my buddies' limbs flying off in front of my face from land mines or grenades.

I had not had to aim my gun at soldiers and innocent people alike and pull the trigger, or flatten a peaceful village, or engage in a deadly nighttime raid, which forever more would make me hate myself. I had not been locked in a cage and beaten for years and had two of my fingers chopped off and my back whipped into bacon.

I had not had to come home, only to relive my Vietnam nightmares and fight with the monstrous visions my overwrought brain did not have the capacity to withhold. I had not returned to a condemning American public and a government unwilling to help, or even acknowledge, the hellacious, ongoing impact of the Vietnam War on its soldiers.

My dad had left us because he woke up one day to a loaded, cocked gun pointed at Momma's head, his finger on the trigger. He thought he had left plenty of money for us to last the rest of our lives. He thought he had provided for his family, as he believed a man should.

I focused on that new, white picket fence.

Forgiveness was definitely a possibility.

* * *

We all thought the bakery needed a makeover, but we hadn't had time to do it.

Enter: Dad.

After hours, we repainted the walls a butter yellow, scrubbed and shined the black and white floors, emptied and cleaned the display cases. We added yellow flowered curtains and bought new tablecloths. We reorganized the back and cleaned out pantries and cabinets.

We bought new red canopies for the front, and Dad had BOM-MARITO'S BAKERY written in gold on the front window. He worked tirelessly with, what seemed to me, great joy. He insisted on paying for the repairs.

"A small gift to the Bommarito Family," he said quietly. "One small gift."

When we were flooded with customers one day, we gave him an apron and an invitation, and he went to work. He came back the next day when we asked, and the next. I cried into my mixing bowls as I saw my dad flip open his old cookbooks and bake the desserts we'd baked as children, his face at peace.

All of his desserts looked exactly like the pictures.

Sometimes I caught him gazing at me, Cecilia, Janie, Henry, or the girls and I was stunned by the expression on his face: Gratefulness. Happiness. Wonder.

And, the most important emotion, love.

I saw it.

I felt it.

I felt that love.

I had missed that love more than I would have missed my own heart.

When Bao and Dad had a break, they played chess.

I couldn't hear what they said to each other, but one day I saw Bao make a slitting motion across his neck, so I knew he was telling my dad what happened to his throat.

Another day I saw my dad making a karate chop slice with his hand and I knew he was telling Bao what happened to his fingers.

And one time I heard Bao say to my dad, "I wish you peace, Carl. That what you need. That what I need. Peace."

My dad nodded.

Bao moved his knight.

Dad moved his bishop.

"Peace for us, peace for them," my dad said. "Checkmate."

"The girls are exactly like us," Janie said, rinsing a bowl after Blow Your Mouth Off Chili Night. Each of us sisters had made our specialty chili, with our personal secret recipe. All of them were spicy enough to bring tears to our eyes.

Cecilia's won for spiciest and best. No surprise there. It 'bout blew out my eardrums.

"Hopefully the girls will end up saner," I mused, as I stared out the window at Kayla and Riley under the willow tree.

"At least less angry," Cecilia said, with anger. "That's what I wish for them. Less anger." She dropped a glass and the shards spun over the counter. "Damn. That makes me mad."

"I think loss makes people angry," Janie said. "And fear. It's a psycho-emotional shake-up that gets us out of balance with the universe. That's why I have my healing herbs."

"Herbs scherbs," Cecilia said, blowing hair out of her eyes.

"Herbs will bring you into focus, into your own softness and gentleness, so your body and mind will harmonize." Janie shook her red hair out of her bun. Her hair sure was getting long.

"Harmonize this, Janie: I'm a fat, angry mom who will burn all your herbs to a crisp if you don't stop with that New Wave herb crap."

Here came the peacemaker. Again. "I remember when you started being angry all the time, Cecilia."

"When? Damn!" She sucked on her finger where glass had punctured the skin.

"When Dad left."

"Well, gee. I didn't know you were so bright, Isabelle!" She clapped her hands to her head. "You shoulda been a rocket scientist!"

"You've transferred your anger to Parker."

"Whoee! More brilliance!"

"And to Dad."

"You're Einstein, Isabelle."

I dried off a pan. "When are you gonna get rid of your anger, Cecilia?"

"When? Never."

"Let's not fight," Janie said. "We'll ruin our inner spherical balance."

"We're not fighting," I said. "I'm worried that your anger is going to kill you, Cecilia."

Cecilia shoved her hands in the soapy water. "I am, too. I've been angry for decades."

"And you hate, Cecilia. You hate this person or that person . . . there's always someone you hate. Our whole lives, there's been somebody."

"They deserved it."

"That's not the point. You've gotta get rid of your hate. It's a living, breathing parasite in you."

"What about you, Isabelle?" she snapped, flicking a dish towel against the counter. "You've battled depression forever—"

"I'm enjoying the fight."

"You've been with a truckload of men."

"Probably two truckloads. I'm not proud of it."

"You travel to horrible places and it unglues you even further."

"I was unglued to begin with." And I missed my photographic jaunts, I finally admitted to myself. How I missed photography. I missed it like I'd miss my soul.

"Don't be a hypocrite, Isabelle."

She had a point. "Okay, I'll try to stick it to my depression if you try to stick it to your hate and anger."

Cecilia whipped that towel against the counter again.

"Well, let's get the tapper-counter in on this. Janie, you gotta stop it with all your checking and hermit behavior and tapping."

"Oh, I don't know . . ." she wobbled.

"Come on, Embroidery Queen," I said.

She put her hands on her hips.

Cecilia whacked her with the towel. "Should I hit you four times?" she mocked.

"I'll go upstairs to my serenity corner and think about it," Janie said.

"Tap, tap, tap, tap," Cecilia mocked.

"Shut up, Cecilia," Janie said, slamming a glass on the counter. "I don't refer to you as fathead or meatball butt or thunder thighs or Queen Double Chin or Sag and Drag, so stop making fun of me."

Whew. That silence was rigid and tight, tight, tight, once again. I moved between them so Cecilia would not annihilate Janie.

"My therapist says I need to become stronger with my social-familial conflicts and stand up for myself with womanly courage, so I am!" Janie declared. "If you're going to be mean, I'll be mean!"

Electrifying silence.

I braced myself to physically defend Janie when Cecilia leaped for her throat.

Janie waited with bated breath for Cecilia to lash out at her.

But a surprising thing happened then: Cecilia laughed. She whipped that towel against the counter and laughed. "I'm so mad at you, Janie, I could . . . I could spit!"

"Spit?" Janie asked.

"Yes, spit!" She spat in the sink. "But I am fat! I do have thunder thighs! I think I have three chins, not two; my boobs are always sweaty; my pits smell no matter what I do; and my mouth is out of control, so who am I to argue? But I'm still so *ticked off!*"

"You gotta stop, Cecilia," I said quietly. "Your anger could kill me. I feel it all the time."

Cecilia's eyes widened, and her chin wobbled. "You feel it all the time?"

"Pretty much, Cecilia," I said. "I feel my own depression, but I feel you, too."

She rested her head on the counter, straightened up, cracked the towel twice. "I'm sorry, Isabelle."

"It's okay. I'm sorry you have to smell the vague scent of a cigarette after my one-night stands."

"Me, too. I get none of the fun."

"But you don't smoke, Isabelle," Janie observed.

"It's a strange tie we have, odd, inexplicable . . ."

"What do you think will happen when one of us dies, Is?" Cecilia asked.

I knew she was referring to our freak twin connection. "I don't know." I hardly wanted to think about it.

But since we are so attuned to one another, when Cecilia died, would I? Or vice versa? Probably not. But it wouldn't feel good. "Okay, Cecilia, we're gonna make a pact. If you or I get terminally ill and our brains are fried, our bodies are rotting, or we're in grave pain and the other twin is feeling the same thing, the sick twin needs to get one of the .45s out and get it over with."

"Let's get off this unpleasant subject of dying with its unpleasant aura!" Janie said. "Cheerful, soul-feeding subjects only!"

Cecilia wiped her hand on the dish towel, then flicked it again. She held her hand out and I shook it. "Deal."

We both knew we were completely serious.

～ 24 ～

Wednesday night I was back singing on stage at the church for the teenagers.

Father Mike bopped around in the front row, smiling, dancing. His dancing resembled that of a puppet and a Gumby doll. The kids loved it.

"Isabelle," Father Mike said to me when all the kids in that giant gang were off at their classes, "I have to tell you again, my girl, it's so good to have you back in the church! It's so good!"

I cringed. I was not exactly back in the church. In fact, on Sunday mornings I was usually sleepin' my sorry ass off, exhausted from the week. "Well, Father, I've been meaning to get to mass, I have." I stopped. Don't ever lie to a priest. It's not a good idea. "Well, I've been thinking about going to mass." Sheesh. "I may come to mass sometime in the future."

"Thatta girl," he said to me, fists raised in triumph. "We're lucky to have you and I know the angels above are appreciating that voice of yours."

"The only way the angels are appreciating my scratchy voice is if they're half-deaf and like the sound of broken glass."

Father Mike laughed, then he patted the pew and I sat next to him.

For a long time we stared at the cross on the altar.

"What's on your heart, Isabelle?"

The familiar question I'd grown up with was my undoing. It's how Father Mike dug deep into all his flock. *"What's on your heart?"*

I started out slow, then the words flew out faster, and I held my head, hiccupping along with my tears, Father Mike's eyes compassionate and forgiving. "I don't think I'm good enough for God."

"Dearest Isabelle! All of us are good enough for God. Every one of us. He made us, he created us. He has a plan for us. And you, Isabelle, are a gift to everyone who knows you. God's gift."

"God's gift has sinned so much. Father Mike, I have hated my momma. I have run from my family . . ."

"Your family, your momma, is complex, the relationships often difficult, made more difficult by circumstance. God gave you this family so you could take what you've learned and help others."

"I think I've broken near to all the commandments, except I haven't whacked anyone off."

"And beyond those broken commandments you will find God's grace and mercy."

"I left God."

"He never left you, Isabelle Bommarito. Never. Not for a minute."

"I walked away from the church."

"He stayed with you on your walk."

"I have sinned a million times."

"And beyond those sins you have God's love. You always did. His love is infinite. It is eternal."

It was midnight when we were done.

"You are a child of God, dear Isabelle. Don't let your past regrets and guilt and the memories of who you *used* to be ruin one more minute of your present or your future. It's done. Go on knowing you're forgiven. Walk with God, Isabelle. He's put out his hand to you many, many times. All you have to do is put your hand out to him."

I put my hand out to Father Mike. He held it.

We sat in front of that cross for a long time.

"We're not going to let him back in our lives just like that, damn it," Cecilia raved. "No way. He thinks he can leave for years and then slip right back in to the family? Pick up where he left off. Be Dad again? Forget it. Asshole."

We had closed the bakery and the three of us were cleaning up. Henry had handed out samples of peanut brittle and was sitting in a booth drawing a bird. His stomach was hurting again, so I'd brought him milk.

The girls were doing their homework next to Henry. Riley had not pulled out any hair that I'd seen. She had not run from her current shrink, either, for two weeks, which was a cause for family celebration. We'd had a "Hooray, She Hasn't Run" party last night at home with steak and potatoes and a huge pink cake.

Kayla was wearing an orange monk's outfit and chanting softly.

"But Cecilia," Janie protested, rinsing out a bowl that had been used for truffle cake, "he's so nice! He makes us laugh! Spiritually, he brings harmony to our lives!"

"No, spiritually he's manipulating us," Cecilia hissed, words dropping out of her mouth like teeny tiny swords. "He's getting to each one of us one at a time. He's going for you, first, Janie, because you're a sucker for sob stories."

"I am not a sucker for sob stories!"

"Yes, you are," Cecilia and I said.

Janie took out the sprayer from the sink and sprayed us, the water arching into the air.

"Stop it, Janie!" Cecilia threw a wooden spoon at her.

"You started it by saying I'm a sucker." She sprayed us again.

I ducked behind a counter. "I don't need a shower, Janie."

"All I'm saying," Cecilia said, wiping her face off with a towel, then throwing it to me, "is that we can't let him come back again."

"He's already back," I said. "And I thought you were going to work on your anger."

"Come on, Isabelle, give me a break. I would think you'd want to break his neck, like I do."

I joined Janie at the sink and started cleaning a pan that I had used for pastries.

"What? You're not talking to me, Isabelle?"

"I'm talking to you."

"Then why aren't you answering my question? Does your mouth not work?"

Watching Cecilia's anger is like watching a fire take hold. It simmers, it grows into tiny orange flames, then it leaps, and it burns down the whole darn forest, taking Bambi and all those furry friends with it.

"Helloooooo . . ." Cecilia mocked. "Yoo-hooo."

I turned off the water and crossed my ankles as I leaned against the sink.

Cecilia glared, feet apart, stomach heaving.

How to start? My hair was dripping from where Janie had sprayed me. I had flour on my arms. My apron was smeared in orange and yellow icing, the colors I'd used today on a birthday cake I'd made in the shape of a monarch butterfly.

My braids were gone, my hair was short. I was almost completely detached from my life in Portland and, after a few stark and brutal realizations about myself after the attack, I didn't think I'd ever live there again. I was checking in on Momma, visiting with Henry, watching over Grandma. I was working with my sisters, running a business, and fighting with the lingering blame/guilt/nerve-shattering fear from the attack.

But I was also so settled . . . so, dare I say it, *content* in Trillium River.

I didn't even feel like my old self anymore.

Where had she gone?

Where was the old self?

I didn't know. And here's a fact: I didn't miss her.

"What?" Cecilia noisily rearranged metal mixing bowls. "You're gonna stand there like a baboon? Forgot your brain somewhere?"

"I haven't forgotten my brain." I stopped weighing my odds for this conversation and decided blunt was best. "My depression has blocked out the light in my life for years. It was a part of me, a part of my life, a part of who I was, starting when we were kids. It was like infected, toxic sludge running through my veins. I isolated myself except from you two and Henry. I slept around. I have lived almost solely for myself, by myself for twenty years. I have been miserably lonely and alone for most of my adult life."

"But you've had us!" Janie squealed, looping an arm around my shoulders.

"The only time I'm not lonely is when I'm with you two and Henry," I said. And that was the truth. The utter truth.

Cecilia bent her head.

"Goodness! Me, too!" Janie agreed. "Me, too. I'm lonely without you three! My spirit alone, wandering, searching."

"I shut down on the rest of the world. Shut them out, including my responsibility to you here, Cecilia, and the family."

I wiped my hands on my apron. I didn't think the girls were listening, but I wasn't sure. Riley was fiddling with her hair. Kayla fiddled with her monk outfit. At least she did not have her burka on.

"If Dad wants back into our lives, I welcome him back. Will he stay forever? I don't know. Probably not. People are people. But I'm not going to base my own happiness on whether or not he stays."

Janie fluffed her pink apron. "I hope he stays . . ."

Cecilia snuffled and sniffled.

"I can't be angry anymore. I cannot spend one more day of my life being angry. I can't be angry at you two, at Momma, at Dad, our past. I can't do it. I almost died with that creep in my loft. I think I'll struggle the rest of my life with what happened, but I finally saw how much I don't want to live in a grave."

This was going to be the hard part. I tightened my jaw and tried not to lose it.

"I actually believe I can be happy here in Trillium River. For me to believe I can be happy, *at all,* is a miracle. I like it here. I like the people. We're going to a barbeque next week at our ex–English teacher's house." I smiled. I had loved Mrs. Lary. "Lin Chi is pregnant and we're all going to a damn baby shower. We're going to Tommy and Kathleen's wedding in September." I matched a sniffle with Cecilia. "And I have you two and Henry and Grandma and the sweet River." We all laughed at that. "I love you, my sisters. I truly love you both."

"Oh, oh, oh, you're talking serenity, Isabelle! Serenity!" Janie said. "And I love you, too! I do!" She brought her apron to her face and sobbed out her love.

Cecilia snuffled, her mouth twisting, face flushed.

"I'm not mad at Dad anymore," I admitted, throwing up my hands. "The man's a Vietnam War vet and he flipped out when he got home. You know I spent months in Vietnam, interviewed ex–Vietnamese fighters and Vietnam War Vets here for that documentary on the war. I heard the most gruesome, hair-raising stories, and I know this: If we had been in combat in Vietnam we probably would have flipped, too."

In fact, I would have flipped and flipped again.

"When he killed that man and went to jail, he'd been over the edge a long time. The man's brother, for heaven's sakes, Joseph Corelli, was the person who hired Dad right out of jail. Dad wrote to Joseph when he was in jail to apologize for what he did. They started writing letters and he forgave Dad. Apparently Joseph's brother had been arrested several times for assault before that incident with Dad and was a real hothead. Dad's worked for Joseph this whole time, until he was offered the position of Chief Financial Officer of TechEx."

Cecilia put her hand to her heart. My heart jumped two beats and sped up.

"It's the love of the world going around!" Janie said, fluttering.

"So what has Dad done since he came back? He's taken Henry

fishing and hiking. He's taken us all out to dinner several times. We went on a boat ride last weekend. He's helped us fix this place up, he's baking up a storm, and he won't let us pay him. He's hung out with Grandma and is making a model airplane with her and Henry. He drove Velvet to her colonoscopy appointment. He's read drafts of Janie's new book. Should he have come back sooner? Yes. No. Maybe."

"We had a great time getting scared together!" Janie exclaimed. "I thought we'd have to get in a closet, but we didn't!"

I hardly knew what to say to that, so I plowed on. "There were extreme circumstances here that led to him abandoning us. He was suffering in a way that we will never, ever get. And if we accept that, accept that his suffering was caused by stupid men running a stupid war, and his mental state was in tatters, then here's the next question: Who are we not to welcome him home?"

"I'll do it! I will! I'll welcome him!" Janie said, flapping her apron. "I like him! He's great!"

Janie hugged me.

Cecilia snuffled again, pushing her hair out of her teary face. "I *might* give him one shot to be a dad again. One shot."

"I think that's a good idea," I said.

I hugged Cecilia. Janie hugged me. And when they were both relaxed, I grabbed the sprayer and soaked them both.

Cecilia somehow gave Dad a sign that she *might* give him another shot. I could tell he was delighted, not only to see Cecilia but to be with his granddaughters.

The girls were surprisingly enthused one day about a neighbor's vegetable garden and how cool it was, and Dad took that idea and ran.

He asked Cecilia if she would like a vegetable garden and where, rented a rototiller, and he and the girls built raised beds for vegetables, flowers, blueberries, and strawberries. I noticed that our dad did not let that bum leg of his get in the way of anything.

As Riley said, "He's one cool old guy. We even discussed astrophysics and the Hubble Telescope."

A brainy dad, then. "He understands astrophysics?"

"Oh, yeah. He said he loves to study astronomy. He even bought me a couple of books on supernovas, spiral galaxies, and meteorology." She rolled her lips in tight, then said, "I told him about my hair pulling. It's not like he couldn't see I'm going bald."

"How did that conversation go?" I braced myself.

"He was, like, cool about it. I told him sometimes I wear ski hats at night so I don't pull at my hair and that I tried wearing mittens, too, but that didn't work. You know, the mittens were supposed to make pulling hard, but all you have to do is take 'em off, so, yeah, like, that didn't work."

"I'm sorry, Riley." I knew better than to tell her to stop. It would be like someone telling me to stop having depression as in—voilà—okay! Now it's gone! Thanks for telling me to stop! Now I'm cured!

"I told myself that when I pulled a hair out, I'd slap myself in the face, and I tried that, but it didn't work. Then I tried giving myself an award like I could have ice cream if I didn't pull or I could spend my allowance money on a science book, but that didn't work, either. I have to pull my hair out. It's like it lets out my stress. Dad thinks I'm ugly and he's embarrassed, I can tell, and so does Constance. You think I'm not embarrassed? I know I'm ugly."

"You're not ugly, Riley. You're beautiful."

"No, I'm not, but Carl said I'm smart and funny and pretty and generous and I'll be more compassionate toward other people and their problems because of my own."

"Smart man," I said. "He gets it."

"Yeah," Kayla interrupted. "He's cool. He said I could wear my sari or my crosses or my fig leaf hat and say the rosary while we were planting the seeds or do some monk chanting. He's rad-

ical." She paused. "He said no to the burka. He said that me
dressed all in black scares him."

I laughed.

The next day I rode my motorcycle to the Columbia River before opening the bakery. I was calmed by the golden lights
streaking over the horizon, trails of pinks and yellows and a slash
of orange swirling around the breaking sun like a dancer's dress.

From the side of that rushing river, I studied my windsurfer.
At another time in my life, I might have wandered over to say
hello. Chat. Get laid, if necessary. He was male and, from a distance, he was attractive. He was athletic.

That would have been enough for me to drown myself in for a
few hours so I could bury my pain, then get rid of him. Plenty
enough.

But I didn't need any more drowning. I had done that for too
many decades.

I think I was finally finding Isabelle.

She'd been hiding, arms over her head, curled up in a ball, in a
closet in my mind, but she was there.

The wind puffed on by, soothing my face and, I do believe,
my soul.

I tried going to church on Sunday. Cecilia and the girls always
go, but I told them I'd go only if we could sit in the back and disappear.

We sat in the back. Velvet, Janie, and Grandma came, too.

The disappearing part didn't work too well.

At the beginning of mass Father Mike spread his arms out and
said, "Welcome, everyone! Welcome if you're here weekly. Welcome if you come once a month or once a year. Welcome welcome welcome if you've never been to church at all but here you
are today! And, ladies and gentleman, I would like to put a *special*

welcome out there for the Bommarito Family, Amelia Earhart, and Velvet Eddow!"

The whole church turned and stared.

Grandma stood and saluted, left, center, right.

Henry stood up in the first row and shouted back, "Hi, Isabelle! Hi, Janie! Hi, Cecilia! Jesus loves you!"

The clapping of the congregation was quite welcoming.

When the clapping congregation turned toward the front again, I rolled my eyes at Father Mike and spread out my arms like—*what the hell?*

He grinned.

He's a sneaky priest.

"Daddy and Constance had a huge fight this weekend. They thought we were at the neighbors next door, but we weren't. We got the whole meal deal," Kayla said. She was wearing three giant wood and metal crosses on her neck. ("I am reviewing my study of three religions this week: Judaism, Catholicism, and Lutheranism.")

She leaned against the porch rail. It was twilight and the three Bommarito sisters were almost comatose with exhaustion. Henry was running around with Grandma like a plane on the lawn, although slower than usual. Velvet was asleep on the lounge, snoring like a southern lady.

"We heard the whole yucky thing," said Riley. She was wearing a green bandana and a shirt with Einstein's picture on it. "Seems like whenever we're there they get in a fight and start in on each other like colliding asteroids."

I dipped some chips into mango salsa and muffled my chuckles. The neighbor up the street gave it to us. His name was Chance Dickey, he was eighty, and he winked at Velvet when he came by.

"Dad was sweating he was so mad because he said he gave Constance a 'shitload' of money—he used that word, Mom, I'm just repeating it—from his retirement accounts to pay her credit cards off before they got married. They also opened accounts together," Kayla said. "What's that called?"

"Joint accounts," I said, settling into the porch swing with my strawberry daiquiri. This was gonna be good. I smirked at Cecilia.

Janie hummed over her teacup. She had a journal on her lap where she'd drawn a noose.

"Okay," Kayla said. "That. So, like, he had the bills for their credit accounts on the table and he was so awesome pissed at Constance."

"Yeah," Riley chimed in. "Daddy and her are renting that place in downtown Portland, they don't own it, and I heard Daddy say they weren't going to be able to buy a house unless they could get rid of the new credit card bills and Constance yelled, 'You better get a raise at work then, Park,' and I thought he was gonna throw Constance out the window. He said his boss was already on his back anyhow because he got divorced. His boss liked you, Mom."

"When I was studying to be a Mormon, I called him and he told me all about their religion. He's so cool," Kayla said. "They got nine kids."

"Dad yelled at Constance," Riley said, "that his boss hauled him into his office because you called him, Mom, because Dad hadn't paid his child support and the boss told Dad he couldn't trust him morally anymore, whatever that means, and to pay the child support immediately."

"Now isn't that a shame," I muttered.

"Shameful," Cecilia drawled.

"Constance told him she wasn't Betty Crocker, like Mom," Kayla said. "And she wasn't going to stay home and cook dinner and she sure as hell's bells—that's what she said, 'hell's bells'—wasn't going to take his shirts to the dry cleaner or take his car in for an oil change, like he'd told her to since she doesn't work.

Dad got even more mad and madder. He said, 'Cecilia always did it and she worked and had two kids!' and Constance threw a fireplace poker at his head. It broke a window."

"Constance wants to go to spas all day and get her hair done," Riley said. "She says she has a business, but all I saw were hundreds of shampoo and cream rinse and lotion bottles stacked up in their storage space. They were labeled Constance's Creams and Dalliances."

"Her business sucks," Kayla said. "She told Dad before she married him that she had so much business she could barely handle it all and Dad said he was going to help her with it. They were all excited about it. They said they were going to take her company international and make a bunch of money."

"Like, she doesn't even use it on her own hair," Riley said. "I saw her shampoo bottles in the shower."

"How was your behavior with your father?" I couldn't resist. I had to ask. Bommarito Power!

I watched the girls squirm.

"I felt like furthering my education as a Muslim again," Kayla said. "So I wore my burka."

"I told Constance her boobs were out and she should put them back in," Riley said.

"I prayed five times a day on my mat to Allah," Kayla said. "Out loud."

"But other than that and telling her she was too old for the outfit she was wearing and that you, Mom, would never dress like that," Riley said, "I didn't speak to her."

"You spoke to Constance when you two had that fight," Kayla corrected her. "Actually, you yelled at her."

Riley sighed heavily. "Constance was bugging me. She doesn't know anything about the European Union or what's going on in the Sudan. She doesn't even know what macroeconomics is. She thought physics was spelled with an *f*. She's stupid. Most of the time I glare at her."

A puff of wind puffed by. I tried not to laugh at how Parker was being filleted.

"When I go to Dad's I feel spiritually driven to be a Muslim woman."

"And I'm going to pluck out my hair in the kitchen."

There was a fully loaded silence as we digested this hilarity.

"To hair plucking and burkas!" I cheered, holding up my daiquiri. "Cheers!"

❦ 25 ❧

I drove out with Cecilia and Janie to see Momma about a week later.

When we arrived, we found Momma square dancing, her head back, laughing, her face lit up like a Christmas tree. She was even wearing one of those flouncy, lacy skirts.

Clearly, she had forgotten her daughters were coming.

I had not seen her so happy in years.

I watched her for a while, remembering all we had been through.

Sinda leaned over my shoulder.

"She's having the time of her life," I said.

Sinda nodded. "They all do here. What's not to like? These people are older, not ill, not dead. They still want to laugh and dance and have a good time. We have activities all day. They don't have to do any housework, their meals are cooked for them, they can go on outings whenever they wish. Yesterday we took them to an action movie and out to dinner. There's a group of them who want to go to a water park and slide down the slides. We're getting signed consent forms from all of them before we go so we don't get sued if they get hurt—and their families have to sign, too—but all the forms but one are back in, so it's a go."

I smiled as I watched an older gentleman spin Momma.

"Is Momma one of the water park people?" Janie asked.

Cecilia threw up her arms, "Whaddya think?"

Sinda handed me the form.

I signed it.

We decided to stay in Portland that night, so we headed over to my loft. It was the first time I'd been back since I was attacked. I felt ill down to my toes, almost feverish, and my sisters held my shaking hands in the elevator on the way up.

Cecilia inserted the key in the lock. Since the police had busted the door down, management had arranged for a new one.

When Cecilia opened the door, it was like she was opening the door to Demon Hell. I didn't want to go in.

I started to shake from the inside, as if my lungs were shriveling from fear. The deathly memory of that night came rushing back, the stark, hopeless, raging terror. I could feel my face getting pounded in, my braids being yanked from my head, my ribs splitting, my chin cracking, and my own hot blood spurting out of me.

I could hear him, his spine-tingling giggles, his off-key singing, his explosive anger, and I heard my own muffled screams, the thunk of my body hitting the floor, the punches he'd rained on me. I smelled his body, his breath, his groin, his danger. I could almost feel the tooth he'd knocked out in the back of my throat.

"Now, don't forget," Janie said, ruffling her beige skirt, "smile when you go through the doorway."

Janie's sweet voice, her innocent, eager face, cut through the churning, paralytic fear of my hideous memories.

"You're kidding, Janie. You want me to smile before I go into a place where I was attacked?"

"Yes, honey, please, it'll feel better in there, it will."

"She's got a point," Cecilia said, bending over double with me, feeling what I felt. "That bastard took so much from you, Isabelle. From all of us. Let's say to shit with him, hope the electric chair malfunctions and he has to fry for hours, and walk on in here. Smiling."

"Yes, let's do!" Janie said, cheerleader-like. "Smile, sisters!"

I straightened back up. Damned if they weren't right. I was not going to let that demented criminal take one more thing from me.

The three of us sisters linked arms, turned sideways, and went right through the door of my loft.

Smiling.

Even when I saw the bloodstains on my floor, I kept smiling.

When I sagged, my knees sinking into themselves as too many horrifying visions collided in my brain, both my sisters caught me.

And hugged me close.

That night we dragged three loungers onto my deck to check on the stars.

We couldn't see as many stars in the city as we could in the country.

That bugged me.

I heard cars and horns.

That bugged me, too.

And I couldn't see through the skyscrapers around me to any towering trees.

That bugged me big-time.

I was in a modern loft instead of Grandma's gracious Queen Anne with the nooks, crannies, stained glass, sunroom and wrap-around porch.

That made me feel cold.

I wanted to hug Henry and get to know the White Dove better and salute Amelia and laugh over Velvet's throat-burning lemonade.

I wanted to make a peach upside-down cake and apricot brandy muffins and hear more outrageous stories from Kayla and Riley.

Dare I say it? I wanted to go home and home wasn't here.
Home was not here.

No phone call at two in the morning is going to be good.
You know that.

All three of us boinged up in my bed at one time as the ringing
echoed off the walls of the night and the steel skyscrapers. I tried
to climb over Cecilia to get at the phone. Cecilia fumbled for it
blindly. I got tangled in the covers and slid off the bed while
Janie pleaded, "Get the phone, get the phone."

"Dammit," Cecilia muttered. She knocked over the last of the
gin and tonic she'd been drinking in bed. Janie knocked the
lamp over on her side.

I hopped to the light dragging the sheet, flicked it on, grabbed
my phone.

The news was not good.

No phone call at two in the morning is going to be good.
You know that.

"He's in the hospital," Dad said, his voice controlled, but the
worry zigzagged through his tone.

"We're coming," I said, panic charging like a bull in my gut.
"Right now."

Cecilia was on the floor, her hand on her chest. "Holy shit,
what is it?"

"Oh dear oh dear," Janie whispered.

"It's Henry," I said, choking back tears. "Dad and Velvet don't
know what's wrong. He's in pain. Says it's his stomach. They're
headed for the hospital in Trillium River. Velvet's staying with
Grandma."

We jumped into our clothes and flew out the door.

Sweet, sweet Henry was hooked up to IVs, pale, weak, his
eyes shut in a way that almost-dead people's eyes start to shut.

In typical Bommarito fashion, we hugged and kissed Henry,

then the three of us sisters went back into the hallway of the hospital and had our meltdowns.

Pancreatic cancer are two words you never want to hear.

It's when the pancreas, this organ that we're not aware of at all, this six-inch *thing* that lies sideways behind the bottom part of your stomach, is infested with cancer. The cells mutate supersonically fast and live a long time, forming tumors that suck the life out of their host. The host being your: grandpa, aunt, sister, father, and so on. The cancer usually spreads quick, insidious and cruel.

And by the time you find out you have it, things are not good.

With our Henry, our sweet Henry, things were not good.

"It's metastized," Dr. Remmer told us in a conference room late the next afternoon. She was thin, about sixty years old with gray hair pulled back in a ponytail. Knowledgeable, friendly, professional. Exactly who you want when you're in the crisis of your life.

Dad leaned his head back, covering his white, pasty face with his hands.

"I don't understand," Cecilia snapped off, already angry. "He's had stomachaches all his life. We've always had him lie down, given him milk and cookies . . . how did this happen? How did Henry get pancreatic cancer? He doesn't drink, doesn't smoke, never did drugs. He eats healthy. He's a little fat, but that's it. He's even lost about fifteen pounds in the last couple of months!"

Janie started hiccup crying, tapping the table in sets of four. She'd already found herself some lemon tea.

"Unintended weight loss, actually," the doctor said, calm and controlled, "can be a sign of pancreatic cancer."

The doctor glanced down at her notes and the lab tests that she had spread out on the conference table.

"How could it have metastized already?" Cecilia said. "This is the first damn second we've even heard about the damn thing!"

"It's a terrible beast." The doctor showed us a scan. The scan was a black-and-white blur of pancreatic disaster.

"The cancer has spread to his liver." Another scan.

"It's spread to his stomach." Another scan.

"We think it's in his lymph nodes."

Janie threw her hands up in the air in defeat and sobbed.

Tears ran silently down Dad's well-lined, white-as-a-sheet cheeks.

I could hardly move.

Devastation, bleak, utter and all-consuming, filled my entire being. How could this be happening? *How could this be happening?*

Cecilia's anger notched way up. "We have to fix this. Can he start chemo today? What about radiation? Can you operate and take the damn thing out? What's the plan? We need to start this immediately. Right now. Like, tonight." I don't even think she noticed that her whole body was shaking, her head wobbling from stress.

I put a hand on her hand, even as the room seemed to swirl and spin.

"Stop it!" she rasped out, standing up. "Don't touch me! You're all sitting around, doing nothing. *Nothing.* And Henry needs help!" She pounded both fists on the table. "What are you going to do, doctor? How are you going to help my brother?"

The doctor was used to this. "We can do chemo . . ."

Cecilia interrupted. "That's a given. Now get your nurse, or get another doctor, and tell her to get things set up right away. If this is spreading fast, we need to stop it. Why aren't you calling her?" Cecilia pounded the table again, her head wobbling. "Why aren't you calling her? *Why aren't you doing something?*"

"Cecilia," I said. My heart felt as if screws were being drilled into it.

"Cecilia," Janie said, tap, tap, tapping.

"Don't patronize me!" she shouted, kicking her chair against the wall. "Don't do that! Don't tell me to calm down. I am not going to calm down until we get Henry help. Help him! *Help him!*"

"Honey," Dad said, getting up and putting a hand on her back.

"Don't honey me!" She shrugged off his arm. "I want a second opinion. Who knows if you even know what you're doing . . ." She put her hands on her face. "Who knows if you even know what you're doing . . ." She bent over at the waist as if she'd been slugged in the stomach. "I think you're wrong. *You're wrong.*"

Dad put an arm around her, urged her to sit down.

"This can't be true," Cecilia half screamed, wrenching away from Dad. "You have the wrong scans. Henry isn't sick. He was outside the other day running around with Grandma. They were planes. He helped with treats on Wednesday night at church. We made giant whale cookies at the bakery because they were studying Jonah and the whale. I'm telling you!" she screamed. "He is not sick!"

The doctor's eyes welled up. "I am so deeply sorry."

"You're not sorry enough! Not sorry enough!" Cecilia's voice ended in a wail. She didn't even bother to try to land in a chair. She sank to the ground, forehead to the floor, keening, crying.

I grabbed her and rocked her, her head in full-throttle wobble. "He's not sick! He's not sick!"

Janie stood up to help and I saw her sway, vision unfocused. "Dad! Get Janie!" I yelled.

The doctor and Dad moved at the same time as Janie pitched straight back.

Cecilia moaned, low, guttural, grief-stricken.

Destroyed. I felt her. I felt that destruction.

I thought of Henry in that bed, his sweet face, his kindness, the only sane person in the Bommarito family.

The tears came like a wave, an angry, frothing, hateful wave.

Cecilia said, "She's wrong! She's wrong! Our Henry isn't sick! He's not sick! He was petting the dogs the other day!"

But the doctor was not wrong.

Our Henry was not only sick.

Our Henry was dying.

"Go and get Momma," Janie whispered to me the next morning, her voice weak. "Go get her."

She was lying in a lounge chair next to a hospital bed where Cecilia was resting. The doctors were concerned about her heart.

I hadn't been surprised. My heart was skipping back and forth, and I knew Cecilia was doing it to me. It was I who told a doctor to check Cecilia. He had done so, against her wishes, and she was wheeled out on a stretcher seconds later. She was currently sleeping, but her sleep was restless, her chest rising up and down, body trembling.

Janie had fainted twice and was sickly pale. Dad was sitting next to Cecilia, holding her hand.

"I'll go get Momma," I said. I dreaded it like nothing I had ever dreaded before.

"I'm coming with you," Dad told me.

"No, I'll go alone. It would be too much of a shock to Momma."

Dad put his chin up. "Honey, it will be a shock to your mother to see me, there's no doubt. But I have not been there for your mother for almost three decades. I will be there for her when she hears this news."

"But Dad," I said, "you left her, left us. She may be furious with you still. Hurt, angry. You know Momma. She lives on full-blast. Forgiveness is not her forte. Neither is forgetting a grudge."

"I know River," he said. "I loved her. I still love her." He paused, swallowed hard. "River knew why I left, honey. She also knew I was in jail."

I felt like I'd gotten another hit in the face. "She did? She never told us."

"You didn't need to know that your daddy had landed himself in jail. River knew not to hurt you more than you'd been hurt. I know how to handle River and I know I can be of comfort to her. It's time for me to go to her. Please. Allow me."

There were too many emotions in my head to argue. There was no doubt that Dad was a calming presence to us. He would know how to handle Momma better than I, of that I had no doubt.

He kissed Cecilia and Janie, who clung to him.

We hurried in to the retirement center, our despair heavy, dreadful, and I immediately saw Sinda. I told her about Henry, who we had brought to the center many times. She got teary-eyed, shook hands with Dad, then led us into a library, where Momma was deep into a bridge game with three other ladies.

For a second Momma didn't see us and I studied her. She was still so beautiful. Bright eyes, soft bell-shaped hair, trim figure. She had a bone structure that would never give. At ninety she'd still be a stunner.

I felt sheer pain radiating through my body. Pain for us all. Pain for Henry and what was in store for him. Pain for Dad, who would soon lose the son he had only come to know recently. Pain for Cecilia, who needed Henry so she could live, and for Janie, who loved Henry to distraction.

Pain for me. Pain for Momma. This news would break her in half.

She laughed at something one of the ladies said, and it startled me. Momma had so seldom laughed after Dad left, our struggles overwhelming any hint of amusement.

She laughed again, her face relaxed, carefree.

I was about to take all of this away from her because her son, her beloved son, who she was always faithful to, and had always fought for, was dying.

Momma chatted with the lady next to her but, like a magnet, her gaze skimming right off Dad, our eyes locked.

I watched as a myriad of emotions galloped across those fine, classic features: surprise (Isabelle isn't supposed to be here! She didn't make an appointment), joy (I was glad to see that), guilt (because she'd been pretending to be such a sick, *sick* Momma), and annoyance (Yikes! The game was up!).

She excused herself from the game over the other ladies' protests and walked stiffly out of the room, right past Dad. I followed her.

"I don't want you to think, Isabelle, that because I took a little break away from my pain, my exhaustion, that I'm better. I struggled out of bed this morning, I could hardly get up. Swanson had to come and help me—" Her eyes finally flittered to Dad.

I don't think Momma could have been more shocked if I'd brought in three ostriches by leash.

All the blood drained out of her face.

"Momma . . ." I put a hand out to steady her.

I expected Momma to recover quickly from this shock and show so much condescension, anger, and coldness to Dad it would freeze the entire room into a giant icicle.

I expected this because I thought I knew Momma.

"Hello, River," Dad said, his voice gentle, soothing. "You, as always, you are still . . ." He paused, gathered himself together as he choked on his words. "Still so beautiful."

I waited for the icicles to drop from her mouth. I waited for her to decimate him, listing the litany of abuses he had inflicted on her by leaving us.

After years alone and struggling she would have words for him, her famous temper breaking free and mean. I would not have been surprised had she hit him. I knew this because I knew my momma.

Her face softened into lines of love, and she put out her arms and stepped right into his warm embrace.

"River Bommarito," Dad croaked out, his voice breaking as he cuddled her close. "I have missed you every day. Every single day, sweetheart. Like I told you I would."

"You're staying then, Carl?" Momma asked, her voice filled with hope, blossoming, cheery, flowery hope.

"Forever," Dad said, rumbly and deep. He kissed her forehead. "Forever, honey."

I dropped into a chair as Momma kissed Dad's cheeks. He tenderly wiped away her tears, then his own.

I clearly didn't know Momma at all.

I hardly knew what to do.

My dad had abandoned us.

He went to jail for murder.

My childhood was filled with chaos and poverty and disruption and humiliation.

And Momma, one of the most vindictive, critical people I have ever met, was hugging Dad, her smile wide and pure and sweet.

It was heartbreaking that the smile did not last.

"River," Dad said, voice gruff and rough. "Perhaps we could have a few minutes of privacy."

Momma's friends grinned at her, waving their cards. One older lady declared, "He's hot! How is he in bed, River?" Another one cracked, "Bring him to the beach with us tomorrow! I'd like to see him in his bathing suit!" She thumped her walker.

Momma escorted us to her room, her head up. I think she was proud of my dad.

She insisted on going into her room by herself. I could hear her moving around in there and I pictured her picking things up, opening the blinds, a window, straightening the bedcovers.

When she opened the door, I could tell that she had added a little lipstick.

"I'll speak to your mother alone for a few minutes, honey," Dad had told me. "We'll tell her about Henry together, but I think she might need a little time to get used to my being here."

I made noises indicating I agreed, and waited outside Momma's door. I heard her laughter; and her voice, which had always been so strident and demanding, was gentle, even soothing, funny, lovely.

I leaned against the wall and wrapped my arms around my body. Momma loved Henry to the Big Dipper and back. She would never be the same. I wasn't sure she'd live through this.

I held myself tighter as the tears tracked down my cheeks.

I wasn't sure I'd live through this, either.

"Momma," I said, as gentle as I could about thirty minutes later. I put my hand around hers across a table and Dad did the same. "Momma, Henry had a stomachache the other day."

Momma smiled, gazed at Dad. "Henry always gets stomachaches. You remember that, Carl? Poor boy."

I cleared my throat. "Momma, it's more than a stomachache this time." My eyes filled up with tears. "It's more than that."

"River, honey," Dad said, clearing his throat. "Henry is at the hospital. Janie and Cecilia are with him."

He declined to mention that Cecilia was lying prostrate in a bed and Janie could barely breathe, but Momma did not need all the gory details at once.

"What?" she squeaked. I could feel her fear poking through. "What do you mean? What's wrong?"

Dad steadied her with his voice. "Henry is not well, River. He's ill and he's under a doctor's care. I'm sorry, honey, there is no easy way to say this." He paused, held her gaze. "Henry has been diagnosed with pancreatic cancer." He waited for his words to sink into her denial. "I am so sorry, River."

She slumped back in her chair. "Pancreatic cancer? *What?* What do you mean? I don't even know exactly what that is!"

Dad explained it to her, explained what a pancreas does and where it is in the body.

"But how did he get that? Henry is a young man, he shouldn't have cancer."

"They don't know," Dad said. "The point is that he has it."

"But he'll be okay? They'll treat it. The doctors will treat it, right?" I saw the bleak panic growing in her eyes by gargantuan leaps and bounds.

"We're consulting with the doctors about that, River, and we're going to bring you back to the hospital now so you can discuss this with the doctors yourself."

"You can bet I'm going back right now!" A fight was coming, I knew it. "You can bet I'm going! We're going to treat this and Henry is going to be fine! He is going to be fine!" She stood up, her body quaking, and slammed both hands on the table. "Do you hear me, Carl Bommarito? *Henry is going to be fine!*"

✌ 26 ✍

Cecilia had checked herself out of her room and was dressed and standing near Henry when we arrived. Standing as if on guard, shoulders back, blond hair bound in a ponytail.

Janie was playing checkers with Henry. She had found a CD player and classical music wafted through. Henry was propped up against the pillows, his slanted eyes tired but happy.

Janie and Cecilia moved out of the way for Momma, who came flying in.

"Momma!" Henry whooped, his arms out, checkers flying.

"Henry," Momma said, hugging him close as the checkerboard fell to the floor. "My boy. My big boy. I love you, baby, and you're going to get better soon."

"Yeah, yeah," Henry said, giving her a kiss. "The doctor say I sick. It a lady doctor. She has a dog. A dog named Snickers. Snickers!" He laughed. "Like the candy bar, get it! And she has another dog, Rex. Rex and Snickers..." He dissolved into laughter. "It silly! Rex and Snickers are in love, that what the doctor said. She have two doggies in love!"

He thought this was hilarious. We all tried to laugh. It's hard to laugh when you're staring down death in the face. Not impossible. But hard.

Momma always knew how to relate to Henry. "Are they married?" She smiled, but I could see the tears in those bright emerald eyes.

"Married!" Henry cackled. "Are the doggies married! I ask the doctor! They should get married if they in loooovvee! Hey! Maybe Jesus can marry them!"

He was pale, sort of yellowish, but that smile beamed. "The doctors and nurses say, 'How you are, Henry?' I tell them, 'I fine. Jesus loves you.' Hi, Dad! Dad back, Momma. Dad back."

"He sure is, sugar," Momma told him, brushing his curls back with such tenderness it almost brought me to my knees. "He sure is."

"Yeah, Dad back. There the doctor!" Henry smiled, his mouth open wide as Dr. Remmer came in. "Hey, doctor, are Snickers and Rex married? Are they married?"

We finally persuaded Henry to take a nap. It hadn't taken much; his eyelids were closing, and when he was asleep we all trooped out to the conference room across the hall to speak again with Dr. Remmer and about three other doctors and nurses whose names I did not bother to learn.

"Tell me about my son," Momma said, her hands laced tight together as the tear dam finally broke. Dad kept his hand on her back.

"Mrs. Bommarito," Dr. Remmer started. "As you know, Henry was recently admitted and diagnosed with pancreatic cancer. I understand that Henry has lost some weight lately—"

"I knew it," Momma said, glaring at the three of us sisters. "You weren't feeding him enough, were you?"

"Yes, we did feed him enough, Momma," I said. "He had lost his appetite."

"You should have made him his favorite meals, then," Momma snapped.

"All we cook are Henry's favorite meals, Momma—" Cecilia protested.

"They've taken wonderful care of Henry, River," Dad interjected. "Wonderful. You've raised beautiful, caring daughters."

"If I had been home—" Momma said, angry.

"If you had been home, Mrs. Bommarito," the doctor interrupted, "the result would have been the same."

Momma wriggled in her chair. Janie put her hand on Momma's shoulder. I stood behind Janie to catch her.

"So you're going to treat it and we'll get rid of it," Momma told the doctor, her tone hard. "You're going to get rid of it."

The doctor glanced down at her papers. I knew she was gathering her thoughts. The doctors around her suddenly found a need to shuffle their papers.

"We need to discuss that," the doctor said.

"What?" Momma spat out. "There's nothing to talk about. Treat the cancer. Get rid of it. People live through cancer all the time. I know two women in Trillium River who had cancer more than twenty years ago and they're still alive. Put him on chemo. We'll bring him in. You can do that radiation thing, too. Or operate. Can't you cut the cancer out?" She arched an eyebrow at the doctor. "Surely you can do that?" I knew Momma and I knew what she was trying to do. Intimidation by condescension.

This doctor was not intimidated, though, as she was used to working with people who were half out of their minds. Momma did not ruffle her at all.

"Unfortunately, of all the cancers one does not want to have, this is it." The doctor paused. "Pancreatic cancer is seldom caught in time to do anything about it. There aren't symptoms until it's too late."

"It's not too late to treat it," Momma insisted, her voice broken, leaning forward. "People have always wanted to give up on Henry. Always. His teachers. His schools. The doctors. Don't give up on my boy. *Don't give up on my boy.*"

"Mrs. Bommarito," the doctor said, "I would never ever give up on any patient, especially not Henry."

"You're going to now," Momma accused, tears dripping onto the table. "You're going to now. I can tell."

The doctor reached a hand across to Momma.

Now I thought Momma might hit that hand, but she didn't. She grabbed the doctor's hand like a lifeline.

"You can save my boy for me, doctor. I know you can."

"Mrs. Bommarito," the doctor said, clasping both her hands on Momma's, woman to woman. She took a deep breath. "We've done a number of scans and tests. Henry's cancer is too far metastasized. We can't operate. There's no point. It's . . . the cancer is all over . . . I am terribly, terribly sorry. I have no miracle cure for this."

"A miracle? A miracle?" Momma's voice pitched. "I don't need a miracle. I need you to do your job and fix my son!"

The doctor did not take offense.

Who could? A mother was sitting across from her, holding her hand tight, tears dripping off her chin and forming a puddle on the table in front of her.

"What are you telling me? There's no cure, there's nothing you can do?"

Cecilia slapped her hands over her mouth.

Janie moaned and swayed, and I linked an arm around her skinny waist.

Dad put both hands around Momma's shoulders.

"Mrs. Bommarito, because of the advanced stage of Henry's cancer, I am giving him, at most, even if we do try chemotherapy, a few months."

I couldn't swallow, couldn't move, this cold despair shooting through my body, cutting off my air, cutting off my blood flow, killing me.

"A few months? *A few months?* What do you mean? What. Do. You. Mean?" Each word was higher pitched until she lost it. Momma was done. She had controlled herself as long as she could.

"I mean . . ." The doctor braced herself. "I mean that I believe Henry has only a few months to live."

There was a charged, trembling, interval when no one breathed, the hideous sentence hanging over our heads like an eight-foot ax. That was it. Momma was gone.

Gone. *Gone.*

She stood up and screamed, "No! Noooo! God, no! *Oh, God, no!*" That scream echoed through the halls and corners of that hospital, primal, raw, hideous. "Oh, God, no!"

She screamed.

Janie and I stayed all night with Henry. We didn't sleep. The sun went down, the bright colors spread across the sky, the light disappeared, the moon rose, the moon disappeared, the sun came back, the bright colors spread across the sky, and we felt like crap.

Cecilia had gone home to be with the girls. Dad had taken Momma home. She was about a half inch from collapse.

We all gathered together in Henry's room the next morning, the shock wearing off, our new reality crystal clear and mind-boggling.

"I go home today," Henry told us as he ate his applesauce. He had had five applesauce containers.

"Henry," I said. "Not today."

"Yes, today!" he said, he karate-chopped the little table in front of him.

I could tell he was going to get belligerent. He was a Bommarito, after all. "I think if you went home in a few days it would be better. The doctor wants you to stay and rest and watch cartoons."

"I no watch cartoons." He frowned. "I go home. I no like hospital anymore. I bored. I see Grandma and we go on a flight. I have job at bakery. I give samples out and say, 'Jesus loves you.' I go home today. Right now I go home."

"In a few days, Henry," I told him, firmly.

But he was not to be coddled. "No. Isabelle, you drive me home on the motorcycle like on Tuesday. I love that motorcycle."

I slid a glance over to Momma. She put a shaky hand on her hip and glowered at me. She did not want Henry on my motorcycle ever.

"If you stay here, they'll bring you more applesauce and you can eat in bed and Cecilia or Momma or Janie or Dad or I will be with you the whole time."

Cecilia brushed his curls back with wobbly fingers.

"No, no. I go home and pet the dogs and I help Father Mike." He pushed back the covers. "I help with the doughnuts. He don't know how to do that. Father Mike don't know how to do doughnuts. At the church. Jesus loves you. He need me."

I snuck a glance at Momma. She'd aged overnight. She was wearing the same outfit. I knew she hadn't slept. Dad stood with his arm around her waist. I knew he was propping her up.

"How about if I bring Father Mike to you here?" I said. "I'll bring him here and you can tell him exactly what you do."

Henry considered that. "I dunno. I pet the dogs. The dogs miss me. Bark, bark. Lacie a new, nice dog. So will Paula Jay. I go see her so she won't miss me." He swung his feet over the bed.

"Henry, I will go and bring Paula Jay to you so she won't miss you so much." I put a hand on his shoulder.

Henry's face lit up. "On the motorcycle? You'll bring her on the motorcycle?"

I snapped my fingers. "That's a good idea. I'll bring Paula Jay on the motorcycle!" She'd do it. That daredevil.

"Hmm." He put a fist under his chin. "No, not work. I help with Bunco." His feet hit the floor. "They need me at senior center. They need Henry. I serve lunch and clean up and put forks in the box and bring Bommarito Cupcakes. Yummy."

"Now, Henry, how about if I bring Mr. Howard to you and you can tell him how to run things when you're not there? That would help."

He thought about that.

"No. You need my help at the bakery." He stood up. He didn't notice that he needed my help for balance.

I put on my most serious expression. "You're right, Henry. We need your help. But I'll hire someone until you get back to help us. How about that? I'll hire someone."

"Hmm." He cupped his chin, then tapped my nose. "You hire my friend, Lytle?"

"Lytle?" I knew Lytle. He was Henry's checker-playing friend. He was in a wheelchair and had trouble moving his hands in the right directions. His parents and four brothers adored him.

"Good idea!" I smiled. "I'll hire Lytle."

"Good. And you bring Lytle here play checkers?"

"Yes, I'll bring him here."

"Hmmmmm . . ." he said.

We all waited. No one wanted to wrestle Henry into bed. "Okay dokay. Henry stay here for few days. But you bring Henry's friends to Henry!"

He smiled.

I promised.

"I love you, my sister, Is."

"I love you, my brother, Henry."

I had no idea how many friends of Henry's would come and visit Henry.

None.

None of us did.

We should have gotten him a larger room.

Two larger rooms.

That night I again stayed and slept by Henry's bed. Momma and Dad stayed until eleven when Dad insisted Momma leave. She was a grayish-white, her eyes were swollen, and her face was lined with grief, as if the tear tracks had dug tunnels into her skin.

"I'm staying with my son," she protested for the third time, but her protest was weaker.

"River," Dad spoke, his voice brooking no argument. "You are coming with me. We are leaving now." He dropped her sweater over her shoulders and pulled her up. She bent to kiss Henry, who was sleeping.

She turned to me and gave me a hug. "Stay with your brother, Isabelle."

I was surprised at the hug, but I held on tight. Hugs were few and far between from Momma, and though I had schooled myself not to want them, I was brought to tears by this one.

She hugged Janie, kissed Henry on the lips again, and left, her walk unbalanced.

Cecilia had left earlier to be with the girls and Janie and I settled down. The nurses had brought in two lounge chairs. Janie and I held hands between the chairs. Within a few minutes we were both asleep.

It was the sleep of grief.

I woke up around three in the morning to Henry singing the "Jesus Loves Me" song.

For a while I listened, the room illuminated only by the tiny lights on a couple of machines, his IV line eerie in the blackness. The song was almost haunting, each word lonely, coming from far away, the notes pitch perfect.

"You have a good voice, Henry," I told him when he finished the third round. *I'm going to miss your voice.*

"Isabelle?"

"Yep. It's me." *It's me, Henry. I'm here for you.*

"You and Janie still here?"

"We sure are, Henry. We're not leaving." *I would never leave you.*

"I was in my dreams and I woke up because Jesus told me to sing the song. So I did. I sung the song."

I sat on the side of his bed. He reached his arms up for a hug and I hugged him, laying down with him on the bed. We held hands. *I would miss holding hands with Henry.*

"Go back to sleep, Henry, it's late." I kissed his cheek.

"I know. I see the star shine. I see the moonbeams. You know how to go to heaven, Is? You gotta get on a sun ray or a moonbeam. That the way up."

"I'll remember that, Henry, I will." *And I'll remember you, Henry.*

His face grew serious. He whispered, "I gotta tell you something, Isabelle."

"Okay, Henry. Tell me anything."

He whispered, "I sick. The doctor told me. I bad sick."

"I'm sorry. I'm sorry you're sick." A sob stuck in my throat. *I wish it were me.*

"I know that, silly Isabelle. I know you sorry. No one want Henry sick."

I patted his hand. I thought the pain in my chest was gonna kill me.

"I got pain-cree-at-ick cancer. Say it like that. Ick. Because it's icky."

"Yes, it is icky."

"Isabelle"—he raised himself to whisper in my ear—"I no get better. I sick."

I paused midpat. No one had told Henry that he wasn't getting better.

"Why do you say that, Henry?" The pain in my chest got worse, spreading like the wings of a sick eagle.

"Because in the dream Jesus said I come to him soon." He smiled.

I could hardly move. "Jesus told you that?"

He bit down on his lip, a big grin. "Yep. I go to heaven soon. I go see Marles."

Marles was a cat we had when we were younger. It was gold. It had gotten hit by a truck.

"Yeah, yeah. Jesus smile at me. He said I done good. He said I go up up up to heaven."

What do you do when someone's dying and they talk about dying? Deny it? Dismiss it and miss out on an honest conversation the dying person needs to have? Offer up hope of a miracle when there is none coming? Henry was special, but he wasn't stupid. The tears started sneaking out of my eyes and I snuffled and I coughed. *I wish you weren't going to die, Henry.*

"Hey, Isabelle! You no cry! No cry for Henry."

That made me cry harder. I knew I had to be strong, but inside I felt like I was folding in on myself. I was devastated beyond devastated. The only reason I believed in hope was because of Henry. He was the only constant joy in my life. My truest friend.

"I love you, Isabelle." He stroked my cheek. "Don't cry or I cry!"

I couldn't stop.

So Henry started crying. "Don't cry, Is!"

I couldn't stop. "I'll miss you, Henry." *I cannot tell you how much I'll miss you. I can't tell it to myself because then I will die of grief.*

"Yeah, yeah!" He wiped his tears. "Me, too. But you silly, Isabelle. I right here." He touched my heart with his pointer finger. "I right here. All the time. I right there."

My heart thumped and thumped and I reached for Henry and hugged him tight.

"You my sister." He smiled. "I your brother. We the Bommaritos. We always be together."

I buried my face in his shoulder. *Why Henry? Why him? So many horrid, murderous people in the world, why not them?*

"Jesus loves you, Is, and he take care of you when I in heaven. I catch a moonbeam or a sun ray!" He grinned. "That fun."

No, that not fun. Because I would be here, at the end of the moonbeam, at the end of the sun ray. Alone. Without my hope.

"I sleep now, Is. I go back to sleep. Night Night, Isabelle. You pretty."

"And you're beautiful, Henry, so beautiful."

He touched the tip of my nose, then slept.

I grieved, deep, seemingly endless grief. "I love you, my brother," I whispered.

Henry being in my heart wasn't good enough. I wanted Henry with me. With us. *With the Bommarito Family.*

More test results came in over the next few days, which confirmed what we already knew.

Janie and I alternated days at the bakery along with Cecelia, who often brought the girls. Dad also took shifts, when he wasn't at the hospital, his hands flying as he made one confectionary miracle after another.

We kept our word and hired Lytle. He came with a different brother each day and they cut out cookies with cookie cutters. Lytle smiled the whole time.

Momma was at the hospital every day, going home when exhaustion took over or she was too overwrought to function.

If we went to the hospital to keep Henry company, we were hardly needed. I had called Father Mike and Janice at church, Mr. Howard at the senior center, and Paula Jay at the animal shelter and told them the situation and that Henry wanted to tell them exactly how to do things in his absence.

Shocked and saddened, they all understood the situation exactly. They came with pencil and pen and wrote down word for word what Henry said.

"I don't know how we'll do it without you, Henry," Father Mike said. Father Mike does not believe in hiding emotions from Jesus or anybody else. He blew his nose in his handkerchief. "I can't wait until you come back."

"Yeah, me, too, Father Mike. But you can do it!" Henry cheered. "You can do it!"

"Thank you for telling me about Bursom, King Nap, and Lady Elizabeth, Henry," Paula Jay said, her hair messed up from the motorcycle ride. "They have tricky personalities. I didn't know that Lady Elizabeth was stealing King Nap's treats. Do you know how I should handle Scotty?"

"Okay, let's go over it one more time," Mr. Howard croaked. The man must have been eighty-five. He had come with three other people who could not have been any younger. "Help us out, Henry. Tell us the order again for getting ready for lunch, then Bunco."

Henry had told his visitors, "Visit Henry! Tell all my friends I happy to see them!" So they did, and people came.

Lytle arrived with his brothers who brought a checkerboard and checkers for him and Henry to throw.

People from the senior center came in groups, and the staff and volunteers at the animal shelter visited in shifts, as did three noisy groups of teenagers from church, many sporting Mohawks and pink hair. Customers from the bakery, Bao and Belinda, friends from his day center, neighbors, and most of the rest of the town, including the mayor and town council, firefighters, police officers, and teachers from Cecilia's school, also visited.

It was a good thing he ended up being there for six days, or we would not have had time for all his visitors.

When Henry was released from the hospital. He hugged his doctor. "Hey, you get those dogs married! They in looooove!"

Dr. Remmer assured him she would.

He high-fived the nurse, a man with tattoos up his arms of his mother and grandmother. They were homely women. "You be good, Henry. Hang gently."

"Hey, hey. I good. See ya, Mac. Mac the Big Mac." He laughed.

Outside the hospital, I handed Henry a helmet.

"Here goes Henry! I on a motorcycle with Is!"

"I still can't believe you're doing this," Momma protested.

Dad put a hand on her shoulder. "It's what Henry wants to do."

She tried to protest again.

"Let him, River," Dad told her. "Let him go."

Momma snuffled as Henry got on the back of my bike.

I started the motorcycle and pulled out, slowly, with Henry holding my waist, whoo-hoo-ing. Carefully we pulled away. In my rearview mirror I could see Momma waving and waving.

Waving good-bye to Henry and me.

Henry, for his part, was holding on tight, screaming, laughing, smiling. "This fun, Is! This fun! Go fast! Faster!"

When we pulled in front of the house, Grandma and Velvet were waiting on the porch. Velvet was waving, Grandma was saluting.

As soon as Henry saluted back, Grandma ran down to the motorcycle.

"My copilot has returned in victory!" she shouted. "In victory! I've kept our secret hidden in the tower!"

Henry guffawed and hugged her, then hugged Velvet. "You need some mashed potatoes and gravy to put some meat on your bones, Henry!" Velvet twanged. "And some of my grandma Ellen's pecan pie!"

"Yeah, yeah," Henry said, still weak but fighting. "Henry home. I home!" He put his arms straight out like a plane and hobbled after Grandma.

ᗏᗏ 27 ᗐᗐ

We met in the sunroom that night, the moonbeams shining through the trees. I hated the moonbeams now, I did.

For three sisters who talk almost incessantly while together, or fight, or laugh, we were strangely, ghastly quiet.

About five minutes later, I heard Janie muttering.

"What are you counting?" I asked.

"I'm counting the tiles in the floor." She made marks on the journal she was holding.

"You've already done that," Cecilia said. "Many times."

"I'm counting them again," Janie said, her voice wispy, like wind. A lost wind.

Cecilia was gobbling down a cherry pie, as if it would fix her life if she ate fast enough. Her mouth opened and I watched her shove one bite in after another. Maybe that's why I was rarely hungry: Because Cecilia ate so much, I always felt full.

Her hair fell forward and one of the gold strands dipped into the red gook. When she put her head back, the gook landed all over her sweater.

"You have cherry gook on your sweater, Cecilia," I said.

"Who cares?"

I sat there for a second. Who cared? *I cared*. I cared that Cecilia was inhaling a pie. An entire pie was going straight down her mouth. I cared that she was huge.

She took another bite, her mouth stretching like a rubber band. This time, hair on the other side dropped in the red gook.

All of a sudden I was ravingly, smokingly, enraged. Did Cecilia *want* to kill herself? Would Henry die and then her?

"For God's sakes, Cecilia, *stop eating!*"

Her head snapped up in shock, cherry juice dripping onto her chin when the fork wobbled. A cherry fell to her lap.

Janie stopped counting.

"Stop!" I yanked the fork out of her hand, then snatched the pie pan.

She instinctively grabbed for it, sputtering through the food in her mouth. "What the hell are you doing, Isabelle?"

She yanked it back, but I was not going to let go. "You are gobbling up an entire cherry pie, for God's sakes, that's enough!"

She stood up and glared at me, her hand still on the pan. "It's enough when I say it's enough—"

"No." My voice was shrill and naggy. "It is enough now. Now, Cecilia."

She pulled at the pan again. Cherry juice splattered onto my shirt. "Give that to me. And don't you ever, *ever* tell me what to eat or not eat. I don't need you, you sanctimonious slut, to tell me what to do with my body."

I hate that word, *slut*, especially when it's aimed at me. "You are the meanest person I have ever met, and you can't do this to yourself anymore, to your health, to your body, you can't do it to your girls—"

"Do what? Embarrass them because I'm so fat? Puff when I walk down the street? Have a face the size of a cow's? Enough fat to warm a group of Eskimos? I can't do that? You think I don't know that?" she shrieked. "You think I don't know all that?"

"You know and you keep inhaling food like a garbage disposal." I fought for the pie pan. More cherry juice splattered. She hauled it right back and we were nose to nose.

"Isabelle, Cecilia, I hate fighting. Please stop," Janie whispered. "We've had such a bad week, come on—"

"Shut up!" we both told her.

"Don't call me a slut again."

"Don't call me fat."

"You are fat, Cecilia."

"And you are a first-rate slut, Isabelle, don't get hoity-toity with me. I have been with one man, *one,* and you've been with enough to fill a U.S. submarine."

"That was a bitchy, bitchy thing to say," I yelled.

"And saying I'm fat isn't bitchy?" she yelled back.

"You're so thick into denial you can't see straight. Cecilia, you've been hospitalized because of your heart! You weigh almost three hundred pounds! Don't you get it? You are going to die, Cecilia, you are going to die, like Henry, if you don't stop eating!"

Her face paled. "Maybe I should go on the spinach and pineapple diet again? The liquid-only diet? The fourteen-hundred-calorie-a-day diet that made me feel faint? The fruit diet that gave me diarrhea so bad I had to take a sick day?" We struggled with the pie plate, cherry filling sloughing around. "All so I can lose weight and gain it all back plus some? Give me the damn pie."

"No." I can shout as loud as her. "You are fat enough as it is! Fat enough and that is enough!"

Her face flushed, her jaw tightened, and she reached in the pie pan, picked up a handful of pie, and smashed it into my chest. The cherries slipped down my shirt.

I thought I was going to shove her I was so mad. Mad at her, mad that Henry was sick, mad at being attacked and my scary nightmares, mad at the whole damn world. I was suddenly so mad, I felt as if a blowtorch had lit from my insides, the flames racing from my hair follicles to my toenails.

I picked up a hunk of pie and palmed it into her fat face.

"You bitch," she seethed.

"Negative choices, negative choices!" Janie said. "Please stop. Take a minute to reharmonize, rebalance yourselves with each other—"

"There. Now you won't eat it. Or will you?" I clutched the pie plate again. "Maybe you will." I picked up another handful and rubbed it into her shirt.

She slapped my cheek with crust and cherries. I felt pie juice run down my chin.

"Reach inside yourself for peace," Janie fussed. "The atmosphere is charged with acrimony—"

"Shut up!" we both shouted at her, battling for the pie plate.

I thought I was going to explode. I picked up a handful of gook and this time I went straight for that blond hair.

She returned the favor and I felt cherry juice on my scalp, slipping down the collar of my shirt. "Dammit," I breathed. I smushed some onto her face.

She did the same to me. It covered one eye, but I could still see well enough to rub some into her hair before she did the same to me again.

I shoved Cecilia and she caught the back of a chair with her heel and I shoved again. She grabbed me on the way down, and it was a rolling, twisting, cherry-gooked mess with Janie pleading with us to "be loving, be sisterly."

When there was nothing left to smash, we pulled apart, gasping, panting, and I got on all fours and glared at her.

"Well, that worked out well," I heaved. "Now you can't eat any more. Most of it is up your nose."

"Oh yeah," she puffed out, struggling up. "Perfect. Next time I'm eating too much, make me wear it instead of eat it. That'll work."

Cecilia was covered in cherry filling. I had shown her! I picked a cherry off my forehead and ate it.

"One two three four," Janie said. "Let's be loving!"

I felt hot, hot tears searing their way through the cherry pie on my cheeks. "God, I'm going to miss Henry," I whispered, choking on my own roaring grief. "I'm going to miss him."

Cecilia wiped pie off her face as gurgly, strangled sobs erupted. "I don't know what I'm going to do, I don't know. I can't stand this. *I can't stand it.*"

"Henry's my favorite person," Janie said. She sunk down between us, uncaring that cherry pie was now on her butt. "No offense." She ate a bit of crust off the floor.

"None taken," I weeped out. "He's mine, too."

We held each other, tear to tear, right there in that cherry pie.

A moonbeam lit the porch and I threw a handful of cherries at it. Oh, how I hated those moonbeams.

The world stops when someone has cancer.

The days start to swirl around that person as if he's the center of a tornado. Your life? Gone. Your schedule? Don't even think about it. Your plans. Put 'em aside.

Henry was to rest for a few days before going back to the hospital for chemo.

The problem was that Henry didn't want to rest. The morning after leaving the hospital, Henry woke up and insisted on going to pet the dogs and cats.

"They miss me! Even Barkey. He bites! Watch out! Ouch!"

Janie went with him while I went to the bakery.

"They all love him," she told me later. "The people in reception, the vet that came in, the other volunteers. He brings light and inner harmony to them all. And the dogs. As soon as we went to the kennels, the dogs went crazy. He takes four dogs at a time and leads them to play in the field out back. It's spiritual, cosmic love—"

"How did he feel?"

Her face crumpled a little bit. "He didn't seem like he had his usual energy, but he was so happy. He told everyone there about the cancer."

I nodded. I wasn't surprised. Henry didn't have a filter. He said what he thought. Most of his thoughts were pretty angelic in nature, so it worked out.

"He went around and said, smiling, 'Henry sick. Henry has pancreatic cancer.' You should have seen people's faces, Is. It was awful. The vet hugged him, then cried into her lab coat. The receptionist kept patting Henry's arm and blowing his nose, patting his arm and blowing his nose. And one guy in there who came in on his motorcycle wearing leathers—he volunteers with the cats once a week—he put his head in his hands and had to sit down."

I could imagine that scene all too clearly.

"So they're all upset and Henry shouts, 'Hey, no crying, no crying or I cry. I cry!' No one stopped, so Henry burst into tears."

"Sheesh."

"Yes, absolutely, sheesh. But you know how Henry is. He got upset, but then all of a sudden he was done with all that worldly sadness and he started his job. He got the dogs out and took them into the field."

I thought for a minute. "You're doing incredibly well, Janie. You're a new Janie."

She knew what I was referring to. "I was scared to death to come to Trillium River, but now I hardly recognize myself. I work in a bakery and I take Henry to the animal shelter. I actually talk to people. You know how I'd get stuck on a scary thought and couldn't get it out of my head? Like I'd be dying, or you and I would be in a train accident with no help around for miles and you'd be bleeding to death, or Cecilia would have a heart attack and I'd be doing CPR but there was no one to help and what would I do? I'm so busy I don't even have time for those thoughts to swirl around anymore." She pulled at her beige bra strap. "I feel a lot better."

"How's the writing going?" I had heard her working on her laptop last night about two in the morning.

"Better. My positive energy is gone and my negative energy is boiling over and somehow all that emotion is coming out in my writing, and I wrote this great scene last night for my book. Jack's trapped in this ship container, you know the type they load up on boats? The killer locked her in there and she's going to get loaded up and sent to China and by the time she gets there, she's gonna be dead, so she's got to figure her way out before she starves to death or suffocates—" She went on for another ten minutes and she explained the graphic parts graphically.

"Okay, I got it." I held up my hands. "Please."

"Well." She fumbled a bit, deflated, disappointed. "Well, okay."

I didn't want to hurt her feelings. "I want to save all that excitement for when I read the book."

Her face brightened. "Right! I don't want to spoil it for you."

"No, no, please don't."

How does she think of these things?

The next day Henry went to the senior center to help with lunch and Bunco. I went with him while Janie went to the bakery. He didn't need me there, but I didn't want to let him out of my sight yet. He was pale and yellow around the edges.

It was like being the bodyguard of a celebrity. He was mobbed by senior citizens.

"I have pain-cree-at-*ick* cancer," he announced to a group of older people leaning on canes and in wheelchairs. He smiled. "Henry sick. Henry sick."

He said this with a smile.

The room suddenly froze, the quiet rocking off each wall and back into the middle.

"Dear heavens," one man muttered, pulling on his tie.

"Oh no, honey," a woman with pure white hair whispered.

"I'm sorry, son. I'm sorry," an old man, wrinkled as a prune, said.

"Young man!" a woman shouted. "I couldn't hear you. What did you say?"

"Hi, Grandma Tasha!" Henry waved. "I said I have pain-cree-at-*ick* cancer! It icky!"

"Holy shit," she said, shaking her white head. "Holy shit."

On Sunday at mass, Father Mike announced a special time of prayer for Henry. We were all there. Cecilia, the girls, Janie, Momma, Velvet, Grandma in her green flight outfit, Dad, and I. Henry got up from the front row and stood beside Father Mike and he smiled and waved at people, smiled and waved.

"Ladies and gentleman," Father Mike said, his tone low, gruff. "Today we're going to put our hearts out there to God and we're gonna pray for Henry." He stopped. I saw his jaw working. "Henry"—he cleared his throat—"has been diagnosed with pancreatic cancer—"

"No, no! You not say it right," Henry said, smiling. He put his face close to the microphone. "It pain-cree-at-*ick*. Like that, Father Mike. Pain-cree-at-*ick*. You have to say the '*ick*' part because it's *icky*."

"Thank you, Henry," Father Mike said. "You're right. Bow your heads. Let's pray so the good Lord hears us."

Father Mike prayed and prayed. He prayed. It was a long prayer, which was surprising, because Father Mike believes that God does not like to listen to prayers that go on and on. "Say what you want," he told our congregation once. "He knows your heart. No need to blather on."

I heard muffled snuffles and tiny gasps and little sobs, and they weren't only from the Bommarito gang. When Father Mike was done, Henry said, still grinning, "Hey! Father Mike. I do a prayer. I pray."

Father Mike was a mess, so he wiped his eyes and handed the microphone to Henry.

Henry grinned at all of us. "Hi, everybody." He waved. "I Henry. I pray now. I pray for you." He did not bend his head, he did not shut his eyes.

"Dear Jesus! Hi ya, Jesus! I pray for all my friends and my sisters, Henry's sisters, and my momma and my dad, my dad back, he right there, my dad back." He pointed at Dad. Dad clenched his jaw, but the tears came out on their own accord. Momma reached for his hand.

"I pray for Amelia, we fly the planes together and Velvet, she my friend, hi, Velvet." Velvet waved, then held her lace handkerchief tight to her face.

"And I pray for you. I pray for you. All my friends here I pray for you." He grinned. "I pray for you to be happy. Happy like me. Henry. I happy. I happy because you all my friends. That why I happy. Not all the people my friend when I little kid. Some bad people. They do mean things to me." His face got red and crumpled up a bit, but then, in a flash, it was gone. "You my friends." He clapped his hands. "But I sick. I have pain-cree-at-*ick* cancer. Like that. *Ick.* Jesus tell me in my dream I go home to him. I go soon. Up the moonbeam. Up the sun ray. That how you get to heaven."

On the altar, Father Mike turned and knelt in front of the cross.

"I love everybody here. Ha Ha! I love you guys. Amen amen."

And all those muffled snuffles and tiny gasps and little sobs become big sniffles and big gasps and big sobs.

"Jesus loves you!" he yelled, waving again. "Yeah, yeah! Jesus loves you!"

It was as if the whole town was rising up in mourning, a giant, screaming wave of pain and all they knew how to do to alleviate that pain was cook.

We were bombarded with food.

On the dot at five, the brigade would begin. Lasagnas, casseroles, fruit salads, desserts. It was Henry's idea to have people come in who were bringing food in on huge platters. "Hey! It the Wongs! The Wongs. You come on in!" he'd shout or, "It the kids! From the church! Hey! You brought Henry pizza? I love that pizza."

Now, at first, this put Momma into a tizzy. Momma did not entertain. Between Henry, Grandma, a house, and the bakery, she simply didn't have time and, worse, she didn't have friends. She was raised in Trillium River, but when she returned, she shut the friendship door.

If she did entertain, I can assure you it would have been with china and starched white tablecloths. But she couldn't manage that now. She was grieving, she was sleepless, she was hopeless.

And yet.

And yet.

I saw Momma change over the next few weeks. At first she was anxious about the visitors, uptight, and did not know how to handle them and their gifts and their kindness.

But as one person in town after another reached out to her, reached out to us, I swear I saw Momma's heart soften like melting butter. We were brought meals by old high school friends of hers still in the area. Neighbors. Cecilia's students' families. Acquaintances.

For a woman who had seen, close up, the ugliness of humans and human nature, she was seeing the beauty of sincere friendship.

Under the deluge of generosity and concern and the grief that people felt for her Henry, her special loving boy, who had not always been treated fairly or right, she started to open her heart up.

When Grandma would march into a room in her flight uniform and announce, "The weather's perfect for flying. Please step outside to admire my new plane," or "The Natives are back. Guard yourselves! They're usually friendly, but not always. That's why I carry a spear," and no one batted an eye when she did, indeed, swing a spear about, it further softened Momma.

This was her family. A special-needs boy, a mother who thought she was Amelia Earhart, and three daughters with varying problems who had become infamous during high school for any number of things. She had a history with much that she was ashamed about and needed to keep secret, poverty that almost killed her, and extreme depression she had fought back for years that finally seemed to settle itself out. (With a drug or two. I'd found the bottles.)

For the first time in her life, she and her quirky family were embraced.

We sat on the swing together one night after we'd had no fewer than thirty guests and she said, "Margaret Tribotti, the woman who owns the bike shop, brought me baked salmon with lemon butter sauce," then burst into tears. "Eduardo Chavez brought me homemade chocolate chunk ice cream. My girlfriend, Joyce Gonzales, from second grade, brought me a coconut cake made from her grandma Consuelo's family recipe!" She covered her face with a hankie.

I reached out and held her hand. To my surprise her fingers curled around mine, and we kept rocking under the light of the moon.

Shortly after that I saw Dad kiss Momma on the lips.

She bent her head after the kiss and I saw a tiny smile. He hugged her close.

The meals kept on coming.

Momma's heart kept softening.

One morning, before I went to the bakery, I walked down to the river and sat in my usual spot. The windsurfer was there. Gliding, catching air, smooth. Thinking about nothing but the water, the sail, the wind.

I wanted to be him.

I really did.

Momma, Janie, Cecilia, and I took Henry to the hospital to try the chemo. To do or not to do chemo caused an earth-scorching family fight. I can only compare this to Mt. St. Helens blowing her top. It was pointy before it exploded, but when that giant ash cloud cleared, the top had been neatly slashed off and hellfire had scorched the mountain.

Our family hit the hellfire stage pretty damn quick.

Cecilia and Momma wanted him to do it. "It could save his life," Cecilia hissed, determined. "He could be one of the lucky ones, a miracle . . ."

"Cecilia," Janie pleaded, hands twisting, four times this way, four times that way. "The doctor said there won't be any miracles . . ."

"Doctors schmocktors!" Momma roared. "He's doing it. My son is doing the chemo." She emphasized this by tossing an old purple bevelled bottle to the floor.

"Momma, Henry has a limited number of days left," I said, hating the pain that streaked across her face. "The chemo is not going to cure him. I don't want the last weeks of his life filled with doctors' appointments and needles up his arms and throwing up and fatigue . . ."

"This could slow the cancer down, Isabelle," Cecilia snapped. "It's his only chance!"

"You would rather see him dead?" Momma shrieked, rising into irrationality at the speed of light. "Would you? Would you?" She stepped over the broken glass to me.

Is there a worse argument to have with family? Chemo or no chemo for a terminally ill member?

"I don't want Henry to die, Momma, you know I don't." I clenched my fists. She was awful. Uncontrollable. Critical. Mean. "How could you say that to me? How could you? I love Henry, you know that, or have you been so blinded by what you want, *what River wants*, that you weren't able to see that?"

"What I see is that you don't want your brother to have treatment! You're giving up on my son!"

"Hell, Momma." I'd had it. Her son was dying, but I was at my limit with her. No, I'd crossed it. "I'm not going to take any more of your cruelty. *I won't*. I know you're hurting, I know you're lashing out, which is what you've done our whole lives when things haven't gone your way, but I won't take this shit, your meanness—"

Momma's face froze, as if I'd slapped her with a table leg. "I am not being mean," she insisted, but her voice faltered.

"You are." I clenched my fists. "You say things, Momma, and they hurt so much, and it lasts forever, but I'm done taking it with my trap shut. I love Henry and I would never give up on him, but I know reality, Momma, I know it and I know the chemo will do little for him, if anything at all." I hated being so honest. Hated it. "It will probably make him bald and sick and not add a day to his life."

Cecilia slapped both hands to her face in frustration. "Argh! You don't know that."

"Cecilia, wake up. You know what I know." And we knew a lot. We'd done research on the Internet. Now, this drives doctors crazy. People cruise like maniacs through the Internet and suddenly they're experts on their disease and think they know more than the doctors, but metastasized pancreatic cancer doesn't have much leeway in terms of survival or treatment, no matter where you cruise to.

"Momma," Janie said, her voice surprisingly strident. "You heard the doctor. Take a second and think about what you're asking him to do, how he may suffer! Do you actually want Henry— *Henry*—to go through this?"

I turned toward Janie, my breath held. She rarely stood up to Momma. Her usual reaction was to lie down, take the potshots Momma threw, and attempt to make peace.

"No!" Momma yelled, her face a bleak mask of unrelenting loss. "No, dammit, I don't! But I don't want my son to have cancer, either! I don't want my son to be sick! I don't want my son to die, for God's sakes! Can't you see that? Can't you? We should fight. We should fight this cancer!" She threw a short, red glass bottle to the floor. "We have to fight!"

"No, we don't have to fight," I interjected. "We have to choose the best possible route *for Henry*. Not for us. He deserves to live a life worth living as long as possible without the needles and the side effects."

Momma's body was shaking, head to foot. "Am I the only one who believes in Henry?"

Oh my God. Is she the only one who believes in Henry?

"That isn't fair, Momma!" Janie raged, face red. "We have believed in him our whole lives! Don't you dare say that!"

Whoa, Janie!

"We changed his diapers when he was four, believing one day we wouldn't have to because Henry would choose not to shit his pants!" She clenched her fists and charged up to within six inches of Momma's face, crunching glass beneath her feet. "We believed he would recover from being attacked by bullies his whole life because we comforted him. We taught him to read when his teachers said he couldn't. We took him to the doctors for all his health problems and believed he would get better because we took care of him. We believed he would start talking again after Dad left and after he was raped, and he did, because we helped him. We believed that even though you spent half our childhood rotting in bed, or being mean to us three, that Henry would still turn out to be a great man, because we were always there for him! Don't you accuse us of not believing in Henry! Don't you do that, Momma!"

The silence in that room about blew my eardrums out. Janie panted, and Cecilia, for once, couldn't find her voice.

"This isn't the time, Momma, for you to be bitchy," I told her, my chin up. "For once, don't attack us when you're unhappy. We're all dying here."

Momma covered her blond bell-shaped hair with her arms. "He can do this, he can live through this," she raged, her body sagging against the wall. "My Henry is going to get better..." She started to slide down the wall, sobbing. "My Henry will go to the doctors and the medicine will heal him..." She swatted away Cecilia's hands. "The doctor is going to fix this," she moaned.

"Shit!" Cecilia said. "Shit! Why did you have to upset her?"

"Why did I? How about this, Cecilia? Why did she upset me?" I said. "Why does she always feel that she can upset all of us, accuse us of terrible, untrue things, and get away with it? Do you think you're the only one hurting here, Momma? Do you?"

For a second, Momma stared at me, her face collapsing. "No," she whispered. "I don't. Not only me."

"I'm hurting, Momma!" Janie cried. "I hurt all the time!"

"I am, too, Momma. *We all love Henry,*" I said. "I believe in him. But I believe that this disease is not beatable. *By anyone.*"

Momma whimpered, a sound of utter defeat, then did something unpredictable, as she so often does. She reached out her hands to us. I hesitated, so did Janie, still so furious at her, so furious.

She saw our hesitation, and she bent her head, then looked us straight in the eye, her face awash in hot tears. "I'm sorry, girls. I'm sorry," she whispered. "I'm sorry. For you. For me. For Henry. I'm so sorry."

Cecilia shot us darts from those blue eyes of hers until we grabbed Momma's hands.

We ended up rocking Momma back and forth, her cries coming from the depths of a mother's broken soul, this lost, hideous, thundering grief. "I don't want my son to die, I don't want my son to die, I don't want my son to die."

I buried my head in Cecilia's heaving shoulder, Janie leaned on me as her tears burned my neck, and we all held tight to each other and to Momma as she keened back and forth.

❦ 28 ❧

Henry smiled as we took him into the hospital, greeting the receptionists by saying, "Hi. I Henry. I have the cancer. You gonna put some juice in me to kill it?"

One of the receptionists, smiling as if she were a restaurant hostess, took us to the Cancer-Killing-Chemo area, bright, window filled and clean, with yellow walls.

"Does she think she's seating us at some damn wedding or something? What's with the weird, maniacal smile?" Cecilia muttered.

"Can we please be nice to the people who work here? We need to be tranquil," Janie pleaded.

"All I'm saying is that Miss Merry Sunshine doesn't need to grin like a Cheshire cat. We're here for chemo not to tip some champagne down our throats."

"Cecilia, chill out," I said. "Chill."

"She doesn't need to be so happy," Cecilia sneered. "It makes me feel like hitting her."

"Lots of things make you feel like hitting," I said. "Why don't you go hit yourself in the face? Knock yourself out, then we won't have to listen to you complain about a smiling person."

Cecilia nudged me. "I think I may hit you in the face . . ."

I whipped on her. "Do it. Do it hard. As hard as you can—"

"I would if we weren't in a hospital. I'm so sick of you taking over, taking control, yapping your mouth—"

"And I'm sick of . . ." I paused. What was I sick of with Cecilia? "I'm sick of . . . sick of . . . I'm sick of *something* that you do, Cecilia, I'll think of it in a sec!"

Janie giggled.

As soon as I realized what I'd said, I giggled, too.

Cecilia's scowl dropped and even she laughed. "I'll think of something, Isabelle, that I do that makes you sick of me and I'll tell you what it is so you'll have something to throw in my face next time . . . Hey! Maybe it'll be blueberry pie next time!"

I laughed. Oh gall. Life is ludicrous. Here I was at the hospital, and my sisters and I were laughing *and* fighting.

Laughing and grief. They are not always mutually exclusive. I reached for Cecilia's hand. She held it.

Henry went right over to a coffee/hot chocolate cart they had set up. "Hey, sisters! Hey, Momma! We get free hot chocolate! Free! I have some. I have hot chocolate. I make you some!"

Momma nodded weakly. After we all had our free hot chocolates, mostly chocolate, hardly any water, we made our way back to a comfy blue leather armchair. Momma sank into the chair next to it, as if her knees were made of straw and the straw bent.

"Hi!" Henry said to a weak, pale woman with a blue headscarf in another armchair. "Hi. I Henry. Jesus loves you."

She tilted her head up at Henry, the circles under her eyes purplish and puffy. Perhaps this was not her best day. "I don't believe in Jesus."

That did not throw Henry at all.

"He believe in you. He believe in you."

The woman glared. I did not think she wanted to have a conversation about Jesus, and I gently pushed Henry away from her.

"What you reading?" he asked the woman, grinning, undaunted.

She tipped the magazine cover up.

"That a dog!" Henry announced. "I take care of dogs at the shelter. I love dogs."

She nodded. "I love dogs, too."

"You have a dog?" His eyebrows shot up, curious and excited about this.

I tried to nudge Henry.

"Yes, I have a dog."

"What his name? The dog. What his name. My name Henry."

"His name is Kermit."

"Kermit!" Henry laughed and bent over to be eye to eye with her. "Kermit! Kermit the Frog, Kermit the dog! You have a dog named for a frog. I like that dog."

The woman smiled a little. I could tell she was relaxing. "I like the dog, too."

"Kermit the Frog is a dog," Henry said. "Does he croak or does he bark? I go now. I have to get some juice in me so I get rid of the cancer. I got pain-cree-at-*ick* cancer. Bad."

The woman's tired face stilled. "I'm sorry to hear that."

"Yeah. All the people's sorry." Henry was still bent down eye to eye with her. "Okay. I go. Jesus loves you. Bye-bye. Bye-bye to the mommy of Kermit the dog." He chuckled. "Kermit the dog!"

Henry said hello and chatted to a young man hooked up to an IV. His two young kids were sitting by him. He was bald. The kids were wearing Donald Duck baseball hats and he quacked at them. The young man was more cheerful and wished him a happy day.

"You have happy day, too. Happy day."

He had to say hello to the nurses. "I Henry. Who are you?"

They were Eric, Randy, and Bonnie.

"I get some juice," he told them. "Juice me!"

We finally got Henry settled in the blue leather chair. Momma patted his shoulders. Janie stood to the side and breathed deep. I knew she might faint. Cecilia panted.

Henry loved the "magic chair" and used the lever to lower the armchair up and down. He practiced putting his feet on the footrest, taking them down, putting them up, down.

"This good chair." He released the handle, which pushed him back up again. "Ha-ha! A magic, moving chair."

Dr. Remmer arrived, her gray hair back in a loose bun. She smiled at Henry. I could tell she was exhausted. What a pleasant job, being an oncologist.

"Hey, hey. Dr. Remmer. You pretty."

Dr. Remmer thanked him.

"You got a dog name Snickers. He in looovvvee. Rex in love. Hey, your dogs get married yet? They marry?" Henry laughed.

"Not yet, Henry," she told him. "But soon. I think they're engaged."

"Ha! Engaged! Two doggies. That funny!" Henry hit the armrest and grinned. "You gonna put some juice in me to get my pain-cree-at-*ick* cancer?"

We had explained the chemo to Henry by telling him the medicine was like juice and it would be put into him to kill some cancer.

"That's what I'm going to do, Henry." The doctor held his hand.

Momma held his other hand, her eyes half shut, as if she couldn't bear to watch this part.

"I get it. Where the juice?"

"I have the juice up here in these bags," the doctor said, smiling.

Henry tilted his head to examine the IV pole and smiled. "Haha. That a joke. How you gonna put the juice in those bags in Henry? You gonna put a straw in them? Juice taste good?"

Momma rubbed her forehead. Janie swayed. I got her a chair. I hoped she wouldn't faint. This was not going to be fun.

"No, Henry, that's not what we're going to do. Me and Eric and Bonnie, we're going to put this little tiny needle in your skin and the juice is going to go in you that way."

He scrunched up his face. "I don't get it. I don't get it. I drink the juice. Free hot chocolate here, Dr. Remmer. I had hot chocolate. My sisters and Momma, too. You want hot chocolate? I make it for you."

"I'm sorry, Henry, this is a special juice and it has to go into your body right here." She tapped the inside of his elbow.

I could hear Cecilia breathing heavily. Momma turned her head away.

He turned his arm and eyed that vulnerable spot. "No. Not there. You no do it there. I drink it." He grinned.

"Henry," I said. "It'll be fine. The doctor is going to give you the juice through your arm while you drink your hot chocolate and we play checkers."

"No. I don't think so, Is. No. Thank you." He grinned as he played with the magic chair again, up and down, up and down.

"Let me show you, Henry." The doctor unwrapped the IV. She showed him the tiny needle that would be inserted into his arm for the chemo.

"That not go in my arm!" Henry's eyes flew open wide. He shook his head.

"Yes, it'll hurt only for a second and that's it! All done."

"What?" Henry's voice pitched. "No. I no do that. No needles. Nope nope."

"Henry, it'll only take a second," Cecilia pleaded, her eyes shiny with tears. "One second."

"I no take a second. I no want a shot. Hot chocolate!"

"It's not a shot," Janie said. "It's the way the juice goes in. Think of it as a straw. An elbow straw."

Henry stared at the needle. "That not a straw."

"Remember when you were in the hospital, honey?" Momma said, leaning forward. I could tell she was an inch away from losing her mental grip. "You had something like this in your arm. It made you feel better."

That was true. But Henry had had a sedative when they put that in.

Momma was shaking. "It'll be fine, Henry, over quickly. As

quick as you can make one of the dogs at the shelter roll over. As quick as you can get one of them to dance on their hind legs. It's that quick. Quick as a lick!"

"Let me show you," the doctor said, so helpfully.

In a flash, Henry flipped down the footrest and stood up. "No no no. I not doing this. You not put that in my arm. That hurt. Ow!"

"Henry, this is the juice you need to get the cancer," Cecilia said, "so you need to sit down and take it."

"I no take the juice in the elbow with no needle." He shook his head back and forth, back and forth. "That shot."

"Henry, please," Cecilia begged, her voice down at a whisper, desperate. "Please. It won't hurt. We'll go get ice cream afterward. Two scoops. Whipped cream. Chocolate sauce."

"No. I go now." He turned to leave. I was not prepared for this wave of thick despair to cover me as he headed for the door. I hadn't wanted him to do the chemo, but this was so . . . final. This was it. All there was.

He walked over to the father and the girls. "Have a happy day. Quack, quack."

The girls quacked back at him.

He said to the woman with the dog magazine, "Say hi to Kermit the Frog dog for me. I go pet the dogs tomorrow."

She assured him she would. A slip of a smile pulled on her mouth.

Cecilia impatiently swiped at her tears. "Henry, sit down. Sit down, now." She didn't say it in a patient voice.

He whipped around, eyes wide. "You mad at me, Cecilia? Don't be mad at Henry."

"I am mad at you. You need to get your medicine." Cecilia crossed her arms, her face flushed.

"No." Henry crossed his arms back at her. He so seldom got angry, but he had the Bommarito temper and I knew it was igniting.

"Yes!" Cecilia said. "Yes, sit down right this minute!" She pointed at the chair.

"No! I no sit down!" Henry shouted.

I saw Janie try to stand, then sink back down. Momma buried her face in her hands.

"If you don't sit down, I will pick you up and put you there!" Cecilia raged.

"No!" Henry yelled. "No! I go home. I fly with Amelia. We go to Hawaii."

"Cecilia, please," I said. "It's not going to work. Back off."

But Cecilia wouldn't listen. She loved Henry like no one's business, and if she had to drag him over to that chair and strap him down while he had chemo pumped into his body, she would do it.

"Cecilia," the doctor said. "He's an adult."

"He's an adult with disabilities," she spat, blinking another set of tears out. "He can't make this decision for himself!"

"He can," the doctor said. "Morally and legally."

"He can't." Cecilia was shaking. "He doesn't get it. He doesn't get that if he doesn't take the medicine, he's *going to die*. He doesn't get the correlation."

But Henry got it and he heard her. He spread his hands out. "I know I die, Cecilia! I already know it! Jesus told me in the dream I go see him soon and I not taking that juice in a needle!"

"Cecilia," the doctor soothed. "I can't force him to take this."

"You can't or you won't?" Cecilia argued.

"I can't, and I won't," the doctor said. Firm. Resolute.

For a moment I thought Cecilia was going to hit her, she was so angry, so I grabbed her arm again and stood in front of her. "Calm down, Cecilia. For once rein in your anger, okay? Think about this, think about what you're asking him to do."

She fought against me, but I held firm, held tight. She swore; I shook her and told her to get a grip. "This is not about you, Cecilia, not about what *you* want." It was ugly.

Cecilia's face crumbled. "It's his only chance, *his only chance,* Is."

"It is. But it's not a good chance. It's an infinitesimal chance, at best. You know that. *You know that.*" I pulled her close to me.

"But I love him," Cecilia said, as if that was all that was needed. *"I love him."*

Janie stumbled over and put an arm around Cecilia. *That's sisters, fighting one minute, hugging the next.* We were pathetic in our grief.

Momma swayed in her seat, her face gray, and a nurse leaned down to take her pulse.

"I know you love him, Cecilia. We all do." Oh yeah, we all did. We loved Henry best.

"Hey! Hey! Why Cecilia crying?" Henry shouted. "Cecilia, why you cry?"

"Because, Henry—" She inhaled, wretched and broken. "I love you and the medicine could give you some more time to live. To fly with Grandma. To make a model plane with Dad. To help at the bakery icing cupcakes with us sisters and petting the dogs and you could serve doughnuts at church and sit in the front row."

"Hmm." Henry put his fist under his chin, then clapped three times. "Hmm. Okay, I do it!" He charged back to the magic chair and stuck an arm out. "I do it for Cecilia." He grinned at us. "I do it for my sisters. Henry's sisters. No more fighting. I love my sisters."

And that was that. Henry took the chemo. Was it ethical the way this was handled? Probably not. Moral? Probably not. Well-intentioned? Yes.

Janie fainted when the needle poked Henry's arm and he squirmed and fussed, but we soothed him, Momma rocking Janie on the floor.

We played checkers with him. He took a nap. We drank the free hot chocolate and coffee Henry was so excited about. When we were done, we left. Momma leaned on me for support, Cecilia was close to keeling over (I knew this because I could feel her exhaustion), a pale Janie clucked and fretted around Henry, and I felt as if I wanted to die. Right there die. I think a blend of stress and grief does that to you.

We went home. The Columbia River was the same as always, little waves frothing with white, the sun was headed downward, down to sleep, as Henry would say, the trees danced a stiff dance, and when we drove up the drive, the wind lifted our hair and swirled it around.

All was the same in nature.

All was ruined for us.

When Henry saw Grandma, he darted out of the car. She met him midway, arms outstretched. They flew around the yard.

"My copilot has returned!" Grandma yelled. "My copilot is alive!"

Late that night I pulled out my favorite camera.

It was as if I'd rediscovered my heart. I held it close to my chest and remembered everywhere I'd been with that camera slung around my neck.

I had quit photography after my brain self-electrocuted and I'd lost a large chunk of myself. I needed that chunk back. Pronto.

Why? Because I needed to photograph Henry. Henry and our family. Together.

And I didn't have much time.

Unbelievably, after that first chemo treatment, our lives resumed as if we were normal people for a few days.

We sisters worked at the bakery. Momma stayed with Henry and Grandma. Velvet helped with both. Dad came over after work to visit and baked up his incredible treats at the bakery. We insisted on paying him. He declined. We insisted. He declined again.

"My greatest happiness is to be with you all in the bakery.

Allow me to have that happiness," he said with a gentle smile. "My time there is a gift. A gift for me."

Momma and Dad made crepes for the whole family one Saturday morning. They swung in the porch swing. I wouldn't say that Momma was doing well. She was a wreck, anxious, shaky, and, as always, hysteria was brewing, but Dad visibly, clearly, steadied her.

Janie and I were hired out to handle a number of weddings, and as brides are not famous for their forgiving natures if their cakes don't turn up, we couldn't stop working.

For a wedding for two eighty-year-olds, we asked them if they wanted a traditional cake with layers and flowers.

"Hell no," the bride creaked out. "I had that at my first wedding. I stayed married for fifteen years to that monster. Flowers on wedding cakes still make me feel like my face is in a headlock. Now, can't you girls come up with something more original? Come along, now! Don't be old fogies!" She prodded me in the knee with her cane, then Janie.

"I'll be damned if I'll conform to tradition," the groom growled, who had been married to his first wife for fifty-one years until she died of a heart attack on a hang glider in Italy five years ago. His fiancée was her sister. "Bah! Not for me. Boring! Restrictive! Put your thinking caps on!"

Well, we girls put our thinking caps on with the bride and groom and came up with a rather splendid idea based on a gift the two lovebirds had planned for the family.

"This'll knock their socks off," the groom cackled.

"It'll be a honeymoon no one forgets," the bride creaked out. She prodded me in the knee with her cane again, then Janie. "A humdinger."

It was an immediate-family-only wedding. The bride and groom invited their children—who were all first cousins—and their children's spouses and the grandkids and a passel of little great-grandkids, out to their sprawling-view home near the gorge on Saturday morning. They told their family the wedding was on

Thursday evening but had them come five days early for family time.

The families noisily arrived on the dot at ten in the morning on Saturday. (The groom, Clarence, insisted on promptness. He had not been in the military for "nothin'. Be on time or don't come at all!")

By twelve the minister had arrived, and Clarence and his bride, June, were no longer officially living in sin. Since Clarence had "no patience for little, pretty food," he insisted the caterers serve steak and potatoes on two long tables on the huge deck.

They were a boisterous, laughing group, clearly delighted to be together and loving that June and Clarence had played a joke on them and gotten married earlier than they'd said.

At the appointed time, with great fanfare, I brought the wedding cake out, a giant white cruise ship.

I must say Janie and I were proud of this particular genius. The cake was strawberry flavored—June's favorite—the icing white, little windows were formed with slices of licorice, gumdrops outlined the rails, the "pool" was filled with blue icing, and the lounge chairs made from chocolate.

That noisy family clapped and cheered. Clarence and June put their arms around me, then kissed right in front of my face. I struggled not to drop the cake.

But we weren't done.

I put the cruise ship cake in the middle of the table, then Janie and I delivered to each person a box made out of frozen chocolate. The lid of the box had a ship's anchor drawn on it with black icing.

"Don't you be eating your boxes yet," Clarence growled. "Don't even touch them."

When everyone had their box (no touching), June creaked out, "Here we go, kids! Now, no screaming! Open your box!"

Inside of each box, Janie had written this note, on instruction from Clarence: "Congratulations! You are coming with us on our honeymoon, a seven-day cruise in the Caribbean! We're leaving in one hour. Get moving."

Pandemonium.

And there was screaming, too.

The bride and groom for another wedding wanted a traditional cake.

The young bride, with a tattoo of a cobra on her chest, wanted all chocolate.

The young groom ran a hand over his shaved head, then scratched his left pit. "I'm sick of chocolate. It gives me hives. One time I got a hive on my ass. You want that on our honeymoon? A hivey ass? My mother wants lemon."

"What kind of flavor is lemon for a cake, we wanna make the guests sick or somethin'?" the bride whined, the cobra squiggling.

We offered to do each layer a different flavor. Neither one of them liked that idea. "Then it'd be a schizo cake," the bride said. "Like his brother. Schizo."

"My brother isn't as schizo as your aunt. God. She should be committed to a Looney Tune place."

We offered champagne cake as an alternate. They didn't like that idea, either.

"You drink champagne, you don't eat it," snarled the bride, "and my parents said if your family wants to guzzle champagne, they're footin' the bill."

"My family's not gonna guzzle champagne. They like beer, and your family better get a keg."

We offered white cake.

"We got a nice, white virgin cake," the groom muttered. "Virgin, get it?"

We asked about the colors of the flowers and they couldn't agree on that, either. The bride told the groom that he was "so sick rigid, don't you care what I want for my own wedding cake?"

and the groom sulked and said, "It's my wedding, too, although your mother wouldn't know that."

The bride defended her mother and said that at least her mother had bought a nice dress to wear and wasn't going to resemble a blue tent. To which the groom almost choked on his tongue and said he would control his mother and her tent if the bride could control her drunken brother.

Her brother was not a drunk, she insisted, but the groom made him nervous so he drank more and what about his sister who was Miss Goody Two-Shoes with that weird smile stuck on her face like glue? Talk about an overdose of Prozac! How in hell was she supposed to handle having to spend all the damn holidays for the rest of her life with that bitch?

She's a bitch? the groom asked. What about you?

No, I'm not a bitch, you're a control freak with a remote control stuck up your ass.

And we stopped things right there.

Janie said, her hands gently patting theirs, "Are you two sure you want to get married?"

The bride and the groom gaped at Janie, seriously baffled, as if she had told them there were three-headed aliens from Pluto under the table.

"Hell, yes," the bride said, her cobra swaying. "Why would you think we don't want to get married? We're here, aren't we?"

"Jeez. I thought you guys sold cakes." The groom scratched his pit again. "What are you, bakery psychologists or somethin'? She's my woman!"

"He's my dude!" the bride said, completely flummoxed by our question. "My dude!"

They shared a tongue-wielding kiss.

No, I thought tiredly, we're not bakery psychologists.

But businesswomen we were, and we got the full payment, nonrefundable, up front.

⊰ 29 ⊱

"**P**arker lost his job," Cecilia told me as we squirted cake batter into giant cupcake molds for our überpopular heavenly cupcakes.

I stopped the squirting.

"His boss told him he was disgusted with his professional performance since the divorce and even more disgusted with his personal life. He told Parker he was running a family-friendly business for family-friendly people. He told Parker it was totally inappropriate for Constance to appear in a shirt unbuttoned to her waist and a miniskirt at the family picnic." She squirted. "The girls told me."

"Well," I said, adding a touch of sanctimoniousness to my tone. "Parker may not have a job but at least he has Constance and her love."

"And his Corvette. Don't forget the midlife crisis car."

"And a big-screen TV."

"Nope," Cecilia said, squirting again. "Constance threw a chair at it and broke it when they had a fight. No big screen anymore. Poor Parker."

"Yes, poor, poor Parker."

We were quiet for a second and then we both burst. The hilarity could not be contained.

We laughed all day.

During the weekend, I grabbed my camera and slung it around my neck. It felt so . . . right. Like I'd refound a piece of myself.

I took photos of Henry with Amelia flying, Henry with Cecilia's daughters standing on their heads. Henry with Janie and Cecilia and me, and Henry with Momma and Dad. I took photos of Henry with his friends, especially Lytle and Velvet, the seniors, Father Mike and Janice, and Paula Jay and the dogs and cats.

I took photos of our whole family together on the porch.

And I felt myself coming back to me.

On a windy, blustery night, Henry woke up and vomited on himself.

His wail, his pathetic, sad wail, woke all of us up and had us sprinting into his bedroom at a dead run, but it was Henry's crying, his choked, broken crying, that bowled us over.

"He's asleep," I told Momma, Janie, and Velvet about two hours later. "Finally."

Henry had had his health problems over the years and vomit was the only thing that could get him really upset. "I hate throw up," he always said. "Make me sick."

Momma was sitting at the kitchen table with her shaking hands wrapped around her coffee cup. She'd tipped in Kahlúa to steady her nerves. I poured a cup of coffee and added Kahlúa myself. I drank it rather quickly.

When we were growing up Momma rarely drank, but when times were bleak, when we were evicted, or Henry was in the hospital again, or when there was no money and no food, she'd pull a bottle out of the back of the pantry and have a glass. Our love of Kahlúa was one thing we shared.

It was raining outside, gray, heavy, cloudy, windy. "How are you, Momma?" I asked.

She didn't answer at first, and Janie and I braced ourselves.

"How do you think I am?" She stared at me with empty eyes. "The chemo is making my already-sick son more sick."

Velvet patted Momma's back, poured her a little more coffee, and tipped in a wee more Kahlúa. "Take a breath now, love. Settle your feathers . . ."

"He is on chemo because he has cancer." I saw her body start to shake.

"He has a cancer that is incurable." A splatter of rain hit the windows.

Janie tapped the table, put her hands in her lap, twirled her thumbs four times, and tapped the table again.

"The chemotherapy will not save him."

I pulled my sweatshirt closer around me. Cold. So cold.

"My son will die, maybe in pain that we cannot control."

I felt my whole body ache. Throb. Ache again.

"How do you think I am, dammit?" she shouted as she swept her arm across the table. The coffee cups, the creamer, the sugar bowl, and the Kahlúa bottle plummeted to the floor and shattered. She stood up, her whole body trembling. "How do you think I am? *I am in hell*. I am in total, complete hell." She lifted the table up with both hands and slammed it back down. "Dammit!"

"Momma, please. Calm down," I said. I stood up.

"River," Velvet said, "let's you and I, sugar, have some of my lemonade . . ."

"Calm down?" Momma hissed. "Calm down? *How can I calm down?* Are you stupid, Isabelle? Are you?"

I knew Momma was devastated. I knew her heart was breaking in two. But the word *stupid* still hurt, always had.

"My only son is being eaten, eaten, by *cancer*. I am going to grow old, without Henry, without my son. I will not be able to watch him run around like a plane. I will not be able to see him in church. I will not be able to hug him and hold him, and take him to the animal shelter, nothing. *Nothing!*"

I closed my eyes. I was exhausted to my bones, crushed emotionally, and did not think I could take one more ounce of free-ranging pain in my life.

"I love that boy, and you know what?" She squeezed her head with her hands. "When he dies, I will have nothing. I will have nothing at all. Nothing."

She fell back into her chair, sobbing.

At first I couldn't move. Neither could Janie or Velvet.

Her searing pain hit first, but I couldn't help feel this utter, selfish desolation. Momma had said when Henry died she would have nothing. *Nothing. Nothing from stupid Isabelle.*

What about me and Janie and Cecilia? Weren't we something to her? *Weren't we something?* Didn't she know that she wasn't the only one grieving?

I heard my voice, in the midst of that wave of despair, attacking her. I hated myself, then, but decades of smashed-down anger does not always erupt at the most appropriate of times. "What about us, Momma? What about us?"

"What about you?" Momma said. "This isn't about you, Isabelle, it's about my son!"

"And our brother!" Janie said, her face mottled. "What are we to you, Momma? Nothing? You say that when Henry dies you'll have nothing? I'm here. Cecilia's here. Isabelle is here. You've always treated us like nothing, Momma. Is that how you feel?"

Momma tilted her pale face up.

"Tell us!" I screamed at her. "We have done everything we could for you, Momma. *Everything.* You've rarely hugged us. Do you realize that? You've hugged Henry. You've rarely told us you loved us, ever. You've told Henry you love him. Is Henry the only person you love? We're nothing?"

Her face was stricken.

"We're your daughters!" Janie shouted, her face flushed, hands clenched at her sides. "You have criticized me my whole life. Nothing I have ever done is good enough. You can't stand my books. You think I'm strange. I embarrass you. No one will ever want to marry me, I'm odd. I'm frumpy. You can't stand my tapping and counting. Well, you know what, Momma? I can't stand being with you, Momma. You make me nervous. I can't stand *you*."

Momma's mouth open and shut. For once, wordless.

"You know what's the saddest? Do you, Momma?" I hugged my arms around myself and my loneliness. "Do you? All we ever wanted was for you to love us. That's it. We wanted you to love us, hug us. It never happened. So tell me, Momma. Do you love us or are we nothing?"

"My son is sick—" she shouted.

"We know!" Janie and I shouted back.

"What do you want from me?" she spat out. "*What?*"

"Maybe we want you to tell us that we're something," I said, my breathing heavy. "That you love us. Maybe that's all it is. But you can't do that, can you?"

"Oh, for God's sakes!"

I felt my insides crumble. Momma could not even say those three words.

"Well, Momma, when Henry's gone, we'll be gone," Janie said, her face a rigid, red mask. "You'll be happy then, won't you? Then you won't have any 'nothings' around you anymore. You can have your home and your flying mother and we nothings—I think you said you raised a fat girl, a slut, and a wacko—we *nothings* will let you die and rot and decay and do whatever else it is that mean people like you do, all by yourself."

"Don't speak to me like that, Janie Bommarito, don't threaten me!" Momma said, eyes flashing.

My anger soared and dipped and crash-landed. "You don't get it, do you? You'll never get it, Momma."

She never would. I had always known that.

Truth, in your face, though, is hard to take.

Janie turned and stumbled outside, heading toward the willow tree.

I followed her out.

"I'm never having kids," Janie said later that night when we were in bed in my room. We'd finished off a half gallon of chocolate ice cream and a bag of popcorn. "I'd be a terrible mother."

"You'd be a great mother," I told her, licking the spoon. "Your kids would know how to count before they were one. And tap. And worry."

She elbowed me. I chuckled.

"I'd love to see the stories they'd write in first grade," I said. "They'd probably be scary enough to stand their teacher's hair on end."

"I would teach them about love and serenity and peace and the delicate balance of our planet—"

"And how to hang someone without getting caught."

"Stop it, Isabelle." She pulled a pillow toward her chest. "What about you? Do you think you'll have kids?"

"No." That was a fact.

"You can't be sure about that—"

"Yes, Janie, I can." That ol' pain blasted me in the stomach. Right about where I would have held a baby.

"Why?" She turned toward me, putting two flowered journals and a book on how to hypnotize yourself on the bedspread.

"Because, Janie, as you know, I do not have a real healthy sex history. I would label my behavior as semi-suicidal."

That was the truth. I had been reckless, unguarded, a loose cannon. I could almost feel my veins and arteries clenching with pain as I spoke. I had never told Janie, or Cecilia, this one devastating . . . *thing.* "I got a disease years ago." I choked up. I could hardly say it out loud. "I'm healthy now, but I can't have kids."

Silence.

More silence.

"Never. I can't have kids." The pain of that statement seemed to engulf my every cell.

We didn't move for a minute, then Janie did what only the best sisters know how to do: hug, and don't ask questions. "I'm sorry, Isabelle, I'm really, really sorry."

"Me, too," I whispered. "Me, too."

She wiped one lone tear off my cheek.

We slept like spoons that night, me and my sister, and she rocked me when my body shuddered with grief. The area where a baby might have been, but never would be now, felt empty and lost.

But at least I had my sister. I did. I had Janie.

And Cecilia, too, the fire-breathing, foul-mouthed, Tazmanian she-devil kindergarten teacher.

Henry's decline was initially slow, then it sped up like a freight train zipping through the night to heaven. He stopped eating and lost more weight. His stomach hurt, "like there's a knife stuck in it, Is." His smile was not as ready as it was before, not as quick. It was as if the smile was getting ready to hide for good. I felt like I was being run over by a tractor eight times a day as I watched, helpless, furious.

We set up a table and chair for Henry to hand out bakery treats and say, "Jesus loves you," to people walking by. He visited with Belinda and Bao, and on his break, he and Lytle threw checkers around.

Henry still went to pet the dogs. They set up a comfortable chair for Henry to sit in while he watched the dogs play. Although it was a sunny day, we brought a blanket for his shoulders because Henry said he was cold and having trouble breathing.

He still went to hand out doughnuts at church and to listen to me sing. He helped out at mass, but wore a sweater even when the wind turned warm. When he had trouble walking up and down the altar steps, Father Mike helped him and the congregation waited.

During Bunco at the senior center he dropped a couple of trays because they were too heavy, so they gave Henry lighter things to carry and a pat on the back.

But Henry, our favorite, the sunshine of our lives, the laughter and the hope, the only thing that had ever held the Bommarito family together, started to melt away, inch by inch.

My nightmares increased and I was bone-ripping exhausted, but as so many people do who are dealing with cancer, I kept my chin up.

It about killed me.

But I did it.

Three weeks after his first chemo Henry woke up screaming again, his brown curls on the pillow.

Within two days, Henry was bald.

He did not take it well, and the tears rolled.

He moaned pathetically when he stared in his mirror, moaned again when his hair stuck to his fingers. "I sad. I embarrass. I have no hair. Henry ugly. I ugly. Big head. Bumps. Funny ears."

And he refused, for the first time in his life, to go out. No church on Sunday, no animal shelter, no Wednesday night church, no helping at the senior center, no playing checkers with Lytle, no going to the daylong events with his friends.

He went up to his bedroom and got in bed and shut the door. He didn't want to eat. Didn't want to play, didn't want me to read to him. He started to slide, quick and sure, right into death.

"We have to do something," I told Cecilia and Janie on Sunday afternoon when we met under the willow tree, the wind ruffling the three of us.

"I tried to get him to wear a wig," Janie said, anguished, wringing her hands. She'd brought her photo of her therapist, a journal, and her Yo-Yo Ma CD, but not a CD player.

It had been a disaster. "No! Gross," Henry said, waving his hands. "I don't want a fake hair, I want Henry hair."

I had tried a baseball hat.

"I still bald! I still bald! No hat in church. I no wear hat in church. That bad."

So he lay in bed. Dad came by for hours each evening pale and withered, exhausted, but he couldn't interest Henry in any garden projects or hikes or bike rides, as they'd done before.

"I tried to get him to go flying with Grandma," Cecilia said. "She misses him."

"The other day I saw Grandma wiping tears off her cheeks on the porch," I said. "She was hunched over, her goggles dangling off her fingers. I said, 'What's wrong, Amelia?' and she said, 'I miss my copilot. He's ill. Jungle fever, I think. Maybe typhoid.' "

We were silent for a while, that ruffling, never-ending wind swirling my hair. Poor Grandma. Poor Henry. Bald and hiding. Dying quick because he had no hair.

I put my hands to my own hair, ran my fingers through it with the wind. It was hair. Only hair.

"I think I'll shave my head," I said.

I expected Cecilia and Janie to freak. They didn't.

"If I'm bald, Henry won't feel so embarrassed. He'll go out. He doesn't have much—" I had to stop. Heartbreaking. "He doesn't have much more time. I want him to enjoy what time he has."

"My hair has always been the only thing that's pretty about me," Cecilia said as the wind twirled her hair. "The only thing. But what's it brought me? Nothing. I'll shave mine off, too."

"Me, too," Janie said. "In fact, I think in my next book the killer will be bald." She thought for a sec. "And it'll be a woman. A bald woman. This'll be good research for me. I'll get the scissors."

We did not waste much time.

Dad came by to see Henry and we told him what we were going to do. "Count me in," he said, instantly.

Cecilia's girls were dropped off by a neighbor as Cecilia slung a pink towel around her shoulders. I had the scissors and razor ready to roar.

"Are you cutting Mom's hair?" Kayla asked. She was wearing a beautiful orange-and-gold sari. I did not ask her where she got it.

"Actually, I'm shaving it off," I said.

"Cool," Kayla said. She crossed herself.

"Yeah, way cool," Riley added. She twisted a hair around her finger. She was wearing a shirt that said, $E=MC^2$, and a red headband. It did not completely cover her spreading baldness.

They thought. "Why?"

"Because your uncle Henry is embarrassed about being bald and he won't come out of his room, so we're shaving our heads so he'll live his life again," I said.

"Rad," Kayla said. "It's monklike. I'll do it."

"Me, too," said Riley. She yanked out a hair, studied it, let it drop to the floor. "I love gravity," she muttered.

I held the scissors. "You don't need to do that," I said. "We're Henry's sisters . . ."

"So, like, you're saying we're not part of the family?"

Kayla was so quick.

"Not important because we're young and not old?"

Riley was quick, too.

I did not take offense to the old part. "No . . ."

"That's what it sounds like," Kayla said. Her sari swished around her. "It sounds like you don't think that if we shaved our heads it would matter."

"Like our relationship to him is less than yours." Riley stuck her chin out.

"You always argue," Cecilia said. "Always. Must you always argue? All your aunt Isabelle was saying was that you don't have to shave your heads. You're kids."

"Henry's a kid at heart and he's lost all his hair."

"Yeah."

"So we want to do it, too," Riley said. "I always pull out my hair because I'm stressed. I hate myself. If I shave my head I can't hate myself, right?"

"You shouldn't hate yourself anyhow, sweetheart," I told her. All Bommaritos were whacked. Except for Henry.

"We'll do it for Henry," Kayla said.

"Yeah, for Henry."

Janie snuffled. "Oh! Oh! I love you two girls! You're true Bommaritos!" She hugged them close.

"You are wonderful young ladies," Dad said.

"Aw, Grandpa, are you going to start blubbering again?"

"No," Dad blubbered. For a manly man, tall and strong with a tough face that practically shouted, "Don't screw with me," he sure was an emotional guy. I wiped a tear off his scar. He seemed surprised by my gesture, which set off another round of tears.

Cecilia said, wonder in her tone, "By damn. I think I've raised good kids."

I hugged those girls tight. We are off our rockers as a family and they all drive me insane, but I love them, I do.

Even Momma, the Mean Grinch, who had not been mean at all since she'd sent the coffee cups flying.

We all swung pink towels around our shoulders and got ready for the razor.

"We should all shave a little bit of everyone else's hair," Riley said. "You know, family like."

"Right. And you can pray or dance or hoot, whatever your religious preference," Kayla added.

"Let's do it," I said, gung ho. "Razors ready? Say hello to baldness!"

"To baldness!" We all cheered, scissors and razors and fists thrust into the air like champagne glasses.

So we did it. Those razors hummed and purred as we each took turns shaving the others' heads. We went straight down the middle first and laughed at our skunkhood. Then we made stripes of baldness on either side. We thought about leaving it at that, but no, we had to be bald, bald, bald. When we were done, we were totally bald. Six bald heads, our hair piled up on the ground—blond, reddish, white, brown.

"Come out and play, Henry," Kayla whispered. "Come out and play."

Momma came home from the grocery store about one minute after we'd cleaned up the kitchen.

She dropped a bag of groceries on the floor when she saw our coneheads. I heard the eggs crunch. "Oh my Lord," she breathed. "My Lord. And you, Carl!"

I braced myself.

"You're all bald! You've . . . you've shaved your heads!"

"Now, you girls let me handle your mother," Dad said. "You all step on back."

"We had to, Momma," I told her. "It's the only way that Henry will leave his room—"

"How could you—" She slammed her purse on the counter.

"How could we?" I shot back. "He's embarrassed about his head, about losing his hair. If we're all bald—"

"How could you—" Her mouth was tight, hands on hips in fists.

"We don't need your approval, Momma," Janie said. "We've set our boundaries, and within our boundaries we made a family decision together."

"River, we did this for Henry." Dad's voice, always so smooth, seemed to reach her. "We did it for him. He needs to leave the house, he needs to live."

"Chill, Grams," Kayla said. "Pray you won't flip out."

"Bald is cool, Grams," Riley added. "I was almost there anyhow. You know. With my hair-plucking problem."

"How could you," Momma started up again, her voice pitching. "How could you do this without me? *Without me?*"

We shaved Momma's head.

She was still beautiful.

"You are more beautiful today, River, than you were when we met," Dad said to her, his voice ringing with this quiet, loving sincerity. "You will always be beautiful."

"Oh, stop it, you old dog," she said to Dad and, by gosh, they kissed. On the lips. In front of all of us. Two bald people kissing who were clearly still in love.

Even after all we'd gone through without Dad.

I would never completely understand my momma, this I know.

We waited until Henry woke up from his nap before we trooped into his room, one by one. Dad, me, Cecilia, the girls, Janie.

Momma came in last, arms outstretched, a smile hiding the tears that were ever present since Henry's diagnosis. "Your bald momma has arrived, Henry!" she announced, bowing to him as he clapped and laughed and kicked his feet with delight. "Now get your bottom out of bed. The bald Bommaritos are going out to dinner to celebrate our baldheadedness!"

Henry got out of bed, gingerly, giggling, and took us to the bathroom, where we all crammed in and admired ourselves in the mirror.

"Now I not the only bald one." He grinned. "I bald. You bald."

I stared at myself. I had a skinny head. Cecilia's was perfectly round with a curve at the back. Janie's was smooth. Momma preened to the left and right, admiring her profile. I swear my dad was even handsomer than before.

Kayla said, "We are the weirdest family I know."

Riley said, "It's like we're so weird I'm past being able to get embarrassed about us."

"I have never, in my life, met better people," Dad said. "You're the best. The best people I know."

Momma leaned over and kissed his cheek, and he linked an arm around her shoulders.

I studied myself. I had gone from braids and a wild, traveling, nomadic, alone life to short, curly hair to nothing.

I almost thought I liked nothing best. I was a new me.

A new Isabelle.

I kissed Henry's bald head. "We love you, Henry."

"Yeah, yeah. I love you guys, too. We the Bommaritos! We the *bald* Bommaritos! Family hug! Bommarito hug!"

I gathered the family and Velvet outside and snapped photos. I shot Dad kissing Momma, Momma's bald head tipped back for the kiss. I shot Cecilia with an arm linked around Janie, and Grandma saluting and Velvet dancing. I shot Kayla running around with Riley on her back, and I shot all of us together, with a timer, in a pyramid.

But my best photo was of Henry, arms outstretched, flying across the lawn, his face beaming.

We created a jaw-dropping stir when we bald people entered Davido's Italian Pizza joint located in downtown Trillium River in an old brick building.

For our outing, Grandma tied a pink ribbon to the top of her flight hat. When she first saw all of us bald people, she muttered, "It's an ancient tradition in Indonesia, but these natives are friendly."

Velvet said, "Well, shut my mouth! I am chugged full of love for you people," and then hugged everyone.

Davido's is always full because the pizza crust is thick and tastes like northern Italy on a blue spring day. All eating and drinking shuddered to a stop as the customers stared in shock at our family, forks and knives clattering to the plates and floor, the silence noisy enough to blow my eardrums to Venice.

Together, we probably knew all the humans in that joint. Between Momma and Grandma's history in this town, our high school years, the bakery, Cecilia's teaching, the girls' friends, church families, seniors from the senior center, Henry's friends and their families, well, I don't think there was a single stranger in there.

But it was so dead quiet.

Not a word.

Then Grandma announced, her pink bow wobbling, her voice strong, "I am Lady Lindy, queen of the air, and these natives will not hurt you! They are peaceful." She saluted.

"We'll need a table for ten," I told the hostess with spiked green hair, who was grinning at Henry.

"Hey, Henry," she said to him, her thumb up. "You rock, man. You rock."

Henry laughed, his old laugh back, gone when he was in his bedroom, death sneaking in step by step, stealing his cheer. He stuck both thumbs up and announced, booming loud to the whole restaurant, "Yeah, yeah. I Henry. I rock! We rock! We the Bommaritos! We be bald! Yeah, we be *bald!*"

Like I said, we knew everybody and they went wild. "Bommarito!" they shouted and hooted, "Bommarito!"

"We the bald family!" Henry announced, both fists churning in the air. "The bald Bommaritos! See? No hair!"

We were mobbed.

It took us half an hour to get to our table.

Grandma prayed at dinner. "Dear God, this is Amelia. I told you to heal my copilot. What are you, dumb? He's still sick. What are you, deaf?" She shouted that last part. "Get it right, God. Don't screw up. What are you, blind? Amen."

Somebody took up a secret collection that night and we did not even have to pay for our meal.

When Momma found out, she bent her bald head and cried, right there in the restaurant.

❦ 30 ❧

We made the front page of the local paper the next day. A reporter had been at the restaurant with his family and raced out to his car to get his camera and take a picture.

There was an article about the Bommarito family and how Henry was fighting pancreatic cancer. The reporter noted that Henry was embarrassed about not having hair and wouldn't leave the house. It detailed how we wanted him to continue his life and to enjoy the time he had left. (He got ahold of Janie; she always spills her guts.)

The article mentioned that Janie was the famous crime writer, Cecilia was a popular teacher, I was a nationally famous photographer, and our family owned Bommarito's Bakery in town.

Henry giggled when he saw the photo of all of us at the restaurant. "We famous. We like the movie stars."

The next morning I took Henry to the senior center to help with Bunco. Janie and Cecilia went to the bakery.

A rumbling, grumbling pickup truck stopped next to us and Henry rolled down the window and waved, both hands, both arms. There were two tough dudes in the truck. Longish hair, hard faces. Mean. One had a face that looked as if he had fought through one too many knife fights.

"Henry, get in here," I hissed. "Roll up the window."

"No, I say hi! I say hi." He leaned out the window. "Hey, hey!"

"Henry, get in here!" I pulled on him.

"No, I say hi to Sammy and hi to Petie!"

"My man Henry! Henry!" the driver boomed and smiled. Gone was the knife-fight face as his eyes tilted up, his yellowy smile almost cute.

"Henry, dude," the other one drawled, flashing him some sort of hand signal. "I dig the hair, dude. Dig it."

"I be bald!" Henry laughed. "I got the cancer. Pain-cree-at-*ick*. It icky! That's it. That's all."

I saw their faces drop. "Oh man, that sucks," Knife Fight Face said. "That sucks."

The light turned green. A car honked behind us. I didn't move, though. Henry was talking!

"Hey, dude," the Hand Signaler said, crushed. "I'm sorry. I'm sorry, Henry."

"Hey! All my friends sorry."

"Can we do something for you, dude? Can we help?"

The car honked again.

"No. No. I good. Jesus told me I go home soon. I like seeing you today! *I like it!*"

The car honked again. I heard both men swear.

Henry whispered, "That bad words."

The men with the bad words got out of that grumbling, rumbling truck, slammed the doors, and glared at the driver who was honking, their leather vests stretching across deep chests.

The honking immediately stopped. I turned around. It was four young male teenagers. They were now slouched in their seats, mouths gaping in fear.

The tough guys turned back to Henry. "You fight it, Henry,"

Knife Fight Face said, swiping a rough hand over the tears in his eyes.

"No, I not fight. I going to heaven! Pretty quick. Jesus tell me. I gotta go do the Bunco. I see you in church. Okay? I see you in church?"

Surprisingly, they nodded.

"Okay, Henry. We'll see you in church," Hand Signaler sighed, grabbing Henry's shoulder.

"Okay dokay. Jesus loves you."

"Yeah, man, he digs you, too."

"Yeah, yeah!" Henry laughed. "Jesus digs you!"

In my rearview mirror, I watched one of the tough guys sling an arm around the other one, patting him on the back.

"Who were they?"

"Oh, that Father Mike's cousins. They so nice and friendly."

Okay dokay.

"You pretty, Is."

I reached out to hold my brother's hand.

Bob The Man in Charge had seen the article. He called again. Kayla took the call. She told him she'd pray about his reason for wanting to speak to her aunt Janie and blessed him.

"Don't you want to see him again?" I asked Janie. "His English garden? Read classics together? Scarf down a few scones with your lemon tea?"

"I do. I don't. I do." She checked the stove, the oven, anguished. She took deep breaths. "I'll have to sit in my serenity corner, light candles, commune with my therapist."

"You've already communed with your therapist," I drawled. "What did she say, for the hundredth time?"

"She told me to call him." Janie sighed, hands to her temples. "I need my embroidery."

"Then do it, Aunt Janie," Kayla said. "Here, wear my sari when you call. It's good luck." She handed Janie the orange sari she'd been wearing.

Janie put on the sari.

It didn't help. She couldn't pick up the phone and dial. Too scary.

The next day, Henry and I went to the animal shelter. He wore a blue shirt with a picture of a black, grinning cat on it and his Velcro shoes.

I noted again that the shelter needed a major face-lift and more room.

"Paula Jay," Henry sang. "Paula Jay, where are you? Henry here. I here to pet the doggies."

No one answered, so we headed toward the back and the kennels.

In the back, we found Paula Jay and Dawn. They were putting leashes on a few dogs to take them for a walk.

"Hi Paula Jay, hi Dawn," Henry said, delighted he'd found them.

"Hello, Henry!" They smiled.

My breath caught midway in my throat, stuck there.

Paula Jay and Dawn were both bald. Not a hair on their heads.

"Hey hey!" Henry yelled. "You bald!"

The ladies laughed. "Yep. No hair. No more shampooing and curling. We're like you, Henry!"

He clapped his hands, his smile lopsided, endearing. "Now we be bald together. We all be bald!"

Yeah, we all be bald.

I hugged those ladies close.

The dogs barked. The cats meowed.

I sniffled.

Henry wanted to go to the bakery later in the afternoon, but I took him home first for a nap. He argued with me and Velvet for a while, but we got him fed and upstairs. Halfway through reading a book to him, he fell asleep.

I ran into Grandma in the hallway. I saluted. "Hello, Mrs. Earhart."

"Greetings," she told me. She was wearing her green flight uniform today and had tied a jaunty yellow scarf around her neck.

"How is your day?"

"The weather is fine for takeoff. I will be leaving soon." She went into Henry's room on tiptoe, one toe at a time. "Don't wake the native," she whispered, after patting Henry on the shoulder. "This native is sick, perhaps malaria or snakebite. He needs his rest."

She grabbed two blankets from a closet and a pillow and lay down on the floor next to Henry's bed. This was not new to me. Since Henry became sick, Grandma often slept on his floor.

I wondered, feeling this black depression start to steal over me again, how Amelia Earhart would do without her native. Without her copilot. Without her friend.

I closed the door quietly before Grandma's pain became too much for me to breathe through.

Bommarito's Bakery was jammed. It was Mommy Wednesday. We had about sixteen Mommies and their kids. The Mommies were passing around white wine in Thermoses. I pretended not to see it.

I went to the back and shook my head at the orders. Birthday cakes, wedding cakes, and the usual cookies, treats, breads, and so on. We had hired two teenagers headed to college in the fall. One studied microbiology and the other wanted to be a brain surgeon. For now, they iced.

Bao's hands were flying. Belinda cut out cookies. Lytle and a brother rolled dough.

Janie was ringing people up like there was no tomorrow, chatting as if she was a normal person who didn't usually hide in a houseboat. The girls were making cranberry nut bread and Cecilia was filling orders.

"This is crazy," I said aloud.

Cecilia laughed. It was great to hear that laugh. It had been too long.

The girls' bald heads snapped up in surprise at their bald mother's laughter.

I saw Kayla smile at Riley. They wriggled in their seats.

Henry did not want to eat dinner that night or the next. Day to day he continued to waste away. He still had his smile, but the wattage was dimmed, his breathing labored, his walk slowing, his plane sputtering.

The decision to not do chemo again had been easy. Dr. Remmer had shaken her head after seeing Henry one afternoon. "Get the dogs married, Dr. Remmer!" Henry wheezed, leaning heavily on me.

So that was it, we were done. We moved to what is gently known as "palliative care," which means you make the person comfortable on their way out the door.

On Wednesday night I asked Henry if he still wanted to go to church. "Are you okay, Henry? You tired? We don't have to go.

Henry's mouth opened. "Is! You silly. We have to go. Henry help at church Wednesdays. What Father Mike do without me? He need help. I help him!"

"You're right, Henry. You have to go. Father Mike needs you. I thought that if you were too tired, we could take one night off."

"No. Not night off. I help."

We got in the car and drove in silence. Henry put a hand out and I drove with one hand, one hand in his.

"Henry," I asked. "Are you scared?"

"Am I scared?"

"Yes."

"Am I scared of church?" He was perplexed.

"No, no."

"What scared of?"

"Nothing, Henry. I got confused."

"Ha! Ha! I get confused, too. But you mean am Henry scared to die?"

Sometimes he has these flashes where he cuts through to the hard truth. Bulls-eye. On target.

"Yes. Are you scared to die?"

He squeezed my hand. "No, you silly, Is, I told you. I not scared to die. Jesus will come and get me. We fly up to the angels on a moonbeam or sun ray and I get some wings on my back and I go live in heaven and I come and visits you."

It was dark, so Henry didn't see my tears tearing straight down my face.

"How will I know when you're visiting me, Henry?"

I didn't think he'd have an answer to that one, but he did.

"Hmm . . ." He put a fist under his chin. "Hmmm. Lemme see. Let Henry think. Hmmmm. I think Is, you know I'm visiting you when the wind picks up your hairs and swirls it all around all around all around." He mimicked my hair flying even though I had no hair. "That from my angel wings."

"You're gonna be my favorite angel."

"Yeah," he snickered. "I your favorite angel. I fly around. Zoom. I always there with you, Is. I there."

"I love you, my brother, Henry."

"I love you, my sister, Is."

We held hands the rest of the way to the church.

My grief was so overwhelming I could feel it crushing me from the inside out.

We were late to church on Sunday. We all went, the whole gang, including Dad. Henry headed, slowly but smiling, to the front of the church and sat in the front pew so he could help Father Mike. We found a place at the back of the church and knelt down, exhausted.

We were stressed and rushed and tired. Henry had had a bad night again. He'd felt sick and alternately I, Momma, Velvet, or

Janie had been up with him. Dad had come at three in the morning when Momma called him and had stayed the night and helped us get Henry ready for church when he insisted on going.

So we dropped to our knees and said our prayers in church. Dad bent his head, somberly, slowly, his jaw locked. Momma held her rosary. I watched her lips moving a mile a minute.

Grandma prayed out loud, her flight goggles on top of her head. "God, this is Amelia. Today I'm praying for you. I pray that you help all the natives out there who need help and my copilot who has malaria fever or baboon bite instead of sitting back on your butt and doing nothing. Does the devil got you or something? Amen."

She sat back and twirled her thumbs. No one said anything about Grandma praying out loud. She had lived in that town forever and they were used to her. Many had commented that they sure liked this Grandma better than the other one.

"I would like the Bommarito Family and Amelia Earhart to come up."

Father Mike's words broke through my raggedy thoughts like an electric bolt, most of my thoughts centered around my encroaching depression, and how I would live without Henry. I was fighting back, but I was weakening, I could feel it.

"Come on up," he boomed, smiling.

I felt Momma freeze beside me.

"Momma, come on," I whispered to her. "Get Grandma."

No need. Grandma had heard the invitation and she was up and striding down the aisle, saluting people. Cecilia and I pulled Momma to her feet.

Janie put a hand on my back and I felt it tremble. Janie does not like big crowds, had only agreed to go to church because of Henry, and she sure as heck didn't like being the center of attention.

Cecilia and the girls came up behind me after Cecilia whispered a little too loud, "What the *hell?*"

It wasn't until later that I realized Dad hadn't come with us to the altar.

But I was distracted by Henry, who was standing next to Father Mike, who was . . . *bald*. I felt my mouth drop open.

We helped Momma up the stairs to the altar. Bald Father Mike smiled at us. When I knew that Momma had her footing, Grandma was not pontificating at the podium, Janie had not fainted, and Cecilia's girls were standing next to her (Kayla was actually wearing a dress today with only three giant crosses), I turned to the congregation.

Baldness.

Not complete baldness, but many, many heads, including a huge group of teenagers, and young children who I learned later were Cecilia's students.

I heard Momma's intake of breath. "Good Glory," she whispered. "Good glory God. Good glory God."

"The natives have lost their hair!" Grandma shouted, arms outspread. "The natives have lost their hair!"

Janie made a squealing sound and fluffed a lace hankie.

Cecilia put her hands on her face and made these long, sobbing sounds.

Riley said, "Sweet. Now I'm not the only bald dude in school."

Kayla nodded. "Cool. Way cool."

And me.

Well, I'm a regular mushpot now. All those people. I saw baldness and I saw kindness. I saw a shiny head and I saw caring eyes. I saw the lights shining on those head cones and I saw generosity of spirit. I saw people I'd recently met and people I'd known since high school, all smiling.

I saw Knife-Fight Face and the Hand Signaler. Bald people from the animal shelter and the senior center. Our neighbors and Bao and Lytle and his brothers.

All bald.

And for a second, I saw a tiny gold light prick the darkness around me.

"Folks, we're going to pray today for the Bommarito Family. Please bow your heads."

And bow our bald heads we did.

After church, Henry served doughnuts and the Bommarito Family all trooped downstairs to socialize with other people for the first time ever.

Soon Momma was chatting, introducing Dad. Momma had never socialized at church, but that wasn't the strangest thing going on. The strangest thing was how she introduced Dad. "This is my husband, Carl."

I raised my eyebrows, and let my smile out. Janie sidled up to me. "For my entire life I have felt that I didn't fit in. It was like the whole group was playing in the river and I was the weed on the side of it. Or the dead duck. Or the invasive plant that didn't belong. I wanted to be normal."

I wrapped an arm around her. "We're not normal."

"But I always wanted to be normal. I've made an observation, though."

"What is it?"

"No one's normal. There's Chin Marko. His wife is the shoplifter. She took the piano out of the Baptist church, remember? She pulled it down Cherry Hill Street with ropes at two in the morning. And the Goyas' sons. They're geniuses. But they do odd stuff. Explosions. Dynamite. That sort of thing. People know when they hear a big bang that it's the Goyas.

"Danika Tobias is wearing a hat with two birds and a nest in between. The nest came from the tree in her backyard."

She tapped one hand against the other.

"So I write about gruesome killings and kidnappings and have a few obsessions. It's the way I am."

"Odd."

"Yep. Odd. Who gives a shit."

"I don't. I don't give a shit."

"Good. Wanna doughnut?"

* * *

So we had a bald town. Many bald people. Henry loved it. We loved it.

Loved it while our hearts broke into teeny, tiny, miserable pieces.

"Parker came over yesterday afternoon," Cecilia told me and Janie a few nights later. We were in our usual position on the grass under the willow tree with our friend the wind whipping about, the moon glowing. "Asshole dropped in without telling me."

"Did you grab your ax and make swishing motions toward his groin?" Janie asked eagerly.

"No . . ."

"Did you reach for your nail gun and shoot at him for self-defense purposes?"

"Damn, Janie, no. No, I didn't do that. Actually"—Cecilia shifted—"when he said he wanted to talk to me, I told him I didn't want to talk to him."

"Good. Screw him," I said.

"If I were there," Janie said, "I would have grabbed a wire, you can use one that is right off a stereo, and I would have—"

"Yes, we know, Janie. That one was in your last book," Cecilia drawled.

Janie humphed.

Cecilia crossed a heel over a knee. She'd dropped weight since Henry's diagnosis. "I said, 'What is it, asshole? And remember I'm not required to take any more of your abuse and how's Bimbo Boobs?' "

I snorted.

Cecilia laughed. "He said, don't call her Bimbo Boobs, and he started getting all fired up . . . and then he sighed. Big sigh. I crossed my arms and waited. It was the funniest thing, too. Because I was able, for the first time, to step back and study him without all the emotions. When I was living with him, I was always upset, always tired, always trying to please him or manage

him and his moods. I knew that he had secrets, I knew he was
lying to me about one thing after the other. He always denied it.
It makes you feel like you're a paranoid wife. Like you're losing
your mind. Like you're a nag and seeing things that aren't there.
He always made me feel like I was the one with the problem, not
him. And yet, I was right all along. I was right. He was lying,
cheating on me, gambling, drinking. Plus he was mean to me."

I squeezed her hand. The sky was sure pretty tonight. A frost-
ing of stars. I hoped that one would fall out of the sky and conk
Parker in the tonsils and he would die a strangulation death. Gee,
I sounded like Janie.

"I hated having sex with him. He made me feel so ugly. He'd
sigh when he was on top of me, like he was so disappointed. Or
he'd groan in a way that I knew he was frustrated. I felt this
small." She held up her fingers a quarter inch apart. "I felt like
nothing. And what makes me so mad is how long I took it. I hate
him for making me hate myself because I didn't have the gump-
tion to leave him."

I wished Parker's face would explode.

"Don't hate yourself, Cecilia," Janie pleaded. "Don't. I love
you, Isabelle loves you. So many people love you. You're this
strong life force, a ray out of a rainbow."

"Thank you, Janie." She faced Janie. "You're a sweet person,
you know that? Gentle and lovely. Except for all the murdering.
Anyhow, Asshole said, 'Cecilia, you've lost weight. Finally, you're
listening to me.' And I said, 'What do you want, Parker?' And he
told me that we had had a lot of problems in our marriage but we
could start to fix things here and now if I got rid of my attitude. I
laughed. He scowled and crossed his arms over his chest, all
authoritative-like."

"I wished I could have been there. You should have invited
me!" I protested.

"I wanted him to hang himself. He said that our marriage didn't
work because I was always nagging at him and starting fights. That
I didn't take care of him. I'm too fat and I would have to change

that because my fat was repulsive. He told me that Constance was great but he was willing to get back together for the sake of the family if I would behave better the next time. He actually used that word, 'behave.' "

My, how we laughed.

"And I said, aren't you still in love with Constance? And he sighed again like he was gravely wounded. It was funny how I could actually predict what he was going to do and say. That's how far I've gotten away from that sicko. He said that Constance was a beautiful woman, charming and sweet, and it would kill him to give her up, she was wildly in love with him, but he would sacrifice for the family and the girls. 'You got that, Cecilia?' He actually said that. 'I'll sacrifice for the family.' "

"Please don't tell me you agreed to try it again, Cecilia," I pleaded. "Or I will have to hire a hit man. You know I wouldn't do well in jail. I can't bring my Porsche."

"I said to him, 'Parker, I know what you're doing. You're broke. You have a mountain of credit debt. You have to pay me for monthly child support and payments to the kids' college accounts. You have no home. You have no job. You don't even have enough money to bet or gamble anymore, do you?' He got all pale when I said that."

"Pale," Janie mused. "Perhaps his life force was draining out of him."

" 'You don't want to get back together with me,' I said. 'Constance is cheating on you. The girls told me they overheard you fighting about it. And I hear you have a new boat?' I loved telling him I knew about that boat! Constance and her boats! 'No, Parker,' I said, like I was some calm self-help guru. 'Never will I get back together with you. And if at any time you stop paying child support for the kids, I will sic Cherie on you again like a pit bull with rabies.' "

"Did he leave?"

"Not before I told him that I had hated being married to him and hadn't realized how much I hated it until he'd left. That once I got over being mad that he had cheated on me, and once I got over that I was furious with myself for staying married to him, I loved my life. If only he would die a painful death with lots of blood spurting from his mouth, then things would be perfect."

"Ohhh, gory," Janie breathed. *"Nice."*

"So, anyhow, he charged off to get his tools from the garage after swearing at me and using the female dog name in reference to me, and I went and got the hose."

"Why did you get the hose?" I asked, anticipating her deviousness with delight.

"Because his car needed watering on the inside."

I sputtered. "Was he driving the Corvette?

"Yes. And since he had been screaming at me, I feared for my life, so when his car was being watered, I called the police station and got Charlotte and told her to come—you remember Charlotte from high school? She was the prom queen. Now she's a lieutenant in the department. She refused to wear a dress, only jeans when she got the crown. It took her five minutes to get to the house. Parker came back to the driveway and she was there with Lieutenant Sho Lin, is Grandma's best friend's nephew."

"Oh yeah, Sho," I said. Nice guy.

"Parker doesn't care they're there, he's still screaming at me and I told Charlotte I was so glad I didn't have to live with a verbally abusive jerk anymore and she nodded at me and told Parker to 'cease his communications immediately' and she stood right in front of me, so did Sho.

"I will never forgive you for not having me over on that day," I said. "Never."

"Parker bad-mouthed Charlotte and scowled at her like she's a parasite and said, 'What the fuck are you going to do, anyhow, Charlotte? You're gonna side with her, aren't you? All you shitface women side with each other.'"

I sucked in my breath like a siphon. Even I know better than to get into it with police.

"So the shitface Charlotte grabbed him and shoved him to the ground and handcuffed him. I am not kidding, girls, Charlotte had him down in seconds. Facedown, head in the dirt. I couldn't believe how fast she moved. She's not that big, either. Parker tried to get up and she put a couple of holds on him until he sank into the ground like a squished slug.

"Then Sho and Charlotte hauled him up and shoved him against the police car. I decide to show Parker how well I'd watered his car and I opened the door to the Corvette and all this water rushed out. Parker started to scream again and said, 'Charlotte! Are you blind? Can't you see what that bitch did to my car? I'll get you for this, Cecilia. You hear me? I am going to get you. You will live to regret this for the rest of your very short life. Say good-bye, Cecilia! Good-bye!' Parker always told me I'd have a short life because I'm so fat.

"Anyhow, Charlotte read him his rights and told him he was being arrested for verbally and physically assaulting a police officer, menacing and trespassing, and threatening to kill his wife.

"And Parker's screaming, 'Look at my car! Can't you see what she did to my car?' And Sho said to him, no smile at all, 'I don't see anything wrong with your car, Parker, do you, Lieutenant?' And Charlotte said, 'Nope, all I see is a car a man would buy who's having a midlife crisis. You should roll up your windows when it's raining, Parker.' "

I sighed. "This is one of the most rewarding moments of my entire life. I will treasure it always."

"I laughed until my fat hurt," Cecilia said. "Too much jiggling."

"I feel joyous, free, like I'm flying," Janie sighed.

A star shot through the sky.

Splendid

So splendid.

❦ 31 ❧

Dad was with us each evening. He and Henry bent their bald heads together and made another model airplane together and a submarine. They swung on the porch swing together, too. When Henry fell asleep with his head in Dad's lap, I saw Dad raise a hand to his face. It was the one with only three fingers left.

Dad had lost so much.

And he was about to lose more.

The slide into heaven was quick. Henry, almost overnight, became too tired and nauseated to get out of bed. He refused to drink, or eat, saying he wasn't hungry or thirsty anymore. He became more jaundiced.

His bedroom was almost always full of people.

Friends from his day center came and patted his head and hugged him. Lytle brought his checkerboard and put it beside Henry on the bed. "When you ready, Henry, we play." Lytle knew they weren't going to play again. I knew that because he went and banged his head in the corner of the bedroom so hard he bled and his brother dragged him out.

Henry, who was fading rapidly, barely able to lift his head, smiled. "You my friend, Lytle. I see you."

Father Mike gave Henry last rites, the intoned words sinking into my grief, deepening it, making it final. Complete.

Late one night, Momma bent over Henry. His eyes were halfway open, his smile only halfway there. "You are my special boy, Henry," Momma rasped. "You have been my light."

I tried not to feel hurt. These last words were for Henry and about Henry. Not me.

"I love you, Momma," Henry whispered. "You a good momma."

"You're a won . . . won . . . wonderful son," she sobbed.

"Hey, Momma. Be nice to sisters. Okay dokay."

Her face registered her shock, but then she leaned her cheek against his. "I will, Henry. I will. I promise."

See? Henry gets it. He always had.

Dad's hands shook as he held his son's hands in his own. "Henry, I—" He stopped. "Henry, I—" Dad couldn't speak.

"You my Dad. You back," Henry whispered. "I love my Dad."

"I love you, son." Dad's voice cracked in half, as if the pain had split him in two and the two parts couldn't get close enough together to sound human anymore. "I'm sorry I haven't been here with you . . . all these years . . . all these years."

Henry reached out a hand, slowly, carefully, and patted Dad's head. "It okay, Dad. It okay."

"Cecilia," Henry said. "Where the girls? I say good-bye to the girls. Jesus tell me say bye-bye."

I wrapped my arms around my stomach and leaned my head against the window. How could Henry be so brave, so cheerfully courageous? He had known from the start he was dying, but he had never flipped out, never gotten hysterical, never grieved. I would never, ever be as brave as Henry.

And now, tonight, he just wanted to say good-bye. A loving good-bye from Henry with the frog hat and the shirt that said "Boo!" A loving good-bye from the most compassionate, caring person I had ever known. A loving good-bye from a man who believed he would join God and the angels and get his wings.

"Okay, Henry, okay. I'll get the girls," Cecilia said, rushing out. Within minutes she was back with Riley and Kayla. Riley and Kayla came in slowly, then burst into tears.

"Oh, no!" Henry said, his voice weak. "Oh, no! No crying. No crying. I go to Jesus. I see you again."

"Uncle Henry," Riley said, so sweet, so sad, as she put her bald head on his chest.

He patted her.

"Uncle Henry, I love you," Kayla said. Today she was wearing a crocheted floral kipot on her head, like Jewish women might wear.

"Nice hat, nice hat, I think Jesus like your hat, Kayla."

Both girls cried and held him.

"You be good. You be good." Henry sighed.

Momma tried to stifle her sobs, but she couldn't do it.

Grandma must have heard the cries of her daughter's heart, because she marched in, straight to Momma, who was keening by Henry's bed, and rocked her back and forth.

Seeing the two of them together like that, bald head next to white hair, after all their decades of fighting, brought steaming hot tears to my eyes.

After twenty minutes, Grandma stood and ceremoniously bowed at Henry and put her goggles over his head.

"I am honoring you with my goggles, young man," she intoned. "You have earned them. Wear them wisely."

Henry grinned at us through the goggles. "Hey, I love you. I love my family. Dad back. See. Dad back." His eyes started to close. "We a family. Bommarito Family."

We turned out the lights and sat in the night as the moonbeams shone through the fluttering curtains.

We got quieter and quieter until all we could hear was Henry's labored breathing, the space between each breath longer and longer.

Momma was about ready to collapse, so Dad and she kissed Henry on the forehead and Dad put Momma to bed. Cecilia settled the girls in the guest room they always stayed in.

I put Grandma in bed. "Leave my goggles with my copilot," she ordered. "He'll need them to get out of the jungle. There are lions where he's going and they'll offer him protection."

I assured her I would. I turned off her light but whirled back because of a muffled noise coming from under the covers.

Grandma was crying, softly, straight into her pillow. I picked her up, she weighed so little, and put her on my lap and rocked her. Somehow, in what edge of sanity she had left, Grandma knew that her copilot was dying.

"Remember what I told you," she instructed me, as I hugged her close. "Leave the goggles with him."

"I will, Amelia. I will. The goggles stay with Henry."

I rubbed her back and covered her up, my heart heavy, then stroked her hair, white and curly and soft.

"Keep the goggles on him," she whispered as she fell into a soft sleep. "He needs my protection."

I went back to Henry's room and tucked myself in by Janie who was next to Henry, Cecilia on the other side.

When dawn came, Henry woke up.

We got him some water, more pain medication, settled him back down.

"I see the angels," he told us, his voice wispy.

I pulled the blankets to his chin, Cecilia stroked his head, Janie rubbed his feet.

"What do they look like?" I asked.

His eyes were only half open. "They white. Gold. Smiling."

"They sound beautiful, Henry."

"Yeah, they beautiful, Is. They right here."

"What do you mean they're here?" Cecilia asked. Her face was tight and drawn.

"They here, Cecilia. Behind you. Behind my sisters."

Janie was the only one who snuck a look over her shoulder. She was sickly white, the circles under her eyes like mottled bruises. I felt like I was watching her decay.

"I know why they here." Henry sighed. "You sisters, I tell you I love you."

I dropped my head. One wonders how much grief a body can take before it caves in on itself.

"We love you, too, Henry." Janie leaned forward, her body jerking. "I don't know how I'm going to live without you, Henry."

I shushed her, but Henry wasn't bothered by her honesty.

"Hey, Janie, I with you all the time. I with you at the bakery making the whale cupcakes. I with you at the shelter when you pet the dogs. Will you pet the mean dog for me? You know, Stevie. He sad that why he mean."

"I'll pet him."

"Yeah. He good dog." He tilted his head to see Cecilia. "I with you, Cecilia, in your class making play dough. You be extra nice to Phil. He sad boy. Yeah, he sad."

"I'll be extra nice to Phil, Henry, I promise," Cecilia said, choking back a sob.

I could feel Cecilia's barely controlled grief. It was going to suffocate me. It was going to suffocate her.

"I with you, Is." He held my hand. "I with you all the time. Don't be sad no more. Angels love you."

"I'll try not to be sad anymore, Henry." Impossible, I thought. How could I be happy without Henry? "You think the angels love me?"

He sighed. "They love you, Is, because you Isabelle. That why they here. They here for my sisters. Not me. For Henry's sisters. They with you because you sisters sad. Their wings around you now. I see it."

This time I peered over my shoulder and so did Cecilia. Just in case. Janie's head was practically doing 360-degree turns searching for the angels.

"You good sisters." He smiled, a weak smile. "We laugh. We cry. We play. We work at bakery and have spaghetti with stringy cheese. Happy life. I say this word, Hallelujah."

"Hallelujah?" I asked.

"Yeah, yeah. Hallelujah. Happy life."

We sisters didn't bother hiding our tears anymore. Our grief took over, demolished us. Henry brought his hands out from under the covers and we held on all together as his eyes started to shut. "I loves you, my sisters. Henry's sisters. I loves you."

Two nights later, after hardly sleeping at all, Cecilia and Janie and I lay on the bed next to Henry, who hadn't spoken in twenty-four hours and hadn't opened his eyes in the same amount of time.

We held Henry's hands and held each other's, too, through the night, through the moonbeams, through the shiny stars, through the utter bleakness of our lives.

And when morning came, and the black turned to pink and yellow, and a sun ray dove right into Henry's bedroom and glided softly to his bed, that's when Henry sighed one more time and off he went, right on that sun ray, which disappeared a minute after it came and got Henry and pulled him up to heaven.

Momma's primal scream came from the soul of her despair. Dad held her, tried to soothe her, but how do you soothe someone who's lost her son?

The scream woke Grandma up and she rushed into Henry's room. When she understood he was dead, she ran out of the house announcing, "My copilot is dead! SOS! SOS!" She is speedy, but I am speedier, and I managed to catch her before she darted off the property.

When I caught her she hollered, tried to hit me, and landed a few stunning blows. I tackled her again, but she belted me, right on the eye. That would be the second shiner this year, I thought.

She twisted away again, still screaming that her copilot was dead, dead, dead, and I rolled her to the ground. She swore and struggled, but then gave up, lying underneath me as she wailed into the grass, "My copilot is dead, my copilot is dead! Oh, SOS! SOS!"

Our tears mixed together, mine and Mrs. Earhart's.

Momma's mouth opened and she began to scream. I could tell, after a while, that she wanted to stop screaming but she couldn't. When she started knocking her head on the wall, we called an ambulance and a man we'd gone to school with, Avery Jordan, drove up with another man and was so kind and gentle with Momma I wanted to kiss him. Dad, limping, emotionally crushed, went with her to the hospital.

Velvet stayed with Grandma, who was now in bed. It appeared that Velvet needed to be in bed, too, and I told her to get in bed with Grandma. "Lordy, I don't know if my heart can take all this grief, I don't know, sugar. I sure loved Henry. I did, he was a gift. A gift from the heavens."

It was Janie and Cecilia and Henry and I in Henry's bed. Again. The four of us.

But one of us wasn't breathing and he was the best of the four of us. The most extraordinary, the most beautiful. The best of the Bommaritos.

Two nights later, after arrangements had been made and tons of people had been in and out of the home, Cecilia, Janie, and I lay on the grass and stared at the moonbeams under the willow tree.

We held hands.

And we cried.

And cried.

And cried.

I hated those moonbeams.

The church was jammed for Henry's memorial service, with people standing all around the sides.

Father Mike's eulogy was beautiful, but he struggled through it. He would barely compose himself, read a few more lines, and have to harden that jaw again before he spoke.

"Henry lived the life Christ wanted us to live. He was good. He was kind. He forgave. He helped others. I do not know a single person who volunteered more than Henry. He helped people every day, with no expectation, ever, of any return. He reached out to others in goodness, in love. We all"—he paused, composed himself—"We all must strive to be more like Henry Bommarito. We must. It is what's right. It is what's good. It is what Henry would have wanted. It is our command from Christ."

After a couple of songs, and prayers, it was my turn.

"My name is Isabelle Bommarito. I am Henry's sister."

I glanced down at Henry's other sisters. Cecilia was shaking, but her chin was high. Janie was shattered, and weak, and white as a crayon, which was nothing compared to Momma, who was leaning heavily against Dad, her eyes half shut. She had taken the road straight up to hysteria this morning, her eyes glazed, as she made, alternately, these small animal shrieking sounds and guttural moans.

She was in a cold, Henry-less hell and had gotten to the funeral only by sheer will to honor her son.

"Thank you for coming today." I stopped as I took in the people in that church, many of them bald, the vast majority familiar to me.

Keep it together, Isabelle, I told myself. *Keep it together.* "Three nights ago, Cecilia, Janie, and I were lying on the grass, under the willow tree, outside Grandma's house. We were holding hands below the moonlight and we were crying about Henry." I bit my lip. "We're the Bommaritos and we do strange things like that. Our Grandma is Amelia Earhart . . ."

Grandma stood up and saluted and sat back down.

"Janie writes frightening, graphic books and likes her houseboat a little too much." Janie nodded, wiped her eyes with a hankie. I let my gaze rest on Bob The Man in Charge, who had come for the service. How kind he had been when he saw me, giving

me a hug and handing Janie a tiny, old book. *Wuthering Heights.*
She'd clutched it to her chest, grateful beyond measure.

"I take pictures of people living in hell and suffer from depression. My reputation in Trillium River during high school was not stellar." I heard some laughter. "Cecilia is an incredible teacher and mother with a mouth that could put a trucker to shame and a temper that could knock a roof off a house. You all know our momma. She is not exactly meek. Our parents have gotten back together after nearly three decades apart. Kayla and Riley are quirky, too. They inherited it in their genes."

The girls nodded. Kayla flashed me a peace sign.

I took a deep breath.

"The Bommaritos are not normal. I told Cecilia that it would have been cheaper for our family to keep a shrink on a monthly retainer than to make individual appointments. It wasn't a joke. We are often half crazed and together we become fully crazed."

I paused.

"Except for Henry," I said softly. "Henry has never been crazed. In fact, Henry is the only sane, completely stable person in our family. He's the one who brought us together and kept us together. He's the one who kept the peace. He's the one who softened all of us when the world made us too rough, too hard, too jaded. He was the center of our family."

I shuffled my notes. "Henry loved many things, but he loved God, he loved Christ, he loved his family, and he loved his friends—all of you, the most. He loved all of you so much."

I heard the sniffling start then—someone blew his nose, another muffled a moan. "Henry knew what friendship was all about. He knew what it took to be a friend." I waited so my voice wouldn't wobble. It wobbled. "From Henry I learned what kindness and selflessness looked like. From Henry I learned how one kind word, from one person, can change the day, maybe even the life, of someone else. From Henry I learned to be. Be there. Be in the moment. *Be in life.*

"There was no show with Henry, no airs, no false values, no

pretenses. He was our family's constant smile during the hard times in our lives, the constant hope." I had to stop. "Henry brought us hope, and without hope, we have nothing. Nothing. Henry prevented us from buying into the nothing."

I struggled with a wave of emotion. "Henry told me that he was going to be with me after he died. I know he told many of you the same thing."

I saw heads nodding.

"So let's assume that Henry is here with us now. That he's here, in the front row, right where he always sat, helping Father Mike at church."

I didn't know how this part was going to go over, but I figured I would try it. What the hell. I knew Henry would love it.

"I don't think I always gave Henry all the appreciation I should have. Why? Because I wrongly assumed he would always, *always*, my whole life, be here with me. With us. I never envisioned that he would die first. I actually never envisioned he would die at all. I never imagined my life without him and I have to say—" I had to stop again. "I have to say that I don't know quite how to go on here."

Momma moaned in her seat and rocked back and forth.

"In about thirty seconds I'm going to start clapping for Henry. For the innocent and pure love he brought into my life, for his laughter and for the way he made each stranger a friend. I'm going to clap for his forgiving heart, his love of pancake breakfasts and for all the times he flew with Amelia Earhart. I'm going to clap for the way he took care of me a few months ago, and all the times when we were kids when we could not protect him, and yet he still loved us. I'm going to clap for the strength he showed then and the strength he showed recently when he was dying. I'm going to clap for the faith he kept in other people, even when people weren't kind, or good to him, and for the way he embraced each day as the gift that it is, then embraced anyone standing around him. No one, and I mean *no one*, has taught me more about living life than Henry."

I walked out from behind the podium and said, "This is for you, Henry. *This is for you.*"

I started clapping. Clapping for Henry.

There was a shocked pause; it did not last long.

Momma was the first to struggle to her feet, with Dad's help, and they started clapping and crying at the same time. Cecilia and the girls sprung to their feet and hooted, and Janie put both hands in the air and waved.

Grandma joined me on the podium, pulled her flight goggles over her eyes, and saluted Henry several times, her eyes at the ceiling, as if she were seeing him.

Didn't take two seconds for the whole church to join in.

We clapped and clapped. A standing ovation. For Henry.

All for Henry.

Before and after Father Mike and I spoke, incense was burned, holy water was sprinkled, Dad and Cecilia and Janie read Old and New Testament scripture, Father Mike led us in prayer, we knelt and stood, knelt again. We took communion. A group of teenagers came up and played two of Henry's favorite Christian rock songs with electric guitars and drums. Kayla and Riley led the congregation in "Jesus Loves Me." Two rounds.

Then it was over and there was Henry's coffin, in the aisle, covered with a wreath with white flowers that Dad had bought.

That was Henry in there. In that box. Gone.

As we filed out, Grandma leaned down and kissed the coffin. "Good-bye, copilot," she announced, then saluted smartly one more time. With solemn care she took her flight goggles off her head and laid them in the middle of the wreath on the coffin. She bowed, slow, deliberate, then zigzagged down the aisle, her back bent over like a pretzel, eyes on the floor.

We helped Momma struggle out of the pew, then she leaned over the coffin, her pathetic, broken wail echoing through the church and off the walls and down into everyone's bones.

Dad half carried her down the aisle with the help of Dr. Silverton, Cecilia's principal, who rushed to help.

Kayla and Riley stood together by the coffin, their bare heads shining. "Bye, Uncle Henry. We love you," Riley whispered. "Thanks for always telling me I'm pretty. You're the only one who believes it."

"I love you, Uncle Henry," Kayla said. "In all my religions, you're going straight to heaven, so don't worry."

Riley slung an arm around Kayla's shoulders as they headed out.

Then it was me and Janie and Cecilia, Henry's sisters, together. We held hands, then bent to kiss the head of the coffin, together, right where Henry's smile would be, our bald heads touching.

"I love you, my brother," I whispered.

We used to be the four Bommarito kids.

Now we were three.

Plus one in heaven, waiting for us, his angel wings flapping.

✺ 32 ✺

Six Months Later

Grandma did not mean to burn the parlor down.

It was, after all, one of her favorite rooms. She stored her airplane books in there and the airplane models she and Henry and Dad built together.

I heard the fire engines zipping past our bakery, in the distance I saw smoke, and within minutes I got a panicked call from a neighbor.

Janie and I rushed out of the bakery. I turned to Bao.

"Go, go!" he insisted, worried. "Go. I come help later!"

"Bye-bye!" Belinda called.

"Grandma's fine," Cecilia shouted at me and Janie as we roared up the drive on my motorcycle. "Momma's fine, too. Dad's coming home from work."

"What happened?" We whipped off our helmets. The house seemed like it was mostly intact, except for that parlor. The flames were gone, but the black smoke still billowed.

Cecilia took a deep breath. Although she'd run toward us, she wasn't winded. Losing seventy pounds and walking endless miles daily ("So I don't crack up") had done wonders. Losing Henry had also killed Cecilia's appetite. It had almost killed her.

"Where are they?" I asked.

"Back of the ambulance."

We ran over, every nerve still jangling with fear.

Behind us we heard Dad's SUV roar up the drive. I tell you, it was a relief to see him. He had been demolished by Henry's death and yet . . . he'd propped us all up, held Momma together, insisted we keep living. His gentleness, his strength, his calm in the face of our spiraling emotions, was the rock that kept us all from sinking back into our own demons. He understood us, he listened to us, his love was steady.

I could see why Momma never stopped loving that man.

I waved and ran for Grandma and Momma.

"Grandma," I said to her, dropping to my knees. She was strapped to a gurney in the back of the ambulance with Momma.

"You're confused!" she declared weakly. "I am Amelia Earhart, United States pilot."

I exhaled. She was covered in soot and smoke. I could see her pants were burned. "Pardon me. How are you, Amelia?"

"Fine. My plane crashed and I inhaled smoke and my pants caught fire. There are some bottom bullet wounds. I have a note for you."

She handed me a pink piece of paper. There was a smile on it.

I smiled. I couldn't help it. "Oh, Amelia!" I hugged her.

"Friendlies," Grandma wheezed. "Thank God."

"You're fine, Momma?" I asked, turning to her.

"Yes, I'm fine! Are you blind? I'm sitting here, aren't I?"

I laughed.

She scowled and smoothed her silk shirt, which had soot all over it. Her face and short, blond hair were streaked with black.

I got up and gave her a hug. She was shaking like a leaf. It was Momma who had dragged Grandma, coughing and sputtering, out of the house.

"Oh, now, stop." She clung to me tightly. "You're getting all gushy on me."

"No I'm not," I insisted, not leaving her clutch. "But I'm glad you weren't incinerated in the parlor. That would have been unpleasant. It would have messed up your military crew cut something awful."

"My crew cut!" she exclaimed. "My hair is growing faster than yours! Isabelle, what do I do with you? Your sweet, dear Grandma could have been burned alive and this is all my fault, *my* fault—"

I heard Dad clamber in behind me and felt Momma's talon-like clutch loosen.

"River!" he said as he shot into the ambulance, his bum leg not slowing him down. He was as white as a sheet. He held Momma close, his scarred cheek next to her smooth, sooty one. "You're all right, sweetheart?"

"Yes I am, young man," she said, pulling back to cup his face. Dad was often "young man." "Yes, I am."

They went forehead to forehead and he reached for Grandma's hand. "Had a plane crash, Amelia?"

"Yes, sir, I did."

See. Dad understood our family.

He winked at me.

You might think that we would have moved Grandma into a home after the parlor incident.

We should have.

We didn't.

The accident happened when Velvet was visiting her girl-friends in Vegas. We decided the next time Velvet was on vacation, we sisters would switch off watching Grandma like hawks. Momma had taken a brief afternoon nap and that was that. Flames went a'leapin'.

Momma had been tired because we'd all gone together to the movies to see one of Janie's books transformed to the big screen and returned home late. The movie was so scary, so suspenseful,

Janie had to scuttle from the theater in fear and tap her fingers together by the popcorn machine. We huddled in her closet that night while she embroidered. I held the flashlight. The movie scared the pants off us and neither one of us could sleep.

It was a blockbuster.

Grandma had stood and said the Pledge of Allegiance at the end of it.

The next day Grandma decided that she needed to build a fire in the parlor to keep herself warm that afternoon after her flight while Momma slept. She found the matches and whoosh. Her fire was made.

After the fire, Momma wouldn't hear of moving Grandma. "We will not put that sweet, dear woman in a home after all she's done for me, for us, after all she's sacrificed."

We sisters did not laugh at that, but a vivid image of those two throwing ornate glass bottles at each other, locked in another power struggle, did spring to mind.

"I'm putting my foot down." Momma literally put her foot down. "Grandma stays here."

So we locked up the matches, the iron, anything else that could get hot, and put funny things on the stove and oven to lock 'em up. We put alarms on all the doors.

Who was to argue with a foot going down? Especially Momma's.

Plus we loved having Amelia around.

Three weeks after Henry's funeral, I started working again. I flew to the Sudan with Stefan Morticelli, an international documentary filmmaker I'd worked with many times who was livid with me for not returning his calls or e-mailing him back these past months.

I endured his screaming at me for about two minutes, then said, "Whaddya got?"

He told me.

We went and shot what we could of the atrocities in the Sudan and managed not to be literally shot. I was worried my mind would collapse again like an origamically folded kite, but it didn't.

I handed Stefan my film when we returned to Paris and he went to work. The world needed to know what was going on— these people were in dire, sick, atrocious circumstances, the women and girls endlessly attacked—and I was glad I went, though my bones were cracking with stress, my soul chipped from the things I'd seen.

But I also knew I couldn't work full time as I had before unless I wanted to re-electrocute my brain and end up muttering in group therapy again.

My solution: About four times a year I leave the tranquility of Oregon and head to a hellhole.

Though I hate seeing people at the lowest levels of poverty and desolation around the world, my work is me. I am my work. I can't give it up without losing a part of myself.

Beyond that, I believe that the work I do is important. Part of our world is smothered in blood.

People need to know.

I held one of my cameras in my hand one afternoon in front of the Columbia River, the wind blowing my short brown curls, and took a picture of myself.

This time, I did not have Momma's handprints on my face.

I was actually smiling.

When the land next to Grandma's Queen Anne went up for sale, Janie and I threw our money together and bought it. Janie and I hired two brothers we knew from high school to build a home for each of us on the five acres.

I also bought the bakery from Momma.

She told me she would accept ten dollars for it. I laughed, paid her a heck of a lot more. She wouldn't cash my check, so I brought her the money, in cash, in a box.

She and Dad sneakily took my bank card out of my purse, asked

Janie for my PIN number, and deposited the cash back into my account via the cash machine, minus ten dollars.

I have sold my loft and am now the owner of Bommarito's Bakery.

Bring on Bommarito's Heavenly Cupcakes.

Bob The Man in Charge and Janie often meet, here in Trillium River and at Bob's house. They read the classics out loud together and have, apparently, gotten into reading poetry. Janie blushed when she told me this. They don't like scary movies or reading violent stories in the newspaper.

"He asked me about my tapping and I told him about that small compulsion," she weeped out one night under the willow tree. "He says he has some obsessive-compulsive problems, too. I was so happy to hear that! A feeling of peace and tranquility came over me then and we put on classical music and reset our inner harmony, after I'd checked his stove."

How delightful.

We all need inner harmony.

Even Cecilia has found some inner harmony. I grasped how far her harmony had grown when I thought she was having a heart attack.

I was simmering the same, luscious spaghetti sauce that Henry loved when my heart started to race, a weight crashed on my chest, and I was hot. Rip-roaring hot.

I slumped against the counter as a wave of breathlessness hit, followed by panic for Cecilia.

I knew the girls were visiting Parker, who was struggling under the weight of giant bills from the long-gone Constance, including a herculean loan for the boat, at least thirty pairs of high heels, and two vacations he did not go on with her during their marriage. He was working as a salesman at a used-car lot and living in an apartment in the suburbs.

"He's a lot nicer now for some reason," Kayla said, who had moved on from studying religions to studying world cultures and often wore a kimono or a grass skirt.

"Yeah, I think it was getting his ass whipped that did it," Riley said. She still struggled with trichotillomania. Probably always would. But the bald spots were certainly less noticeable and she liked her shrink. "Dad's so humble it's sickening."

"Yeah, sickening."

I did not bother to knock at Cecilia's door, sprinting through her house and pounding up the stairs to her bedroom.

This is why you should always knock before entering anyone's bedroom: They may have something personal going on. Intimate personal.

I thundered through the door and flew into her room.

And that's when I had the pleasure of making Dr. Silverton's (naked) acquaintance again, as he was there, in my sister's bed, candles creating a romantic atmosphere. I did note to Cecilia later that he had a well-shaped bottom.

"Uh . . . uh . . . excuse me," I stuttered, waving my hands around. "Cecilia, sheesh. I'm sorry."

She laughed and wiggled her naked shoulders at me. I giggled, then slunk like a skunk right out of that house.

Over my spaghetti, though, I laughed and laughed until my tears mixed with the sauce, the spices, and the stringy cheese.

I still see the windsurfer. I wave at him each morning. He waves back.

Maybe one day I'll stick around and say hello.

But maybe not.

I have come to the conclusion that a man in my life, a relationship with a member of the male species, does not appeal to me right now. I don't need the stress, I don't need the drama. I've had enough of both.

My experience has also led me to believe that men are much

better at a distance, much better in our heads when we fantasize about them, and when we believe what we *want* to believe about them, than they are in real life. In real life, once the sheen is off, they're just . . . men, deeply flawed and exhausting.

Except for my dad, whom I love dearly, and Henry.

On my own, I've found Isabelle after a relentlessly tumultuous journey and I don't want a man along with me for the ride right now. I certainly don't want to share with him my pretty bras. I like Isabelle. I like who I've come to be. Finally, I have found peace. Why let a man mess that up?

But maybe one day I'll say hello.

I'll think about it.

The wedding ceremony took place at the church that summer with the reception at Grandma's house.

The dress was a lavender color, the heels matched, and the groom was gorgeous in a black tux. The church was packed with friends and decorated with white ribbons, giant bouquets of spring flowers, and an abundance of candles.

I was nervous and happy and excited and tearful. Janie and Cecilia held my hands, like always.

"Do you, Carl Bommarito," Father Mike said, smiling, "pledge to love, honor, and cherish your wife for as long as you both shall live?"

"I do," said Dad.

"And do you, River Bommarito, pledge to love, honor, and cherish your husband for as long as you both shall live?"

"Oh, I do," Momma said, for once not ferocious, but soft and loveable. Her new wedding ring flashed. It was a doozer. "I do."

It was a heart-warming, tear-jerking ceremony.

It was unnecessary from a legal standpoint.

Momma had never divorced Dad.

Dad had never divorced Momma.

But they were both adamant that they wanted to renew their

vows. Father Mike thought it was a blessed idea, *blessed*, godly, holy!

"Why, Momma?" I had asked her one night as we swung on the swing on the porch, Janie and Cecilia in wicker chairs. "Why did you never divorce?"

She huffed at me. "Now, Isabelle, why would I divorce your dad?"

"Uh, because he left us?"

"He left because the monster inside of him was making him a monster on the outside. Some quack in Washington sent him to war and that screwed him up good. I loved your dad. I still do. I always will. And I always knew he'd come back." She wagged her pointer finger in my face. "And I was right, Isabelle, don't you forget it. I was right."

"But you forgave him instantly, Momma. How did you do that? Forgiveness isn't your strongest suit, you know." I could hardly believe I was having this conversation with her. Before Henry's death, this subject would not have been broached unless I wanted to get verbally pummeled. But Henry's death had taken Momma down about five hundred pegs in the over-aggressiveness department.

She started loving differently, I think, because she had lost deeply. Dad loved her, she was at peace in that love, and we, her daughters, were still alive and open to that love. She took the opening. Yes, it was a miracle. No, she was not transformed into sweetness—she could still wither anyone she chose into dust, and her grief for Henry was permanent—but kindness seeped out on a more regular basis instead of . . . never.

She had even written us each a note on her pink paper. The notes said, "I love you. I always have, always will. Momma."

Momma was silent for a minute and we let the wind surround us, calm and quiet.

"There was nothing to forgive," Momma said. "We can't imagine what that poor man went through. His knee was broken with a hammer. Two fingers were chopped off with a machete. He was beaten and starved. This was after his *second* tour in 'Nam, after he'd lived in the jungles that time for more than a year, after he'd been shot at, and had shot at others, after watching half of his unit killed during one nighttime attack, to say nothing, young lady, of all the other horrible things that happened there that Vets, *to this day*, won't speak of.

"When he was ready, knew his life was in order, knew he could offer something, he thought about coming back. But he was worried his return was selfish, that coming back would upend our lives, add stress and renew anger and hurt. But I'm so glad . . ." she brushed at those bright eyes. "I'm so glad your dad came home."

"You're still in love, after the turbulence you went through, the leveling negativity!" Janie said. She put down a pile of classics she'd been clutching on her lap.

"I am. I could never stop loving your dad, just like I can't stop loving you three crazy girls and Henry." She glared at us, not wanting us to get all mushy.

She slipped her hand in her pocket. "Anyhow, look what your silly dad gave me the other day." She pulled out a check made out to her and signed by Carl Bommarito. The sum was enormous. "He collected his back pay from the government—which was supposed to forward the money to me when you were kids, but didn't because they lost their brains in their own bureaucracy."

I gaped. We all gaped.

"It's also the money his parents left him, in stocks, when they died. The money was supposed to go to me and you kids, but your dad left with two papers accidentally unsigned, so the money never reached us. He never knew. But see what happens when you leave your money in the stock market for thirty years, girls?"

I leaned back against the swing. Lord, she was rich. She would not have to worry about money again.

"Your dad told me that I deserved it for all I went through.

Silly man. He told me to give a check to you three girls, too. So here they are." She pulled out three checks, signed by Dad, and handed them to us.

I blinked.

Sheesh.

We sisters could forget about working, too.

But all that money got us sisters thinking. I didn't need the money, neither did Janie, who could buy France, and neither did Cecilia.

But we knew something that did.

The Henry Bommarito Animal Shelter opened eighteen months from the day our idea hatched. We donated our checks from our dad, held several fund-raisers, received money from many animal groups, money from the city, money from our friends (I can't believe I can even say "our friends," as if the Bommaritos are normal people), money from Momma and Dad, and Dr. Silverton, who had transferred to the high school before he'd asked Cecilia out on a single date but then . . . tra-la-la . . . Cecilia said, "We couldn't resist." Momma liked Dr. Silverton, calling him a fearless giant, not like Parker, who "thought like a man with a small dick."

We received a chunk of money from Cherie, and an awesome big chunk from Bob The Man in Charge. Bao gave ("Hurting animals, hurting people, all the same," he said), and Belinda pledged two dollars a week for the cats. "I like cats," she told me. "They always smile."

Funny enough, we found out that Grandma actually did have a stash of money. Hearing all the excitement about the Henry Bommarito Animal Shelter, she whispered to us sisters, "Come with me. I'll show you where my secret is hidden." We followed her up to the tower room at the top of the house on tiptoe, as she insisted. She then surprised us by picking up a hammer and smashing a hole clean through the wall.

And there it was. Stacks and stacks of dollar bills. Grandma's secret added up to $22,000.

We pretended to donate the money, but it went right into a savings account for her. "Thank you, Amelia," we said, in all seriousness. "Thank you."

She saluted. "Anything for my copilot. I miss that man in my plane. So do the natives." She sniffled.

"Me, too, Amelia," I said, hugging her close. "Me, too."

"The natives here love me," she said, hugging me back. She farted. "Gas in the tank!"

So we had our shelter.

It was huge and clean and we put Paula Jay and Dawn in charge of it, and Paula Jay declared, "You see, your brother keeps on giving! He keeps on giving!"

Janie and Cecilia and I held hands the night before the "grand opening" party in front of the shelter, moonbeams beaming on down.

The dogs and cats from the old shelter were going to be ceremoniously walked/carried to the new shelter down the street, parade style, with most everyone I knew in Trillium River coming. Janie had bought five hundred T-shirts with pictures of dogs and cats on them in front and "In Memory of Henry Bommarito" written on the back, which we would be giving out for free.

The high school band was playing, the church choirs were singing songs about animals, plus "Jesus Loves Me," the seniors were sponsoring a Bunco game to raise money for the shelter, the church parishioners were holding a silent auction, and the firefighters in town were serving a spaghetti dinner with "stringy cheese," Henry's favorite.

Momma and Dad and Grandma would walk next to Paula Jay. Momma would be carrying a picture of Henry. Father Mike would carry a banner the church made with Henry's name and a shimmery gold cross on it. Cecilia and Janie and I and all the other people we love like crazy would come next. Riley was wearing a dog bandana and a shirt that said, "Scientists are sexiest." Kayla was wearing a grass skirt, and Velvet was wearing a new purple velvet dress and purple velvet hat.

Belinda would carry Joe, that ragged cat, who I had bought a new pink bow for, and Bao would come after decorating the table centerpieces with flowers from his garden. Lytle would wear Henry's favorite dog shirt.

The students and teachers at Cecilia's school made construction paper dog and cat hats with ears. There were also lizard hats, a goat, four cows, six monsters, a Tazmanian devil, King Kong, and a witch hat.

We had invited Dr. Remmer to come with her two dogs, and she agreed. When she arrived the next day, the male dog had a blue bow on, the female pink. A sign on their backs said, JUST MARRIED.

We had dog and cat treats waiting for the four-legged animals and giant cakes in the shapes of mutts, German shepherds, and a big fluffy white dog ready for the two-legged animals. All of the Bommarito family had baked them, together.

We'd commissioned an artist in Joseph, Oregon, to make a bronze statue of Henry for the entry. His curly hair was blowing in the wind, he was smiling and waving, and he was holding a fluffy dog, with a big mutt standing beside him and a cat slinking around his tennis shoes, Velcro snaps visible.

We stood around that amazing statue holding hands, and we three sisters snuffled for our Henry, but we stopped when the wind suddenly kicked up and swished our short/fluffy/curly hair all over our heads.

"I feel Henry," Janie sighed. "He's in the wind."

"Knock it off, Henry," Cecilia snapped, although I saw the sheen in her eyes. "Dammit! I've got a date with Larry right after this and you're messing up my hair!"

I laughed. "You got big angel wings, didn't you, Henry? Yeah, yeah, you did." I put my arms straight up in that windy air and twirled around under the moonbeams, under the stars, under heaven, right by Henry and his smile and his angel wings. "I love you, my brother. I love you. *Yeah, yeah.*"

HENRY'S SISTERS

CATHY LAMB

ABOUT THIS GUIDE

The suggested questions are included to
enhance your group's reading of Cathy Lamb's
Henry's Sisters.

DISCUSSION QUESTIONS

1. Of the three sisters, whom do you relate to most? With whom would you most likely be friends? If you had to change places with one of the sisters for a month, which one would you trade places with? What would you do to change their lives in that month, if anything?

2. How did Isabelle change from the beginning of the book to the end? Cecilia? Janie? What do you think is in the future for each of the sisters?

3. Describe River Bommarito. Do you like her? River made many difficult decisions when the sisters and Henry were growing up. Was River backed into a corner, or were there different decisions she could have made? What would you have done? Is it judgmental to say that we would not have made the same decisions as she did if we were in her shoes?

4. What kind of a man is Carl Bommarito? Do you agree with his decision to stay away from the family? Would you have been able to forgive your husband if he left for thirty years, given the same circumstances, as River did? Would you have been able to forgive your father for an absence of that length?

5. Henry said, "You good sisters. We laugh. We cry. We play. We work at bakery and have spaghetti with stringy cheese. Happy life." Did Henry have a happy life? What made him happy? What could all of us learn from Henry?

6. What role did Father Mike play in this book? How did his words help Isabelle recover from who she used to be? Would you describe Isabelle as religious?

7. Velvet Eddow said, "Men are easily baffled, though, dar-lin', don't ever forget that. Their brains think like porn. That's the only way I can describe it, darlin', like *porn*. . . . One part of their brain thinks, the other part is holding a breast in his hand, at all times." True? Not true?

8. Isabelle said, "You get help for a mental illness? People start to steer clear. They are blockheaded, insensitive, narrow-minded morons who will never get past their own flaming ignorance, but they peg you in a hole, treat you with annoying kid gloves, condescension, and/or like they think you're a weak, perhaps dangerous, eternally sick whack job, unsafe or unhealthy to be around. It's beyond their minuscule minds to accept that people with mental illnesses get better all the time. *All the time*." Discuss this statement. Is it true? What specific events do you feel most helped Isabelle in her battle against depression?

9. Parker, Cecilia's cheating, mean, ex-husband, loses every-thing by the end of the book: his wife and kids, his beauti-ful home, his job, and his new wife. He acquires massive credit card debt from Constance, a boat he doesn't want, an arrest record, a watered Corvette, and a job as a car salesman. Did he deserve these consequences? What did Cecilia learn about herself from that relationship?

10. Janie says, "So I write about gruesome killings and kid-nappings and have a few obsessions. It's the way I am . . . odd. Who gives a shit?" Has Janie finally come to accept herself? Do you think she will ever seek help for her "few obsessions"? Will she be able to maintain a relationship

with The Man in Charge? Do you think you've accepted yourself—faults and idiosyncrasies and all?

11. Cecilia and Isabelle had an intense emotional/physical twin connection to each other. Do you believe that these types of connections exist between twins, siblings, or family members? If so, how does this happen? Did this connection enhance the story?

12. The sisters, and Henry, all suffered from their childhood. In the end, did it make them stronger? More compassionate? Or was the fallout so extreme for all of them that they'll never fully recover? How did their childhoods affect their future careers?

13. Isabelle said, "My experience has also led me to believe that men are much better at a distance, much better in our heads when we fantasize about them, and when we believe what we *want* to believe about them, than they are in real life. In real life, once the sheen is off, they're just . . . men, deeply flawed and exhausting." What do you think of that statement? Is she right? Do you foresee Isabelle choosing to have a relationship in the future with a man? What are some of the stumbling blocks they will have to overcome together?

14. How did Henry hold the family together? Do you agree with the author's decision to have Henry die by the end of the book? Was there any other ending that would have worked?

15. Describe the sisters' relationships to one another. Are they typical sisters? Is the Bommarito family a functioning or a nonfunctioning family? Is your family like this to some extent?